THERE WAS NOTHING
STANDING BETWEEN HER
AND HER DESTINY...
EXCEPT THE MAN WHO
HAD SWORN TO CHANGE IT.

High Praise for
MARSHA CANHAM
winner of the *Romantic Times*
Lifetime Achievement Award

IN THE SHADOW OF MIDNIGHT

"DRAMATIC AND SENSUOUS . . . MARVELOUS
. . . OUTSTANDING . . . A tale of grand proportions
. . . Top notch from start to finish!"

—*Rendezvous*

"NOTHING SHORT OF GREAT!"

—*The Brazosport Facts* (Me.)

"FAST-PACED . . . ACTION PACKED . . . *IN THE
SHADOW OF MIDNIGHT* is definitely one of the best
novels of the year."

—*Affaire de Coeur*

"SENSUAL . . . FIERY . . . LUSTY . . . Filled with
intrigues, mounting dangers and marvelous adventures."

—*Romantic Times*

Also by Marsha Canham

THROUGH A DARK MIST

UNDER THE DESERT MOON

IN THE SHADOW OF MIDNIGHT

STRAIGHT FOR THE HEART

MARSHA CANHAM

A Dell Book

Published by
Dell Publishing
a division of
Bantam Doubleday Dell Publishing Group, Inc.
1540 Broadway
New York, New York 10036

The trademark Dell® is registered in the U.S. Patent and Trademark Office.

ISBN: 0-440-21786-5

Printed in the United States of America

Published simultaneously in Canada

May 1995

10 9 8 7 6 5 4 3 2 1

RAD

This one is for the Crash Queens,
Eleven Lively Ladies from Louisiana
who make me feel like a friend,
not just a name on a book cover.

To Chuck and Lucy Fry,
who have become more like family
instead of just friends.

And to my brilliant illustrator,
Morgan Kane
who shares my boundless love for flowers . . .
as long as they're in a vase where they belong!

strong and turbulent as the currents of the Mississippi. She deserved to be happy. She deserved to be unafraid. She deserved to be loved, for God's sake, even if he had to rap her

Prologue

Montana Rose paused under the crimson and white archway and drew a deep breath. The main gambling salon was alive with the sights and sounds the huge paddle wheelers had become famous for. The tables—blackjack, faro, roulette, and keno—swarmed with patrons of all shapes and sizes. Coins sparkled on the green baize tabletops, glass chips chattered noisily in and out of wooden slots. Great mahogany wheels spun with a feverish energy producing a blood-thrilling hum all their own. The level of noise rose and fell with a distinct rhythm, the sound flowing from one end of the salon to the other as if in keeping with the gentle flow of the river currents beneath her keel.

Montana's extraordinary blue eyes took in the length and breadth of the entire salon in a long, careful sweep as she savored the heady atmosphere she had come to associate with wealth, power, and pleasure. Only the very rich—or the very foolhardy—could afford what the *Mississippi Queen* offered. She was an elegant gambling casino, a queen among queens, a floating palace that catered to all tastes ranging from expensive wine to exquisitely beautiful women.

Montana's gaze rose from the churning activity in the belly of the salon and prowled slowly around the banistered, curtained alcoves that shared the same level as the fountainous crystal chandeliers. Cigar smoke blurred the curtained entrances to the private booths, hanging in thin, diaphanous layers that shifted and swirled in tiny whirlpools as men and women moved from booth to booth in a shimmering kaleidoscope of color. Hostesses, clad in scarlet satin and glittering, feathered headdresses, disappeared behind the plush tapestries carrying full bottles of whiskey and bourbon, emerging seconds later with their trays burdened with empty bottles and dishes brimming with cigar butts. To the novice, what went on behind those tapestries made for curious speculation. To the knowledgeable few, the private booths were where real money was won or lost.

Montana felt a subtle increase in the pulsebeat throbbing through her veins. She had dressed carefully this night, meticulously brushing the dark emerald velvet of her gown until it gleamed with lushness. Her hair was gathered into a mass of honey-gold curls that crowned the back of her head and trailed in shiny spirals over sloping white shoulders, drawing the eye downward to the breathtaking plunge of the scalloped bodice. Contrasting with the translucent whiteness of her skin, the velvet seemed to cling by the merest of promises to the rounded swell of her breasts. There, nestled snugly in the deep cleft, was her solitary adornment; a delicate, heart-shaped gold locket bearing an ornately stylized *M* in fiery pinpoints of etched fire. The long, exotically draped tiers of her skirt hinted at equally long, exotic legs beneath. A frilled back panel of butter-yellow lace spilled from the narrow waist to trail almost a full pace behind her, causing anyone who wanted to gain entrance to the salon to stop and circle a wide berth around her, like dark rushing waters around a glittering gemstone.

A head turned, noting the disturbance. Another head turned, and another. An arm nudged a companion and the mechanical spinning of the roulette wheels was ignored for a few brief moments. The low murmur of appreciation was noticed by the captain of the stern-wheeler, Benjamin Winston Turnbull, whose craggy face split into an immediate grin.

A formidable figure of a man, Captain Turnbull was built not unlike his riverboat—solid of beam and wide across the stern. His full, black beard was liberally shot with silver, as was the thickly waved tangle of hair that surrounded a face fashioned after weathered lava rock. His eyes were deep set and darker than coal, adept at concealing all but the most unexpected reactions. They snapped alive now as he identified the cause of the turbulence at the entryway.

"Well," he said huskily, turning his back on a patron who

had suddenly been reduced to insignificance, "if it isn't my favorite little peacock, out in full feather."

The captain reached the landing in three giant strides. Montana extended both hands and felt them swallowed into Ben's huge bear paws.

"It's good to see you," she laughed softly.

"I wish you'd let me know ahead when you plan to visit us. I could bring in twice the business on your name alone."

"I'd rather surprise you," she answered, her voice as naturally sensual as the rest of her body. "And I'd rather *not* play into anyone else's hands."

The captain's smile took on a hard edge as the lower half of his spine turned to butter. "Come. Humor an old friend by sharing a sip of brandy with him. 'Pon my word, but you get lovelier every time I see you."

He continued to hold one of Montana's hands as he steered her through the crowded tables toward his own private booth. She was as slim and delicate as a porcelain figurine, with the top of her head barely reaching his chin. From his superior height, he was afforded a spectacular view down the front of her bodice, and he could feel the buttery sensation spreading upward to constrict the walls of his chest. He gave the cool, slender fingers an involuntary caress and was pleased to imagine a measure of the intimacy returned.

"Business as usual, I see," she murmured, waiting patiently for the coal-black eyes to lift to hers. "A credit to you, Ben, for I don't believe I have ever found the *Queen* at anything less than full capacity. And only the best people too; where *do* you manage to find them?"

"They find me." He grinned, holding the back of the chair while she settled artfully onto a crush of lace and velvet. "And the reputation of the *Queen* guarantees they keep coming back. Just like you."

"Are there any games going on tonight?"

As he seated himself opposite the emerald-clad beauty, the captain allowed himself a wry glance around the salon. It was crammed stem to stern. Not a table was suffering for want of attention, nor was a space vacant for longer than a few seconds before another eager player jostled to fill it. But Ben knew what she meant, and his blood quickened perceptibly.

"There are one or three might prove interesting to you," he said, lowering his voice to a throaty rasp. "In the corner above the faro table. Five players. Stakes not too high, not too low. Easy spenders who don't seem to mind losing. Been on board for the whole trip upriver from New Orleans. Speculators by my reckoning, with new money to burn."

The drinks arrived and Ben took a deep swallow before continuing.

"Two booths down, pretty well the same thing. Spending greenbacks like they washed in with the tide. Last possibility is on your left in the rear—" He waited for the ice-blue eyes to flick up and over his shoulder. "Three of them have been on board for the week, one since noon yesterday, and we picked up two others this evening. Hot money there, but it all seems to be going in one direction. Looks like a sharp to me, so it would depend on if you were in a mood to test him, see how good he was."

Montana's interest lingered on the last booth for a few seconds, debating the challenge, but in the end, it reverted to the booth above the faro tables.

Ben nodded in agreement and grinned again. "Be my choice too. Easy pickings. Bored with being together so long with nothing to talk about except business. I'm sure they would appreciate some new blood, 'specially if it was packaged right."

Montana's gaze met his with a directness that caused his breath to catch. "Do you think I'm . . . packaged right?"

Ben's chest burned and his belly ached with a fresh, hard surge of blood. Flesh that had been fighting against the constraints of his breeches since he had seen her on the landing tested the tailor's skill yet again, causing him to set his teeth in a wry grimace. "Hell," he murmured, "they'll be so bloody appreciative, they won't even know they're playing poker with the best damned pair of hands to come along since the high days of Billy Fleet. You just wait here and enjoy your drink while I mosey on up and put a bug in their ears.''

He finished his brandy with an audible gulp and pushed to his feet, thankful his broadcloth jacket was long enough to camouflage the reason for his brusque strides.

Montana followed his progress with her eyes and seemed to take no notice as a face she knew as well as her own passed by her table and tossed a casual glance her way. She avoided making any eye contact with the newcomer, but was keenly aware of his presence as he took a seat at the bar and ordered a large whiskey.

A long, fine-boned finger tapped noiselessly on the table-top, then stroked smoothly up and down the side of the brandy snifter. At a table nearby, a player was enthusiastically throwing dice, obviously enjoying a run of good luck. Montana watched him for a moment, but then the focus of her gaze shifted subtly and she found herself staring past the dice player's shoulder, drawn by a pair of smoky gray eyes that seemed to have come out at her from nowhere. The man they belonged to had been staring at her, a not unusual circumstance in itself, but the fact that he appeared to have no other interest in any of the activities around him would have made him stand out in the crowd even if his piratical good looks had not. He was tall and impressively broad across the shoulders, with dark chestnut hair that fell in carelessly handsome waves to the collar of his shirt. A luxuriantly thick mustache followed the curved line of his smile, expanding to embolden a square jawline that needed no such assistance. In response to Montana's casual appraisal, the slash of straight, even teeth gleamed in anticipation. But if he expected her to offer an invitation to join her, his hopes were crushed with Captain Turnbull's reappearance. Montana's brief lapse in concentration ended as well, and she was standing by the table, her drink untouched, when Ben arrived back at her side.

''They said as how they'd be honored to make your acquaintance,'' he advised her. ''Especially after I offered personal assurances as to your character.''

Montana slipped her hand into the crook of his arm and let him escort her up the stairs and along the narrow balcony. "May I assume these . . . personal assurances come with the usual arrangements?"

He lowered his voice. "Five percent," he agreed, nonplussed by the act of discussing his cut of the profits even as he boasted the honesty of his ship.

She smiled again, as comfortable with Benjamin Turnbull's greed as she was with his casual lechery. Neither was a threat to her, and, with a deliberate toss of her tawny gold curls, she passed through the wings of the crimson velvet curtains and entered the smoky alcove. Someone paying very close attention might have seen her turn and glance directly at the man watching from his seat at the bar, but the only one who followed her progress with any interest now was the gentleman with the handlebar mustache, and he seemed more intent on catching a last glimpse of the graceful motion of her hips before the curtain dropped behind her, cocooning her in privacy.

"Gentlemen," Ben announced smoothly, "allow me the pleasure of introducing Miss Montana Rose. She was hoping there might be some space for her at your table."

Montana scanned each face in turn, noting with a practiced eye which of them seemed amused at the prospect of having a woman join their game and which of them were deciding their evening of hard gambling, hard liquor, and hard language was more or less over.

As she did at the outset of every game she joined, she set their minds at ease with a small laugh and a practiced speech. "Nothing you say or do during the course of the game will shock me; neither my ears nor my imagination has been virginal for quite some time. I give no quarter and ask for none in return. I am not like any of your mothers, I am not like any of your sisters, and thank the good gracious God, I am not like any of your wives."

She waited for the round of gruff laughter to end and took her seat near a portly, red-faced participant who watched the glitter of coins that spilled from her reticule with almost the same amount of interest he bestowed on her cleavage.

"Ten-dollar ante," he mused. "No limit on the raises, dealer's choice. Is that acceptable to you, Miss Rose?"

"Montana. And yes, it's quite acceptable."

"Good. Best of luck then. Newcomer deals."

Part One

DEALER'S CHOICE

Chapter 1

"**D**amn and blast, I've got you again!" William Courtland's gravelly voice cut through the silence with a smug chortle. "I've got you with three little Jakes."

Alisha Courtland glanced sharply at her father. His bushy white eyebrows were crushed together over the bridge of his nose, his mouth bristled with undisguised mirth as he leaned forward to fan his cards on the table.

"Three!" Her vivid blue eyes narrowed in disbelief as she glared first at the royal winners, then at the gloating smile that puffed her father's cheeks.

"Three Jakes," he repeated, thrusting a stubby finger at each pasteboard in turn. "One . . . two . . . three . . . Which means the pot is mine. Again."

Alisha bristled as she watched her father rake the heap of matchsticks to his side of the table.

"You did it during the draw," she scowled. "You must have. I was watching the deal too closely, and you couldn't have done it then or I would have seen it."

"You have been known to miss a trick or two, young lady," he said, immensely pleased with himself.

"But not during the deal," she insisted. "Ryan—did you see how he did it?"

The eldest Courtland offspring spread his hands innocently. "I saw nothing. All I know is I drew three cards and each was worse than what I discarded."

Alisha sought her sister's support. "Amanda?"

"I'm afraid not. I'm with Ryan this time; nothing higher than a king."

Alisha sighed and leveled the full power of her eyes on her father. "All right, how did you do it? *When* did you do it?"

"Tut-tut." He wagged a finger like a lecturing dean. "If you couldn't see a switch, how do you know it happened?

Perhaps it was just the luck of the draw. Luck has been known to favor a hand now and then."

"Not around you," she retorted. "And wasn't it you who said luck was just a bit player, and if a man didn't know how to turn it to his own advantage, he shouldn't be sitting at the table?"

"I said that?" William asked, admiring his own wisdom.

"You did. And how am I supposed to learn how to turn luck to my advantage if you won't teach me all your tricks?"

"They are not tricks, young miss," he protested with an arching of an eyebrow. "They are skills. And you are supposed to acquire them through acute observation and diligent practice. Not by throwing out your lower lip and sulking." He scooped up the loose cards and began to shuffle. "Shall we try again . . . *paying attention* this time?"

"Deal me out." Ryan laughed, tossing his last matchstick into the kitty. He stood and stretched, flexing the smooth muscles in his arms and chest as he did so. He was tall and solidly built, possessing the familial cornflower-blue eyes that twinkled as he looked at each of his sisters in turn. Amanda was the only one who returned his smile—and glowered at him at the same time for abandoning her—but he only shrugged guilelessly and walked around the table to stand behind William's caneback wheelchair. The lamplight caught the sharper angle of his jaw and burnished the dark gold color of his hair, but there could be no mistaking the resemblance between father and son. Even the lines and creases on their faces had formed in similar patterns.

"Please, Ryan, tell me they are not at it again."

Ryan turned at the sound of his mother's querulous voice. She was seated in front of the fire, as close to the heat as she could manage without threat of a cinder catching the hem of her skirt. Her head was bowed over her sewing, but as Ryan joined her, she tilted her face upward to peer through the owlish lenses of her spectacles.

"They aren't, are they?" she asked again, sighing with the futility of a false hope. "I thought you were playing a friendly game of whist."

"We were," he said, and stretched his hands toward the warm blaze. "For about the first five minutes."

"And now they won't let you play anymore?"

Ryan held his smile in check, knowing his mother's concern was, as always, genuine. Sarah Fayworth Courtland was as round and soft as a dumpling, a full head and shoulders shorter than her husband—who was himself a mere inch shy of six feet—and possessed of such tender and easily disrupted sensibilities, there was always a bottle of smelling salts within easy reach. It was a mystery and a constant source of amazement to all who knew them how Sarah had managed to bear her husband five children and survive twenty-seven years of tumultuous wedlock. But survive she had, with the aid of her salts and the fearsomely protective mammy, Mercy.

"It isn't that they won't let me play, Mother," Ryan explained. "It's that I can barely see the cards I'm holding, let alone read what is on them."

"You work yourself too hard, dear," Sarah said, reaching up to pat his arm. "Last night you nearly fell asleep at the dinner table."

Ryan caught her hand in his and studied it a moment, frowning over the fingers that were shiny and painfully red from the unaccustomed hours she had spent working with needle and thread over the past few weeks. But it was her daughter's wedding and she was insisting on doing the delicate work herself, altering the lustrous gown her grandmother, mother, and she herself had worn on her wedding day.

"Will it be finished on time?" Ryan asked gently.

Sarah's sigh displaced a wisp of silver-gray hair that had escaped her cap. "I sincerely hope so. If my eyes weren't so bad and my hands not so clumsy . . ."

"And if she didn't keep changing her mind every time she tried it on," Ryan whispered, bending so that only his mother heard.

"Oh. Pish." She swatted his hand away. "She just wants everything to be perfect, that's all. A girl *should* have everything perfect on her wedding day. She should look perfect and feel perfect—'' Sarah sighed again and ran a trembly hand over the watered silk sateen. ''Your grandmother Fayworth would have been so proud. And your sister will look just like an angel sent from heaven, don't you agree?''

''An angel,'' he agreed dryly, and glanced at Amanda over his shoulder, noting the faint smile she cast back in reply.

''Check or raise?'' William barked. ''Pay attention, girl. The evening is not long enough to squander twenty minutes each time the play comes your way. You have to be quick! Decisive! Assured! Otherwise your opponents will read you like a book.''

Amanda felt a blush creep up her throat at the chastisement. She had two pair, aces and queens, yet she guessed it would not be nearly good enough. Her father was in rare form and Alisha seemed to be out for blood.

''By me,'' she sighed, throwing down her cards.

''Bah! Amanda, you surprise me. There was nothing wrong with your hand.''

Alisha arched a finely shaped eyebrow and did not trouble herself to look over at her father as she murmured, ''Is that just a lucky guess, or do those nicks and scratches on the edges tell you something the rest of us don't know?''

William opened his mouth to refute the charges, but thought better of it and grinned instead. ''Merely a test of your powers of observation, m'dear. Happily, you have passed it.''

''Small wonder, since you practically sawed the edges with a file. Being shot for a cheat was not one of the skills I was interested in learning, Father,'' Alisha added caustically. ''Although at your age, I suppose your peers would be more apt to tar and feather you by way of example.''

William feigned a look of mortification. ''Are you implying I practice my hobby on anyone outside the confines of this family?''

''She's not only implying it, William dear,'' Sarah chided from her seat by the fire, ''She is warning you against doing it again any time soon. We shouldn't want to have to go and fetch you out of jail again, regardless if the Judge is locked up with you or not.''

William glared over at his wife. "I have never taken advantage of a man unless he knew what he was getting into— or unless he deserved it. And Judge Moore asked me—*asked* me, mind you—to teach that young whip of a solicitor a lesson in mocking his elders.''

"He was a lawyer?" Ryan asked, choking back a laugh. "You didn't tell us that."

"I don't tell you a great many things"—William harrumphed—"if I don't think they concern you. Besides." His brow pleated and he studied his cards with grave intent, adding "—He was a Yankee," as if that was all the explanation required. "Now, where were we?"

Alisha toyed with a long coil of golden blonde hair. "I was in the process of calling your bluff."

"In that case"—her father slammed his cards down— "you owe me another twenty for a full house: Kings over tens."

He saw the look on Alisha's face and crowed delightedly. "Thought you could distract me, eh? I saw that little switch you did up your sleeve. You should be careful, Missy. If this was a real game, you would be deuced uncomfortable explaining where that fifth king came from."

Amanda leaned forward to stare at the glaring pair of kings her father plucked out of Alisha's hand.

"Saw me mark 'em with a file, did you?" he snorted.

Amanda leaned back and shook her head.

"Oh . . . don't look so scandalized," Alisha snapped crossly at her sister. "I was only doing it to rile him."

"Rile me, eh? Judging by the diminished state of your matches and the growing health of my own, it certainly appears to be working. By Jove, I'll have you shucked down to your bare fanny soon if you keep riling me like this."

"William!" Sarah gasped as she stabbed her finger soundly with the needle. "Must you be so crude?"

"What is crude about a bare fanny? Nothing at all, I

warrant . . . unless, of course, it belongs to Old Blisterpuss, Mrs. Nelly Weems. A sight like that would be downright brutal.''

Sarah sucked belligerently at her finger. "I am simply suggesting, William, that you might show a little more decorum in your speech, especially around your daughters."

"Their own father, their own mother, and their own brother—who, I'll wager, has seen a bared fanny or two along the way himself. Why should I not say what I damn well please to say in front of them?"

"Upon my soul," Sarah declared, her voice wavering and her bosom swelling with indignation. "If you carry on so at the wedding, I shall die. I shall simply wither away and die."

"Bah! You're as healthy as you were the day I married you. Healthier for it, I'd say, and twice as fractious now that Alisha is finally marrying—*and* marrying into titled money to boot. All this fuss and bother. Lecture me in my sleep, you do. The right fork to use, the right spoon. Lecture me on how to chew and when to speak and what I can and cannot say. I am still the master of my own house, am I not? The last time I looked, I was only crippled, not gelded! Should I choose to drink my soup out of a cup and eat a fine roasted haunch of beef with my fingers whilst I scratch an ear or adjust a hitch in my trousers, I might jolly well do so, my dear. Jolly well do so.''

Sarah's mouth dropped open and her eyes rolled beseechingly in Amanda's direction.

"Don't worry, Mother," she said. "I will see to it that he behaves."

William's eyebrows flew to his hairline as he considered this new affront. "Is that so? A sprout like you taking it upon yourself to act as my watchdog?"

"If you need one, yes."

"Damn and blast! Has the whole household turned against me?"

"Not so as you would notice," Alisha said wryly. "Are you dealing, or shall I?"

"Go right ahead," he snorted again. "I should not want to be accused of acting out of turn."

"Amanda? In or out?"

"I think I was out before the evening started."

Alisha dismissed her without a thought. She shuffled the deck, gave it to William to cut, and dealt each of them five cards apiece in a quick, efficient blur. Her hand, when she fanned it open, showed a nine of spades, a three of hearts, the four, five of diamonds, and the eight of clubs.

"Cards, Father?"

He straightened in his chair and puckered his lips, his gaze fixed like glue to Alisha's hands. "Two, if you would be so kind."

She flicked two pasteboards across the table and turned her attention to her own cards. "Dealer takes . . . one. And, since it is only between the pair of us, shall we bypass the formalities and wager the lot of your matches against the lot of mine?"

"A paltry enough wager," he pronounced sarcastically, "without the added incentive of cash."

Alisha drew a deep breath and stared at her father through clear, cerulean blue eyes. "Ten Yankee greenbacks from me," she agreed, "and from you . . . a promise that there will be no shenanigans on the day of my wedding. Further: that you will behave yourself between now and then and do nothing whatsoever to draw any unwarranted attention to yourself or to this family."

Amanda glanced sidelong at her father and tried her valiant best to suppress a smile. Alisha was referring to a rather spectacular bout of drinking he had embarked upon with his closest friend and ally, Judge Frederick Arblaster Moore, whereafter he had declared to all and sundry that since his daughter was marrying a German baron, he supposed he would have to learn how to eat pickled cabbage and fart a fugue.

"I will want your word on it," Alisha insisted. "Your word as a gentleman."

"You have it," William scowled. "And you may also have

these, Miss High and Mighty!'' He spread his cards with a flourish, showing another full house, kings over queens this time. Muttering a colorful oath, he leaned back and folded his arms over his chest. ''Treat your father like a buffoon, will you? Beat that, if you can, and if you can't . . . be prepared to count out the cash. And I will take it in gold, if you don't mind. Yankee greenbacks lack substance and I don't care to tolerate them.''

Alisha narrowed her eyes and fanned her cards—four aces and the missing king. She kept her face blank and her voice cool enough to chill a pitcher of julep. ''Will this do, Father?''

William looked. Then started forward and looked again.

''Your word, of course, is worth its weight in gold or greenbacks,'' Alisha remarked, her eyes sparkling in triumph over her father's astonishment.

''But just in case the temptation is too great on the day of the wedding,'' her sister Amanda added, ''you will have my undivided attention for the entire afternoon and evening.''

William glowered at each of his daughters in turn.

''Blast it anyway,'' he spluttered at length. ''And blast my luck that it should be only one of you moving away. Were it the pair, I should be inclined to celebrate my way into blissful oblivion.''

''Were it the pair of us leaving Rosalie,'' Amanda said lightly, ''who would be here to watch over you?''

''The devil himself! He did well enough on his own before the lot of you came along to plague me.''

''Now, William,'' Sarah said solicitously. ''Remember your condition. Dr. Dorset says you mustn't become agitated.''

''Dorset is a quack,'' William declared flatly. ''And my condition would be much improved if I was not so damnably henpecked. Daughters are an aggravation I could well do without in my declining years. I should have had nothing but sons; a few licks from Old Charley always set them straight.''

"You are not suggesting you should have whipped your daughters!" Sarah cried, aghast.

"Not until they bled," he qualified gruffly. "Just until they stood up and took notice."

Sarah's shock was downplayed by Ryan's chuckle. "It probably wouldn't have helped, Father. If you will recall, you tried taking a switch to them a few times when they were younger and the only one who felt worse for it was you."

William's piercing blue eyes narrowed. "That was because I was younger then myself and suffered from a soft heart. I was under the mistaken impression they would acquire common sense with age. I can see now the error of such lenient thinking. Old Charley it is. First thing in the morning. You may tell your brothers they are welcome to come and watch if they have a mind; it would not hurt Stephen and Evan to learn a thing or two about handling women instead of always fussing over those horses of theirs the whole blessed day long. As for you, young lady—" He wagged a sausagelike finger under Amanda's nose. "You may be sure I will inform that rapscallion husband of yours if he is too slack in his discipline, he will find himself condemned to the same sorry state your mother has badgered me into now."

It was so sudden, so completely unexpected, that for a moment no one moved. Even Alisha lost some of her high color and turned pale at the mention of the absent family members, dead now these many years. North and South alike had lost many of their sons and husbands, and in that respect, the Courtlands were not alone. Mississippi had called on her men early in the fighting between the states, and there were few of hot blood and hotter tempers who could resist the lure of gaining glory and honor in defense of their land.

Evan Courtland's glory had come in the form of a bullet in the stomach the first month he was at war. Stephen had found honor in an unmarked grave somewhere in the Virginia foothills barely a year later. Amanda had married Caleb Beauregard Jackson on his last leave home from the fighting; he had died of a saber wound the week he rejoined his cavalry unity.

The surviving Courtland men, Ryan and William, had been among the lucky ones to return to Adams County at the end of the war, but neither one had come back as completely whole as when they had departed. Ryan had lost the toes of his left foot to frostbite—a condition he suffered often during the year he spent incarcerated in a Yankee prison camp. William's spine had been severed by a minié ball, but he had had his pride shattered in more ways than the one. There were days when he was lucid and in general command of most of his faculties, but there were others when he suffered great gaps in his memory and refused to even acknowledge there had been a war at all.

For the most part, the family had managed to steel themselves against these lapses. But references to Stephen and Evan, especially dropped out of the blue like this, were jarring reminders of an easier time, a happier time when the laughter of the two tow-headed rakehells rocked the elegant manor house from floor to ceiling. And although Caleb and Amanda had only lived together as man and wife for less than a week, they had known each other all their lives and the loss had left a deep, lingering void.

"Well?" William demanded, suspicious of the lengthy silence. "What have you to say for yourselves?"

Amanda Courtland Jackson lifted her head and smiled. "Yes, Papa. Old Charley, first thing in the morning. Will that be with bared fannies and all?"

Sarah transferred her frozen gaze to her daughter. Ryan's mouth curved slightly in admiration, for Amanda usually could be counted upon to draw William back from the brink.

Their father's stern expression held a moment longer, then collapsed with a hearty guffaw of laughter. "Naturally. What would be the point of lifting a skirt if there was nothing to admire?"

"Well! I never!" Sarah stabbed herself again, this time hard enough to draw a bead of blood. "Mercy," she croaked. "Fetch Mercy at once with my salts. I . . . . I believe I have a faint coming on."

"Then faint and be done with it," William commanded.

"In all my years of bondage, woman, I vow we have never once finished an argument with you standing on both feet."

"Oh! You are a cruel man," Sarah wailed, cradling the stabbed finger as if it were proof of her husband's tyranny. "Mother was right all those years ago. I never should have married you. Why, I had the choice of—"

"—any young blade east of the Great Beyond," William concluded by rote. "And I, for one, shall be forever in awe of the reasons why you chose me over all the other possibilities."

"Certainly it was not because of your genteel nature or bearing," she retorted with an indignant sniffle. "And I vow . . . I positively swear on everything I hold sacred or dear, that if you, William Andrew Morrissey Courtland, make one single scene or cause me one solitary second of grief on the day of our Alisha's wedding—"

"Have I not already given my word?" he roared. "Have I not already pledged to be a host of unimpeachable grace and good behavior?"

"Good behavior? By whose standards do you judge good behavior? We have two fine, lovely daughters, and how do you encourage them to spend their summer evenings? Strolling in the gardens? Practicing their stitchery or their music? No! No! You teach them card tricks and sleight of hand!"

"Both highly specialized skills that develop intelligence and wit," William protested, his hand thumping the table for emphasis.

"Intelligence to do what? Cheat without being caught? Gamble with impunity? Alisha is getting married in three weeks' time. What will her husband think of such goings-on?"

"Karl enjoys a friendly game of chance now and then," Alisha remarked blithely. "He might just appreciate a wife who can partner him with intelligence and wit."

"Or he might not," Ryan interjected dryly. "He still has time to change his mind, God help him."

"Have no fear," Alisha assured him. "Wild horses could

not keep Karl away from the altar now. He is more afraid I might change my mind."

"Again?" Sarah shrilled, almost beside herself. "Surely you . . . you are not contemplating such a thing. *You have not done anything to discourage him, have you?*"

To a woman like Sarah Courtland who had given birth to three of her five children by the time she was Alisha's age, to be teetering on the brink of twenty and still unwed, regardless of the circumstances, was flirting with catastrophe. Men were scarce, true enough. And the ravages of war had drastically altered the rules as far as when one declared a single, unwed female consigned to spinsterhood. But Alisha had been engaged three times over the past two years and all three times had broken off the engagement when a better prospect came to light. Baron Karl von Helmstaad, while falling critically short of her requirements in some areas, was as rich as he was infatuated with the most sought-after belle in Adams County.

"Discourage him? On the contrary, Mother dear, it will pose a genuine challenge to keep my eager groom at arm's length for the next three weeks. Perhaps I should be asking Amanda how she does it; how she manages to keep herself so detached and cool a man would sooner stake his chances on winning the Queen of England."

Amanda looked up and found her sister's smug, teasing grin waiting for her.

"Amanda does no such thing," Sarah protested. "Not deliberately anyway, I'm sure. She has her Mr. Brice, after all, who is a fine young man, and not at all unhandsome. Moreover, he is reliable, trustworthy, dependable—"

"Boring," Alisha murmured under her breath. *"Poor."*

Ryan glanced up from the fire and frowned. It was hardly a flattering thought to have about one's own flesh and blood, but if anyone had ice water flowing through their veins it was Alisha. She had culled Karl von Helmstaad from the herd with as much emotion and affection as she would a bull at auction . . . with the bulk of her consideration based on the size of his estates and bank accounts.

"There is nothing wrong with Joshua Brice," he said, rising to Amanda's defense. "Or with Amanda waiting until she is sure of what she wants."

"What she wants?" Alisha set aside the deck of cards she had been fidgeting with and squared them neatly on the table before she stood. "Surely it cannot be too difficult a decision to make to want more than . . . than this—" She waved a hand airily to indicate the large, empty room, devoid of any carpets or curtains, any furniture not of the most practical design and purpose.

Once a richly decorated, lavishly appointed parlor used for entertaining guests of high social standing, the room, like most of the rooms in Rosalie, had been stripped and looted to the bare boards by marauding soldiers from both armies. Situated close to the banks of the Mississippi River and boasting its own jetty and deep-water bay, the Courtland home had played host to Confederate troops as well as, in the latter two years of the war, headquarters for the series of Yankee generals who passed through Natchez. Forced to relinquish their home to unwanted guests, the Courtland women had watched their possessions and priceless heirlooms disappear one by one, even to the carpets and throw rugs that had once protected the polished oak floors.

"I am well aware of what all of you think of my upcoming marriage," Alisha continued wanly. "And I'm telling you it doesn't matter one wit to me. I'm tired of being poor. I'm tired of living off pride and stubbornness, tired to the bone of being scorned and looked down upon by trash to whom we would not have given the time of day before the war. This house . . . it isn't a home anymore; it's just a big, empty shell with empty rooms and no future. You want your daughters to stroll in the gardens, Mother? We would trip on the weeds if we tried, or break our legs on the rubble that has never been cleared away. You want us to sew and practice our music? What use are fancy stitches on frocks that have been patched and mended so many times it is hard to recall what they once looked like? As for music, the only sound you can hear in this house, other than the sound of empty bellies grumbling for food, is the sound of the wind howling through the broken window boards.''

"Alisha, please," Amanda breathed. "Father—''

"Yes, indeed. Father. I am especially weary of playing these silly games, always having to pretend in front of him that nothing has changed. Always having to pretend we are still *The Courtlands,* still of the noble d'Iberville stock. Surely to gracious God, he still has the use of his eyes if not his full sensibilities. He must see Ryan riding out to the fields every morning and coming home every night bone tired, dragging his feet like a plowhorse. He must see we have no slaves left, that we are practically destitute—''

"Alisha, by God, that's enough!" Ryan's voice was dangerously brittle. "You have said what you wanted to say, now leave it alone. There is no need to lower yourself further.''

"Lower *my*self?" Her eyes screwed down into vindictive slits. "I'm not the one who spends fifteen hours a day crawling through muck and slime to pick cotton like a common darky.''

"Maybe you should. Maybe it would teach you to be thankful you still have two good hands to work with; something not all of our neighbors and friends can say.''

Blue eyes clashed with blue eyes, the sparks flying between the siblings like lancets of fire.

"My, how we do love to play the role of noble hero," Alisha mused. "Turn yourself into a slave, sacrifice everything, shun anything and everyone whose ideals are not as pure and unsullied as your own. In the end, though, you know you'll have to do the same as everyone else along the river. You will have to sell this place and no one—not one single solitary soul—will blink at the news.''

Ryan's handsome face went white beneath the ruddiness of his tan. The defeat of the Confederacy had brought all of the rich Southern states buckling to their knees. Emancipation had freed the slaves, but without the hundreds of strong black hands to harvest the miles upon miles of cotton and tobacco, the financial backbone of Mississippi and others like her withered and died in the fields. The rule of the day, after the Yankee victors had swept triumphantly into power, was to see the stately plantation homes confiscated for taxes and debts. A few—a very few—had managed to hold out longer than the rest by mortgaging, borrowing, breaking their backs, and splitting the flesh on their hands to plant and harvest a crop that would haul them away from the brink of ruin. With the price of raw cotton soaring through the roof, one good crop was all that was needed.

Ryan Courtland had gambled everything, mortgaged everything there was left to mortgage, even their good name, to put such a crop in the field, and for the first time since the smoke and charred remains of the war had been cleared away, there was a chance blossoming to pay off some of the staggering debts and keep Rosalie afloat.

There *had* been a chance, that is.

For almost a month straight, the skies had opened and poured wrath on the banks of the Mississippi. From early dawn until late dusk, and often right through the night, the roads were churning quagmires, the fields were rivers of rainwater, the fertile lowlands were turned into a bog of rotting crops and mud washes. Some folks in the cities might have welcomed the cooling downpours as a relief from the scorching heat of August. Others, like Ryan, saw the cotton bolls ripening on stalks that were turning to mush, struggling to gain nourishment from roots that were rotting under a foot of slimy water. His family's salvation was out there and it was drowning in front of his eyes.

Amanda saw Ryan's fists clench and unclench by his sides, and she spun angrily on her sister. "You have no right to say such things to Ryan. Everything he does, he does for this family. You, of all people, should be the last one to criticize him."

Alisha's mouth curled with scorn. "If you are referring to my wedding plans, dear Amanda, you can stop right there."

"Why? Why can't I say what I'm thinking?" she asked, using Alisha's own capricious attitude against her. "Why *shouldn't* I say that the money you are planning to squander just so you can be the talk of the county for *one day* would ease the burden of this family for a year?''

"Karl gave me the money to spend on *myself.* He expects a grand wedding. He is a baron, for pity's sake!''

"His title might mean something in Europe, perhaps, but here he is just another rich speculator lording his wealth over those who gave up so much to end up with so little. How many of your guests will feel comfortable watching such a display of arrogance? No one has grand weddings anymore. And even if they could afford it, most would be too conscious of the feelings of their less fortunate friends and neighbors to rub their noses in it.''

"I don't care,'' Alisha insisted evenly. "I don't care if they're all sick with envy. And anyone who does not feel comfortable—including anyone in this room—can damn well sit at home and enjoy their own sour company!''

With that, she whirled on her heels and stormed out of the parlor. The draft of her passing caused the flame in the oil lamp to flicker and shudder, and until it steadied again, that was the only movement in the room. No one dared to breathe or make a sound. Sarah Courtland's hands lay motionless on the crush of watered silk, her lower lip was sucked between her teeth in an attempt to keep the quivering from spreading down into her chin.

Amanda knew she had allowed her temper to get the better of her, knew she should have let her sister run on unchallenged—but the pain on Ryan's face had driven her past her usual limits of patience. The pain was still there, pulling the smooth skin across his cheeks taut, pulsing in the small vein that traced along his temple.

She stood and crossed over to the hearth. She touched his arm, but it took several more moments of concentrated effort for his eyes to lose the glaze of outrage and for him to focus on her face and realize he was no longer confronting Alisha. It was a difficult task at the best of times, for aside from the few slight differences only a handful of people could discern, Amanda and Alisha were identical twins.

Chapter 2

Ryan's fingers were visibly unsteady as he lifted his hand and brushed the soft curve of Amanda's cheek.

"I'm all right," he murmured, sounding anything but. "She hasn't said anything I haven't heard before."

"Still, she had no right to say those awful things. Not after everything we've been through, everything you've done for us. For her."

"It doesn't matter," he insisted wearily. "We should save our sympathies for von Helmstaad. In another three weeks, she'll be his problem."

Amanda bit her lip and glanced over to where her father had retrieved the deck of cards and was laying them one by one on the table, studying each picture and number as if it were crucial they be placed in precisely the correct order. He kept blinking, fighting to keep the cards—and the world—in focus, and for that, Amanda would gladly have slapped Alisha to tears.

She turned her head to hide the anger in her eyes and stared at the blackness outside the curtainless French doors.

"It seems as if the rain has stopped," she remarked tautly.

Ryan followed her gaze to where the moonlight was shimmering on the wet grass, turning the wide puddles into sheets of molten pewter.

"As usual," he said. "When we least need clear skies."

Amanda studied his face a moment, then addressed her mother. "Will you and Father manage without us for a little while? I think I might like a breath of fresh air."

"Of course, my dear," Sarah replied, her hands fluttering back to her sewing. "Your father and I will just sit here and chat. Mind you take a shawl with you, the dampness could put a chill in your lungs."

Amanda barely paused to snatch up a knitted wrap before

exiting hastily through the French doors. Ryan was a brief pace behind, his face grim and his mouth set as he watched Amanda dash a hand across the tears that splashed down her cheeks. He remained a silent and discreet step behind her until they were far enough away from the house for her to unleash an unflattering litany of adjectives applied to their sister's sensitivity and compassion.

Her vitriol lasted until they reached the cobblestone circle that had once formed the heart of the formal gardens. It was, as Alisha had so artlessly pointed out, one of the harsher reminders of the state of disrepair into which Rosalie had fallen. Weeds twisted treacherously through the cobbles. The paint on the summerhouse was peeling from lack of use and attention; the structure itself was missing spindles, rails, and a whole section of the roof. Leaves clogged the floorboards and the vines that crept along the banisters were slowly choking the ornamental carvings and open grillwork. The summerhouse had once been an elegant, cool retreat from the sun, a place for lovers to exchange whispered promises under musky, sensuous bowers of honeysuckle and magnolia. Now it stood under the moonlight, a skeletal monument to a rich and easy lifestyle that was gone forever.

"You cannot blame Alisha for not wanting to marry here," Ryan commented, looking around. "It would take longer than her engagement period just to weed and reshape the gardens."

"I would take the time," Amanda said stubbornly. "You would too."

"Well . . . you and I are different. We don't seem to need the same things Alisha needs."

Amanda stopped at the foot of the wide steps leading up to the summerhouse. She glanced over her shoulder at the sound of a match scraping over a bootheel and studied her brother's face in the sharp, bright glare of the flame he touched to his cigar. His was a face of planes and angles, softened only by the startling blue eyes that were incredibly wise and honest for his twenty-six years. His hair was tawny blond, normally the color of chamois but now bleached al-

Straight for the Heart

most white by the daily exposure to the sun—exposure and
~kbreaking work that kept him lean and fit and finely tem-
ered her with. gave him little time to fuss over the limp he had

"She isn't all up and smoothed a stray lock of hair off
quietly. "I suppose it was a he, the unselfconscious gesture and cov-
we could save Rosalie from falling to the a dream to think

"I won't listen to that kind of talk," Amanda insisted,
withdrawing her hand. "Not from you. It isn't a dream.
You've proved it can be done. There is still plenty of time
before harvest, and if the weather clears—"

"The weather isn't going to clear in time, and there isn't
going to be any harvest. There isn't any way to repair the
damage that has already been done. The cotton is black with
rot; there is hardly enough tobacco to roll a cigar. We would
need a long, hot dry spell to even start to think about salvag-
ing enough to seed next year's crops."

"There," she said brightly. "You see? You're already
talking in terms of next year's crops."

"I could talk about growing wings and flying, but that
won't happen either."

"Everyone along the river is in the same position—even
the damned Yankees who thought they knew so much more
than we did. It isn't just us."

"There isn't a plantation within a hundred miles north or
south that isn't drowning under the floodwaters," he agreed
glumly. "As for Yankee know-how, the man who owns the
most property hereabouts doesn't seem to give a damn if the
land drowns or not."

"Wainright," she said on a despairing sigh.

"Wainright. And if I didn't know better, I'd say he played
a hand in this somehow—" He tipped his head up and waved
his cigar at the moisture-laden clouds where they were once
again drifting back to blanket the moon. "He's just waiting
there, like a vulture, knowing we cannot possibly buy back

our bank note unless we have something close ... the
crop this year."

"He can't force you to sell." ... the dollar.

"He doesn't have to force me. He ... all the price of a
bank forecloses, then steal it f.. burn just to think of it."

Twenty thousand prime ... another six months."

fence to enclose it. M...

"The loan is... to show in the fields, it might as well be

"With ... days. The fifty thousand we owe . . . might as
due in...
well be fifty million."

Amanda frowned and tore a leaf off the trailing end of a
vine. Fifty thousand dollars. Before the war, they had
thought nothing of paying fifty thousand dollars for a pair of
prime broodmares. Now they had to deliberate carefully over
spending five dollars to replace a sway-backed workhorse.

"There is . . . another way to clear our debt *and* stop
Wainright from sniffing around Rosalie."

Ryan drew a deep breath, pulling the harsh cigar smoke
into his lungs at the same time. "No."

"It's probably my fault anyway that he is so persistent. I
was the one who slapped his face and called him a lowdown
cowardly worm."

"If the shoe fits . . ."

She glanced up from the shredded leaf. "It wouldn't be so
very terrible."

"I would burn Rosalie to the ground first," he said suc-
cinctly. "With you in it."

"I could do worse."

"Than marry E. Forrest Wainright?" Ryan spit out a
shred of tobacco and thrust the lit end of the cigar under her
nose. "Anything worse would be slithering through the grass
on its belly and you know it."

"I know it," she sighed. "But if it's the only way—"

He swore and threw the cigar aside, then grasped her
roughly by the shoulders. "Now you listen to me, young
lady, and listen well. I'm telling you *no*. Not while I am in
charge of this household, and not while I have a sound breath

left in my body.'' He saw the sudden shine the harshness of his words brought to her eyes and his grip relented somewhat. ''Having one addlebrained sister marry for all the wrong reasons is hard enough to swallow; having another swanning about, threatening to sacrifice herself for the good of mankind, would just about put me over the edge. I wouldn't be responsible for my actions. Would you want *that* burden on your shoulders too?''

''I think you're almost over the edge anyway,'' she said, smiling haltingly. ''And if you want to talk about sacrifices, what are you playing at each day when you ride out into the fields and each night when you come back with your hands split and bleeding, the skin burned from your shoulders, your clothes so ragged and filthy a darky wouldn't wear them? If Alisha was right about anything, it was about calling you the noble hero. Why are you so determined to do this alone? Rosalie is as much my home as it is yours; I'm entitled to swan a little, even to make sacrifices if it means keeping our home in our family.''

''You have already helped more than you should. And for Christ's sake, don't start throwing Alisha's words in my face. She wouldn't know the meaning of the word sacrifice if it jumped up and bit her in the nose. Were you not the one who pointed out that what she is squandering on a party for one day would keep a family in bread and meat for a year? And as if it wasn't enough to watch her sharpening her claws for von Helmstaad's fortune, I gave you money for a new dress last month and where did it end up? On Alisha's back.''

''The world will not end if I am seen twice in the same frock, whereas she . . . she needs to look pretty. She needs to have pretty things around her.''

''Whereas you,'' he said sardonically, ''are unscathed by any such heinous character flaws? You prefer wearing rags and languishing in poverty.''

''I am not perfect,'' she admitted softly. ''But I am content with who and what I am.''

''And what are you? A proud, stubborn woman who refuses to let herself fall in love with a man who clearly worships the ground she walks on, but who would, for all the wrong reasons—including that of ignoble martyrdom—be willing to sacrifice herself to a slimy, weasel-faced carpetbagger. If that isn't the perfect irony, I don't know what is.''

Amanda sighed extravagantly. ''Not you too. Is that what all this is about? Me and Josh?''

''All this is about wanting to see you happy and safe.''

''I am happy. And I'm perfectly safe here at Rosalie.''

''Hiding behind your widow's weeds,'' he added pointedly.

''I'm not hiding. And I stopped wearing black last year, in case you hadn't noticed.''

''Only because it confused and upset Father, not because you wanted to appear in public without your armor.''

Amanda squared her shoulders at the stab of truth that came with her brother's words and turned away, climbing the two wide steps that took her into the summerhouse. She walked to the center of the small pavilion and paused in the blue-white shaft of moonlight that filtered through the broken slats of the roof. Her hair, bleached silver by the uncertain light, tumbled around her shoulders in a soft cascade of loose curls.

Watching her, Ryan's heart ached with pride for her beauty . . . and at the same time cursed Alisha for sharing it, for despoiling it somehow. Amanda should have been the one marrying a baron or a duke, even a king, by God. She was honest and unselfish and good. Her smile could brighten the gloomiest of days, her laugh could lighten the darkest of thoughts. How rarely she smiled these days, however. In spite of the brave front she showed most of the others—that of the good daughter, the loving widow, the embodiment of Southern grace, pride, and honor—there was a streak of loneliness in her a mile wide and a fathom deep, its flow as strong and turbulent as the currents in the Mississippi. She deserved to be happy. She deserved to be unafraid. She deserved to be loved, for God's sake, even if he had to rap her

on the head, bind and gag her, and prop her at the altar
beside Joshua Brice.

If that was what she wanted, that is.

"Are you in love with him?" Ryan asked quietly.

"Josh and I grew up together," she replied without turning. "We have known each other all our lives."

"But are you in love with him?"

Amanda felt her cheeks grow warm despite the cooling
dampness in the air. "I . . . don't know."

"Well, you don't hate him, do you?"

"No, of course not. I mean, he has almost been like another brother to me. He was one of Caleb's closest friends
and . . ." Her voice trailed off miserably and her head
bowed under the weight of her thoughts.

"And you are worried he thinks he owes you some kind of
loyalty because he was with Caleb when he died?"

The silvered waterfall of her hair rippled slightly as she
shook her head. "No. No, it isn't that. Not exactly."

"Then what . . . exactly . . . is holding you back?"

"I don't know. I don't know what I feel for Josh. I don't
know what he feels for me."

"He's here nearly every other day putting up with
Mother's attempts at subtlety and Alisha's lack of it; he must
feel something. Has he asked you to marry him yet?"

"No."

"Would you agree to marry him if he did ask?"

"Why? Are you planning to hold a shotgun to his back if
he doesn't?"

"I might. I would if you wanted me to."

Amanda lifted her shoulders and dropped them again.
"Why is everyone so eager to see me married off again?"

"Because it's time," Ryan said gently. "Because you
need a husband . . . and Verity needs a father."

She twisted her hands into the folds of her shawl and
pulled it closer around her shoulders. Verity Leigh Jackson
was a month away from her fourth birthday. She was the only
good thing that had come out of the hardships, terror, and

deprivations of the war, and Amanda's love for her was as fierce and uncompromising as her love for Rosalie.

"Josh adores her," Ryan pointed out.

"Everyone adores her, that doesn't count."

"She held his hand the other day. And *talked* to him . . . without leaving his ear full of spit."

Amanda frowned and looked over. Verity's infancy had not been one of carefree days and lush excesses. A tiny, delicate little thing at birth, she had been born into a world of gunfire, tramping boots, rough language, and leering, unshaven faces that belonged to strangers who were as likely to shout at her as kick her out of the way. Even now, with the war behind them, she spoke mainly in whispers and took to hiding in dark corners if there were tall, booted men around.

"You don't play fair," she murmured.

"Life hasn't been very fair lately. To any of us. It is your decision, however, to marry or not to marry."

"Thank you very much for saying so. I was beginning to think it was everyone else's decision *but* mine."

"Mother is only concerned for your, ah, declining years."

"I am hardly on the threshold of senility."

"A few years ago, you would have considered yourself to be on the threshold of antiquity, and an unmarried lady of so many years to be almost beyond redemption."

"I've been married," she reminded him sourly, casting him a look that suggested she was not beyond boxing his ears. "And if I have to be 'redeemed' again . . . well . . . I would rather do it with my eyes wide open and my expectations grounded more firmly in reality."

"You were barely sixteen when you wed Caleb, and there was a war going on. What did you expect? Stardust and choruses of Hallelujah?"

"Maybe just some honesty."

It was Ryan's turn to frown. "In what way was Caleb *dis*honest? You knew he was returning to the fighting. You knew there was a chance he wouldn't come back."

"No." She shook her head slowly. "No, I didn't know he wouldn't come back. It never occurred to me he wouldn't come back. It never occurred to him he wouldn't come back and insofar as that goes, I guess we were both too young and starry-eyed to make promises we couldn't keep.''

''Promises? What promises?''

She bowed her head again and the movement sent a shiver of silver light down the length of her hair. ''He promised to kill every Yankee who dared set foot across the Mason-Dixon line. He promised to keep me warm and safe and happy, to fill me full of children who would comfort and keep us in our doting old age. And me? I promised I would love and cherish him forever.

''Forever?'' she repeated in a whisper. ''It didn't seem like so difficult a promise to make when we were standing in the candlelight and roses, but now . . . now I can barely remember what he looked like. As for stardust and Hallelujahs, we were both virgins on our wedding night. Maybe if we'd had more time to practice, we could have apologized less and enjoyed it more. As it was, it was a lot of sweat and bother with nothing much to show for it at the end but wrinkled sheets.''

''For Christ's sake, Amanda,'' Ryan muttered.

''Well, it's true. It wasn't the grand, passionate experience I was led to believe it was supposed to be. It was clumsy and painful and . . . and rather embarrassing, if you must know.''

''I never said I *must.*''

''But you did ask.''

''So I did. I guess I just wasn't expecting as blunt an answer.''

''Or that particular answer at all? Don't worry, I don't imagine every woman feels the same way. Dianna, for instance: You can just about see her heart leaping out of her chest every time she gets near you.''

Ryan was thankful the darkness hid the flush that crept up his throat. Dianna Moore, the Judge's daughter, was about as close as he would ever come to making a complete and utter fool of himself over a woman. She was beautiful, genteel, sweetly tempered, with an inner radiance that made a man melt at the knees and stumble over the thickness of his tongue.

"She loves you, Ryan Courtland, without a doubt or hesitation. Almost as much as you love her. She wouldn't blink if you asked her to marry you tomorrow."

"I can't. I can't ask her to marry . . . this." He spread his arms helplessly. "Or me. She deserves better. A fine home and servants, not reclaimed cotton fields and a husband who comes home at night looking worse than a darky, too tired to worry if the sheets get wrinkled or not."

"You're doing it again," she warned evenly. "Equating everyone's values with Alisha's. Do you honestly think Dianna cares if you have money or not? Do you think any of this matters to her?"

"It matters to me."

"Then you deserve to lose her to the Yankee."

Ryan's jaw tensed into a hard ridge. A "friend" had told him Dianna was being escorted around Natchez on the arm of a Yankee who had been an acquaintance of the Judge's before the war. This "friend" also said the Yankee was as handsome as the devil himself, as rich as Croesus, and eager to ingratiate himself with the local populace by marrying one of their own.

"My, my, big brother," Amanda mused, signaling an end to the conversation as she descended the stairs of the summerhouse and started walking back toward the house. "So easy to pontificate on the choices someone else should make . . . but how difficult to take it when the finger is pointing at you."

Chapter 3

Alisha Courtland stretched and purred with delicious contentment as she listened to the rush of leaves stirring in the wind. It sounded like muted applause and made her skin tingle, adding to the heated waves of satisfaction already flooding through her body. It had been a performance worthy of applause, and absently she let her fingers trail across her full breasts, down the smooth indent of her belly, and finally, with a kind of adoring fondness, into the moist, silky thatch of curls at the juncture of her thighs.

She was still throbbing, and so dewy her fingers slid through the golden triangle and elicited a moan of pleasure.

"You're only asking for more trouble by doing that."

Alisha smiled lazily and turned to admire the sleek, hard body reclining alongside her. His skin was glistening from the strain of his own performance—one equally deserving of rapturous applause. A large, callused hand covered hers and brought it to rest at the base of his belly, and she felt a thrill course through her blood. He was not as completely spent as she might have expected him to be, and even as her fingers wrapped teasingly around him, there was a distinct stirring of interest.

"I suppose we must get dressed soon," she murmured with genuine reluctance.

"I'm in no hurry to leave."

Alisha snuggled against the curve of his body and draped a cool, bare leg over his. "Nor am I. But we have been out here for well over an hour and I might be missed."

"You'll be missed more if you leave now," he said huskily, pushing himself up into her hand.

She laughed and released him, then sat up and gave her tousled mane of hair a shake. The exhilaration she was feeling was due to more than just the wild lovemaking of the past hour. There was the added element of risk, daring to do it so close to the house, that had aroused her to unbelievable heights. They were in the summerhouse, and although it was late and most of the manor was in total darkness, she could see the ghostly silhouette of the gabled roof and tall, jutting chimneys etched against the sky.

She suspected . . . no, she knew damned well she had screamed at the peak of her orgasm, despite his efforts to keep her mouth covered with his, but she had seen no flicker of light, no glow of a lamp moving from room to room.

"It would serve them right if they heard me," she muttered petulantly, still bristling over the heated exchange in the parlor.

"What?"

"Oh . . . nothing." Alisha glanced down at her lover and smiled through the ribbon of heat that slithered between her thighs. He was broad across the shoulders, his muscles incredibly well defined from the hours he spent working under the broiling sun. His hair was auburn, his eyes jade green. His face was handsome in a brooding, aristocratic way, with a straight, Romanesque nose and a mouth that promised as well as delivered a multitude of carnal pleasures. In all, he was a prime specimen of pure animal magnificence—with his clothes off. Dressed, he became a reflection of his position in life: the fifth son of a man who had lost everything in the war. A well-bred Southern gentleman, he had been raised to excel in riding fine horses, drinking good whiskey, charming beautiful women into compromising positions. Stripped of his home, his horses, and the money to buy anything more than cheap, raw spirits, he still possessed the magnetism to find his way into Alisha Courtland's bed, but he could hardly hope to aspire to anything more. As much as she enjoyed his body, Alisha could no more have considered a more serious tie to Joshua Brice than she could to a common field hand.

"Has anyone ever told you you resemble a cat when your eyes are half closed like that?"

"Not recently," she purred.

"You behave like one too when your claws are bared and you feel the need to defend your territory."

Alisha's body tensed perceptibly as Josh's hand slid up the length of her thigh. "I wasn't aware I was being challenged to defend anything tonight. If you truly prefer Amanda over me—"

"If you truly preferred to marry me instead of that larded German toad," he countered with a growl, "neither one of us would have to sneak around in the dead of night."

"We don't have to now," she said in a pique. "I can just go on back inside and—"

He rose up beside her and silenced her with a kiss that was deep enough, long enough, brutal enough to scatter any thought of resistance when he pushed her back onto the crush of clothing that had served as their mattress. His hand glided between her thighs, winning a husky groan as he stroked deftly through and into the pearlized folds of flesh. He slipped two fingers inside her and, after a few moments of admonitory, teasing pressure, thrust them deep enough and hard enough to bring her hips rising up off the floor with a raggedly mouthed oath.

It was indeed a pity, she lamented inwardly, but how could she, Alisha Courtland, possibly allow herself to become the wife of a fifth son of a bankrupted plantation owner? A lover, yes, but a wife? His father had turned them all into sharecroppers, for pity's sake, barely scraping together enough of a loan to rent out a miserly few acres of what had once been their own sizable plantation. Josh had, naturally and honorably, pleaded with her to marry him, but she had had more than her share of tired old dimity frocks and red, chapped hands. Josh was handsome and virile and insatiable—exactly the kind of mate she craved physically. Karl von Helmstaad, on the other hand, was old and rich and infatuated with her. He owned a grand and stately manor that was sorely in need of a woman's extravagant touch, and if his generosity thus far had been any indication of things to come, he would be more than able to provide her with a lifestyle that would keep her young, beautiful, and pampered forever.

She also needed Karl Kristoffer von Helmstaad for another important reason. It had been three months since the first glorious tryst with Joshua Brice, and God only knew how many times they had been together since. She did not know on which occasion she had been careless enough to let his seed take root within her, she only knew her time had come and gone and she needed an obliging husband quickly. Karl was convenient, gullible, and as impatient to be done with the civilities as she pretended to be. In three weeks' time, she would have a rich, doting husband, a father for her unborn child, and a lover who would go to almost any lengths just to hear her cry his name in ecstasy.

She gasped it out now as the wet heat of his mouth closed around her nipple, suckling the flesh with the same lusty rhythm his fingers were using to debilitate her senses elsewhere.

Defend her territory, indeed! As if it needed defending from her cloyingly naive, ingratiatingly wholesome twin. Why, it almost brought a laugh to her lips to imagine Amanda sprawled naked on the floor of a ruined summerhouse, her body running wet with desire, her breath coming in broken gasps, her hips moving in a blur beneath a man who grunted words of encouragement at each clenching shiver.

It *did* make her laugh each and every time she remembered pressing her ear to her bedroom wall and listening to the sounds the bride and groom had made on their wedding night. Polite conversation. Polite whispers. A sudden and oh-so-brief sawing of bedsprings that ended in more polite murmurings. She doubted if either Amanda or the doting, doe-eyed Caleb Jackson had even taken off their nightclothes.

Alisha would miss none of them. Not the simpering silliness of her mother, not the exasperating foolishness of her father, or the glowering hostility of her brother. Most decidedly she would not miss Amanda. In fact, when the time for pretenses was over, it would give Alisha immense pleasure to tell her dear sister that her beau had only been playing a game—a game Alisha had devised and encouraged shortly after she and Josh had become lovers.

"I can't deceive Amanda by letting her think I am courting her," he had protested. "I can't give her false expectations."

"Amanda expects nothing from you but your friendship. She never has and never will. It is only the rest of the family we will be deceiving. They are so determined to see me wed to Karl, they would spirit me away at the first hint of rebellion."

"I wouldn't feel comfortable."

"Do you love me, Josh? Do you?"

"You know damn well—"

"Then you mustn't abandon me now. Oh, please, Josh! It was Ryan's idea to arrange the marriage with Karl. He knows the baron would not allow his wife's family to become homeless and destitute, and it is Ryan's intention to save Rosalie at any cost—even my happiness."

"How can he force you into the marriage when he knows you don't love the man?"

Alisha had bowed her head sorrowfully. "Land, property, the honorable Courtland name has always been of supreme importance to Ryan. He is adamant the plantation must be saved. And as much as I loathe what I am being forced to do, I cannot stand by and see my family driven off our land. The d'Ibervilles have lived here since the Trace was just a footpath between Natchez and Nashville, and the only boats on the Mississippi were birchbark canoes. I cannot stand by and watch my poor mother cruelly turned out of the house she and her mother and her mother's mother were born in. I just can't! You couldn't either, if the situation was reversed. If it was *you* the family hopes depended upon, would you be able to run away and leave them? Would you be able to live with the guilt and the pain, knowing you had left them in ruin and despair?"

Alisha had flung herself tearfully into his arms and Josh had succumbed like a hapless schoolboy. He was so desperately in love with her she could have asked for the moon and he would have flown straight up to fetch it. He had played into her hands more perfectly than she could have hoped, and he still did, sweet merciful Jesus. He still did.

"Josh," she gasped. "Josh!"

Alisha bit her lip against the scream that was threatening to tear from her throat as his hands and mouth worked her body into a frenzy. She clutched at his arms and dug her nails into his flesh, vowing to rake him into bloody ribbons if he didn't replace the dancing, teasing fingers with something of more substance.

When he did, she welcomed the first savage thrust with an eagerness that left them both gasping for the wit to muffle their cries of pleasure. She met each successive thrust with shuddering breathlessness, wrapping her arms, her long legs around his plunging body, urging him to a near-brutish demonstration of his skill as a lover.

She was not disappointed. His strength and power filled her, even frightened her a little as the force of each thrust slammed her closer and closer to the splintered edge of the stairs. But the fear was an added elixir and she arched up in an agony of pleasure as her climax tore through her, the spasms so powerful, they shocked her body into a hard, tight curl of ecstasy. She heard Josh's strangled groan and felt the heat breaking within her, and she held him locked in her arms, rocking and writhing with each throb of sensation until the last heated pulse was wrung from their flesh.

"Alisha . . . Alisha . . ."

She swallowed hard and gulped at the air needed to clear her senses. He was still moving inside her as if reluctant to admit the finality of the act. She stroked her hands down the length of his back and kept her limbs twined around his waist, sharing his despair at feeling him slowly diminish.

"Tell me you love me," she whispered. "Promise me you will never leave me."

"You know I love you," he rasped, dragging his head out of the crook of her shoulder. "You know I could never leave you."

His mouth descended with a fierce passion and when the

kiss ended, Alisha's eyes were glazed with pleasure and triumph.

"I . . . want to be with you so much. Promise me we'll be together one day, Josh. Only promise me this and I know I can endure anything. Anything," she added, her voice catching on a sob.

Josh lifted himself free and rolled beside her. He gathered her protectively against his chest and felt the sting of outrage burning behind his eyes, not even wanting to think of what lay ahead, only three weeks away.

"Are you absolutely certain you want to go through with the wedding?" he asked tautly, his body rigid with anger.

"You know I must. The situation is even more desperate now that the crops are a total loss."

Josh pressed a fevered kiss into the silky blonde crown of her hair. "I can't bear to think of that bloated, loathsome toady touching you. Sometimes . . . sometimes I think I'll go mad just imagining what he'll want from you."

"What he wants and what he gets are two different things," she insisted.

"He'll be your *husband,* for God's sake. He'll have certain rights."

"He will never have the right to my heart," she whispered, tilting her head up so that their eyes met. "For it belongs only and always to you, my love. Only to you."

His hands shifted and he grasped two streaming fistfuls of silvered hair, holding her mouth against his until the salty taste of her tears broke them apart.

"I must go," she breathed, and started to collect the scattered articles of her clothing.

"When will I see you again?"

"Tomorrow," she said, deliberately misinterpreting his question. "You are still coming to tea, are you not?"

"You know what I mean."

Alisha shook her head. "We will have to be careful from now on."

Josh laughed dryly and glanced around the summerhouse. "You call this being careful?"

"You were the one who came tossing pebbles at my window. If I hadn't come down, you probably would have climbed that rickety old trellis and crashed straight into Ryan's room.''

''I needed to see you. I *probably* wouldn't have been able to make it through tomorrow's little farce without telling them all to go to hell and lifting your skirts right there in the parlor.''

Alisha let a small rush of breath escape her lips as his hands pushed up beneath the camisole she had just slipped over her shoulders. Her nipples constricted instantly under the pressure of his fingertips, but she drew determinedly away and set to work fastening the ribboned closure.

After a long moment of frowning concentration, she looked up and smiled. ''You wouldn't dare do something so scandalous . . . would you?''

''Wouldn't I? It isn't me who is insisting we keep our feelings for one another a secret. And it certainly isn't me who's afraid to tell Ryan what a bastard he is.''

Alisha's smile froze. ''You're not planning to do something . . . rash . . . are you?''

Josh pulled his shirt over his head and raked his hands through his hair. ''If you want to know if I plan to demand satisfaction on a dueling field, the answer is no. Unfortunately, Ryan is a far better shot than I, and the baron . . . well . . .''

Alisha held her breath. ''Yes?''

He ground his teeth together as he dragged his breeches over his ankles. ''The baron has a purpose to serve. After that, I won't guarantee anything.''

''Wh-what do you mean?''

''I mean, I will do whatever I have to do to make you mine,'' he said quietly.

''But I am yours, you know I am.''

''Mine *completely*,'' he said with grim emphasis. ''In every way. Even if it means making a rich widow out of you.''

''A widow? Oh, Josh, no! No, you mustn't even think such a thing. If anything went wrong, or if you were caught!

No, Josh. No! You must promise me you won't even consider—''

''Hush,'' he commanded, pulling her into his arms. It was the first time he had dared to voice his turbulent thoughts out loud, and he cursed his error in judgment, especially when he felt the tremors of fear racing through Alisha's body. ''I'll think what I want to think, and if I *think* there is some safe way to hasten your toad prince along to his kingdom in the sky . . . well . . .''

Alisha clung to him, unable to suppress her shivers of excitement. It was working! It had taken him long enough to work himself into such a state that the only logical solution had finally presented itself. For all his boldness and brawn, he was somewhat lacking in the area of initiative, and she had begun to think she would have to spell out the obvious answer to all their problems. But now that the idea was firmly rooted, she would see that it flourished and grew, and in seven or eight months' time—after the baby was born, of course . . .

A low throb of sound, still distant, yet familiar enough to raise the tiny hairs along her arms, echoed through the darkness, distracting both occupants of the summerhouse. As they stared motionless at the velvet blackness that stretched out toward the river, Alisha's fingers curled around the gold locket that hung between her breasts and she rubbed it as she would a talisman.

A second plaintive wail reverberated over the waters of the mighty Mississippi and Alisha groped the shadows for Josh's hand.

''The *Contessa*,'' he guessed, returning the questioning squeeze in her fingers. ''She is due to dock in Natchez tomorrow.''

''The *Contessa*,'' Alisha repeated in a hushed murmur. ''We missed her on her last trip upriver.''

Josh looked at her with some surprise. ''Didn't you just finish saying we had to be careful from now on?''

Alisha's eyes were shining. Josh had introduced her to more than just sexual adventures. Like most of the Southern gentry, he had learned early that to a planter's son—especially one who was groomed to marry into money rather than earn any of his own by honest means—the sound of a riverboat whistle was the beckoning call to easy women, smooth-flowing whiskey, and high stakes games of chance.

He had taken her on board one of these floating casinos, intending only to amuse her with a few hours of harmless diversion, but the diversions had grown less and less harmless when she realized she could put her father's clever parlor tricks to good advantage. Over the course of the past few months, the meager handful of hoarded dollars they had started with had grown into enough to pay for the rent on a small hotel room and to outfit them both in the fancy attire needed to gain entry to the best games on the best boats.

"It may be our last chance for a while," Alisha said breathlessly. "It may be our last chance *period* to luck into a big game. If we won enough, we could give Ryan the money he needs to stave off the bankers and I wouldn't have to go through with the marriage to Karl von Helmstaad."

Josh drew in a slow, deep breath along with the bait. "It's too risky. What if someone sees us? What if someone recognizes you?"

"If the *Contessa* is up from New Orleans, there won't be anything but Yankees on board. Rich, bored Yankees who have nothing better to do than play poker and stare down the front of my bodice."

"I don't know," he said, hesitating. "Didn't you say the last time you thought someone was staring at more than your bodice?"

"They were," she agreed, leaning against him. "But then so were you. I could feel you undressing me all the way across the salon. Why, it almost put me off my game the whole blessed night long."

He was weakening, and he knew it. Her breasts, clad only in the thin layer of her chemise, were pillowed against his chest, warm and soft and ripe with entreaty as she tickled his chin with a kiss.

"Besides," she whispered, trailing her lips down his throat. "You *know* how enthusiastic I get when we win."

Josh knew. He also knew the risks of becoming too familiar a face along the waterfront. He had already heard the rumors concerning a beautiful lady gambler whose "luck" was beginning to annoy the owners of the riverboats. He dared not tell Alisha, however. The challenge, the thrill, the danger would only whet her appetite more.

"Hasn't anyone become suspicious about you making so many trips into Natchez?"

"Au contraire, my darling. I'm sure they're happy not to have me underfoot all the time. Furthermore, I have a trousseau to buy, don't I? And they know I'm well chaperoned by my dearest friend Olivia Ward. She's such a mouse, they think me quite admirable for spending any time with her at all. Not that I have," she giggled. "I doubt I would recognize her if I tripped over her in the street. Oh, Josh—" She laced her fingers behind his neck and covered his face and throat with tiny, feathery kisses. "Can't we go? Can't we at least *pretend* we are still just as rich and bored as all those damned Yankees? Just one more time?"

"Alisha . . ."

She pouted prettily and thrust her tongue between his lips. His breeches had not made it above his knees, and she was more than a little aware of his weakening resolve. She left his mouth wet and still wanting, and trailed her tongue down onto his chest, stalking his nipple like a hungry predator. Sharp white teeth plucked at the raised nub, winning a jolted curse before they prowled lower on his belly.

Josh threaded his fingers into her hair, his teeth clamped around a half-formed protest as he felt the greedy tug and pull of her lips. She would get her way again. She always did. He would take her into Natchez and help her dress in her velvets and ruffles, and he would be there to watch her back if something . . . anything went wrong. She was good with the cards, there was no question of that. Even counting the ups and down, the wins and losses, the extravagant meals and hotel rooms, he knew there was enough to buy their way into one big game where five hundred could become five thousand in a matter of minutes.

"Hell and damn." He gasped and looked down at the silken crown of her hair where it rose and fell with vigorous determination over his groin. His hands tightened and his head arched back, his body began to shudder and jerk with the persuasive power of her lips.

His own lips moved rigidly through a ragged promise, one that echoed harshly on each gust of his breath. It was a promise that he would never let her go. Never. Not for any reason. Not to any other man. Not ever.

It was a promise he vowed to keep if it cost him his life.

Amanda was wide awake, seated on the cushioned window ledge of her bedroom. She was not sure what had wakened her, only that she had been feeling restless and warm for the past hour or so. The chamber was steeped in heavy shadow, the guttering lamp on the nightstand too miserly to throw off more light than what puddled on the table beneath it.

There was a time when lamps and fires were kept burning in every room day or night. There were servants to fetch a shawl at the slightest hint of a chill, to run a pan filled with hot coals between the bedsheets so that tender pink feet would not suffer a moment's worth of discomfort. These days it was up to each member of the family to see to their own needs. If Amanda forgot to fill her kindling box, she spent a long, cold night shivering. Each drop of precious whale oil was guarded as if it were pure liquid gold, and if a lamp was lit past sundown, it was done so only out of absolute necessity.

Of the hundreds of slaves and servants Rosalie had boasted before the war, only Mercy and her husband Obediah had remained, both of whom had declared themselves too old and set in their ways to regard emancipation as anything but a threat. They had stayed on of their own free will, scorning the masses of newly freed slaves who were starving and unable to find work with their new Northern masters. Promises of jobs and plenty of money to buy their own homes and hire their own servants had proved to be no more than that: empty promises. Every day Ryan went out to the stables he found more and more hungry mouths huddled there, offering to work his fields in exchange for food and a place to sleep. He had not refused any of them; he could not afford to, but the cost of feeding and clothing them only added more strain to his already limited reserves.

In some ways, Amanda did not mind the hardships. She did not resent having to cook or sew or sweep the rooms; it gave her a sense of accomplishment, of usefulness. Granted, there had been times—and there still were—when she felt like crying from exhaustion and frustration, but there were more times when she experienced a sense of satisfaction at having learned to bake sourdough bread and cook a firestorm cajun creole that set even Mercy's eyes to watering.

The hard times came with watching Verity make do with dresses that were cut from her own, or seeing her clutch the rag-filled doll in her arms and pretend the gingham face had eyes instead of buttons and a mouth instead of a row of thick black stitchery. Her own youth had been so full of excess that it made Amanda want to weep with the injustice of it all whenever they passed by a shop window brimming with porcelain dolls and fancy wicker prams.

She sighed and leaned her forehead against the window sash. The clouds had blotted out what slender hopes there were of a clear morning, and it wouldn't be very long before the mist thickened into rain. Poor Ryan. Of all of them, he had worked the hardest to keep Rosalie on its feet, scratching out gardens to keep the family fed, mucking out the stables to keep the livestock healthy. If nothing else, the rain had forced him to slow down a little. To catch his breath. In the event the weather did improve and the cotton did have a chance to recover, he would need every last ounce of stamina he possessed to oversee the harvest.

A sound outside the window caught her attention. She listened closely for it to come again, and when it did, she lifted the heavy sash and leaned fully out into the night air to follow it.

If the night had not been so hazy, the paddle wheeler would have been visible when it reached the bend in the river less than a mile away. As it was, Amanda closed her eyes and pictured the sight as she had seen it so many times: the deck lights twinkling and sparkling through the trees like a cluster of slow-moving fireflies, the huge rolling paddle wheel cutting into the river's current, pushing a wash of white, foaming water into its wake.

As a child, she had let her imagination fling her across the open spaces and carry her away on one of the huge, floating monsters, leaving nothing to mark her passage other than the fading eddies of music and the trailing plumes of black boiler smoke.

Her fantasies were not entirely of her own making, she knew. William Courtland had been no stranger to the riverboats, and he had regaled his family with many a colorful story of the grand salons, the high-stakes poker games, the thrill of watching fortunes won and lost on a throw of dice.

Amanda flinched as a fat splash of rain bounced off the window ledge and startled her up off her elbows. She started to lower the sash again, but a blurred movement in the gardens below made her stop and shrink back against the wall. It looked like someone running. No . . . it was two people running, and one of them, her skirts hiked high in front and belling out like a canvas sail behind, was Alisha.

What on earth was her sister doing outside at this time of the night? And who was the man in the garden with her?

The two figures ran beneath the shelter of the roof overhang and Amanda lost them. They were too far away to hear more than a whispered exchange before the man emerged and slipped away into the darkness, leaving Amanda with the distinct impression of someone hastily tucking in clothes and refastening buttons. The shadows made it impossible to identify him, but she did not think it was Karl von Helmstaad. Alisha's fiancé resembled a large, squat bloatfly, and would

many wild stretch of anyone's imagination, have been
as quickly or as agilely as this late-night par-
mind on ha... ...ha was having second thoughts about
nobody was going to ...anda dismissed the thought with-

It had to be a lover, then, ine... ...and title. Nothing and
shadows of midnight. Having a young..., ...estinely in the
certainly explain why she was so indifferent to the... would
heaped on Karl von Helmstaad. Nor was the notion all that
shocking or difficult to accept. Alisha attracted men like a
cake attracted ants. Armies of them had passed through Mississippi wearing the blue and the gray, and Alisha had
thrived on the attention lavished upon her by both.

Amanda turned her head slightly, catching the faint sound
of tiptoeing feet in the hall outside the door of the adjoining
bedroom. Her glance was intercepted by the ghostly reflection in the cheval mirror—a reflection that might have been
Alisha herself save for the minuscule variances in their features. When it was not pressed flat in approbation, Amanda's
mouth was a shade fuller. Her nose was a breath thinner, her
hair a glimmer lighter. All of their lives, however, they had
been mistaken one for the other, and there had been no lack
of suitors eager to win the favors of either twin when such
things were considered to be of monumental importance.
Moreover, truth be told, it had been a game of sorts to trade
places with this beau or that—a game that had rapidly lost its
charm when Amanda realized her sister was decidedly freer
with the liberties she allowed.

It was possibly one of the reasons why Amanda had accepted the marriage proposal from Caleb Jackson. His reserved demeanor had never appealed to Alisha, and she had
found his strict sense of honor too stifling and far too boring.
The Jacksons had owned the Mercantile Bank in Natchez, so
the families had both been pleased when they had announced
their intentions to marry on his next furlough home. Amanda

had, it seemed, always done the right thing.

Caleb Jackson had been her _____ nights. He had been both g_____ tant to vilify her in any_____ urgency that always _____ helplessly in her _____ring impression of bony arms and legs singing the pr___er in the sheets.

_____ Brice was neither bony nor modest. He was lean and hard and exuded a vitality that could not be easily dismissed . . . or, she suspected, too easily forgotten.

Amanda's gaze sought its own accusing stare in the polished surface of the mirror.

She had not meant to be quite so candid with Ryan in the garden earlier, but she had spoken the truth when she had admitted she could scarcely recall Caleb's face anymore. She had to rely more and more on the daguerreotype of him she kept on the bureau, a glossy gray-and-white image of a stiff-backed young man proudly standing in his Confederate uniform, too wary of the newfangled photographic process to spare a smile.

When she had been told of his death, she had held his picture against her breast and wept for the loss. She had wept over Stephen and Evan too, and the countless other friends, neighbors, and acquaintances whose names appeared on the long rolls of casualty lists. After a time, their faces had all started to blend together, but none, other than her brothers, took precedence in her sorrow.

Was Joshua Brice partly to blame for this growing indifference? Was it because Josh was here and real and vibrantly alive that she could conjure his handsome face in the blink of an eye?

There was no answer forthcoming from her reflection, and Amanda's gaze slipped down the length of the shapeless cotton nightdress she wore. It was mended in places and so threadbare the muted glow from the lamp was strong enough to outline the shape of her body beneath. It was the same shape as Alisha's, with the same voluptuous fullness across the breasts, the same slender waist and long, lithe legs. So what was different about them? Why was Alisha returning breathless from a tryst in the garden while she stood in a dark bedroom resenting it?

Maybe Ryan was right. Maybe she had been hiding behind her widow's weeds too long. Josh cared for her. He would love and protect Verity as if she were his own child. He was not afraid to bend his back to the land or to be seen with calluses on his hands and dirt under his fingernails. She was comfortable in his company. While it might not be love she felt for him, it was certainly a deep fondness.

For E. Forrest Wainright, on the other hand, she felt only disdain. An admitted speculator and profiteer, he had made his fortune during the war selling blackmarket goods to fools who were willing to pay exorbitant prices for silk underpinnings and English wool. He had come to Natchez two years ago from Charleston where, it was rumored, the military government had begun to frown on his less than lily white business ventures.

Wainright would never bend his back to the land; he was far more interested in buying up every spare acre he could lay a hand to then turning around and selling it again at a 500 percent profit. He had been trying to buy Rosalie for several months now but had met a formidable obstacle in Ryan's stubbornness. Wainright was unaccustomed to losing at any match of wills, and Amanda guessed it was no longer even a case of wanting the land so much as wanting to see the Courtlands humbled.

He was arrogant, possessive, and cold-bloodedly ruthless. Amanda was decidedly uncomfortable in his company, but then she had stopped believing in stardust and Hallelujahs long ago. Marriage to Joshua Brice might make her and her family happy. But marriage to Forrest Wainright would keep them safe.

Chapter 4

A lone rider was coming slowly up the winding approach to Rosalie. Amanda strained to see through the soupy fog, having heard the hoofbeats long before the horseman came into view. It had rained all night and well into the morning, and the August heat pressed down from above while the earth steamed sulkily from below; anything trapped in the middle—people and objects alike—ran wet with moisture and fought the urge simply to wilt where they stood. The silence, save for the sharp chirping of crickets and the shrill hum of cicadas, was equally oppressive. This was the time of year when the fields should have been echoing with the singing and wailing of the slaves harvesting cotton. The steady barking of dogs should have caused as much clamor as the children running around the open-pit barbeques where sweat-slicked, grinning darkies stoked the fires for smoking meat. The skies should have been a bright blue, the cotton a snowy contrast as it was baled and stacked in the flatbed wagons to be transported to the jetty.

This morning, like so many others, the fields were too muddy to venture into and were empty but for the shifting blanket of fog.

Amanda grudgingly left the only corner of the wide veranda where a hint of a breeze was teasing her skin. A slim white hand adjusted the errant wisps of blonde hair at her temples for the twentieth time, then smoothed the folds of her skirt so that the carefully stitched patch along the hem did not show. She had dressed and groomed herself with special care this day. The lavender frock she wore had been one of Caleb's favorites, close-fitting in the bodice, with the soft folds of muslin crisscrossing in front and outlining the shape of her breasts. She had but one sorry crinoline to wear beneath the full skirt instead of the three or four it had been designed to embellish, but such frivolities had long since ceased to hold much importance in Amanda's eyes.

And yet her hair reflected a new determination. Rather than being scraped back and twisted into a severe chignon at the nape of her neck, it was gathered softly at the crown of her head and bound with a delicate cluster of ribbons. Her cheeks were dusted pink, not entirely due to the heat. As much as she tried to deny it, she was impatient for Josh's arrival, and as she walked to the edge of the veranda, she visualized the long, pebbled laneway flanked on both sides by towering cypress trees, their boughs bent and trailing beards of gray moss.

If she closed her eyes, she could picture the grand avenue as it had once been, with the velvet lawns and sculpted parterres that formed a circle of elegant plantings enclosed by the crushed stone drive. Now, of course, there was only ruin. The shrubs and roses in the rotunda had long ago been trampled into the ground, and the only tree left standing close to the house was an ancient oak, its topmost branches glossy and arched like an umbrella.

The sound of hoofbeats came closer, the crunching distinct and slowing as the rider emerged from the milky wisps of fog. And as the visitor himself took shape, Amanda's anticipatory smile was transformed slowly into a thin, compressed line of shocked disbelief.

E. Forrest Wainright savored both the reaction and the hard pulsing response that rippled through his own body. The one identified immediately which twin stood before him so fetchingly dishabille in the heat and humidity; the other was purely a physical reaction to something so perfect, so exquisitely beautiful, a man would have to have ice water flowing through his veins not to feel himself rise to the occasion.

"Mrs. Jackson." He doffed his tall beaver hat as he reined his horse to a halt at the foot of the steps. "A pleasant surprise, by any measure."

Amanda resisted the urge to turn and run into the house. The last time she had seen Forrest Wainright, he had just finished proposing marriage and had been wearing the imprint of her response on his cheek. It was not so much that he had dared to suggest marriage as an alternate way of resolving the Courtlands' financial difficulties, but that he had done it in such a way as to make her feel as if she was just another piece of property that afforded him the possibility of a quick profit. It was time, he had arrogantly declared, for him to start thinking of putting down permanent roots, and there was no one more perfectly tailored to his needs than the great-great-great-granddaughter of Jacques Lemoyne, seigneur d'Iberville, the French nobleman who had founded Fort Rosalie on the present site of Natchez.

The union would not only ingratiate him with the old society of Natchez—something that would be as formidable to breach as the fossiled walls of Jericho—it would impress the powerful and influential members of the new Federal Government, who were more inclined to bestow political favors on those who seemed sincere in their efforts to make reparations with the South.

The slap had come without thinking, as had her rather inelegant suggestion as to who and what she would rather marry in his stead. And now, even though her palm was stinging as if she had just struck him, he was smiling up at her with a lazy indolence that suggested the incident had only served to whet his appetite more.

He was handsome in a stark, brutish way, with a high, wide forehead and a nose that would have done a hawk proud. A finely shaped mouth molded very deliberately around each word, as if he did not want to be misunderstood . . . or he thought his listener to be beneath his intellect. Hair redder than flames flowed in thick, well-oiled waves to the top of his collar, a disconcerting contrast to pale white skin and copper eyelashes. He was tall and lean, with thin, long hands that were well suited to tallying his wealth at the end of each day. He dressed expensively and always had a look of money about him—other people's money—wearing it unashamedly in a land where the majority had to scratch from one meal to the next to survive.

Without waiting for an invitation to do so, Wainright dismounted and casually tethered his bay to the hitching post.

"A warm day," he remarked offhandedly. "I suspect there will be rain again before too long."

Amanda was at a temporary loss. Was it only last night, her mind wandering in the wake of the passing riverboat, that she had actually contemplated marriage to this man?

"I'm sure you haven't ridden all the way out here to discuss the weather," she said coldly.

"I'm sure I haven't either." His watery hazel eyes lingered on the crisscrossed folds of muslin, staring at her as if he could see clear through the layers of her clothing. "You're looking lovely," he murmured, "as always. Not that such a simple, homespun frock does you the justice you deserve, my dear. Silk, I should think, in the same stunning blue as your eyes."

"As it happens, I prefer simple things, Mr. Wainright. Like simple answers to simple questions. Why are you here?"

He mounted the wide, flat stairs until he stood a single tier below her, a level that put his eyes even with her bosom. "I don't suppose you would believe me if I say I have come to prostrate myself before you in the hopes you will reconsider my offer of marriage?"

Amanda arched a delicately shaped brow and fought to keep her expression as civil as possible. "I don't suppose I would."

He expelled a short, soft chuckle. "A pity, then, for I warrant we would make a most handsome couple."

"Marriages should be based on more than appearances alone."

"Do you also prefer your men with shiny round heads, protruding bellies, and hair growing out of the tip of their bulbous noses?"

It was an apt description of Karl von Helmstaad, and Amanda bristled. "If they were not afraid to show affection, tolerance, and *kindness*, I would not be so quick to judge their outward beauty."

"My dearest Amanda—" He took her hand in his and raised it to his lips. "There is not a man alive prepared to show you more affection than I. And I assure you, I am a most tolerant man. My continued devotion in the face of such . . . overwhelming odds should be proof enough of that."

Amanda withdrew her hand and resisted the urge to wipe it clean on the front of her skirt. His only devotion was to money, to the acquisition of wealth and power regardless of whom he had to destroy or humiliate to get it. "I am in no hurry to marry again," she said curtly. "And even if I was—"

He closed his eyes and held up a thin white hand to cut off the rest of her sentence before she could expound. Again. "Spare me the details," he laughed. "I have an excellent memory."

"Then I'm surprised how quickly you seem to have forgotten," said a gruff voice behind them, "that I said I would shoot you where you stood if you set foot on our land again."

Ryan stepped out of the shadowy front entrance of the house. The door had been left open to entice what little air there was to flow through the hall, and Amanda wasn't sure how long he had been standing there; she was just relieved to see him. He had obviously been in the fields recently. His boots were caked with mud, his hair was wet and slicked to his forehead. His clothes clung in damp patches to his skin, emphasizing the bulk of muscle across his chest and arms that, in turn, left Wainright sorely lacking by comparison.

"What the hell are you doing here, Wainright?" he asked.

"I have come on official business, actually, although"— the pale watery eyes flicked to Amanda again—"it is always a pleasure to engage Mrs. Jackson in verbal intercourse."

He mouthed the words with such obvious relish, Ryan took an angry step toward him. "What *official business* can you possibly have with us? Rosalie is not for sale. Neither is my sister."

"Ah." He lifted his eyebrows more for effect than sur-

prise. "So she told you I offered an amiable alternative to
bankruptcy and foreclosure?"

~~she~~ told me you proposed. She also told me she gave
if any~~~~~ver."
be passionate ~~~~, yes indeed. And I wanted to assure her
~~~~ward her . . . impetuosity. I find it,
ile." ~~~~ trait in women that they should

"I'm sure we'll all sleep easier ~~~~ther than dull and doc-
forgiven her. Now, if that was all you had to saying you've

Ryan took Amanda's hand and started to lead her back
into the house, but Wainright's voice stopped him.

"Actually, I have a good deal more to say. And directly to
the party responsible for the debts and mortgages incurred
against this property. I presume that would still be your
father?"

"Presume all you want, Wainright. I have been entrusted
with the running of this plantation—all quite legally, I promise you. So when I tell you I have no intention of selling, you
can take it to be the final word on the subject."

"This legal authority extends to *all* matters pertaining to
finance?"

Ryan's eyes narrowed. "It does, as if it was any affair of
yours to know."

"As it happens, it is very much my affair," Wainright
said, smiling tightly. "You are indebted to the Natchez Mercantile, are you not? To the sum of nearly fifty thousand
dollars?"

He said the amount with an almost respectful awe in his
voice, for most plantations had collapsed long before now on
amounts that were minuscule by comparison.

"You have a point to make, Wainright?"

"The *point,* Mr. Courtland, is that your father signed several notes with the Mercantile. Notes supported by not much
more than the strength of your father's good name . . . and
a certain familial connection."

He was referring, of course, to Amanda's marriage to

Caleb Jackson. But Horace Jackson, even if his only ~
not married into the Courtland family, would ~ profits
tended the necessary funds to William on l:~
signature, for Sarah's father had bee~
original clients and the family h~ ~ne bank has changed
for the Mercantile for over ~ns."
"You must be aware ~
ownership in the l~~~ce vultures have moved in and taken
"Meaning~appened to most of the banks in the South—
over. It :~
w~~~ of it? The terms of the loan are legal and binding, no
matter who is in control."

"That would be true," Wainright agreed, "if it were a
business loan backed by solid assets as collateral. At the
time, as I understand it, Rosalie was a ten-thousand-bale
plantation, with several hundred head of prime Thoroughbreds in the stables. I have no doubt Rosalie was worth ten
times the amount borrowed, but now? A flooded plantation
on the brink of ruin is hardly worth the taxes being levied on
the land assessment alone."

If Ryan had any inkling of what was coming, he did not
betray it through any change in his expression.

"Moreover, a personal note—little better than an I.O.U.,"
Wainright explained blithely, "comes due and payable upon
the holder's discretion."

"There are six months left in the terms of the loan," Ryan
said evenly.

"The *original* terms, perhaps. But as I said, the bank has
changed ownership since the notes were negotiated. The new
management has found such a shocking laxness in the area
of outstanding debts, it has been prompted to sell some of
those they deemed to be too high a risk to warrant keeping.
In other words, they don't believe there is a hope in hell of
some of you Southerners coming up with the money you
owe, so they have decided to cut their losses and salvage
what they could. Your father's notes were, needless to say,
some of the largest, and although I will admit to being forced

a higher price than I intended, I still look upon it as
now he... not spent."

repayment in cash—flesh and blood and muscle was all
around it, with screws being tightened
breathe. His chest felt as if there were

Horace Jackson had indeed . Beside him, Amanda felt the
tending credit on a mere signature, and no... have.
was a father-in-law and friend to the Courtlands. He w... ...
a loyal and fervent supporter of the Confederate cause, and if
any of the big plantation owners needed cash to supplement
their efforts toward supplying the war machine, he gave it
freely and without question.

Horace Jackson had let sentiment interfere with sound
business practices—something Wainright was obviously not
going to be guilty of doing. He would take Rosalie from
them if he could. Any way that he could.

Some of what she was thinking must have been swimming
in her eyes, for Wainright's smile took on a sardonic curve.
"If nothing else, your husband and father-in-law both died
believing they had helped your cause. Passion, however, has
never made a businessman much profit."

"Why, you bastard—" Ryan started forward, all but dragging Amanda with him since she refused to let go of his arm.
It was only this added weight, along with her sharp cry, that
prevented him from launching himself off the edge of the
veranda and going for Wainright's throat.

"Ryan! No!"

"Let me go! Let me at the son of a bitch!"

"What good will it do? He has the note! He has all the
thieving Yankee carpetbaggers on his side!"

Ryan's mouth was white, his eyes blazed with a murder-
ous rage, and E. Forrest Wainright was enjoying the experience immensely.

"I have been advised," he said calmly, "that I may give

you thirty days' notice of intent. If, with[...][...]t of him
to repay the entire amount outstand[...] "it would
land it sits on will be forfeit." [...]wn appeal, "it would

"Thirty days!" Ryan sp[...] for you to at least honor the
Amanda's hands, and she[...] Six months cannot mean much to
to keep him from flyi[...]. Six months cannot mean much to us

"Surely," she c[...] whereas six months to us
not be too grea[...] ition and means, whereas six months to us
original ter[...] difference between surviving and losing every-
a man o[...] the difference between surviving and losing every-
coul[...]

"Which is exactly what he is counting on," Ryan spat
past her ear.

"A gentleman"—she paused long enough to put the
proper importance on the word—"would do nothing less
than honor the agreement."

"My dear Mrs. Jackson." The burnt umber of Wainright's
eyes glittered maliciously. "As a gentleman, I have offered a
fair price for this land in the past. The offer still stands if
your brother chooses to accept it, and if he has the business
acumen to walk away from this situation with enough cash in
his pocket to begin again. If not, if he is too stubborn to sell
outright, and if in thirty days he does not appear before me
with fifty thousand dollars in hand, then it is his conscience,
not mine, that will suffer from his obstinance."

"Is there no way to change your mind?" Amanda asked,
horrified.

The glowing eyes raked down the length of her body and a
smile twisted the corners of his mouth. "There are always
ways," he murmured. "A husband, for instance, would
never see his wife's family turned out into the street."

Ryan's voice was brittle enough to shatter. "I would burn
this house down and poison every acre we own before I
would see my sister married to you, Wainright. Now get off
my land or by Christ I'll see you grinning in hell."

Wainright's smirk flattened marginally in response to the
threat, but his eyes never left Amanda's face as he settled his

hat firmly on his head and walked back down the steps. At the bottom, reins in hand, he gave the house and the figures on the veranda a last lingering look that suggested it was only a matter of time.

"Thirty days," he reiterated. "One way or another."

Amanda was shivering visibly by the time Wainright was swallowed into the fog again. Ryan had his arm around her shoulders, but it did little in the way of offering her comfort or reassurances.

"What are we going to do?" she asked in a whisper.

"I don't know. I need time to think."

"We don't have time. And what is there to think about? He owns the notes. He intends to foreclose. Perhaps . . . maybe if we spoke to Father about it?"

"What good would that do?" Ryan blurted out angrily. "He thinks the stables are still full of horses and the fields are still ripe with cotton. He can barely keep the days of the week straight anymore, and when he sits out here in the mornings, he still nods and chats to the slaves as they go off to work the farm."

"He's only *pretending* to speak to them," Amanda insisted fiercely.

"He's in another world. A better world. A world he knew and loved and felt safe in."

Amanda bit her lip and started to pull out of his embrace. She turned her face so he would not see the wetness brimming along her lashes, and found she had to cover herself again, for Sarah Courtland was bustling around the side of the house, her face flushed from hurrying, her hair flying out like soft gray wings from beneath the rim of her bonnet.

Trailing in her wake, her own oversized bonnet askew over one blue eye, Verity Jackson was struggling valiantly to maintain the balance of the huge wicker basket she was clutching in both hands. Her tongue was thrust out of the corner of her mouth in grim determination. Her cheeks were pink and puffed up with air, and her little feet were tangling over each other as she scuffled side to side on the path. In the basket were a handful of scrawny, underdeveloped carrots and onions still covered in black mud from the garden—a good deal of which was streaked down the front of the child's pinafore.

Ryan smiled despite himself as he went down the stairs and relieved his niece of her terrible burden. "Heavens above, you didn't carry this all the way from the garden by yourself, did you?"

Verity looked up at her uncle's great height and shoved at the brim of the drooping bonnet. She was an exact replica of her mother at that age, with a bow-shaped mouth and enormous cornflower-blue eyes that seemed to fill her whole face. Her long blonde hair had been properly braided earlier in the morning, but with the strain of playing and gardening, and the constant worrying of the bonnet, it looked as if it hadn't been brushed in days.

She answered Ryan with a huge grin as he pretended to groan under the weight of the basket.

"Dear me," Sarah fretted. "I thought I heard a horse and wondered if your Mr. Brice had come early. I said to Verity, 'My word, but Mr. Brice must have come early,' didn't I, child? but then I said, 'No. No, it could not be Mr. Brice, for it has barely gone noon and he would have to be dreadfully eager to have come out in all this wretched fog.' It wasn't Mr. Brice, was it?" she asked, peering into the settling mist.

"No, Mother," Amanda replied. "It wasn't Mr. Brice."

"Well, who was it then?" Sarah demanded, her gaze having found a fresh pile of steaming horse dung. "Who on earth would visit at this time of day and why did you not invite whoever it was to sit for a cup of coffee or a cool glass of water? Surely to goodness we haven't forsaken all of the amenities!"

She glared expectantly at her son and daughter and Amanda sighed, knowing there would be no putting her off.

"It was Mr. Wainright, Mother, and he wasn't visiting, he was just . . . consulting Ryan on a business matter."

"Wainright?" Sarah frowned, trying to place the name. "Wainright? Not that dreadful man with overlapping teeth and eyes that go their own separate ways? Well, thank goodness he didn't stay then, for I declare it exhausts me just trying to figure out which eye to talk to.''

Amanda and Ryan exchanged a glance, but neither one made any effort to correct Sarah's identification. Ryan offered his mother his hand to help her up the last two steps, then passed her into Amanda's care.

''If the three most beautiful ladies in Adams County will excuse me now, I have some chores to tend to down at the barn. Amanda—try to smile a little. It might help to bring out the sunshine.''

Sarah presented her upturned cheek for his kiss and nodded in agreement. ''Indeed, yes. It wouldn't do to look so glum when your Mr. Brice arrives. It wouldn't do at all.''

Amanda attempted a halfhearted smile, but her thoughts were with Ryan as he descended the steps and headed along the path toward the dilapidated sheds that now served as stables for the livestock. His shoulders were squared and his stride was firm, but his hands were shoved deep in his pockets and balled into tight fists.

Fifty thousand dollars in thirty days. No one had that kind of money. No one but Yankee speculators and the vultures appointed by the government whose job, it seemed, was to drive every honest Southern family to the brink of ruin.

She thought again of Wainright's marriage proposal and shuddered. It would resolve all of their problems, certainly, but was it something she could actually go through with? The narrowed, glittering eyes and spidery thin white hands made her flesh shrink just to imagine waking to them each morning and submitting to them each night. She had felt weak with relief at Ryan's adamant refusal even to consider allowing the unholy alliance, but in thirty days' time, they might be left with no other alternative.

Chapter 5

J oshua Brice was not the most avid conversationalist at
the best of times, and certainly not when the topics cen-
tered around flowers or hats or precisely which shade of
yellow velvet would most likely flatter the peach moiré gown
Sarah Courtland would be wearing to her daughter's wedding.

Alisha was doing it deliberately, he had no doubt, chattering on and on about who was wearing what and bemoan-
ing the fact that several crucial articles were still missing
from her trousseau. To her credit, she acted as if he were not
even present in the room when she declared she had so many
things to do, she simply had to go into Natchez the following
morning, and, if the strain of a full day's worth of running
from store to store was as telling as it had been in the past,
she would be best off staying the night with her dearest
friend, Olivia Ward.

Sarah had initially protested, which was how they ended
up talking about hats or, more specifically, the cunning little
yellow bonnet Alisha had ordered for her mother on her last
trip into town, intending it as a surprise.

Josh hoped he smiled in all the right places and made the
appropriate sounds of approval when his opinions were
called upon. His hands shook only a little and his palms were
only moderately slippery from the pressure and tension
seething within him. He should have been used to Alisha's
games by now, he supposed—her feigning an almost rude
disinterest in him in front of the rest of the family—but after
last night . . . after the passion and the wildness and the
pleasure . . . half the time he couldn't hear what they were
saying over the incessant pounding of his own heartbeat.

Making matters worse, he felt like a complete fool balancing a delicate cup and saucer on his knee while the sweat

gathered between his shoulder blades and poured in rivulets down his back. The jacket he wore belonged to his brother and fit snugly across the shoulders—not as snugly as his breeches each and every time he risked a glance at Alisha and watched the way her tongue glided across her lips to moisten them. He was sure she knew whenever his eyes were on her, certain she exaggerated the need to keep her lips so shiny or mold them so deliberately into a soft, seductive pout.

Thankfully, no one else appeared to notice his discomfort. Sarah Courtland was too distracted by the thought of a new bonnet, and Amanda . . .

Amanda looked as uncomfortable and miserable as he was to be there, not touching her tea at all or even pretending to follow the conversation. Normally she was the one to suggest an escape from the clutches of such civility, but today it fell on Josh's shoulders finally to ask if she might want to take a stroll outside with him.

"I understand one of Ryan's mares is in foal."

"Yes indeed," Sarah replied, breaking briefly away from an exchange with Alisha. "And we are all quite proud of the coming event. It will be the first birthing since the war."

Once renowned for breeding the best horseflesh south of Kentucky, the stables of Rosalie had been emptied in order to supply the Confederate cavalry with every advantage of speed and stamina. Upward of three hundred of Ryan's pride and joy, his Thoroughbreds, had been sent onto the battle-fields, and he had come home to find one stallion and two mares strapped in front of plows, all three half starved and near crippled.

"Ryan will fill the stables again in no time," Josh predicted as he walked by Amanda's side, his hand cradling her elbow. "Hell, he and your pa started out with a handful of knockkneed breeders. All he needs is a turn of luck."

"Luck," Amanda said wryly. "And a few thousand spare dollars to rebuild the barns, buy stock, and purchase the oats and hay to feed them."

They lapsed into silence again as they cut through the

garden on their way to the old slave quarters, the only outbuildings not ruined beyond use of anything other than firewood. Josh felt more than a small twinge of alarm as they
approached the summerhouse and he tried to hasten his steps
to carry them past before Amanda noticed the white lace
handkerchief snagged on a broken spar of the railing.

Amanda did just the opposite, however, slowing when
they came abreast of the once-elegant structure and stopping
altogether before they reached the fork in the path that would
take them in the direction of the makeshift stables. She was
feeling foolish and awkward, not because she had seen any
flapping white squares of lace, but because she had suddenly
become very conscious of Josh's hand on her arm. The encounter with Wainright was still raw in her mind. The cloyingly sweet odor of the hair oil he used came to her as freshly
as if the Yankee's narrow face were still before her.

But beside her, smelling of nothing more threatening than
sunshine and hard work, was Joshua Brice. His lean hand-
someness was as familiar and warming as a slow fire on a
cool evening, and, as she looked up at his clean, strong
features, she wondered why she had had any doubts at all
that Josh could make her happy.

"Josh—?"

His head jerked around and he frowned. "Mmmm? Sorry,
I must have . . . ah, drifted there for a minute. Did you
want to ask me something?"

She looked down at the path and kicked at a pebble. "No.
No, not really."

"Well, I want to ask you something," he said softly.

Amanda held her breath. "Yes?"

"Do you remember"—a grin spread across his face and
he tilted his head in the direction of the river—"the night
Stephen, Evan, Caleb, and I snuck out of a Christmas party
your folks were throwing? We sat here and shared our first
full jug of whiskey together, drinking until we couldn't
hardly stand, then caught the bright idea of going on down to
the jetty and sailing a boat all the way to New Orleans."

Amanda laughed easily. "I remember. The current was

stronger than you counted on and Evan fell overboard. He sobered up enough to come tell Father where you had gone, but they still had to ride nearly twenty miles before they could get a line to you and drag you ashore.''

''Christ, our butts were raw meat for a week after that.'' He turned, his hands shoved into his pockets, a lock of brown hair fallen over his brow. ''The four of us were always getting into one sort of trouble or another together. We went to the same schools, got expelled the same number of times for the same reasons, fell in love with the same women . . . even managed to ride in the same unit for a while. Damn,'' he added in a whisper, ''but I miss them. It's like someone cut off both my arms and a leg, and I just can't seem to find my balance anymore.''

Amanda caught her lip between her teeth. ''I know exactly how you feel. You and Caleb were as much a part of this family as any of us.''

''Yeah, well, Caleb was the smart one. He made it official. He said it came over him all sudden-like, that you weren't the yellow-haired brat with big blue eyes who used to follow us around with dirt on her face and holes in her smock. You'd grown up when we weren't looking, and old Caleb there, he worried himself into a lather every night thinking someone else might have noticed too.''

Amanda shook her head. ''He shouldn't have worried; no one did. Or if they did, it was only because Alisha set their heads in a spin and they figured one twin was as good as the other.''

Josh stiffened perceptibly and she hastened to add ''I didn't mean to sound catty. It's just that . . . Alisha has always seemed to know what she wanted, what was out there waiting for her, what she could expect to find around every corner. And if it wasn't there, she knew how to go out and get it. She still does.''

''Amanda—'' Josh placed his hands on her shoulders, but in the next breath, the words died in his throat and all he could see was the startling blue of her eyes, the tempting

softness of her mouth. Alisha's eyes. Alisha's mouth. And it
was Alisha's hand that lifted and rested lightly on his chest.

"What a terribly serious expression, Mr. Brice. What can
you be thinking about?"

"I'm thinking . . . Caleb was a mighty smart man."

Amanda felt a small thrill spiral through the length of her
body. She was conscious of the breadth of his shoulders and
the muscular leanness of his waist and thighs. His jade-green
eyes were like a second pair of hands, warm and soft and
sensual as they caressed her temples, her cheeks, her lips. A
stronger wave of light-headedness, tinged with impatience,
coursed through her, and she swayed even closer, wondering
why it was taking him so long to see that she wanted to be
kissed. The thought had startled her, to be sure, but now it
was there, forthright and urgent, and she wanted more than
anything to be gathered into his strong arms and told that
everything was going to be all right.

Josh felt the gap closing between them. The liquid, pulsing heat in his belly refused to subside. His eyes remained
intent upon her face . . . Amanda's face . . . Alisha's
face. They shared the same flawless complexion, warm as
velvet, smooth as fresh cream. Their eyes were the same
evocative shape—wide and slightly uptilted, surrounded by
the same thick fringe of lashes. Their bodies were as lithe, as
seductive, their hair as fine and silky to the touch. He knew
exactly what lay beneath the thin layer of lavender muslin,
knew the shape and firmness of her breasts, knew they would
be rose-tipped and succulent . . .

"Josh, what is it?" she asked in a whisper. "What's
wrong?"

"Nothing. Nothing, I just—" The air he sucked into his
lungs was heated with resentment and frustration. Alisha was
marrying someone else. She was sitting in the parlor now,
laughing and making her plans to wed a paunchy, randy bag
of money, not even sparing a thought for the torment she was
causing *him*.

"Josh—"

The blood pounded up into his temples, blurring his

thoughts, blurring his ability to reason. His hands found their way to either side of Amanda's neck, his fingers twined themselves into the honey-colored silk, and he brought her lips to within a hair's breadth of his.

Amanda's skin glowed where his hands cradled her neck. Her body pressed eagerly, expectantly into his, and the tiny, tickling thrills became urgent shudders that weakened her arms, her legs, and sent her lashes fluttering closed. His heady, masculine scent engulfed her, and her hands inched higher, boldly demanding the support of his arms. With a smothered groan, Josh crushed her to him, sinking his fingers deeper into her hair and holding her captive to the bruising hunger of his lips.

It was a savage, brutal kiss, not at all what she had foreseen, and the shock of intimacy turned suddenly and frighteningly into the shock of intrusion. She tried to push away, to turn her head and be free of the wet, stabbing insistence of his tongue, but he would not permit it. His grip tightened and his mouth worked more furiously over hers until the sawing of his teeth and tongue wrought a genuine cry of alarm from her throat.

Amanda twisted and pushed with all her might, managing at last to fling herself out of his grasp. Displaced by his fingers, her hair flew every which way around her shoulders and her chest heaved with surprise, anger, confusion. Her eyes were fixed wide, staring in disbelief. Her hand rose instinctively to her mouth, and she scrubbed away the wetness as if to scrub away the taste and feel of him.

Josh had stumbled back a step or two and for a moment it looked as if he were going to lunge after her again and renew his assault. His cheeks were flushed and his gaze seemed to be without focus, bright-hot with a fury she had never seen in him before. But even as she watched, frightened and bewildered, the snarl of his lips started to fade and the rage subsided, draining away to shock.

"Amanda," he gasped. "Amanda . . . I'm sorry. Christ Almighty . . . I'm sorry. *I'm sorry!*"

He advanced a step and Amanda flinched back, not trusting his intentions or her own reactions.

"Amanda . . . you have to believe me . . . I never meant to hurt you."

She swallowed hard. "You . . . haven't hurt me, Josh. You've just . . . startled me, is all. I mean, it wasn't as if I didn't expect you to kiss me, or didn't want you to kiss me. It's been three months since you started calling and—"

"Stop," he groaned, raking his hands into his hair. "Dear God, stop. Please. I never meant to let it go this far."

"This far? I . . . don't understand."

"I never meant to let it go this far! I never meant to hurt you, never wanted to hurt you. If nothing else, you have to believe that."

"Of course I believe you, but I still don't—"

"It was Alisha's idea," he said in a husky, strained voice. "She didn't want anyone to know that she and I . . . that we . . ." The blue of Amanda's eyes was so pure it seared his soul with guilt and brought his confession to a stammered halt. He could not put their deceit into words, could not bear to see each and every one of them reflected in the growing horror that began to turn Amanda's features rigid.

Her skin became ashen and the hand she held pressed to her lips began to tremble visibly.

"It was you," she said hollowly. "Last night in the garden —*here*—it was *you.*"

"God, Amanda, I—"

He reached out again, and again she jerked back. The color she had lost from her complexion resurged with a vengeance, staining her cheeks red and hot.

"You . . . and my sister . . . all this time?"

He could not bring himself to face the accusation in her eyes, and he looked at the ground, at the overgrown hedgerow, at the cracks in the cobblestones. What could he do? What could he say? He loved Alisha. He hadn't planned on it happening, but it had and there was nothing he could do to change it, or to change the way he felt. Amanda *had* always been like a sister to him, someone he could talk to, be comfortable around, and respect for her loyalty and honesty. Alisha, on the other hand, was dangerously wild and unpredictable. She was exciting and passionate and pushed his emotions—love and hate—to the limit each and every time they were together. And although it did not say much for the strength of his own character, he could not imagine a life without that wildness and passion in it now.

"You have to believe, I never meant to hurt you," he said again lamely. "*We* never meant to hurt you."

Amanda's hands fisted around the folds of her skirt and crushed the fabric so hard her knuckles ached from the pressure. She could almost believe he was sincere—naive and ignorant, yes; blind and besotted, obviously—but sincere when he said he hadn't meant to hurt her. On the other hand, Amanda was certain Alisha had known exactly what she was doing. She never thought of anyone's feelings but her own, and if she had to betray her own flesh and blood in order to get what she wanted, she gave it little more thought than stepping on a bug if it was in her way. She clearly had Josh twisted tightly around her finger. It was apparent he was blindly in love with her, and it was difficult for Amanda to feel anything but pity for him.

"You haven't hurt me, Josh," she said calmly. "If anything, you may even have helped me. You see, I had some difficult choices to make, and in a way, you've made it that much easier for me to do what I have to do."

He looked up, his face pale and anxious. "You . . . won't tell Alisha about this, will you?"

It took more effort than she felt like expending for her to paste a half smile onto her lips. "No," she said, shaking her head sadly. "No, I don't think either one of us should tell Alisha about this. You won't mind, however, if we put an end to this insulting little charade. If the two of you need or want an excuse to see each other in the daylight, you will just have to find someone else to use. Good-bye, Josh. And . . . I am sorry for you. Because if anyone is going to be hurt by all of this, it's going to be you. Alisha will hurt you, and use you, just like she has hurt and used everyone else who's ever been foolish enough to love her.''

Josh remained wooden and unmoving as she brushed past him and headed not in the direction of the outbuildings, but in the direction of the river. For the sake of her pride, she did not slow her steps until she was well away from the summerhouse; for the sake of her skirt and shoes, she stopped in the first thick wedge of trees. Out of sight, she leaned against a wide trunk and covered her face with her hands.

Josh had used her. Alisha had used her. And she had been so wrapped up in her own pride and foolish notions of doing what was best for everyone else, she had not even had an inkling of their duplicity. Tell Alisha? Why? So her twin could laugh in her face and say it only confirmed her low opinion of Amanda's gullibility? She couldn't even dare tell Ryan—at the very least he would probably go after Josh with a whip or a gun . . . or both.

Amanda brushed angrily at her tears and turned her face into the humid breeze, letting it drag at the weight of her hair, but she found neither relief nor comfort in the clinging moisture.

Joshua Brice was indeed the fool if he thought Alisha would give up everything the baron had to offer for the sake of love. And Alisha was just a plain fool for turning her back on the kind of emotion Amanda had seen blazing from Josh's eyes. It was a certainty no man had ever looked at *her* that way before, not even Caleb.

It was a further certainty that if any man ever did, she would give up life itself before she would turn him away, and she would die content, knowing the sacrifice had been well worth it.

Chapter 6

With a flourish, Montana Rose fanned her five cards onto the tabletop, showing the three tens that were good enough to bring home the pot of nearly four hundred dollars. She permitted a small smile as she raked in her winnings. Having arrived on board with less than three hundred dollars, she had managed to coax the tally to over four thousand.

Her secret smile became somewhat less secretive as she surveyed the faces of the men seated around the table. Four out of five of them had their eyes fastened speculatively on the deep cleft between her breasts; the fifth, who had been stretching his legs, rejoined them with a loud scraping of his chair and sent a broad wink across the table.

"Good show, Montana," he said, and she was not one hundred percent certain he was referring to her card-playing skills. "It looks to me like Lady Luck has decided to favor her own sex tonight."

Montana ran her fingers caressingly down the final, neat stack of coins and met Lyle Swanson's gaze directly. "You are not doing too badly yourself, sir."

"No, I'm not," he agreed readily. "And I intend to give you a run for your money tonight even if none of these other beggars are up to it."

Her gold locket reflected a flare of light from the overhead lamp as Montana accepted the deck of cards and began to deftly shuffle them. Swanson was a balding, rotund man who developed a tic in one of his bullish jowls whenever he held anything better than a pair. He also had an annoying habit of humming under his breath, a sound that was pervasive and irritating and rarely in keeping with the music that filtered up from the main gambling salon. But he had a stack of greenbacks and gold double eagles in front of him the size of Mt.

Vesuvius and gambled with enough indifference to deter any
of the others from complaining.

"Shall we try a little round of cutthroat?" Montana suggested casually. "Quick and vicious—just the way I like it
sometimes, when the blood needs to flow a little faster."

In the long moment of exquisite silence that followed her
declaration, at least three hearts skipped a beat and more
than one mind's eye had a brief, explicit picture of satin
sheets and gleaming, sweating bodies.

"Fifty-dollar ante, deuces wild," she announced crisply,
and began dealing the cards. Her eyes followed around the
table as each player met the ante, starting with the gentleman
seated on her left.

Norman Smith was a Yankee, like the others, a banker or a
speculator come to scavenge what he could from the corpse
of the South. Short and squat, with no neck to speak of, he
was an officious boor who made it quite clear through unsub-
tle hints and hard stares that he was a wealthy man who
would not be opposed to lavishing his generosity on a fine
Southern-bred mistress—if he could find one with enough
fire and spunk to hold his interest. Adding to his appeal, he
kept an unlit cigar clamped between his lips and as he
worked it side to side, the spittle built up a brown crust at the
corners of his mouth.

Paul Whitney sat next in the circle. He had the lean, rangy
look of a panther, dressed all in black from the toes of his
tall, polished boots, to the top of his wide-brimmed, silver-
banded hat. He was as miserly with his conversation as
Smith was gregarious and rarely showed any change in his
expression. He had the smell of a professional about him,
someone who made his living from cards and other games of
chance. He folded more often than he played, but when he
did stay in a game, it was usually with a hand that was tough
to beat. He also rarely played a hand that required him to
draw more than one card, a sure sign, Montana suspected, he
was leading up to a monumental bluff.

Her eyes flicked to the next player, Michael Tarrington.
Ex-Army, she surmised. A Yankee officer. His voice and

mannerisms bespoke the quiet authority and self-confidence of a man accustomed to giving orders and not having them challenged or ignored. His inordinately broad shoulders were encased in tailored blue-black broadcloth. The whiteness of the pleated linen shirt and the burgundy silk of his waistcoat gleamed with casual wealth. His hair was chestnut brown and rather handsomely unkempt, as if he shunned the services of a barber and preferred to let the wind style it for him. He wore a rakishly thick mustache over a generous mouth that occasionally parted to reveal a slash of strong white teeth. His peculiar trait, if it could be said that he had one, was to stroke a thoughtful forefinger over his mustache whenever he debated a wager of over a hundred dollars— which seemed to be most of the time. He neither won nor lost with any regularity or interest. The latter seemed to be reserved for the scantily clad hostess who hovered in the background replenishing drinks when the need arose.

The last member of the group was Ainsley Scott, the youngest and also the heaviest loser so far. Handsome and spoiled by family wealth, he could not have been a day over twenty, not old enough to have even bruised his callow softness in the war. He was an easy mark, suffering from a combination of poor card sense, a face that read like an open book, and a puppylike eagerness to impress Montana with his boyish charm. She, in turn, responded to all that lavished charm by relieving him of as many coins and greenbacks as he was willing to squander, a pleasure that would not last much longer to judge by the diminishing reserves in his pockets.

She finished dealing and barely glanced at her own hand before turning to the squinty-eyed Norman Smith. "Cards?"

"Two," he grunted, discarding a pair of pasteboards and reaching a fat, clammy hand for their replacements. Following his customary habit, he tapped all five together on the baize and leaned well back in the chair before slowly fanning and peering at the new additions. When he did, he grated his cigar savagely between his teeth and tossed a smug glance at Paul Whitney. "Well, sir, will it be one or none this time?"

A slight tilt in the brim of the gambler's hat was the only reaction to Smith's sarcasm as he held up a long, tapered finger to call for a single card.

Smith grunted again and Montana shifted her attention along the table. "Mr. Swanson?"

"Lyle, my dear. Call me Lyle, and I shall take a pair. Two ladies as lovely as yourself, if you can arrange it."

Montana smiled and thumbed the top card of the deck. Something made her look over at the Yankee officer, and she was mildly surprised to find Michael Tarrington's eyes waiting for her. Nothing so commonplace as gray, they were a smoldering blend of blues and greens and slate that seemed to probe clear through everyone's pretensions—including her own—and lay them bare for his amused scrutiny.

"Mr. Tarrington?"

"Three," he said, not wavering his stare. He made his discard with an irreverent flick of his wrist and slotted his new cards into his hand without looking at them.

"I'm going to stand but for one, Miss Montana," declared Ainsley Scott, his voice pulling her gaze away from Tarrington's. "I'm feeling lucky this hand, sure enough, and one just oughta do it. Oughta fit itself"—he paused and grinned hugely when he saw the card she threw him—"right here, you sweet thing. Right here."

The bluff was so obvious, Montana almost winced.

"Dealer takes three," she said, making the exchange with brisk, efficient movements. When she looked up again, it was to find that Tarrington was still watching her, but his attention was now focused intently on her hands. It wasn't the first time she had caught him studying her movements. The green velvet gown had long fitted sleeves and a spill of lace at the wrists—lace she had made a point of folding back so that her hands and wrists were clearly visible at all times.

"The betting is open, gentlemen," she said, drawing his eyes up to hers. "No limits, no credit."

Norman Smith chewed the cigar from one side of his mouth to the other. "I might as well ride this filly awhile and see where she takes me." He tossed some coins into the center of the table and glared down his nose at Paul Whitney. "Fifty to open."

Whitney called the fifty and raised fifty without comment. Play passed to Swanson, who glowered at his cards for a long moment before counting out his bet. "Your hundred, gentlemen . . . and fifty more. And speaking of fillies, what's your secret, Tarrington? What does a man have to do to get a drink around here?"

The buxom brunette waitress, who had indeed been giving most of her closest attention to Michael Tarrington, sashayed over to Swanson's side and tickled his ear with a few breathy words as she topped up his empty glass.

"Gads," he muttered. "You'd let me do that?"

"If the price is right," Smith proselytized, "I warrant these hot little Southern wenches would let you do just about anything."

Tarrington was the only one of the men who did not respond with at least a dry chuckle. He called the girl back to his side instead and when she was there, he tucked a hundred-dollar bill into her waistband and held up his glass. "Just a refill," he said quietly. "Thank you."

He threw two hundred and fifty into the pot, raising the bet again, and glared narrowly at Smith. Scott, whistling jauntily under his breath, matched Tarrington's bet and added a hundred more.

While Montana debated what to do, she toyed with the length of gold chain around her neck. She kept her face carefully blank as she studied her cards, knowing this was going to be a rich pot. "Three hundred and fifty to cover all raises . . . and five hundred more to see what you Yankees will do for the right price."

Smith guffawed and bit down hard enough on his cigar to sever a soggy clod in his mouth. He swore and spit at the same time as he threw his cards face down on the table.

"Not play the sucker," he snorted. "That much I can tell you for free."

Paul Whitney pursed his lips and riffled thoughtfully through a stack of greenbacks before counting out the required eight hundred and fifty dollars to call Montana's bet, and two hundred more to raise.

Swanson's humming stopped abruptly. He stared at the small hillock of money that sat temptingly under the circular spill of light and his jowl twitched and shivered as if it were possessed. He had a good hand—full house, fives over aces —but was it worth over a thousand to see just how good?

"Bah. Only money." He slid the bet forward and looked expectantly at Tarrington.

Tarrington casually stroked the ends of his mustache and seemed to take a close look at his cards for the first time. He suspected Whitney was running a bluff—he had already managed to convince the hummer he would play only if his hand was solid. Swanson's twitch meant he had enough for at least a run at the prize. Scott was running low on cash and would probably fold. The woman was the puzzle. She was good—damned good—and was either bluffing to the tips of her distractingly luscious breasts, or she had them all cold and was reeling them in like fish on a line.

It was worth the gamble, he decided, just to satisfy his own curiosity. He covered the bet, sweetened the pot by fifty more to keep his options open, and patted his jacket pocket, finding and extracting a slim gold cigar case.

Ainsley Scott's hands trembled visibly where they cradled his cards. A fine sheen of sweat glistened on his upper lip, and his eyebrows arched up and down as if he was having an argument with himself.

"That's eleven hundred to you, boy," Smith said impatiently. "And that's why it's called cutthroat. You either show the balls to stand behind them cards of yours, or you toss 'em in and let the grown-ups finish playing."

Scott's flush deepened. He flexed one of his hands into a fist then started to count out his cash.

"Are you certain you want to do that?" Tarrington asked with a sigh. "He's only goading you."

"Yeah, well, I guess that's all he's got the balls to do. And I can play my own hand, if you don't mind. Eleven hundred? Why not take it up to an even two thousand?"

He pushed his money into the middle and Tarrington shrugged. He withdrew a thin black cheroot from his case and smiled his thanks at the brunette as she leaned over quickly to light it.

The acrid cloud of smoke drifted straight across the table and caused Montana's nose to wrinkle with distaste. Tarrington noticed. He also noticed that she covered the bet without so much as blinking an eye.

Play went to Whitney, who again riffled the small stack of cash in front of him as his eyes, shadowed by the brim of his hat, flicked around the table doing a rough calculation of the money remaining in everyone's stash. Satisfied, he counted out two thousand to call and a thousand more to raise.

Swanson started shaking his head even before he conceded and threw his cards down in disgust. Across the table, Scott mouthed a particularly graphic oath that stopped play before it even went to Tarrington.

Norman Smith chuckled deep in his throat and picked at a cavern in his tooth with a wooden matchstick. "Looks like you ain't going to have enough to bluff out this round, boy," he said, indicating the few bills and coins Scott had left. "Should have got out last round, like Tarrington advised, while you still had enough to maybe buy your way into a game of Old Maid."

"I can write a note for the amount I'm short. I'm good for it."

"No dice," Whitney grated. "The rules were stated plain enough at the outset. Cash on the barrelhead. No notes. No credit."

"A personal loan then," Scott countered. "Between players. There was nothing said about that."

"True enough," Swanson agreed. "But just who are you going to get to spot you, son? I don't believe anyone here is willing to throw good money after bad . . . unless, of course, Mr. Tarrington here has another soft spot?"

The Yankee officer studied the end of his cheroot a moment before spitting out a shred of tobacco and crossing his arms over his chest. "I believe he told me he was capable of playing out his own hand."

Scott surged to his feet and threw his cards on the table. "You raised on purpose just to shut me out!"

"The game is poker, boy," Whitney said, his voice low enough to scrape the floor. "You win some and you lose some. No one is going to coddle you because you smile real pretty and boast about your daddy's fortune."

"At least I'm not a cheap cheat," Scott countered furiously.

The brim of Whitney's hat came up again and his dark eyes screwed down to slits. "You accusing somebody of something . . . *boy?*"

Scott's flush deepened and his breath, laboring in and out of his lungs, sounded like bellows. His hand, rigid with indignation, inched back toward his waist, and Montana wondered if he was truly stupid enough to try to draw on a man like Paul Whitney.

Luckily, he wasn't. He did push away from the table, however, sending the chair flipping backward onto the floor. He snatched up the meager remains of his cash and stormed out of the curtained alcove, consigning all their souls to rot in hell.

Montana released a slow sigh of relief and reached uncharacteristically for the as-yet untouched glass of whiskey that sat at her elbow. Norman Smith dug in his nose in lieu of any verbal comment, an act that was frozen rather comically midway when he saw Whitney's hand emerge from under the cover of the table. It was not the sight of the small, pearl-handed derringer that was the most unnerving. It was the fact that he had palmed it and aimed it at Scott without anyone noticing.

Or almost anyone.

A second muted *snick* came from the gleaming Remington revolver that Michael Tarrington uncocked and returned to his hip holster.

"I see we both had the same idea," Whitney said with a crooked grin.

"A similar idea, perhaps," Tarrington agreed, "but I doubt our intentions were the same."

Whitney's smile faded. "Meaning?"

"Meaning . . . I wasn't aiming at the boy."

"He accused me of cheating," Whitney snarled.

"A poor choice of words on his part. Manipulating would be more like it."

"Because I raised the stakes higher than what he could afford? I didn't notice your heart bleeding too much at the time. Or is it just bleeding now because you can't meet the stakes yourself?"

Tarrington's gaze narrowed through the fine ribbon of smoke that curled up from his cheroot. He smiled slowly and carefully counted out the greenbacks he had in front of him, then, with every eye on him, he reached into the breast pocket of his coat and produced a leather billfold. From it he extracted enough to call Whitney's bet . . . and added five thousand more.

Montana suffered a distinct sliding sensation in the pit of her belly as she followed the motion of his hand. It was a strong hand, she noted absently, with long square-tipped fingers that looked more than capable of crushing her smaller, finer-boned one to pulp.

There was more than twenty thousand dollars sitting within arm's reach. She'd had enough to meet Whitney's raise—barely—but Tarrington's flamboyance left her almost five thousand shy.

Now, as she watched his fine, strong hand retreating again, moving as if it were being dragged through a heavy liquid instead of air, she thought it might well have been an axe he had wielded, not a billfold. And she wondered if anyone had yet noticed the blood.

She looked up and, indeed, the attention had shifted from Tarrington's grandiose gesture to her own meager reserves.

"In or out, lady?" Whitney demanded. "Is that all you have?"

Montana cursed inwardly. She glanced at Tarrington, but

he had obviously used up his quota of sympathy and the gray eyes were as cold and hard and flat as Whitney's.

"It's surely all I have . . . *in cash,*" she murmured, putting every ounce of seductive innuendo she could muster into the last two words.

It had the desired effect. Smith and Swanson both had to breathe through their mouths as she stared at each of them in turn and made her meaning even clearer by trailing her fingers along the deeply scalloped edge of the green velvet bodice.

Smith mashed his cigar to the corner of his mouth as he pulled out his billfold and started counting out greenbacks. "I'd say you're a sweet enough risk to take. How much are you short, gal?"

Whitney flashed an angry glare. "Didn't we just have this discussion with the kid?"

"We discussed credit," Smith countered. "And I ain't offering any. This here is a loan, between friends, with real friendly terms of interest."

For the briefest of moments, Montana hesitated. She had no illusions as to what he would expect in return for the privilege of losing his money, but before she would let herself think about it too long, she used the edge of her cards to push her bet into the center of the table. "I'll just take you up on your offer, Mr. Smith, and I'll call."

Whitney sat back in his chair and, with an angry stab of his finger, thrust the brim of his hat up above his hairline. The act revealed more than just his mounting frustration. It uncovered a wide, jagged scar that ran across his forehead from temple to temple, the kind a knife might make in a botched attempt at scalping. Immediately above and below the scar, the skin was a smooth, shiny pink, translucent enough to see the veins pulsing beneath the surface.

Without another word, he folded his cards and threw them face down on the baize. He gripped his whiskey glass tight enough to shatter it and tossed back the contents. The brunette came forward out of the shadows to refill it, but he snatched the bottle out of her hand instead and pushed to his feet, stalking the short distance to the open porthole behind them before he filled his glass and drank again.

Tarrington stroked his mustache and stared across the table at Montana Rose. With the betting closed, it had come down to the two of them, as he had suspected—hoped?—it would.

He had, from the moment he had first laid eyes on her, been conscious of her intensely seductive beauty—what normal, warm-blooded man would not? The stunning cornflower blue of her eyes, wide and thickly lashed, gazed out at the world from a face as flawless as a Botticelli Venus. Her mouth was lush enough to send the most erotic images through his mind, especially when she sent the tip of her tongue across her lower lip to moisten it.

He would give a year of his life to see her naked. Envisioning her so was costing him dearly enough, for just the thought of her lithe, supple body stretched out beneath him, her skin smooth and white as cream, her hair spread in a soft, silky pool . . . made him ache as if he hadn't had a woman in years. Which he had, of course, the last one being two hours before he'd come on board the *Mississippi Queen*. And perhaps that was what was corrupting his perceptions, for the experience had been mechanical and perfunctory, no more than a pleasant way to release some tension. With this blonde beauty he doubted anything would be perfunctory. And he would need hours, not minutes, to release the kind of tension she was inspiring.

Tarrington blinked. He drew deeply on his cheroot before placing his cards down on the table, displaying four nines with an ace high, and the glimmerings of an I-tried-to-warn-you look in his eyes as he waited for Montana's reaction.

She drew an equally deep, slow breath, and her hand betrayed the slightest of tremors as she reached up to grasp the comfort of her locket.

Norman Smith, leaning over with all of the solicitude of an oiled snake, placed a fat hand over hers and squeezed. "Well now, looks like I saddled me a pretty filly after all."

Montana turned the full, seductive power of her eyes on

him as she smiled and fanned her cards face-up on the table. Three unobtrusive sixes became five of a kind in the company of the pair of wild card deuces she laid beside them.

"Sorry, Mr. Smith. But I prefer to ride barebacked."

Michael Tarrington stared at the cards, then at the faintly mocking smile that still lingered on her lips.

"My compliments," he mused, his tone half admiring, half hostile. "I would have bet everything I owned that you were bluffing."

"I rarely bluff, sir. And never when the odds are so heavily stacked against me."

"Against you, madam?" Lyle Swanson huffed. "I should have thought it the other way around, considering we are all gentlemen here."

"We are all gamblers here, sir. And as Mr. Whitney and Mr. Tarrington have both demonstrated, a very prickly bunch indeed. I hardly consider it a favorable climate for testing temperaments. Now, if you all have no objections, a short break would be much appreciated."

Montana slid her chair back from the table, but before she could move very far, a pale, long-fingered hand reached out and curled tightly around her wrist. Her first instinct was to wrench free. Her second was to hold her arm very still so that her bones were not crushed under the pressure.

Paul Whitney had stepped away from the porthole and now stood blocking her path to the exit. "You are planning to return, I hope?"

She curled her hand into a fist and twisted it slowly out of his grasp. "I am, indeed, sir. If only for the pleasure of relieving you of whatever you may have left."

In truth, Montana's prime desire was to escape both the room and the company with all haste possible. Her blood was singing through her veins, her pulse was thrumming in her temples. The thrill of victory had never tasted so sweet, and she was hard-pressed to control the urge to throw her hands wide and embrace the world in laughter. Discounting the five thousand she had temporarily borrowed from Smith, she had won over twenty thousand dollars in that last hand. She had beaten Whitney at his own game, and she had given the mustachioed Yankee something to ponder other than the brunette's long legs and come-hither smile.

Montana scarcely noticed the clamor of music and noise filling the main salon of the riverboat as she threaded her way through the crowds. She located a familiar face at the bar and gave him a nod, tilting her lovely head slightly to indicate an invitation to join her out on the deck. She waited long enough to see him take a last swallow of beer, then hurried out into the cool, fresh night air.

The riverboat was docked alone at the end of the jetty and on the port side, the waterfront was garishly ablaze with the lights from a legion of cheap taverns, saloons, and hotels that crowded the shoreline. It was not the most reputable part of Natchez, for the merchant district and more prosperous hotels and homes sat on the crown of the hill that overlooked the river. On nights when the big gambling boats were in, detachments of soldiers had to patrol the main roads and safeguard the passage of the wealthy patrons and their fine carriages to and fro.

Montana preferred the relative quiet of the starboard deck. There she could lean against the rail and drink in the beauty of the vast, starlit sky. Overhead, a faint drift of smoke rose from the *Queen*'s boiler stack, spreading outward in long, filmy scrolls. Beside her, the river rolled by like a sheet of molten glass, pewter colored from the starlight, a mile-wide silver ribbon that divided the state of Mississippi from the distant shoreline of Louisiana.

Tonight, for a change, there was not a cloud in the sky, not a trace of haze to blot the opposite bank from sight. If she leaned far out over the rail and looked south, she could just see the twinkling lights of Vidalia across the river; to the north, the dark tip of Natchez Island.

Hearing the anticipated footstep behind her, Montana straightened and spun around with such enthusiasm the luxuriant emerald velvet of her skirt swirled outward and was brought to a frothing halt against a pair of polished black boots.

"Oh!"

"I beg your pardon. You were, perhaps, expecting someone else?"

Montana collected her wits about her as quickly as she could. The *last* person she had expected to see following her onto the deck was Michael Tarrington.

"N-no," she stammered. "No, not at all. I . . . you just startled me, is all."

Tarrington smiled slowly at the succession of rapid changes that came over her expression. The thick wings of her lashes immediately swooped low to conceal the disappointment in the vibrant blue eyes. Her smile—the fullest and loveliest he had seen in quite some time—was repressed to a tight, formal curve. Hands, slender white and delicate, that had been poised for a greeting, flew instinctively to the juncture of her breasts as if to catch a heart that threatened to leap from its confines.

"In that case," he mused, "forgive me again, but for a greeting like that, I would gladly startle you several more times."

"I . . . beg your pardon?"

"The smile. You should set it free more often."

Montana stared for as long as it took to read the mockery in his eyes. "Do you make a habit of following women around to startle them into smiling?"

"I hadn't really thought of it as a worthwhile pursuit . . . until now. Usually I only follow them if they are intriguing. Or enigmatic. Or beautiful." He saw her eyes narrow and her jaw set against what must, he imagined, be a familiar opening gambit. "But in your case, I only wanted to commend you on your flawless performance back there."

She arched a delicately shaped eyebrow. "Performance?"

"Certainly. One of the best I've ever seen. Bluffing successfully is one thing. *Pretending* to bluff is quite another." He paused long enough to strike a match on the deck rail and touch it to the end of a cheroot. "You're really very good."

"You sound surprised, as if it never occurred to you to regard me as a genuine threat."

"Oh, I regarded you as a threat, all right. I just wasn't sure what kind."

Montana felt a tug at the corners of her mouth. "And are you sure now?"

"No." He exhaled a long, slim streak of smoke and offered her the smile that usually had women melting in their pantalets. "I'm not sure about anything concerning you."

To his obvious surprise, she laughed. It wasn't the coquettish titter most females affected with the expectation of having some swain salivating at their skirt hems, it was soft and throaty, definitely feline in nature, and, whether she expected it or not, it won a decided stirring of interest in flesh that was already piqued by the scent of her perfume.

"I'm also hoping you won't assume it will be so easy the second time around," he added. "Those . . . gentlemen . . . you so artfully fleeced back there will be anxious to prove they aren't as foolish as you made them look."

"Including you?"

"I rarely make the same mistake twice. And my manners have a tendency to fall by the wayside when someone deliberately asks for trouble."

"Is that what I am asking for?"

He shrugged congenially. "It might be what you get if you go back in there."

Her smile broadened. "A Yankee with a conscience. How unusual."

"A Rebel still fighting the war," he countered smoothly. "Not unusual at all . . . but a bit misguided, perhaps."

"Really? How so?"

"Because I don't want to fight with you," he said quietly.

His words and the way he said them sent a tiny spiral of heat radiating down her spine. It was an innocent enough statement and said casually enough, but there was an unmistakable air of possessiveness about it, as if by not fighting, he assumed they would aspire to some other emotional relationship.

The notion, surprisingly not an entirely unpleasant one, made her take a closer look at the man who stood so huge and imposing before her. He was handsome almost beyond decency, big with muscles that suggested he was no stranger to hard physical labor. The little creases and lines that life had etched around his eyes and at the corners of his mouth heightened the impression of authority and determination—his was not a face that men scorned with impunity or women rejected out of hand. There was also an efficient grace to his movements, an instinctive balance and agility that implied he was as comfortable walking the decks of a tall ship as he was a smooth road. It was a trait easy to recognize for someone who had lived by the river all her life. His accent? Pure Bostonian. Blatantly upper crust, although his voice was so deep and carefully modulated, the hardest edges had been worn seductively smooth.

Michael Tarrington was not unaware of the close scrutiny, and he thought it only fair he should be accorded equal privileges. But with the silvery rush of the river behind her and the muted light from a nearby porthole bathing her face and shoulders in a soft, pearly glow, he was having difficulty regarding her with anything near his usual state of detachment. He wanted to reach out and touch her, to brush the backs of his fingers across her cheek and down her neck to see if her skin was as supple and warm as it promised. He wanted to keep exploring, to run his hands, his mouth, his whole body over hers, to know if her flesh would be as responsive as he imagined. Would she purr when he stroked her? Would she be sweet when he kissed her? Would she let him kiss her now or would she make him go through all the silly motions?

Now, he thought, and took a measured step closer.

Montana presented him with a cool shoulder and stared out across the river. "You said you would have bet everything you owned that I was bluffing. Why didn't you?"

"Maybe I did."

She cast a glance back under the thick sweep of her lashes and regarded him thoughtfully before turning away again.

"You don't look like the kind of man who would gamble *everything* on *anything*. Or any*one*."

"You don't think so? You wound me, madam."

"Not fatally, I trust."

"You could stop the bleeding . . . by having a late supper with me."

"A late supper," she said, "would imply a desire to become better acquainted."

He drew a slow, deep breath, saturating his senses with the smell of her hair, her skin. He succumbed to an even greater temptation and caught a shiny tendril of her hair in his fingers, fascinated by the slippery, silky texture, wondering how it would look released from its pins and curls. He was directly behind her, his body crowding hers against the rail, his intentions as warm as the softly mouthed oath that brought his lips to within a breath of her ear.

"Would you rather I just come right out and say it? Shall I simply say that I find you a fascinating and irresistible creature, Montana Rose, and have since the first time I saw you?"

"The *first* time?" she questioned with a small frown.

"It was about a month ago, the last time the *Queen* stopped in Natchez. I saw you in the salon, talking to the captain—getting him to arrange a seat in a game? As luck would have it, he was too efficient and returned before I had a chance to introduce myself."

"How unfortunate," she said dryly. "And you have been riding the river, watching for me ever since?"

He defused her sardonic smile with one of his own. "Our meeting tonight was purely accidental, I assure you. I've come back on business."

"And you wish to invite me along on a business dinner?"

"I would like to get to know you better. Dinner seems like an amiable place to start. After that . . ."

"Yes?"

Tarrington cursed through another soft laugh. "After that, I was hoping to perhaps mellow that formidable Southern

pride of yours. Enough to convince you I never wear blue in
public . . . and never talk politics in bed."

The tiny spirals of sensation became disturbingly insistent
—almost as insistent as the glaring looks that were coming
from the shadowy figure who stood not twenty paces away
and who had been observing them—with increasing signs of
agitation—for several minutes now.

"The possibilities sound intriguing, Mr. Tarrington," she
said. "But unfortunately, I prefer to keep my Southern pride
intact. I don't find you fascinating in the least, and the fact
that all of your charm and conversation has been in aid of
procuring yourself a bedmate for the evening . . . well, I
find that amazingly easy to resist."

The gray eyes narrowed sharply. "The war has been over
for two long years, Montana."

"Yes," she said, offering an exaggerated sigh as she
brushed an invisible fleck of lint from his jacket lapel, "but
I'm afraid you will be a Yankee forever."

She swept past him with a regal flourish of velvet skirts
and reentered the brightly lit salon. Tarrington watched her
go, her rebuff keeping him rooted to the spot for as long as
his mind held the image of her framed by the arched entryway. When he realized it wasn't merely a ploy, that she
wasn't coming back, his fingers curled around the cheroot
and crushed it in half before he flung it over the rail and
consigned it to the swirling eddies of the river. He strode
back into the salon without ever noticing the man who stood
watching him from the deck rail, nor did he see the man
emerge from the shadows and follow purposefully in his
wake.

Chapter 7

Montana won two hands easily, folded early in the third, and lost a maddening fifteen hundred dollars on a bluff she should have smelled standing a mile downwind. The atmosphere, as Tarrington predicted, was definitely grittier after the short break. Norman Smith chose the role of observer instead of participant, and while he amused himself winking at the hostess and tossing back shots of whiskey, the remaining four players concentrated all of their energies on winning. The air behind the closed draperies became increasingly hot and smoke-filled. The tension and strain seemed to feed upon itself and build until Montana could feel it in the muscles across her back and shoulders. She had announced upon returning to the game that she would be departing at two A.M. whether she was ahead or behind. With an hour still to go, she wondered if her patience would last.

There was no more light banter. Lyle Swanson had stopped humming, twitching, and tapping. Whitney's glowering countenance dominated the table and set an undertone of mistrust and belligerence. He studied every play like a hawk; he consumed an amazing quantity of liquor, which only served to make his mood blacker, his remarks blunter. It was distracting enough that Montana was more inclined to lean toward caution where she should have capitalized on several glaring opportunities.

She lost the next three hands in a row, one to Swanson, two to Tarrington.

The latter, true to his word, ignored her completely and focused on winning—which he did very well. He swore as fluently as Whitney, drank as heavily, and smoked his accursed little cigars until Montana thought her eyes would catch fire. He lavished tips and attention on the brunette waitress who showed her appreciation by practically spilling her breasts into his hands each time she bent over to replenish his drinks. Once, when a cloth napkin fell in his lap, she took so long to retrieve it, both Swanson and Whitney stared. Tarrington only smiled. And the waitress's eyes grew to the size of saucers.

Montana counted the minutes and held her patience in check. As luck would have it, when it came to play the last hand, she had the deal again and could barely keep the relief out of her voice as she called for the others to ante up. Despite her losses, she was still ahead on the night. It would have given her a warm feeling to see a few thousand more pried out of Tarrington's billfold, but she was more than content with her profits.

"You aim to deal those cards or shuffle the spots clean?" Whitney growled.

Montana glanced over and deliberately shuffled several more times before dealing. She set the deck aside and scanned the hand she had given herself, smiling inwardly when she saw the two aces, two kings, and the six of diamonds, as honest as the day they were printed.

Whitney seemed less pleased, but since he had abandoned his tactic of taking one or none, he tapped the table twice and said, "Two."

Swanson drew two also, but Tarrington only stared across the table at Montana and grinned. "I kind of like what I see; I'll stand pat."

Whitney and Swanson were instantly on guard. He had stood pat twice before and bluffed them out of several thousand dollars apiece.

"They say a blind man only stumbles into the same wall once," Swanson muttered.

"Is that what they say?" Tarrington mused.

"Indeed. And then his instincts tell him when to avoid it. Mine, sir," he said, tossing down his cards, "are buzzing like a nest of hornets."

Montana met the Yankee's gaze as he dismissed the banker with a small shrug.

"Dealer takes one," she said, discarding the six of diamonds and picking up the eight of clubs.

Whitney opened with a bet of two hundred.

"Your two hundred," Tarrington drawled easily, "and two thousand more."

Smith, sitting back in the shadows, leaned forward in his chair and perked to attention. "What am I missing?"

"Nothing yet," Tarrington said blithely. "But you're about to witness the second surrender of the Confederacy."

Montana slid her thumb along the top edge of her cards and glared across the table. She knew he was baiting her and she knew she should have shrugged him aside as casually as he had dismissed the banker's jibe, but it *was* the last hand . . .

"Twenty-two hundred to stay," he reminded her with a soft, whiskey-induced hiccough. "About as much as what was left in the Rebel treasury when we took Richmond, if I'm not mistaken."

Smith guffawed and pulled his chair closer.

"Your twenty-two hundred," she said quietly. "And five thousand more."

Whitney grinned for the first time all evening and displayed a row of childishly small teeth overlaid by thick pink gums. He threw his cards face down and folded his arms over his chest. "I might just sit back and enjoy this. You two deserve each other."

Tarrington drew on his cheroot, clouding the air over the table while he debated the bottomless blue of Montana's eyes. He remembered then where he had seen the color before. Not in the warm, tropical waters of the Caribbean, where he had first guessed, but in the cold heart of an ice flow he had once encountered on a whaling expedition out of Boston.

He counted out the five thousand in greenbacks, then went to his billfold for an additional ten thousand.

Montana curled her fingers around the gold locket, her thumb smoothing over the scrolled letter *M*. The stakes had risen with a breathtaking lack of warning, no thanks to her own reckless behavior. If he *was* running a bluff, it would cost her nearly everything she had just to find out. On the other hand, if she called, there would be thousands of dollars sitting under the glare of the oil lamp.

"Well, Miss Rose? Unless my arithmetic fails me, you have enough to cover the bet, with a little left over for a pretty new frock. I don't know how much experience you have playing this man's game, but I'll give you the same advice I gave young Scott: You might want to play it smart and quit while you still have something to brag about."

Her instincts were screaming at her to back off, that she had been set up as neatly as Paul Whitney in the earlier rounds—as easily as she herself had set them all up. Greed sent her eyes to the center of the green baize tabletop, to the rich pile of coins and greenbacks that awaited her decision. She had the cards. She wanted the money. It was all or nothing.

She pushed her bet into the middle of the table and laid her cards face-up beside it, spreading them to show three aces and two kings.

"Goddamn full house!" Swanson's eyes bulged and his jowls twitched. The balding dome of his head glowed a deep, exuberant red as he slapped his hands flat on the table. "Goddamn aces and goddamn kings!"

Montana smiled, if only to ease the strain in her jaw. She was on the verge of sharing some of Swanson's laughter when she saw Michael Tarrington begin to lay his cards on the table, one by one.

King. Queen. Jack. Ten. Nine. Of spades.

She stared at the flush in disbelief and horror.

"Sorry, Montana," he said easily. "But you can't say I didn't warn you."

"Yes," she agreed, talking through lips that felt numb and wooden. "You did warn me. But then that's all part of the game, isn't it?"

When she had watched his long, elegant hands gather the last of the bills and coins to his side of the table, she collected her own meager sum and stood.

"Well, gentlemen, that has unquestionably finished me for the night. I thank you for an enjoyable and entertaining evening. Perhaps we will meet again another time."

She walked stiffly from the alcove, her heart pounding so loudly in her ears, it drowned every other sound. Voices, movement, laughter, conversations swirled around her as she started down the stairs to the main salon, but she took no notice of anything or anyone. She felt, in fact, as if she were pushing her way through a huge vat of water, with everything moving slowly, and every sound muffled and blurred except for that of her own voice.

"Stupid," she hissed. *"Stupid!"*

"Yes, it was, wasn't it?" a voice echoed in her ear.

Montana whirled around, unaware she had stopped halfway down the stairs or that Tarrington had come up behind her.

The sight of his gloating smile cleared her senses like a cold, hard slap in the face and she spun away from him, hurrying the rest of the way down the staircase. Force of habit made her gather up her flaring skirts, but the sudden forward lurch she took to get away from Tarrington put her toe in her hem and would have sent her sprawling headlong off the bottom landing if not for the hand that was suddenly, firmly at her elbow.

"Allow me," he said, steadying her against the muscled wall of his chest.

"Let go of me this instant," she whispered fiercely.

"Not until you get a grip on yourself. And not until we talk."

"We have nothing more to say," she spat.

"I think we do." His voice was insistent and so was the hand that remained clamped around her upper arm, guiding her out onto the deck. She either had to follow along or cry out in pain and create a scene. Screaming and clawing his face to bloody ribbons would have made her feel better, but they were drawing enough attention as it was.

Once out on the relative privacy of the deck, however, she

wrenched her arm free and put several paces' worth of shadowy distance between them.

"Thank you very much for the escort. Now, will you leave me alone, or must I call for assistance?"

"Are you certain I can't get you a glass of water, or something a little stronger, perhaps?"

"No!"

"Pray, don't tell me the lady gambler with the nerves of steel cannot take a loss in stride?"

Montana bristled at the sarcasm. "I can take a loss, Mr. Tarrington. What I cannot endure is a Yankee scoundrel who gloats over his winnings."

"It was not my intention to gloat. I only wanted to make sure you were all right. You looked a little shaken when you left the table."

"I'm fine," she retorted. "Thank you. Now will you please take your pious concerns elsewhere and find some other poor unfortunate to dazzle with your barbarian wit and charm."

"Yes," he murmured, arching a brow, "you are feeling better."

"Then will you please go away and leave me alone!"

"No," he said quietly. "I may be a Yankee scoundrel, but it has been quite some time since I allowed a beautiful—and somewhat distressed—young woman to find her own way home. This is neither the time of night nor the type of city to wander around without an escort."

"As it happens, I already have an escort," she snapped. "A very impatient one at that, so if you don't mind—"

"Impatient and invisible?" asked Tarrington, glancing pointedly along both lengths of the deserted deck.

"He won't be invisible much longer. Especially if I scream."

Tarrington moved closer, his long legs slicing through the stream of light that escaped the salon window. "Come now, I don't frighten you that much, do I?"

"It would not be fear that prompts me to scream, sir, but sheer frustration!"

He was close enough to see her face clearly, to read the anger, the distrust, the chafing need to flee and be alone somewhere to cry out her misery. She was also frightened of something—or someone—and Tarrington's jaw set itself in a grim line. He should have known.

"So. You have an *escort*. How will he take it when he finds out how much of his money you lost?"

Montana felt the heat rise up her throat and bloom in her cheeks. "I don't know what you're talking about."

"Don't you? Surely you can't take a man's loose change, increase it to over fifteen thousand dollars, then lose it all—and more—in one misguided hand . . . and expect him to be amused. I know I wouldn't be."

Montana simply glared and did not offer comment.

"I suppose my question is, what kind of a temper does he have?"

"What possible business is it of yours?"

"None whatsoever," he admitted with a twist of a smile. "Yet I can't help feeling mildly responsible for what happened."

"Why? You won the hand fairly."

Tarrington laughed softly. "My dear Montana Rose: My flush was about as honest as your three aces. If you were half the card player I was given to believe you were, you should have known that. Moreover, you should have seen it coming."

"You cheated?"

His grin was broad enough to smooth out the dark fur of his mustache and reveal a gleam of strong white teeth. "I prefer to call it *protecting my interests.*"

"Call it what you want," she protested in amazement. "It's still cheating."

"So is shaving kings and queens with your thumbnail, or dealing twos and threes off the bottom of the deck, or *accidentally* dropping an extra ace onto your lap."

Montana opened her mouth for an immediate denial, but she saw a muscle flicker in the hard angle of his jaw and she knew he was not so perfectly composed as he would have had her believe. He was angry—furious, to judge by the jeweled gleam in his eyes. He was also far too big, too proficient with the Remington he wore beneath the long skirt of his coat, and too damned close for comfort.

"I . . . had no choice," she admitted brokenly. "I had to do what I did."

"What do you mean?"

"You wouldn't understand."

"Try me."

She started to moisten her lips and when she saw his eyes drop to follow the movement of her tongue, she knew suddenly that his anger wasn't all caused by her chicanery with the cards. He was still prickly from her curt dismissal of his supper invitation and belligerent because he now knew why.

"When I lose," she said evenly, "my . . . escort . . . becomes *very* angry indeed."

"Are you saying he beats you?"

She bowed her head and lowered her lashes as if the weight of such a confession was too much to bear. She ran her tongue across her lips again, leaving them shiny and wet, and, for added poignancy, drew a deep enough breath to send his gaze—if it was not there already—to the creamy smooth half moons of her breasts where they swelled over the scalloped edge of her bodice.

"Believe me," she whispered, "I did not want to . . . to . . ."

"Cheat," he supplied dryly.

"To *protect my interests,* but there was so much money at stake, and I knew . . . if I won it . . . he would . . . well . . . he would leave me alone tonight."

Tarrington watched her in silence. The tears were there, gathering along the lower fringe of her lashes, glistening like droplets of liquid silver. No doubt they would make the blue of her eyes almost too painful for a man to endure without feeling his insides melt into a sorry, self-deprecating puddle. And here they come, he thought. Brace yourself, lad.

So much time had lapsed without a response of any kind, Montana risked a glance up at him through her lashes. He was just standing there with the devil's own arrogance stamped on his face, not the least affected by her tears or her misery, not even by the breathtaking view he had down the front of her bodice.

"Having already complimented you once tonight on a flawless performance," he murmured, "isn't it rather shameless of you to try it again?"

Montana's eyes widened. "Whatever do you mean, sir?"

"I mean—" He tucked his forefinger under her chin and tilted her face up, bending his own dark head so that their mouths were only a mere inch or two apart. "You're a *very* good actress, but I'm not buying it. Not the contrition, not the quiver in the voice. The tears are a nice touch, but I grew up in a household ruled by five sisters and a mother who could turn their water on and off like spigots whenever they wanted to weasel something from the men in the family. So I would suggest you drop the act or I may just be tempted to beat you myself."

"I don't doubt you would," she said through her teeth.

"On the other hand"—his grip turned into more of a caress than a restraint and his voice became a husky invitation—"if you really wanted to muddy up my mind with other thoughts, you could so something far more inventive with that lovely mouth of yours than sulk."

She lowered her gaze a fraction and it was no longer the smoldering gray of his eyes that held her, but the suggestive closeness of his lips. "I could, could I?"

Instead of answering, he drew her against the hard contours of his body, molding her to him in a way that made her aware of the potent energy he possessed in every muscle, bone, and sinew. She felt crushable. Crushed. And as she watched his mouth descend toward her, she could not help but wonder how many other women he had bent to his will.

The kiss was just a fleeting thing, a teasing brush of his lips to give her the taste and promise of his heat. His mustache tickled and she was not sure she liked the sensation. It smelled of tobacco as well, and whiskey, and it was easy for her to remain detached even as he nibbled here and there as a prelude, she imagined, to a bolder conquest.

He must have felt her eyes watching him, for he leaned back and met her gaze with wry amusement.

"It would be more enjoyable if we both participated."

"I imagine it would be more enjoyable," she murmured, "if I were kissing the hind end of a goat."

If her words, or the honest sentiment behind them, startled him, Tarrington's laugh gave no indication. He released her and straightened to his full height, then, while she watched in wary silence, he pulled out his fattened billfold and started counting out a sheaf of greenbacks.

"Here. This is the amount you came with—five hundred, I believe, or near enough. Maybe your partner won't be *quite* so angry with you if you break even on the night. Go on, take it. And next time, save your acting abilities for someone who does *all* of his thinking from between his legs."

Montana's temper flared hotly in her cheeks as she took an enraged step back. "How dare you! I do not want your charity, nor do I need your sympathy! And I wouldn't take your filthy Yankee money if it was the difference between life and death! It is satisfaction enough for me to know you had to cheat to win it from me. As for what *you* have between *your* legs, sir, I warrant you've had far better actresses than me beneath you wishing you could *think* a little more and boast a little less."

She started to dart past him and almost made it when his hand snaked out, skidding across her bodice before finally catching a solid hold on the edge of her sleeve. She twisted sideways against his grip and his fingers slipped again, but before he could make a second grab for her, she lashed out with a sharply heeled shoe and kicked him savagely on the shin.

Tarrington swore and jerked back to avoid the subsequent flurry of small, bunched fists. By the time he recovered his balance, she was free and running along the deck. He took a step to follow but she was already swallowed into the shadows—shadows that may or may not have been concealing her mysterious "escort."

He cursed again, fluently and graphically, and leaned against the deckrail. His shin stung like someone was holding a lit torch against it, and sure enough, when he looked down to assess the damage, the fabric of his trouser leg was torn, the edges darkening with blood.

He was still clutching his billfold in his hand, and it was while he was replacing it in his jacket pocket and searching out his handkerchief that he saw the bright glint of gold lying on the oak planking. It was a locket. *Her* locket, he was maliciously pleased to discover, probably torn loose when she had erupted like a she-cat. He snatched it off the deck and snapped the two halves open, but the portraits of the man and woman inside offered no clues to the identity of the owner.

He did have a sudden image, however, of long slender fingers caressing the warmth of the gold, brushing over the stylized *M* for luck.

"What a shame," he murmured. "I wonder how you'll manage now without it."

His fist closed around the locket and he was about to throw it over the side, but something made him hold back at the last moment. The locket and the broken chain went into his pocket instead, tucked there with a muttered promise.

"I haven't finished with you yet, Montana Rose. Not by a long shot."

Chapter 8

With Alisha's wedding day approaching, the Courtland family had moved into the graceful, white-columned splendor of Baron von Helmstaad's residence. The plantation itself was less than a quarter the size of Rosalie, but it was far enough from the river to avoid the devastating floods that had played havoc with other farms. So where others were failing, Summitcrest was as prosperous as it had been before the war.

The baron's wealth, like his title, was inherited. He had remained in Europe during the war and had come to the "colonies" only in order to oversee the restructuring of the family business. He did not know the difference between a boll of cotton and a milkweed pod, nor did he care to learn. He was content to keep his land well groomed and the house freshly whitewashed, and the fact that he was soon to acquire a vivacious and lovely young wife to help him entertain in the extravagantly European style he so woefully missed, well, it was the nearest thing to bliss he could imagine.

The Courtlands were ensconced in a private wing of the house (tucked away in a back corner, William had grumbled) where Alisha refused to allow the baron even the slightest glimpse of her. Not because of superstitions or tradition, but because she was far too busy taking inventory of her future domain. She gave the two dozen servants a taste of what was to come, ordering fresh flowers for every room each day and cheerful fires in every hearth to ward off the last traces of mustiness and damp in the unused furniture. Silverware was polished to a rich glow. Everything that was not scrubbable was set out to air and beaten to within an inch of ruination to remove the dust. Mountains of food were prepared and stored in the pantries; chickens were killed and plucked, the suckling pigs were spitted and salted and readied for the enormous cookfires that would be built in a trench at the side of the house.

The weather appeared to be cooperating. Four straight days of scorching sunshine had worked hard to undo some of the damage of the rain. For the first time in many weeks there was dust rising off the roads. A stiff breeze in the afternoons helped to chase the swarms of glutted mosquitoes and horse-flies across the river; bonfires and smudge pots were lit at night to keep them there.

Amanda busied herself in the kitchen, helping Mercy prepare the creoles and gumbos that were foreign fare to the baron and his people, but staples in a Southerner's diet. By the end of the day, her tongue burned from testing sauces and her hands were red from shelling shrimp and crawfish, and she felt a personal, grudging dislike for each and every one of the hundred and fifty guests invited.

"I never thought this day would end." Ryan sighed, joining her on the wide, shaded porch to share a cool glass of lemonade and watch the sun dipping below the rim of trees. "There's the proof, however. Now, if we can just get through tomorrow's wedding with our sanity and our backs intact . . ."

Amanda laughed and kneaded a knot of muscles high on his back, earning an appreciative groan in response. "Look on the bright side. We'll be eating leftover chicken for a month and have enough ham and eggs to send Mercy into ecstasies."

"It's not worth it," he grumbled, and hung his head forward so her fingers could work their magic on his neck. "And I still don't know why I had to be here. I haven't done anything any one of a dozen of von Helmstaad's lackeys couldn't have done. I should be back at Rosalie. I should be—"

"You should be quiet and endure, like the rest of us," Amanda interrupted. "And you're here to look handsome and be charming, and to keep a certain ragamuffin I know from getting under everyone's feet."

Ryan followed Amanda's glance to where Verity was playing under the drooping arms of an old cypress tree nearby. She had been "helping" her uncle Ryan all afternoon, keeping him company on his errands to town, hunting out berries for Mercy's pies and tarts, searching for the prettiest wildflowers to weave into her hair in the morning. Her pinafore was streaked with dust and grime, as usual. Her hair was a tumble of tight yellow curls that would undoubtedly take hours to untangle before bedtime.

Amanda smiled and rested her cheek on Ryan's shoulder. "Thank you."

"For what?"

"For loving her so much," she said softly. "She doesn't really have anyone else in her life she can look up to, and I know how hard it is for you to play uncle and father and hero all rolled into one."

"You neglected to mention mud pie specialist and personal pony," he added wryly. "And it isn't my fault she doesn't have anyone else to look up to."

Amanda sighed and straightened. She hadn't told Ryan the details about her confrontation with Josh in the summerhouse, only that they had they had both come to the conclusion they were better suited as friends than lovers. Ryan had had that look in his eye, however, as if he had suspected there was more to it, but Amanda had remained adamant. There was already enough tension between her sister and brother; something like this might cause an irreparable break.

"Have you seen Dianna lately?" she asked, steering the conversation away from herself. "Do you know if she and the Judge are coming tomorrow?"

"Mmmm."

"Is that mmmm you have seen her, or mmmm they are coming?"

He stalled a little by draining his glass of lemonade before answering. "I saw her in town this morning, and yes, both she and her father will be coming."

"Then why such an overwhelming display of enthusiasm? I would have thought you'd be happy they made it back from Fayette in time."

"I'm happy," he muttered, and looked away.

"Positively thrilled, I can see." She craned her neck forward and her frown deepened when she saw the expression on his face. "Ryan? What is it? What's wrong?"

He sighed again and set his empty glass down on the step beside him. "She also told me some news about her Yankee friend."

"Who . . . ? Oh."

"Yes, oh. It seems he wasn't just here sniffing around her skirts. It seems he has also been sniffing around for land investments. He bought the Porterfields' out. All forty thousand acres."

"The Glen?" Amanda gasped. "A *Yankee* bought Briar Glen?"

"Several weeks ago." He nodded glumly. "I guess the family wanted to keep it quiet as long as they could."

Amanda's shock was justified. The Glen was the biggest estate in southern Mississippi. By comparison, Rosalie was a farm and Summitcrest a homestead. She had not known the Porterfields were in such desperate straits to have had to sell the home their ancestors had lived in for generations—and to a Yankee! It must have broken what was left of poor Emma Porterfield's heart, for she'd lost her husband and both sons in the war.

"Oh, Ryan," she whispered. "How awful. About everything."

He refused to meet her eyes. He watched Verity playing in the grass, her face twisted with concentration as she tried desperately and stubbornly to overcome the disadvantage of uncoordinated little fingers and uncooperative flower stems that refused to weave together the way her uncle had shown her.

Ryan's face reflected a similar desperation and helplessness, and Amanda's heart wrenched in sympathy. Why was everything going so horribly wrong? she wondered. Why could no one in this family be happy? Ryan's strength was not bottomless, and her own, goodness only knew, was on the verge of collapse.

"Maybe she is only keeping company with him to make you jealous," she suggested halfheartedly. "After all, a girl can only be patient for so long before she feels she has to take matters into her own hands."

"Dianna isn't the type to play games. And even if she was, how could I possibly go to her now? I have nothing. By the end of next week, I'll have less than nothing."

Amanda bit her lip. "Have you tried talking to Wainright again?"

"Hat in hand," he spat. "I groveled so low I almost made myself puke."

"He wouldn't extend the deadline on the loan?"

"He wouldn't extend me a glass of water when I was choking on my pride."

Amanda's teeth drew blood. "Have you thought of . . . of asking Karl? After all, he will be part of the family tomorrow."

Ryan snorted derisively. "I didn't have to ask him. While I was discreetly leading up to the subject, he voiced his sentiments in no uncertain terms. 'Never do it,' he said. 'Never loan money to relatives. Never get it back, don't you know. Besides that: develops character. Strengthens a man's resolve if he struggles through a failure now and then.' "

Amanda's shoulders slumped a little further. "And I don't imagine Alisha would ever consider lifting a finger to try to change his opinion. The more he gave us, the less she would have to spend."

She heard no argument from Ryan. Alisha did not even know—or care to know—how much they were in debt. She would probably look on the loss of Rosalie as a godsend, for she had come to associate the plantation with poverty and ruin.

Ruin, loss, and abject poverty aside, Verity approached her mother and uncle with by far the worst calamity of all. Her lower lip had all but disappeared into the bow of her upper and her chin was rigid with the effort it was taking not to give way to tears. She walked right up the short flight of steps and threw herself into Ryan's arms, burying her face in his shoulder, curling her hands tightly around his neck.

"Whoa, now. What seems to be the problem here?" he asked.

Two huge blue eyes looked up at him with the forlorn despair of a cherub given the responsibility of holding up the entire Sistine Chapel. She brought one of her fists down from his shoulder and showed him the tangle of crushed and broken flowers she held.

"Ahh," he said, nodding with understanding. In case there was any doubt, she reached up and pressed her mouth to his ear, whispering a flurry of half words and broken sentences. When she ran out of breath, she thrust the wreath into Ryan's hands and stood waiting for him to use his customary magic to fix it.

He suspected there was not much hope for it, but he made a few corrective twists and turns with the stems and held it up against Amanda's hair. "Almost perfect," he pronounced. "Maybe a few more bluebells. Do we have any left?"

Another flurry of wet whispers had Verity scampering back to the tree, her curls and petticoats bouncing in her relief.

"I don't recall you ever having this much patience with me when I was her age," Amanda noted.

"You were never as sweet-natured as Verity. Or as cute."

She reached over and slipped her hand into his. "We'll get through this somehow," she whispered fervently. "I just know we will."

The day of the wedding dawned cool and clear. Those servants who had not been up all night long were already busy with tasks when the bright pink eye of the sun winked over the horizon. They trooped through the house like ants through sugar, moving the last of the furniture out of the large parlor where the dancing would take place later that night. An archway had been constructed at one end of the formal gardens and was woven with hundreds of roses to frame the dais where the vows would be exchanged. Chairs were set down in neat rows on either side of a central aisle, to be moved back after the ceremony and placed around the long trestle tables that had been erected closer to the house. China was brought out in gleaming white stacks and covered with sheets; trays of food began appearing in astonishing quantities to sit patiently under yards and yards of filmy netting.

The minister arrived and gave the arrangements his solemn nod of approval, then was happily whisked away by William Courtland to wait until the clock struck noon. The hallways, porch, and lawns echoed with footsteps and laughter as carriage after carriage of guests drew up in front of the house and emptied their colorful cargoes. Every room bustled with activity. Chattering, gossiping women preened in front of any reflective surface they could find, while the men gathered over cigars and fine port wine and lamented over the soaring price of cotton.

By noon, the house was in utter chaos with the eye of the storm swirling around Alisha's dressing room. She surely had to be the only one to have the use of a full-length cheval mirror all to herself, and as she stood before it, critically surveying herself from every conceivable angle, there were others in the room with her who held their breaths, waiting for her verdict.

It could hardly be anything but favorable. The gown, which had seen her great-great-grandmother to the altar before the turn of the century, was a breathtaking creation of rose-colored silk sateen, as slippery as water, as light as air. The tight underbodice was cut square and alarmingly low, originally meant to be worn with a delicate gauze scarf, but trimmed now with bands of gathered ruching. The sleeves were tight to the elbow before flaring in successive tiers of white and pink lace. The overskirt was a fountain of silk, again meant to be worn over wire panniers, but modified for Sarah's wedding, and again for Amanda's, with some of the bulk reduced to make a graceful sweep over the six layers of ruffled petticoats worn beneath. Alisha's silvery blonde hair was piled high on her head, woven with ribbons and sprigs of tiny pink flowers.

Sarah Courtland pressed a much-abused handkerchief to her eyes, weeping happily as she watched her daughter turn another full circle in the mirror.

"Beautiful," she sobbed. "Just beautiful. I cannot believe my eyes, Lissy. If only Grandmother Fayworth were here to see you now . . . and your sweet grandfather. How proud they would have been."

Alisha was not so sure as she checked and rechecked her profile in the mirror. Mercy had nearly ruptured a vessel trying to lace her into the underbodice. An odd look had come into the old crone's dark eyes when she realized she wasn't going to get Alisha's waist any smaller, and if she suspected the reason for the added plumpness, she had kept her tongue between her teeth for a change.

After today it wouldn't matter anyway. After today she would eat and eat and eat to her heart's content, and if she started to gain a little weight, why, she would tell everyone it was because she *was* so happy and content. And a few months from now, when cream pies and custards couldn't explain the location of all her gain, she would let Karl give out the happy news, leaving her in modest seclusion until the brat was born and she could get on with her life again.

She could do it. She *would* do it, by heaven. She had Josh, who loved her to distraction, and who would continue to love her even more desperately when he found out she was carrying their child. He would understand then why she had done it, why she had married Karl von Helmstaad, why she was about to allow . . . no, encourage the doughy old pig to consummate the union, why it had been necessary to let him paw her and climb on top of her and push himself inside her enough times to make him believe he was the father of the child. She had heard there were ways of prolonging the time a child stayed in the womb, just as she had heard there were ways to bleed it away before it had firmly taken root. She had been too cowardly to seek out the one solution, but the other might be necessary, depending on the doctor's predictions and Karl's gullibility. Giving birth early to a healthy, robust, squalling babe might be too much for even him to swallow.

Swallow it he would, however, at least long enough to legitimize the brat with his name. Afterward, if he suspected anything, or demanded anything to maintain his silence, she would suggest to Josh it was time to make her a widow.

First, of course, she had to become the baron's wife and get through this day without slapping her mother, screaming at her father, or taking a razor-sharp knife to her sister.

Alisha's gaze narrowed as she sought Amanda out of the shadows. She was standing by the window, lost behind the haze of sunshine streaming through the panes. She'd hardly spoken a word all morning, seemingly too distracted with whatever filled her brain these days to even think to offer her twin a compliment or two on her wedding day. Stuck like glue to her left leg was Verity, her hand fisted so tightly to the folds of Amanda's skirts, the material would be permanently wrinkled from the damp.

They were dressed alike in gowns of pale blue that perfectly matched the color of their eyes. Short frilled sleeves were worn off the shoulders, with ruffles of pleated silk continuing across the bodice in three delicately scalloped layers. The skirts were cut in tiers as well, swagged in back to form trains, the silk so fine the slightest movement sent it rippling like a wash of sea foam. Alisha would have preferred to see her sister dressed in sackcloth and bunting, but Karl had insisted on buying everyone new outfits to complement his bride.

Complements like that, Alisha could live without.

As twins, it should have come as no surprise that Amanda could be a rare beauty when she chose to wear silk instead of dimity and dress her hair in a gleaming cascade of spirals and ringlets instead of scraping it back into a severe, matronly chignon. Today she was not only beautiful, but a visible threat to Alisha's composure.

"Well?" she demanded. "Do I look like a baroness? Karl tells me when he takes me home next summer to meet his relatives, I shall be an honored guest in all the royal houses in Europe. Can you imagine that, Mother? Me? Sitting next to a duke or a duchess or a princess, for goodness sakes, eating little cakes and chatting about the weather.''

Sarah nodded and wailed into her handkerchief. Amanda acknowledged the momentous possibilities with a smile that set Alisha's teeth on edge.

''Well, then,'' she snapped. ''Let's get it over with, shall we? Before Father has the reverend too drunk on Karl's brandy to read the service.''

Amanda led the way out into the dazzling sunlight, smiling only when she saw Ryan waiting at the end of the flower-strewn path. She had indeed been too distracted to do more than go through the motions of getting dressed, sitting still while tongs and irons shaped her hair, answering only if a direct question was asked. She was worried about Ryan, worried about her family, about Rosalie. Not the least of all, she was worried about Verity and her reaction to so many strangers who were bound to frighten her into hiding for most of the day.

The constant drag on the side of her skirt relented only when she came to a halt. Then a small face and body were pressed into the side of her thigh, buried in the crush of silk until the signal came to walk forward again. It was torture for the child, torture for the mother as they walked down the garden aisle. The only good thing about it—the sun was warm on her face, blinding in its brilliance, and served to blot out the faces and whispering mouths of the people they passed on their way to the dais.

At the end of the aisle, Alisha's groom waited beside the imperiously tall, sedate Reverend Mr. Aloisius Kelly. Almost a caricature by comparison, Karl von Helmstaad was short and balding. He stood ramrod straight in an effort to lessen the protruding girth of his belly, but it only made him look like a splay-footed penguin balanced precariously on a sheet of ice.

He turned at a signal from the reverend and saw his bride walking slowly toward him. Flushed with the purity of her beauty, he tipped forward eagerly and extended his arm in greeting. A collectively indrawn breath from the crowd came as Amanda declined the groom's offer of assistance and stepped aside to make way for Alisha's frosty countenance.

Out of the corner of her eye, Amanda saw Ryan struggling to keep his expression blank. He almost succeeded too, until the groom, trying his best to recover from his blunder, missed the step up onto the dais and nearly pitched headlong into the festooned arch.

Thankfully, the rest was short and sweet. The reverend's voice droned out the service, prompting the exchange of vows and rings, and Amanda's concentration drifted again, recalling the same words, the same vows she had taken with Caleb Jackson by her side. Their wedding day had been drab and overcast. The ceremony had taken place in the parlor at Rosalie with only the immediate families to bear witness. Caleb had promised, when the war ended, they would have a proper celebration, with all their friends in attendance, with music and laughter and happiness as far as they could see into the future . . .

Another promise made, she reminded herself with a little shake, was the one she had given her mother to keep an eye on their father, who, even though confined to a wheelchair, usually managed to slip out of sight in the winking of an eye. And true to form, when the vows were duly recited and solemnly pledged, he wasted no time in having some of his cronies roll him back down the aisle toward the long rows of refreshment tables. There they happily laid siege to the baron's supply of expensive bourbon and toasted the health of the bride and groom.

It seemed a harmless enough feint for the time being and Amanda was glad of the opportunity to try to pry Verity away from her leg long enough to return some of the circulation to the limb.

She saw Ryan and caught his arm before he could pass.

"Ryan, thank goodness. Can you see if—" She stopped

and frowned. "What is it? What's wrong? You look as if you've swallowed a peach pit."

"Over by the magnolia," he said tautly. "That's what's wrong."

Amanda followed his bleak stare but had to wait for a parade of feathered bonnets and daintily twirling parasols to pass before she could locate the reason for her brother's sudden pallor. When she saw it was only Dianna Moore standing in the shade with her father, she almost let a curse slip through her lips. But then the last of the slow-moving belles strolled past and Amanda saw the third member of the small group—a tall, broad-shouldered gentleman whose rakish smile and piratical good looks had been the main cause of the women meandering so slowly by. Not only was he standing at ease beside the Judge, he had Dianna's hand tucked possessively into the crook of his arm, smiling down at her as if they were sharing a private joke.

"You don't suppose that could be her Yankee . . . do you?" Amanda asked in a whisper.

"I have a feeling we are about to find out," he said grimly, pulling his mouth into a smile of sorts as Dianna saw them and waved.

"Amanda! Ryan!" Dianna detached herself from her companion's arm and came hurrying over. Petite and dark haired, she did not possess Amanda's classical beauty; a close inspection would even find a smattering of reddish-brown freckles across the bridge of her nose. She had wide, expressive blue-green eyes that filled with adoration whenever they happened to settle upon Ryan Courtland, and today was no exception. Moreover, she took shameless advantage of the happy occasion to thrust her hands into his and surge up on tiptoes before him, brushing her lips across his cheek, leaving them flame red in her wake.

"Ryan . . ." Her voice was as soft as a whisper and shivered along his spine. "You look wonderful."

Which he did. His shock of gold hair was freshly trimmed and tamed into a wave that ended just above the starched formality of his collar and cravat. The many months of hard

work had added a powerful strain to the seams of his coat
and trousers, and despite the slight limp in his left leg, he
carried himself with an easy grace that recalled hot lazy days
long gone by when men and women lounged in the shade of
columned verandas and talked of nothing more serious than
the next horse race on Natchez Island.

The Judge was a beat behind Dianna in taking Amanda
into a jovial bearhug that left them both laughing with affection.

"Amanda . . . by Jove, is that you under all those frills
and fancies? No wonder you had the baron breaking wind up
there; I'd marry you myself if I was thirty years younger.
How's the family holding up under all this stuff and nonsense? Quiet parlor wedding would have done quite nicely, if
you ask me, and if you"—he grasped Ryan's hand in a
particularly hearty shake—"ever do get around to asking me
for my daughter's hand, that's all you had best be expecting."

Dianna went an immediate beet red and lost all of her
breath on a gasped "Father!"

Accustomed to dealing brusquely and frankly with the
drunks and derelicts who came before him in a courtroom,
the Judge had never been one to mince his words, or apologize for not doing so. He looked very nearly like a derelict
himself, with full white whiskers and thinning hair that flew
out over his ears like wings. His frockcoat and breeches were
ten years out of date, and the striped waistcoat could barely
contain his burgeoning girth, a fact that made anyone in
close proximity stand a little to the side in case the buttons
let loose and put out an eye.

William Courtland and Frederick Arblaster Moore had
been friends for over thirty years, since the day they met each
other across the green of a dueling field. It had been deemed
the only honorable way for two Southern gentlemen to decide who should be the one to court the lusty Miss Beulah
Raye Tobina. Both men had missed with their first shot. Two
subsequent attempts had sent their seconds ducking behind
the coaches for safety, the fourth—for they were determined,

if not accurate—killed a wild turkey the first three shots had flushed out of the nearby woods. Aided by a bottle of medicinal whiskey, it was decided the death of the fowl was an omen not lightly to be dismissed, and the two very drunk, very relieved men returned home that day to feast on turkey and discover they were better suited as friends than rivals.

"Where is that old scoundrel?" the Judge demanded. "Is he behaving?"

"Probably not," Amanda answered on a sigh. "In fact, I was just on my way to check up on him."

"Well, before you do, gal, spare a minute more and meet one of my wife's distant cousins—third or fourth removed, I believe. Born on the wrong side of the Mason-Dixon line, wouldn't you know, but then Esther—rest her soul—and her family always were a contrary bunch. Step on up here, m'boy, and meet the son and daughter of the best damned poker player this side of the Mississippi. Ryan, Amanda . . . Michael Tarrington."

Up close, the Yankee looked even more imposing than he had in the shade of the magnolia. A full half head taller than any other man currently on the grounds, his broad shoulders made impressive work of filling a gunmetal gray jacket of the finest merino wool. A collared waistcoat of silver-green silk brocade was set off by a pearl-pink cravat, the latter knotted to within an inch of fashionable perfection and tacked to his shirt with an emerald the size of a giant pea.

He stood hatless under the sun, preferring to hold the rakish flat-top by his side. As he bowed cavalierly over Amanda's hand, the sunlight burnished the thick chestnut waves of his hair, threading it with glints of red and gold and fiery copper.

"A very great pleasure," he said, flashing a generous smile beneath the wide, full mustache. "The Judge and Dianna have told me enough about the Courtland family, I feel as if we have met already."

"We have been hearing a great deal about you too," Ryan said stiffly.

"Michael's mother and Mama were good friends as well

as cousins,'' Dianna interjected quickly, her hands fluttering with nervous tension. It was obvious she had anticipated a reaction from Ryan and wanted to avert any potential misunderstandings. ''I can't tell you how many summers we spent together as children. I mean, Michael and I were never exactly children together, he's ages older than I am, but he has five sisters, two of whom I attended school with for a season. And we used to visit the seaside, near their home in Boston, at least once a year, right up until . . . until . . .''

''Until travel became awkward?'' Tarrington supplied gently, still smiling from the ''ages older'' reference.

Dianna sighed her thanks and glanced up at Ryan, who had no such compunction toward subtlety.

''The war made a good many things awkward, travel being the least of our concerns. You fought for the North, naturally.''

The smoky gray eyes lifted slowly to Ryan's. ''Naturally. A somewhat different war than yours, I would imagine.''

''I beg your pardon?''

''Navy,'' he said easily. ''I commanded a gunboat in the blockade.''

''Broke through the defenses at New Orleans in '62,'' the Judge provided helpfully. ''Barged right on up to Vicksburg with his cannons blazing and his saber clutched between his teeth. Wasn't for him and his damned ironclads, the Union never would have been able to come down the Mississippi and cut our supply lines in half. Saved the Federal Army the embarrassment of being chased on up into Canada by our cavalry. Now Ryan here,'' he added, puffing up his chest, ''rode with Jeb Stuart himself and would have been in the vanguard chasing you scalawags back where you belonged. Rode with Jeb in the first charge at Bull Run and stayed with him until '64, in a battle outside of Spotsylvania.''

''Ryan had four horses shot out from under him that day,'' Dianna elaborated in a breathless whisper. ''The last one fell on his leg and broke his ankle, and the Yankee commander was so impressed by his bravery, he ordered his own surgeon to tend the wound.''

The two men weathered the words of praise swirling around them but added nothing to either encourage or prolong the commentary. They assessed one another in silence, their faces impassive, carved out of stone. And though there had never been a time when they had actually faced each other as enemies in battle, they faced one another now as adversaries, wary and guarded.

Tarrington was the first to relent, his eyes losing none of their intensity, however, as they fastened once again on Amanda. "The Judge is not usually given to understatement, but I find in this instance, when he said you and your sister were twins and difficult to tell apart, he was short by a country mile. The resemblance is nothing less than extraordinary, Miss Courtland. Startling, in fact."

"Then I can only imagine you must startle easily, Mr. Tarrington. And the name is Jackson. Mrs. Caleb Jackson."

"Forgive me for the presumption," he said, bowing slightly at the waist. While he was in the act of straightening and before his gaze had managed to rise above the elegantly smooth arch of her throat, he caught sight of a second small, pale face peeping out from behind the folds of Amanda's skirt.

The change that came over his face was immediate and somewhat startling in its own right. The lines across his brow disappeared, the deep creases at the corners of his mouth were given greater substance in a smile that expressed pure pleasure.

"Well . . . hello there. And who might you be?"

Verity burrowed back into the crush of silk like a mouse scurrying back into its hidey-hole.

"You will have to excuse my daughter," Amanda said, lowering her hand by her side as if to offer further shielding. "Verity is not comfortable around strangers, especially tall, ominous-looking men."

"Am I ominous-looking?" he asked, lifting his eyebrows in mild surprise. "My nieces and nephews all tend to think I look more like a large stuffed pony."

"You have no children of your own, Mr. Tarrington?"

"I have no wife of my own, Mrs. Jackson."

"Implying you have one belonging to someone else?"

He smiled again, his pleasure tempered by the obvious hostility in her voice. "I am not married. I have no children. And I make it a point to stay well away from other men's wives."

"An admirable quality," she allowed wryly. "Husbands everywhere must sleep better at night, I'm sure."

Judge Moore *harrumphed* loudly into his hand and glared under his brows at Amanda. "A mite prickly today, are we?"

She had the grace to flush, although not the compunction to offer any apology, for despite her near rudeness, the Yankee continued to stare at her. If anything, her rebuff had brought a thoughtful new gleam into the slate-gray eyes, almost a determination to know the placement of every lash, every errant wisp of blonde hair.

"Besides," the Judge continued, "Michael won't be a stranger around here much longer. I gather you've heard he's bought himself a prime tract of land."

"We heard the Glen had been sold," Ryan acknowledged. "We just hadn't heard it had been *put up for sale.*"

The implication behind Ryan's words appeared to win a small reaction as Tarrington's eyes narrowed against the challenge. It also brought Dianna rushing into the fray again in an anxious attempt to avoid a scene.

"It wasn't what you think. Emma wasn't forced into selling the Glen. In fact, she came to Father a few weeks ago to ask his advice. She said the plantation was simply too much to handle on her own, and with no one left to inherit, she said she would be just as happy rid of it so she could move back home to England. Michael happened to be passing through Natchez on business and . . . well . . . Father took him to look at the Glen. He met with Emma and arranged terms the same day."

"At a fair and honest price, I can assure you," Tarrington added. "Probably a damn sight too fair in today's market."

"But nowhere near its real value, I warrant," Amanda muttered under her breath.

He did it again. He stared at her openly and far too intimately for such a casual acquaintance. His eyes probed hers with a lazy menace that seemed to be warning her against pressing him too far. As if he had given her a similar warning once before that she had ignored.

"Sir," she demanded point blank. "Are you suffering under the impression we have met somewhere before? You keep staring at me as if you expect me to wink back and acknowledge some private joke we should be sharing."

The bluntness of her query caught him off guard, and even though he recovered quickly enough, she thought she detected a faint ruddiness darken his complexion.

"I can assure you we have not met," she insisted archly. "And the only joke I sense here is the one you have perhaps played on yourself. Briar Glen is indeed one of the largest and grandest plantations in Adams County—forty thousand acres, if I am not mistaken—of good, rich land that produced nearly half the cotton in the region before the war. But the Porterfields also owned over a thousand slaves, a once-necessary evil in our part of the world, Mr. Tarrington, and one I am sure you abhor with as much zeal as the rest of your countrymen. It remains, nonetheless, the only practical way to plant, till, and harvest vast amounts of cotton without bankrupting yourself ten times over."

"Oh"—Dianna gasped—"but Michael doesn't plan to grow cotton, he—"

"He plans to try to live here as peacefully and harmoniously as he possibly can," Tarrington interrupted. "Although it doesn't look as if I am off to a good start."

"Nonsense, m'boy," the Judge said, slapping him on the shoulder. "No one's drawn a gun and shot you yet. I call that downright sociable."

"At the risk of sounding *un*sociable," Amanda said sardonically, "you will have to excuse me now. I would like to take Verity out of the hot sun before she is melted permanently to my leg."

Amanda reached down for the child's hand and started to lead her away, aware of Dianna's blurted excuses and her hasty footsteps following up the slope of the lawn.

"Amanda! Amanda, please . . . don't be angry with me. Oh . . . I just knew it would turn out all wrong. I thought, I hoped if Michael came with us today and if Ryan got a chance to meet him and talk to him, he would realize what a fine, sweet man he really is. I know how you all feel about Yankees—I feel the same way too! But Michael isn't like the rest of them. He's my cousin, for pity's sake; I've known him all my life and he's a fair, honest man who would never have behaved anything at all like the animals who beat and tormented Ryan in the prison camp. I can't be rude to him. I just can't. No matter what people think or what they say about Father and me. And don't try to tell me they aren't gossiping and wagging their nasty old tongues at us. I've seen the way they stare at us and the way they lift their hands and talk about us when we pass. I don't care, I tell you. I don't. Not if they're so petty and cruel and awful that they could have known us all their lives and still treat us this way. But I *do* care what you think. And what Ryan thinks. Oh, God . . . did you see the way he was glaring at me! Do you think he hates me now? Do you think he truly hates me?"

"Dianna—" Amanda stopped walking and stopped trying to follow the breathless rush of questions and conclusions. "What on earth are you going on about? No one hates you. No one is whispering about you. And we all have to deal with Yankees every single day because they aren't simply going to go away even if we vow to ignore them the rest of our lives. As for the way Ryan was looking at you—it should have made you jump for joy. Or don't you recognize a jealous man when you see one?"

"Jealous?" Dianna gasped. "Ryan was jealous? Of whom?"

Her bewilderment was so innocent, so completely without pretense, Amanda had to laugh. "Who do you think, goose? Who has been seen squiring you all around town for the past few weeks and who has set the gossips' tongues wagging so furiously?''

Dianna's mouth dropped open. "Michael? He's jealous of Michael?"

Amanda shook her head in a gesture of hopelessness and started walking again. Dianna was delayed for the length of two pounding heartbeats before she scrambled after her, her expression suspended somewhere between wonder and disbelief.

"But . . . Michael is my cousin," she said lamely.

"Ryan didn't know that. And anyway, cousins marry cousins all the time; he probably would have thrown bigger fits if he had known."

The huge turquoise eyes grew even huger. "Ryan has been throwing fits?"

"Great foaming ones," Amanda said dryly. "He's been quite unpleasant to be around for the past month or so."

"Jealous," Dianna murmured again, obviously experiencing a resurgence of hope. Her complexion took on the hue of a dusky rose and her hand trembled where it touched Amanda's arm. "Do you honestly, truly, sincerely think so? Oh, Amanda . . . I love him so much it hurts. If I only knew for sure he felt the same way—"

"He does. He is simply too proud and too pig-headed to do anything about it."

"He never comes to call," Dianna lamented. "I'm lucky if I see him once a month by accident, and even then I feel as brazen as a hussy when I run up and corner him on the street. Short of my asking him outright if he wants to marry me or not, I don't know what more I can do."

They were hailed by a cluster of Courtland relatives, and Amanda could not pass by without stopping to say hello to her eighty-three-year-old great aunt. But neither could she let the moment escape without offering her crestfallen friend a bit of advice from the heart.

"You can tell him how you feel. You can make him understand how much you want him, regardless of what he does or doesn't have in the bank. And if you don't do it soon, he is noble enough and pig-headed enough to offer to read the banns for you and your Mr. Tarrington.''

''Michael? Good heavens, he's the last man on earth I would expect to see standing willingly in front of an altar. His parents and sisters have been throwing debutantes at him since he was eighteen, and he's either frightened them away or left town himself, taking to the seas for months on end until he thought it was safe to return again. And much as I adore him, I could never contemplate living with him. He is very set in his opinions and his ways, and I daresay a wife would only be considered a nuisance.''

Amanda refrained from reminding Dianna she had only just finished praising him as being sweet and fine and honest. ''Whatever you do, don't tell Ryan any of that or you'll be an old maid before he comes to his senses.''

While Dianna absorbed this last warning, Verity broke away and tumbled into the outstretched arms of her kindly, crinkly old Auntie Rose. She came running back a moment later, her fist clamped around an enormous stick of cinnamon candy that had been brought specially for her. Amanda and Dianna both had glasses of punch thrust into their hands and were cautioned by way of broad winks that there was more in the glasses than apple cider and chokeberry juice. It was strong and warming, a welcome diversion for the two women until they thought it was safe enough to steal respective glances back in the direction of the magnolia tree.

To Amanda's consternation, it wasn't safe at all, for the Yankee's piercing gray eyes were waiting for her. A stray beam of sunlight caught the white, wolfish smile as it spread slowly beneath his mustache, and he had the further audacity, the insufferable arrogance, to acknowledge her interest with a deep and formal bow.

''He *is* by far the handsomest man here, isn't he?'' Dianna commented on a sigh.

''If you like pirates with great hairy mustaches who look at you like they're undressing you without your permission . . . I suppose some might think so.''

''I was talking about Ryan.'' Dianna giggled. ''But yes,

Michael does look like a pirate. And he most certainly does seem interested in you.''

''Me?'' Amanda looked aghast at her friend. ''Don't even say such a thing as a joke. Ryan would rupture something, then murder us both for good measure.''

She changed the subject quickly after that, but the flush stayed warm on her skin for some time. Worse, she could still feel the Yankee's gaze on the back of her neck, and while she dared not risk another glance to confirm it, she suspected his smile had turned into quiet, mocking laughter.

Chapter 9

"**M**rs. Jackson."

Amanda whirled around, startled by the sound of a voice coming out of the shadows.

She had spent the better half of the afternoon and evening overseeing the one hundred and one things that should have gone smoothly but naturally didn't. One whole table burdened under platters of sweet pastries and freshly churned ice cream had collapsed, trapping two children and a dog beneath. The children had been dug out with no ill effects, the dog had vomited a mélange of strawberry preserves and canned peaches all over the hems of nearby guests.

William Courtland, fortified by hefty quantities of spirits, had accepted a wager from his red-nosed compatriots (who by then included Judge Moore among their number) and, with stop watches ticking, had raced his wheelchair along the veranda and literally scooped Miss Pauline Brickley off her feet and carried her screeching to the opposite end of the porch. Sarah had required her salts. Amanda had been stern, William sheepish, and Miss Brickley amazingly forgiving. It had, after all, alerted a large portion of the male attendees to the shapeliness of her calves and ankles.

Dusk had crept over the lawns and shrouded the house in a soft haze of pink and purple shadows. The strings of paper lanterns were lit and most of the activities moved inside to the room that had been cleared for dancing. Wine and champagne flowed. And for a while, caught up in the cocoon of bright lights, laughter, flowing ballgowns, and lively music, it was the same rich and elegant life the South had known before the devastating horror of war. There were no floods, no quagmires of mud, no ruined crops. There were no empty rooms to go home to, no scarred piles of smoke-charred rubble, no deserted slave quarters, no barren, empty cupboards.

Amanda stood in the night air, swaying slightly to the rhythm of the music that flowed out through the open French doors. The veranda wrapped around three sides of the house, and she had deliberately sought out the quietest, darkest corner. Honeysuckle and roses grew in fragrant abundance in the gardens beside her, and if she closed her eyes and concentrated, she could still detect the lingering aroma of the cooking fires, the pungent-sweet smell of cigar smoke . . .

Her eyes popped open a fraction of a second before she heard her name.

"Forgive me, I did not mean to frighten you." The glow of ash at the tip of his cigar flared briefly as Michael Tarrington flicked the stub over the railing. He stood with his back against the wall, one foot propped on the lip of a stone urn, a hand tucked casually in his jacket pocket. His face was entirely in shadow, only the wink of the emerald tie pin reflected any light from the nearby open doors.

"I have been hoping for an opportunity to speak to you alone," he added. "I dislike loose ends . . . or unfinished conversations. If I offended you in any way earlier today, believe me it was not intentional."

Amanda curled her lower lip between her teeth and bit down gently. "No. It is I who should have sought you out. I dislike rudeness, Mr. Tarrington, and I was very rude to you this afternoon. Dianna and the Judge are good friends, and it was unfair of me to place them in such an awkward position."

Several moments lapsed while Amanda glanced longingly at the open doors and the boisterous crowds inside. The solitude she had welcomed not long ago was suddenly uncomfortable—as uncomfortable as conducting a conversation with a shadow.

"Your brother . . . I gather he lived through some bad experiences in the war." It was a statement, not a question, and Amanda did not feel obliged to answer, or to elaborate.

Not to someone who had spent the war sailing up and down the river, snug behind the armored protection of an ironclad.

"Johnson's Island, wasn't it? In Ohio?"

Amanda bristled under his persistence. "He was taken from the Army hospital at Spotsylvania, if you must know, and spent the next fourteen months enjoying the hell of your Yankee hospitality. If you are expecting an apology from *him,* I would suggest you might see flowers growing on the moon first."

"Both sides of the dispute had their hells, Mrs. Jackson. The Confederate prison in Florida was, as I understand it, known for its rate of death by starvation."

"Our army could hardly be expected to feed prisoners beefsteak when they barely had a slice of bread themselves. And what little *we* had was commandeered by your own armies—or dumped in the river to teach us all a lesson in humility."

"Yes," he said, pushing away from the wall and emerging from the gloom. "I can see by the festivities today just how humble you have become."

A hot flush surged through her veins and Amanda started toward the doors. She had to pass close by him, and as she did, his hand came out—first to block her way, then to wrap firmly around the cool white flesh of her upper arm. She was shocked by the unexpected contact, more so by the boldness that prompted it, and she was forced to stand quiet, listening to the faint rustle of her skirt and petticoats settling around her ankles.

"I'm sorry," he said. "I didn't mean to sound so flippant."

"Yes, you did. And if it will amuse you any more to know, half the people here are indeed mortified by my sister's excesses, but they will undoubtedly recover enough to stuff whatever they can in their pockets and reticules when they leave. Do you like oranges, Mr. Tarrington?"

"Oranges?"

"Yes. You probably ate them every day when you were growing up; I know we did. My daughter tasted an orange for the first time not more than six months ago. She took a whole week to eat it, shred by shred, then saved the peels in a jar so she could take them out now and then and remember what it smelled like. Don't tell me about hell, Mr. Tarrington. We have all been there.''

He was standing so close, his vision was filled with the smooth, bare expanse of her shoulders. Her hair, curled artfully tight in the morning, had relaxed into loose, soft spirals that surrounded her face in a cloud of errant wisps and trailed halfway down her back.

She drew a particularly deep breath, alerting him to the fact that she was aware of his scrutiny and had endured more than enough of it. ''Please remove your hand from my arm, sir.''

He did, but not until he skimmed his fingers from her shoulder to her elbow and felt the tremors his intimacy provoked.

''Apologizing to you seems to be becoming a habit,'' he murmured. ''One I'm not sure I'm going to like.''

''Habits require repetition to form,'' she said, clipping her words. ''I doubt very much you have to worry about any part of this day or evening ever repeating itself again. Now, if you will excuse me—''

She was going to bolt again, and again his hand reached out, stopping just short of touching her.

''You had something *else* to say, Mr. Tarrington?'' she demanded impatiently.

''Actually . . . I thought I said it all the other night.''

She raised only her eyes to the face that loomed above her. ''The other night?''

''When I told you I found you fascinating and irresistible. It might amuse *you* to know I broke about ten of my own rules in doing so. I imagine, though, I would have foolishly broken ten more if you had taken me up on my offer.''

Her eyes grew rounder and a single eyebrow arched. ''Mr. Tarrington . . . have you been enjoying too much of the baron's whiskey?''

''On the contrary, I probably haven't had enough. You're

almost too quick for me. And bloody convincing. All that righteous indignation. The hell, the oranges, even the little homily this afternoon about crops and fields and slaves. And asking me if we'd met before—that was a nice touch. As cool as ice too, where most women in your position would likely have fainted dead away."

"Mr. Tarrington—"

"Please—" He held up a finger and pressed it to her lips. "Call me Michael. And I shall call you Amanda. I far prefer it over 'the Widow Jackson,' and 'Montana Rose' sounds like the design of a teacup."

She batted his hand away. *"Mr. Tarrington . . .* I have no idea what you are talking about. I thought you were surly and presumptuous this afternoon, but this . . . this goes beyond patience. For Dianna's sake, I will endeavor to forget this entire meeting took place, and in the future, I would appreciate it if you never ventured to speak to me again. Now, as you can plainly hear by the approaching commotion, my mother appears to be searching for me."

He bowed sardonically as she pushed past him and she heard the chink of metal hitting the wood slats.

"A moment, Mrs. Jackson. I believe you dropped something."

Amanda turned, her eyes sparkling with disdain. He was holding up something small and glittery—a locket—its burnished gold surface gleaming brightly in the light that streamed across the width of the balcony.

"Amanda?" A swirling bell of yellow chinz floated past the doorway, halted, and backed up a pace. "Amanda! Is that you? Did you not hear me calling?"

Sarah Courtland flounced through the door like a woman unaccustomed to wide skirts and frilly ruffles around her neck, tripping over the one and blowing the other off her chin. "Where have you been? I've been searching high and low and—" Her words and her forward momentum stopped abruptly as she caught sight of the tall, boldly handsome stranger sharing the evening shadows with her daughter. "Good heavens . . . a man!"

Tarrington laughed easily. "Indeed, madam, I was the last time I looked."

"Oh." Sarah's hand covered her mouth and her giggle, then stifled her gasp as she leaned forward and peered more closely at his face. "Why . . . you're the gentleman who came with the Moores. The, er, Northern cousin."

"Guilty as charged," he admitted. "I have been staying with them for a few days while I finished some business in town. I am also a business associate of your new son-in-law and have had the very great pleasure of being able to share this happy occasion with them. Michael Tarrington, ma'am, at your service."

He bowed gallantly over Sarah's hand, and she rolled her eyes in Amanda's direction. When he straightened, the thought that was bubbling on her lips was cut short as she noticed the heart-shaped locket twined around his fingers.

"Amanda . . . is that not your lavaliere? The one you thought you mislaid?"

Amanda's mouth went bone dry. Her face drained of all warmth and color and her stomach took a slow, sickening slide downward.

"I found it a short while ago," Tarrington explained, flashing his most disarming smile at Sarah. "But for the life of me, I could not recall being introduced to anyone whose name began with *M*. I was hoping Mrs. Jackson could help me identify the owner."

"Why, it is hers, of course," Sarah said promptly.

"So I have just discovered. She was just about to explain the mystery of the *M*."

Sarah waved a hand airily. "It is no mystery at all, Mr. Tarrington. It was a gift from her dear departed grandfather. He always called her Mandy."

"Mandy." The reflective gray eyes turned to Amanda again. "Yes. I think I like it."

Sarah's overtaxed brain instantly reverted to her reasons for searching out her daughter. "Amanda, you simply must come inside at once. Your father has vanished and I fear he may be up to his *old tricks*. You know you are the only one who can stop him if he is"—she caught her tongue in time and glanced pointedly at Tarrington—*"at it."*

"Yes, Mother," she murmured, her eyes held prisoner by the Yankee's dark arrogance. "I will be along in a moment."

"A very *short* moment, Amanda Elizabeth. You *know* how I worry."

"Yes, I know Mother. I will be right there."

Sarah managed three complete steps before her maternal instincts reasserted themselves. "I don't suppose you are free next Monday evening, Mr. Tarrington?"

"Monday?"

"Yes. I was about to invite the Judge and Dianna to dinner, and if you have no prior commitment, we would be delighted to have you join us."

"Mother!" Amanda gasped.

"Oh, hush, Amanda. It isn't as if your Mr. Brice is too anxious to complete a foursome of whist anymore. Do you play cards, Mr. Tarrington?"

"I . . . have been known to call a trump or two."

"Good. Then it is settled. Amanda . . . are you all right? You're looking altogether too pale to be standing out here without a shawl."

"I will see she comes inside at once," Tarrington promised.

Sarah sighed and swirled away again, the folds of yellow chintz creaming out behind her like the wake of a ship.

Amanda found her voice as soon as her mother was safely through the doors. "I will be equally delighted to convey your regrets and explain that you remembered a previous engagement."

"But I don't have one. And I would not dream of upsetting your mother's blossoming plans for matchmaking. Who is Mr. Brice, by the way? My rival for your affection, I presume?"

She fisted her hands in frustration. "If you were the last man on earth, there would be no room for you in my affections."

"Such harsh words," he chided softly, "considering the circumstances of our last meeting."

She was still of half a mind to deny it despite the damning evidence of the locket, but something—a look in his eye, a steely hardness in his jaw—made her exhale a few choice words of self-condemnation instead.

"Now, now. Don't be so hard on yourself. Your secret is perfectly safe for the time being . . . ah . . . assuming it *is* a secret, that is. Or do all these fine people . . . ?"

"No!" she cried in alarm. Then in a calmer voice, "No. No one knows. No one *can* know, Mr. Tarrington. It would . . . it would kill my mother, ruin our family . . ."

She sounded frantic even to her own ears, and she bit her lip again, trying to quell the panic growing inside. Tarrington watched her, studied her as he would a fly with its wings torn off.

"How did you know?" she finally asked.

"To be honest, I didn't until a few minutes ago. Not for sure, anyway. I *thought* I had it figured out a few days ago, the afternoon following our friendly little game. I was coming out of my hotel and saw a young woman who looked remarkably like Montana Rose walking bold as brass down the street. I trailed her out of curiosity for a while and asked for a name at one of the shops she went into. The shopkeeper couldn't identify her, but he told me her purchases were charged to Karl von Helmstaad. As it happened, I already had an invitation to the wedding—the baron and I, as I mentioned to your mother, share some business interests. And while I hadn't originally planned on attending . . ." He shrugged and left Amanda to surmise the obvious reasons why he had changed his mind.

"You can imagine my surprise when I saw the two of you walking into the garden," he murmured, his eyes taking full measure of the smooth sloping shoulders, the slender gracefulness of her neck, the hint of a tremor in her chin. Light from the ballroom frosted her hair and caused the folds of her gown to glimmer like water. The laurel of withered and crushed bluebells she wore tucked in her hair was even sad-

der than it had been in its prime earlier in the day; the fact
she wore it at all made it that much more difficult to equate
the woman who stood before him now with the one whose
every detail of her appearance had been calculated to icy
perfection on the deck of the *Mississippi Queen*.

"I don't suppose there are too many people who can tell
you and your sister apart at first glance," he added.

"You didn't seem to have too much trouble."

Tarrington wanted to smile at the mutinous set to her
mouth. It was childlike, yet deliciously seductive at the same
time.

"I'll admit you kept me guessing for a while. I'll even
admit you weren't my first choice."

"Really. Why ever not?" she asked dryly.

"A mother with a small child?" He *tsk-tsked* and shook
his head. "Not exactly any man's prime candidate for Queen
of the Mississippi."

"Then how did you know?"

"Instinct," he said. "Yours, not mine. I only remembered
afterward that when we were first introduced you reached up
for the familiarity of something that wasn't there. The locket.
You did it again—and you're doing it now—when I startled
you a few moments ago."

Amanda dropped her hand away from her throat. "That's
hardly enough proof to hang someone on," she said stubbornly.

"Your mother's timely arrival, however, was."

Amanda continued to scowl at him for a moment, then
conceded with a sigh. "I wanted to die. This afternoon,
when I saw you with Dianna and the Judge, I just wanted to
turn and run . . . as far away and as fast as I could. But
then you would have known for sure. I had to take the chance
you might be confused long enough for me to think of a way
out. Or at least a way to explain what I did and why I did it."

"And? Have you?"

"No," she admitted miserably, her eyes too bright and too
liquid for him to feel safe staring into them for too long.
"Nothing you would understand, at any rate."

"Try me. My ability to grasp the truth might surprise you."

She shook her head. "I have no excuses, Mr. Tarrington. I have no one to blame for my folly but myself. Ryan warned me, begged me, threatened me—"

"Ryan?" The dark eyes narrowed. "He was in on it? He *knew* what you were doing?"

"He begged me not to go. He said . . . well, it doesn't really matter what he said. I wouldn't listen. I told him I was going to do it whether he agreed to help me or not. I thought it was the only real chance we had. It almost worked too," she added softly.

A sudden gleam came into Tarrington's eyes. "He was your 'escort'?"

Amanda nodded again and looked down at her hands. One of the dispirited bluebells tumbled off a curl and landed in her palm. It made her think of Verity, of the pride that had shone from her eyes when Amanda had insisted the wreath was pretty enough for a princess to wear . . .

She curled her fingers around the trumpet-shaped blossom and squared her shoulders. "So, Mr. Tarrington, now that you know our dirty little secret . . . may I ask what you plan to do with it?"

"What did you mean when you said you thought it was the only real chance you had? Chance to do what?"

She swallowed hard and he thought he heard her whisper the word "Survive," but her voice was too soft and Sarah Courtland's high-pitched plea for smelling salts came sailing out into the night air, followed by a raucous burst of male laughter.

"You had better go," he advised. "We can talk more later."

"I trust, sir, as a gentleman you will allow me an opportunity to explain. You have no idea of the damage that would result"—her voice faltered briefly—"from anything untoward you might say."

"I am crushed to think you hold me in such low esteem. I am a reasonable man, however, and you have my word *as a gentleman* that not one breath of this will escape my lips . . . for the time being, anyway.''

Her face, already flushed with color, grew warmer. There was nothing more she could do or say. He held all the cards and it was another royal flush. She was not foolish enough or naive enough to doubt what he would expect in return for maintaining his silence—he had made that plain enough on board the *Mississippi Queen.*

"Until later, sir," she whispered, and turned to leave.

"Mandy?"

She froze and her shoulders stiffened at the intimate use of her name.

"Aren't you forgetting something?"

She did not want to look back at him. She suspected she had made enough of a fool of herself already without giving fuel to his scorn by letting him see the threat of tears in her eyes.

But she did not have to look at him. She only had to endure the shock of feeling his hands against her skin, brushing her hair aside so that he could refasten the locket around her neck. His fingers lingered a moment on her shoulder, hinting at a forgone possessiveness as they traced the length of a slippery blonde spiral.

"Until Monday, then," he murmured.

Until Monday, she thought, forcing her legs to carry her back into the crowded ballroom. Oddly enough, in spite of the raw acid burning in her stomach, she felt relieved. The games were over. She knew what had to be done . . . before Monday . . . and she knew she had to do it if she wanted to protect her family and safeguard Verity's future.

And because she simply didn't have any options left.

Alisha von Helmstaad settled deeper into the plush softness of the feather mattress and stretched languorously. Her head was spinning from the amount of wine she had consumed. Karl was still in the dressing room and she could hear the faint shuffling sounds he made as he tiptoed around removing his clothes, folding them just so. She could picture him smoothing his hair, splashing on more of his supposedly irresistible pomade—the one that made him smell like a newly varnished carriage—and she had to stifle the urge to laugh as she envisioned him rolling into the room.

Laughing would definitely not be politic tonight of all nights, and she hoped she had blunted her senses enough with the wine to make whatever he did to her seem to be the height of bliss and ecstasy. It wasn't the first time she had required a performance of such magnitude, nor the first time she had used her body to barter for favors.

The nightdress she had selected was silk, sheer enough she could have read the pages of the *Mississippi Gazette* through it. Her skin flowed like pale cream beneath, leaving shocking little to the imagination. Her breasts gleamed round and firm, crowned in pink rosettes; her limbs stretched out long and lithe, bridged by a thatch of soft golden fur that betrayed just a hint of the dark cleft between.

Alisha smoothed her palms over her breasts, cupping their heaviness in hands that trembled with impatience. She thought of Josh and how he loved to take each nipple into his mouth and suckle her until she thought she would come right out of her skin. He would not have wasted time in a dressing room. He would have torn her clothes off and torn his clothes off and probably not even bothered about having a bed beneath them. He would have known by a single glance how ready she was. For certain, he would never have wasted his time preening and splashing carriage oil on parts of his body he knew she would prefer to slick with her own exotic musk.

Her fingers crept lower and she nearly groaned at how wet she was. Just thinking of Josh had started the juices flowing, making her limbs ache with tension and her body too restless to remain still. She glanced at the door of the dressing room and saw a shadow cut back and forth across the sliver of light at the bottom.

What in God's name was the old fool doing?

She drew the snow-white coverlet up over her hips, dragging the hem of the nightdress with it. She checked the door again and swore softly as her fingers slid between her thighs, wishing with more savagery than she could have imagined that she had let Josh talk her into sneaking into the garden for a few minutes alone together. She had suspected he had wanted one more attempt to talk her into leaving with him before it was too late, and she had refused, not wanting to fight, not wanting to spoil what had been an otherwise perfect day.

It *had* been perfect. She was somebody to reckon with now. She had position and wealth. She had a rich husband and a grand house filled with every luxury she could possibly want or need. Josh would come around. He couldn't stay angry with her forever. After all, she was doing it for *them*. For the child they had conceived together. He wouldn't be able to stay away from her forever either; he needed her as much as she needed him, and he had too big of an appetite to deny himself the banquet he had found in her arms.

She curled her lower lip between her teeth and stifled a groan. Her hips began to arch off the bed and she twisted her head into the softness of the pillow, wishing it was Josh she was waiting for, wishing it was Josh's fingers dancing between her thighs.

A belch followed by an ejection of an even more alarming *pfert!* of trapped air came from the direction of the dressing room. The door opened and the bridegroom padded into view, his corpulent body swathed neck to knee in a tent-shaped cotton nightshirt.

He stopped by the side of the bed, clearly awed by the sight of his beautiful new wife swathed in silk and satin, waiting for him in breathless anticipation, her cheeks flushed red, her lovely moon-shaped breasts heaving in virginal trepidation.

"My dearest Alisha. My bride. My precious beauty. You are more exquisite than—"

Alisha pulled the sheets aside, effectively tying his tongue around whatever poetic comparisons he had been about to make.

"Karl," she said brokenly. "You were taking so long, I thought you had forgotten about me."

"Forget about you?" He moistened his lips and his eyes bulged as they fastened on the sharply defined peaks of her breasts. "It was because I revere you, my lamb, my lovely, my . . . my most astonishing goddess of Virtue . . . that I could not dream of rushing at you like some beast of the forest."

"You could rush . . . a little," she suggested dryly. "I would not think any less of you, I promise."

"You are as eager as I?" he dared to ask.

"More so," she assured him. "I . . . ache for you, Karl. We have waited so long for this moment, I think it cruel and beastly you should make me wait a moment longer."

He swallowed hard and scrambled onto the bed, his knees tangling in the sheets. Alisha caught him as he fell heavily on top of her, her curse smothered under a hail of wet, sliding kisses.

"My dearest one!" he cried. "My darling! How I've waited for this moment! How I've longed for it!"

Alisha cried out as well, not from any sense of unrequited passion, but because his fat, clumsy hands were pulling at her hair, kneading her flesh, straining the fragile seams of her gown from shoulder to thigh. He seemed not to notice or care. He nuzzled and rooted at her flesh like a pig searching for truffles, moaning and grunting as he started to thrust himself against her thigh, stabbing at her through the ungiving layers of their bedclothes.

"Wait," she gasped anxiously, hearing the distinct rasp of tearing silk. "For heaven's sake!"

"It is best to do this quickly, my dove," he declared in a quivering vibrato. "Especially the first time. Afterward"—he panted—"we can take more time to explore and savor, but for now . . . ahh . . . !"

Grasping, spatulate fingers greedily shoved the hem of her gown above her hips. Alisha locked her knees against their rough intrusion, but he was surprisingly strong, as feverishly determined to wedge her thighs apart as she was, suddenly, to keep them together. He won the tussle with a victorious yelp and positioned himself eagerly at the breach, misreading her continuing struggles as passion, her cries as maidenly modesty as he hiked up his nightshirt and prepared to sheath himself in ecstasy.

"Karl . . . wait a moment . . . please!"

"A moment indeed, my love," he trumpeted. "Only a moment more and bliss awaits us."

"But I can't! *I can't do this!*"

"You can, my pet. Hold fast! I have you now! Hold fast to me, my petal, and . . . augh!"

He plunged forward, driving most of the air out of Alisha's lungs as he thrust his bulk over her. Too dazed to do more than gasp for a breath, she tried in vain to brace herself as he started bouncing and slamming her into the mattress. Her fists pounded and flailed at him to no avail. Her curses came on snatched gulps of air each time he heaved his sweating body into hers.

"Ahh . . . ahh . . . ahh . . ."

She sobbed and boxed his ears with the heels of her hands. ". . . ahhhh!"

The balding, beet-red head jerked out of the crook of her neck with a strangled cry and Alisha gave one last mighty shove, managing to twist free just as something hot and wet spurted across her belly. Her groan of shock and revulsion was genuine as the clinging, clammy mass of doughy flesh collapsed on top of her and quivered to a halt, gasping words of undaunted passion into her ear.

"My love, my dearest, my precious one . . ."

"My God! Get off of me! Get off of me, I can't breathe!"

"Of course," he gasped. "Of course. How thoughtless of me."

She groaned again as he hoisted himself free and rolled beside her onto the bed. The rush of cold air was welcomed but she dared not move in fear of discovering that every bone in her body had been crushed to pulp.

"Alisha, my flower. Have you any idea how happy you have made me tonight?"

She turned her head so he would not see the disgust and loathing in her eyes.

"I can't begin to imagine," she whispered hoarsely. Then, remembering the role she had to play, she added through her teeth, "As happy as you have made me."

"No . . . happier. Far, far happier, my swan."

I cannot argue with that, she thought murderously.

"I . . . hope I did not hurt you too much."

"No. No, Karl. You have made me very happy. If I acted foolishly, or afraid, it was because I . . . *I honestly didn't think it could be like this.*"

"Oh, my dearest petal," he cried, and scooped her into the circle of his arms. "This is only the beginning! It will be much better for you the next time, and the next after that. I'm afraid I was so eager tonight I did not take the time . . . but in the coming weeks and months—" He stopped, overcome with rapture at the prospect.

"Months." She shuddered, doubting she could survive another week. "Months, yes. In the coming months I shall try to do my wifely duty and . . . and make you proud of me, and of the family we shall create together."

Karl clutched her hand and squeezed it against his lips. "I am rapturously proud of you already, my dove. You and I are more than family enough."

"Still, I intend to give you sons. In fact, I will not rest until I give you a fine, handsome son to carry on your name."

"Oh, my dearest, if it were only possible," he whispered fervently, nearly putting his teeth through her hand as he caressed it.

"It is not only possible, it is more than likely. You"—she choked back the bile that rose in her throat as she saw the mess on her belly—"are so virile, so manly. The seven children you gave your former wife are proof of that; the fact they were all daughters was no fault of yours."

He rolled onto his back with a despairing sigh and Alisha was momentarily distracted by the sight of his dome-shaped belly heaving to one side, then listing to the other before it settled. She caught the last few words he muttered, however, and came warily to attention.

". . . no fault of mine at all. They were my wife's children, you see. She was a widow with an established family when I married her."

"Well—" Alisha tried to feign a wifely concern as she rearranged the folds of his nightshirt to cover his exposed belly and thighs. "I shall give you sons of your own. I am quite determined."

"It would take more than determination, I'm afraid," he explained in an agony of embarrassment. "I am, my pet, quite unable to father children at all."

Alisha's hand paused in the process of smoothing the cotton. "What? What did you say?"

"I assure you it is the truth."

Alisha sat slowly upright, her gaze fixed on the mole that sat like a wart on the end of his nose. "How can you be so sure? I mean, you seem . . . perfectly healthy."

"Healthy?" he whined. "My heart has palpitations, my legs swell abominably with the gout. You already know my little problems with, ah, gaseous expulsions, although the doctors claim they have had some success with extract of ipecac. On the other hand, it is also true that the von Helmstaads tend to live into their eighth and ninth decades, and after tonight, well, I feel as if I could live forever in your arms, my pet. But children? No. No, I am certain, beyond a doubt, that children of my own, alas, were never meant to be."

Alisha stared at him in growing horror. "Why did you not tell me this before now? If you knew you could not father children, *why did you not tell me before you married me?*"

"Why, precious." He reddened and shrank back on the pillows. "I thought . . . that is, I assumed . . ."

"You assumed what?" she demanded, the fury crackling in her voice.

"I thought you would be relieved."

"Relieved? *Relieved!*"

"I assumed my wealth, my title, the prestige you would

gain as my wife would more than compensate for the loss. It never once occurred to me that you would possess any maternal instincts. Rather the opposite, I would have sworn, seeing how you blossom and flourish under the heady lights of society. Knowing this and knowing how you would sparkle with diamonds at your throat and servants to tend to your every whim, I . . . I foolishly thought only in terms of offering you material happiness. I thought it would be sufficient.''

Alisha was almost too thunderstruck to reply. The flatulent old fool had seen right through her, had known exactly why she had married him and had known what she had wanted out of this unholy union. Almost everything, that is. It had never occurred to him that motherhood was foremost in her mind just as it had never occurred to her that the oaf could be sterile. Well, he had delivered his surprise tonight; hers would be arriving in somewhat less than seven months' time.

He would simply have to accept the child as his and pretend to the world he had fathered it. What man could refuse such an opportunity to boast his potency?

''What is more,'' he was saying, still trying to appease his lovely young wife, ''a child now would be disastrous. Simply disastrous.''

The twist of irony faded from her lips and Alisha glared at him again. ''What do you mean, disastrous?''

''It would ruin us,'' he huffed. ''Utterly ruin us, my love. Strip us of every penny and probably see us tossed out onto the street like paupers.''

''I don't understand,'' she said slowly. ''You said yourself, you are a rich man, with wealth, a title, prestige . . .''

He coughed uncomfortably. ''Well, ah, and so I am . . . to a certain extent. You see, the von Helmstaads are a very old, very revered family in Europe. Descendants of royalty, don't you know, and as such, the family fortune and title are held in trust, safeguarded and preserved for succeeding generations to come. When it, ah, became apparent that I would not be able to sire an heir of my own, my nephew Wolfgang was named as my successor. Upon my death, he will assume the title, as well as possession of all the von Helmstaad holdings in Europe and here in America.''

''What on earth does that have to do with a child? I should think you would want one in order to keep your fortune intact.''

''It is a dreadfully complex matter, my dove. I really don't think—''

''What does it have to do with a child?'' she insisted, startling him with a sharp jab in the ribs.

''W-well, several years ago there were unforeseen circumstances—bad investments and the like—which caused me to, ah, violate some of the terms of the trust. When the discrepancies were discovered, I was forced to sign control of the family businesses and estates over to Wolfgang. It was all done very discreetly, of course; the family would not abide any further scandal, and as soon as the war ended, I was banished here, to America, and given a generous stipend yearly to run the family's export interests on this side of the ocean. It is all fairly complicated and nothing at all for you to worry your pretty head about, but suffice it to say, the appearance of an heir now would nullify the terms of the agreement I made with Wolfgang. At the very least I could be brought to account for the breech of trust. I could be prosecuted, shamed, humiliated beyond endurance and, in the end, probably be forced to flee for my very life. Wolfgang,'' he added with a small shudder, ''is not a nice person to cross.''

''What about your daughters . . . your wife's daughters. They bear your name, do they not?''

''Proudly so,'' he agreed. ''But they were never considered my legal heirs. Arabella was a wealthy woman in her own right and they inherited from her.''

Alisha gaped at her husband and felt her skin shrinking from the bones, crawling with horror. She had married this pompous, bloated ass in order to secure her future, to safeguard her own reputation against the shame of bearing an illegitimate child. Now he was telling her it had all been for nothing. She could end up worse off than she had been before, only this time she would be saddled with a squalling, hungry baby *and* a blubbering, useless husband.

"Don't look so distressed, my sweeting. Nothing is going to spoil our blissful union, now or ever. Wolfgang has agreed to a generous allowance for the both of us." He leaned over and cupped a pudgy hand around her breast, molding it to the shape of his palm as he prepared to claim it with his lips.

"Don't you touch me!" she snarled, scrambling to the side of the bed. "Don't you *ever* touch me again!"

Having fallen facedown on the mattress when she slipped out of his grasp, von Helmstaad took a moment to right himself, and by then, she had jumped off the bed and was half way to the door.

"Alisha? My goddess, my love!"

She screamed out of sheer exasperation and snatched a large crystal decanter of perfume off the dressing table as she ran past. She delayed only long enough to hurl it at the bed and see it smash into a thousand bits on the wall over his head.

Karl had dived for cover when he saw the missile coming. As it was, he was showered in a spray of crystal shards and pungent French perfume. He had no idea what had set his genteel young wife off in such a volcanic display of distemper. He certainly had had no idea that the flighty, flirtatious Alisha Courtland could have cared a fig for motherhood. After all, he had been honest and forthright in confessing his inadequacy as well as his indiscretion with the von Helmstaad trust. He could have simply said nothing and enjoyed her efforts to conceive a child. He could have pretended he was equally determined, equally indefatigable in his quest to produce an heir. Arabella had been cold and unresponsive in the bedroom, making him beg and plead for every minute he spent between her thighs. Alisha promised to be stunning in more ways than one.

Time. Perhaps she just needed time to adjust to everything that was new in her life. A new husband, a new home . . . it was undoubtedly daunting for a young woman of such exquisitely tender sensibilities. She would come around. He was convinced things would look vastly different in the morning when she found his little gift on the breakfast table. She was, after all, born to wear diamonds. The size and worth of the one waiting to be suspended between those perfect white breasts would soothe whatever anxieties she had suffered tonight. He wouldn't have to tell her the pendant, along with the other jewels he would adorn her with, were merely on loan, that they belonged to the von Helmstaad estate and would eventually go to Wolfgang with everything else.

He was, if nothing else, a man who learned from his mistakes.

Chapter 10

E. Forrest Wainright straightened the knot of his cravat and cursed as he brushed the flecks of dandruff off the stark blackness of his frockcoat. He could scarcely believe he had heard his houseman correctly: Amanda Courtland Jackson was requesting an audience with him and was waiting in his parlor this very moment.

The name, when Bentick had first said it, had sent a shiver of anticipation down his spine. That had been half an hour ago and while the initial shock had passed, the pleasure had not. It had grown proportionately with each minute he delayed, each step of his personal toilet he prolonged in order to organize his thoughts and—perhaps—unsettle hers.

He did not want to appear to be either eager or expectant. Curious, yes, for she should surly have known her appearance here, without a chaperone, on a bright church-going Sunday morning would rouse nothing less. No doubt she had been sent by that arrogant, upstart brother of hers to plead yet again for more time. If that was the case, she would be sorely disappointed, for he had about expended his patience with the Courtland family. All of them. He had offered to buy the land outright and the offer had been thrown back in his face. He had made a sincerely genuine offer of marriage and that too had been *slapped* back in his face. If she had come to beg, he would let her. It would, in fact, give him the greatest pleasure on earth to see her humble and meek, her hands clasped in supplication, her eyes filled with tears. Perhaps he would even test her, see how far she was prepared to prostrate herself in order to save her precious brother's pride.

Wainright cast a critical eye in the mirror, tipping his head this way and that, smoothing an errant lock of copper-colored hair over his ear.

He had come a long way in the last seven years. Enlisting

in the Army had probably been the smartest thing he had
ever done, for when they had discovered his talents for
scrounging, bartering, and outright stealing supplies and
munitions for his outfit, he had been transferred into the
quartermaster corps—a veritable gold mine of goods he had
sold for ten times, fifty times its worth on the black market.

He had come out of the war a rich, rich man and had come
South with the rest of the insightful investors, knowing the
devastated, destroyed towns would need supplies to rebuild,
and suspecting the shattered Southern aristocracy would be
hungry to buy goods and luxuries that had been denied them
during the long years of blockades. Wainright now owned
four sizable plantations, several businesses, and held solid
investments in shipping and banking. He had initially wanted
Rosalie for both its prestige and location, although the latter
had lost some of its appeal lately, what with the extensive
flooding and damage to the crops. He might even have
walked away from it, turned his eye to some other plum
prospect, had the Courtlands not risen above the normal level
of arrogance he had encountered, spitting at his offers,
laughing in his face!

No one spit at E. Forrest Wainright. No one laughed in his
face. No one bested him at his own game, and no one—*no
one* humiliated him and walked away unscathed. He was
determined to have Rosalie now if only to let it stand empty
and rot to the bare floors.

He would see Amanda Jackson. He would hear her out,
nod in sympathy, commiserate with her tales of woe and
tragedy. In the end, however, he would slap her down as
coldly, as cruelly, as thoughtlessly as she had rebuked him.

It was a shame, really, for they would have made a magnificent couple. Her beauty, her elegance, her refinement would
have removed the taint of cheap speculator from his profile.
With her by his side, he would have been invited, no, *welcomed* into the best homes in Natchez. With a beautiful
Southern wife on his arm, he might have aspired to the
governor's office, or even higher, attaining heights of power
and influence that made him dizzy just to think about it.

He could have had the other one—the sister—for a song. But then so could every other warmblooded stud in trousers. He had gone that route once, which was one of the main reasons he had enlisted in the Army in the first place and why he had come south after the war and not gone back home to New York. He didn't mind using whores, he just had no desire to be married to one. The lovely Widow Jackson, on the other hand, was a lady. She would have brought out the best in him, he had no doubt, and helped rid him of the taint of his past.

He swelled his lungs with a final deep breath and strode out of his dressing room, glancing at the imported Louis XIV canopy bed as he walked past.

"This shouldn't take too long, my dear," he said. "You will strive to keep everything warm for me?"

The woman smiled and stretched, the motion causing both breasts to rise free of the silk sheets. Wainright returned the smile and closed the bedroom door behind him, making a mental note to bring a bottle of champagne back with him.

The sound of his boots descending the uncarpeted stairs kept the thin smile on his lips. A drum could not have produced a louder echo in the vaulted, paneled hallway, and he hoped Amanda was listening, losing her concentration on whatever little speech she had had prepared. He could imagine the agony of fear clouding her face, the pale delicate hands twisting in dread, the blue eyes rounded and staring at the twin mahogany doors, waiting . . .

He paused a moment to set his expression into one of grim forbearance and pushed the doors open before him.

Amanda was standing in front of the circular window, watching the carriage traffic pass by out in the street. The light was behind her, blooming soft and golden, turning her hair into spun silk and her profile into an artist's envy. She looked amazingly calm. In fact, she looked as if his sudden appearance was as much of an intrusion as Bentick's knock had been on the bedroom door earlier.

"Well. Mrs. Jackson. I trust you will be neither offended nor surprised if I say that of all the people I might have expected to see on a Sunday morning, you were well down from the top of the list.''

''In that case, I hope I am not disturbing you. The list must be very long indeed.''

Wainright smiled tightly as he closed the parlor doors behind him. ''Your sister's wedding went well, I hear?''

''As well as she expected.''

''She is happy?''

''I presume so.''

''And the groom?''

The false pleasantries were grating, and, she suspected, amusing him no end. ''Deliriously so.''

Wainright saw her annoyance and crossed to the sideboard. He took the stopper out of a decanter of brandy and poured himself a small glass.

''May I offer you something? Tea? Coffee? A little wine, perhaps?''

''No, thank you. My business will not take long and I have several errands to run before returning home.''

''Business? How intriguing,'' he said coldly. ''After our last meeting, I assumed you had nothing more to say to me. You and your brother were most insistent, in fact.''

''Ryan has been under a great deal of pressure lately. I . . . did not even tell him I was coming here today; he probably would have stopped me.''

Wainright lifted his glass and sipped. So, the brother didn't know she was here. Did anyone know she was here, dressed in what was probably her best frock—the lavender muslin he had so admired on his visit to Rosalie—putting herself in the lion's den with only her own misguided expectations of Southern chivalry to protect her?

He laughed softly and took another sip of brandy. ''I should warn you, Mrs. Jackson, if you've come to plead your brother's case before me—''

''I haven't come to plead,'' she insisted calmly. ''And believe me, if there was any other way out of the dilemma we find ourselves in, I would not be here at all.''

Wainright lounged against the edge of a writing table inlaid with gold marquetry and crossed his arms over his chest. "So why *are* you here, Mrs. Jackson? I confess, you have me stymied."

Amanda showed the first small fault in her composure as she ran the tip of her tongue across her lips. "I have come—assuming you are still interested—to accept the terms of your offer."

"Offer?" Wainright's bewilderment was genuine. He had made no offers aside from the purchase of Rosalie, which she would not be empowered to accept one way or the other, or . . .

The glittering hazel eyes widened and despite himself, he stiffened in surprise. "Are you referring to . . . the offer of matrimony?"

Amanda returned his gaze steadfastly. "Yes. I am."

"You wish to become my wife?"

"No. I do not *wish* to become your wife, sir. I merely find I have no other alternative but to do so."

"How flattering," he mused.

"But honest. If I had answered any other way, would you have believed me?"

He stared at her thoughtfully for a long moment. "No. Probably not. At the same time, I would want an equally candid answer if I asked what you would expect in exchange? If there were any conditions, verbal or . . . physical in nature?"

Amanda met his gaze steadfastly. "If I married you, sir, I would agree to comply with whatever would be expected of me as your wife."

"And in exchange?"

"In exchange, I ask only that you allow Ryan the time he needs to repay the loan on Rosalie."

"In other words," he said quietly, "exactly what I offered you before."

"Yes," she agreed hesitantly.

"When you slapped me in the face for my impudence."

Amanda's gaze did not waver or falter. The only sign of the extreme stress she was feeling was the thin blue vein that

beat so rapidly in her temple, it appeared to keep the surrounding flesh as drained and pale as wax.

"What makes you think I would still want you, Mrs. Jackson?" he asked, his voice a low and ominous throb in the
silence. "And if I did, what makes you think I would take
you on the same terms?"

She returned his stare without answering, without moving,
and he knew she had come to him fully prepared for his
sarcasm, his anger, his contempt. It was a gift, he thought
with a kind of wonder. A gift he could take and use whenever
he wanted or needed to remind her of his generosity, his
forgiving nature, his complete and utter possession of her.

Wainright tipped his glass to his lips and tossed back the
entire contents in a hard swallow. Keeping his eyes on
Amanda, he went over to the sideboard again and poured
himself another drink.

"What about your hot-headed brother? What is to keep
him from shooting me out of hand before we ever make it to
an altar?"

"He mustn't know. Not until it's too late to do anything
about it."

His eyebrows shot up at that. A furtive, late-night ride to a
preacher's doorstep was not exactly what he had had in mind
as a way of establishing himself as a respectable member of
the community. "Are you suggesting . . . an elopement?"

"I couldn't guarantee your safety any other way," she
said matter-of-factly. "But if you would prefer to stand in an
open churchyard . . . ?"

He laughed and held up a hand. "No. No, an elopement is
fine. Romantic, even. It's just that I was under the impression
most brides craved the pomp, the ceremony, the opportunity
to show themselves off to the world. Especially," he added
softly, "if they were marrying someone who would relish the
opportunity to do a little bragging and boasting himself."

The thought of Alisha's extravagances brought a hint of
color into Amanda's cheeks, and she lowered her eyes for the
first time.

"I would be content with a simple exchange of vows," she said. "The rest . . . does not interest me."

Wainright set his glass down with more care than the act required. He went over to where she stood and waited until she raised her eyes to his again.

"I have already told you," he murmured, "I want someone by my side who will make me the envy of Mississippi. I want a wife I can lavish with jewels and spoil with furs and silks and gold pins for her hair. And I will be utterly, absolutely honest with you when I say I want a wife who will stand by my side, wherever that might be, whether it is here, the county seat, or the governor's mansion—and be able to convince everyone who sees her that she is more than just *content* to be there."

Amanda's heartbeat slowed noticeably. It thudded in her chest like a fist, reminding her why she was here, what she had to do to ensure the safety and future happiness of her family. Her own didn't matter. She was desperate and she was sick at heart, but she would do almost anything at this point, agree to almost anything in order to protect Sarah and William, Ryan and Dianna . . . Verity. She would still have to deal with Michael Tarrington and find some way to appease his thwarted vanity, but there again, if she was married to Forrest Wainright, she would be buying herself a measure of protection. From what she already knew about Wainright, he would be a dangerous man to challenge.

All of this went through her mind between one heartbeat and the next. None of it showed in her eyes, which were round and clear and luminous with her resolve. None of it showed in her manner either, which was suddenly imbued with all of the sensual innuendo that had brought men to their knees before Montana Rose.

"I will be more than content," she promised intently, the movement of her lips dragging his focus and his concentration downward. "If you take me for your wife, Mr. Wainright, and fulfill your part of the bargain, I will do everything in my power—verbally and physically—to ensure you do not regret your decision for a single moment."

Wainright found his mouth was too dry to form an answer right away. All of his cocky plans to leave her groveling and humiliated vanished with the thought of those lips soft and pliant beneath his, those eyes jewel-bright with her determination to please him.

"When?" he asked huskily. "And where?"

Amanda's mind raced ahead. Tomorrow was impossible with Tarrington coming to dinner, but if she waited too much longer, she might find a thousand reasons not to go through with it.

"Wednesday night. After dark."

He nodded. "I will bring a carriage to the foot of the avenue at Rosalie. Shall we say midnight?"

"Midnight," she agreed. "I'll be there."

"Alone," he insisted. Seeing the quick narrowing of her eyes, he added, "It is little enough to ask that we have a day or two on our own—to become better acquainted—without the distracting needs of a child to tend to."

She hadn't considered . . . hadn't even thought of the likelihood of having to leave Verity behind for any length of time, however short.

"Rest assured, Amanda—I may call you Amanda now, may I not?—rest assured I am quite fond of children. Other people's children up to now, of course, but hopefully, in time, that too will change."

Amanda felt her knees begin to buckle. She *certainly* hadn't given any thought to children, and the notion of it now, of bearing a child with carrot-red hair and brown eyes made her stomach rise precariously high in her throat.

"I—I should go now," she stammered. "I will be missed."

He raised a hand and brushed the backs of his fingers along her cheek. Her eyes flickered for a moment, but she did not pull back, not even when he cupped his hand under her chin and angled her face up to his.

"In most business ventures, things that come with a high price tag are usually sampled first, just to prove to the prospective buyer he isn't being sold a bill of goods without substance . . . or potential.''

When she neither balked nor made any attempt to prevent him from doing so, he bent his lips to hers, taking them lightly at first, wary of any delayed sense of propriety or indignation. They were cool—a little dry, he thought—with just enough of a tremor to guard against any further intimacy.

He did not press his intentions, although there was a definite stirring of interest to know what she would have done had he insisted on more. After Wednesday, there would be plenty of time to test the strength of the earnest promises she had made. After midnight Wednesday, she had best not deny him anything, or she would find out the true meaning of humility.

Chapter 11

Amanda found herself looking forward to Monday evening with the same degree of anticipation as she would an infestation of locusts. The Judge and Dianna Moore had come to Rosalie in the late afternoon, and, though she had prayed and willed for a storm to open up the heavens and wash away the roads, Michael Tarrington had been the one holding the reins of the buggy as their visitors drove up the tree-lined avenue.

Looking more piratical than ever, he was wearing a fawn-colored jacket over dark-brown trousers that fit snug to the bulge of muscles on his thighs. His shirt was snow-white linen, left casually open at the throat to counter the humid effects of a hot August afternoon. He wore his flat-top hat at a rakish angle, slightly off to one side and forward to shade his left eye. His boots were knee high and made of supple black goatskin that seemed as comfortably molded to the shape of his calves and feet as a pair of thick socks.

Reflecting her own dark mood, she had deliberately worn one of her mourning frocks, a plain high-necked, long-sleeved dress of dull black cotton with nothing, not a braid or a line of piping, to relieve the severity. Sarah had been dismayed, William had declared she looked like a crow. Ryan had been the only one not to criticize her, saying it was only fitting to wear mourning clothes to mark the day they entertained a Yankee at Rosalie.

Verity had reacted no differently to Tarrington this time than the last, hugging her mother's leg and giving every good impression of being determined to hide in her skirts all evening. But her resolves, along with a considerable portion of her shyness, dissipated a few seconds after Michael Tarrington produced a huge covered and beribboned basket from the floor of the buggy.

"The card says this is for a Miss Verity Jackson," he had announced, frowning over the pink square of vellum. "Does anyone know where I might find the young lady in question?"

An enormous blue eye had edged around a stiff fold of cotton and lingered long enough to catch Tarrington's attention.

"Ahh. Well, if no one knows anyone by that name, I suppose we'll just have to carry this big old basket all the way back to town with us. I wonder, though, if she would mind if we took a peek at what's inside. It's powerfully heavy—too heavy for me to hold like this without spilling. I'll just set it down a minute and maybe we can pull back the cloth an inch or two . . ."

Verity swayed to the side, using Amanda's leg to maintain her balance as she watched the gingham cloth being drawn slowly back. The basket had been filled to the brim with oranges—a dozen or more—and perched on top, her eyes as big and blue as Verity's own, was a doll with long blonde ringlets and a pink velvet pinafore.

The child had capitulated without any further struggle. Tarrington had held up the doll and Verity had walked toward it like someone in a trance. The oranges had been the icing on the cake, buying him a dimpled smile every time he looked at her and a comical, double-eyed attempt to mimic him every time he charmed her with a wink.

Dinner was an ugly pretense at civility. Ryan glowered with open hostility, almost defying anyone to speak to him directly. He was too much the gentleman to cause an outright scene at his mother's table with a guest she had personally invited, but if stares could kill, the Yankee would have been colder than a corpse before they finished the first course of catfish soup.

Ryan's black mood had a direct effect on Dianna, who looked to be on the verge of weeping each time she tried to draw him into the conversation and was met with a dark glare. Sarah was the only one who could be relied upon to jump into the breach. She was always starved for company

and starved for gossip, and having someone there—now that
Alisha was gone—with whom she could share her observa-
tions from the wedding kept her chattering almost nonstop.
Amanda wanted to scream. She did not care that Permalia
Howard had turned into a shocking hussy, or that Dorothea
Prine was as swollen as a ball of dough and should never
have appeared in public in her condition. She did not care
about the petty trials and tribulations affecting other people's
lives; she did not care about anything anymore. She only
wanted to find the strength to survive through Wednesday
night and then it would not matter if she cared or not anyway.

Mercy had done an impressive job of outfoxing potential
scavengers after the wedding feast. She had hoarded several
sacks of meat and savories from the pantries at Summitcrest,
and the catfish soup was thick with vegetables and spices, the
roasted haunch of beef was tender and juicy, the gumbo hot
enough to set the glands in everyone's mouths squirting rivers of saliva to drench the fire. But Amanda's appetite had
deserted her the instant she had seen the carriage rolling
down the avenue. She spent the better part of the meal pushing her food from one side of the plate to the other, eventually earning enough attention to win a not-so-subtle pinch
from Mercy as she carried platters to and from the kitchen.
Tarrington was to blame, of course. He was to blame for
Ryan's sullen resentment and Sarah's babbling foolishness.
He was the cause of Dianna's helpless frustration and Verity's open treachery.

When the meal ended and Mercy had cleared away the
empty plates, Amanda begged to be excused and spent more
time than usual getting Verity washed and ready for bed. She
brushed out the child's hair and told her a long story, staying
by her bed well after she had fallen asleep, her hands
clutched tightly around her new doll. Amanda was half hoping Tarrington would be gone by the time she descended the
stairs again, but no. He was in the parlor with the others,
seated by the fire, his long legs stretched out and crossed at
the ankles, feigning an avid interest in a discussion between
William and the Judge over the proper way to distill bourbon.

Ryan and Dianna, she was informed by her mother, had gone for a stroll in the gardens and *wouldn't it be hospitable* (said with suitable emphasis) of her to invite Mr. Tarrington to do the same?

Tarrington saw the soft pink flush that darkened Amanda's complexion and he caught himself staring again, at the prim black frock, the matronly chignon, the face so pale and devoid of any animation it made it nearly impossible to envision her on the deck of the *Mississippi Queen*. The green velvet gown had been anything but modest or matronly. It had encouraged her breasts to swell voluptuously over the edge of the bodice. It had drawn attention to the smooth white slope of her shoulders and lured the eye downward to marvel over how tiny the span of her waist was. It seemed insane to even think the two women were one and the same. A betting man would have staked his entire fortune on the sister, Alisha, being the one more likely apt to seek her thrills by masquerading as Montana Rose. Tarrington had met the twin only briefly on the day of the wedding, but he had felt those blue eyes stripping him naked and taking his measure in less time than it had taken him to offer his congratulations to the happy bride and groom.

Bristling with more curiosity and intrigue than he cared to acknowledge, Tarrington rose to his feet, acting on Sarah Courtland's suggestion before Amanda had any chance to refuse.

"A pity you did not seem to enjoy your dinner," he said as they exited through the parlor doors. "The creole was exceptional."

"I wasn't very hungry."

"Nothing to do with the company, I trust?"

Amanda gave his attempt at brevity a measured look then searched the shadows until she saw the vague outline of Dianna and Ryan. They were strolling toward the summerhouse, and even in the heavy gloom, she could see that Ryan's limp was more pronounced than usual, a sure sign he was battling more emotions than he could handle.

She turned and walked abruptly in the opposite direction,

leaving Tarrington standing alone in the glow of light from
the parlor.

"Like my daddy always said," he mused wryly, following
after her. "A bad impression is better than no impression at
all."

"You take too much upon yourself, sir, to assume my
mood is entirely owing to you."

"Implying there are weightier subjects on your mind than
your penchant for frequenting riverboats and dealing from
marked decks?"

"Believe it or not, Mr. Tarrington, there are."

Her voice was as soft and thick as the night air, and Tarrington had to steel himself against falling into so blatant and
obvious a trap. She was not the helpless widow, despite the
widow's weeds. Nor was she the innocent, maligned, suffering Southern belle struggling valiantly to hold on to her
dignity and pride despite the hardships of the war and the
humiliation of defeat. She was not afraid to enter a man's
world and call his bluff. Nor was she reluctant to use her
considerable talents to cheat, lie, and steal with the same
impunity she used them to start a man's blood pounding in
his temples and surging through his belly. She could shuffle,
mark, and deal a deck of cards slicker and faster than anyone
he had seen. She was clever and she was cunning. She was a
woman, for God's sake, and that made her the most dangerous and deceptive creature on earth.

Tarrington was determined not to be the one to break the
peace this time, and they walked for almost five minutes in
silence. Insects hummed in the uncut grass and somewhere
in the distance a dog bayed at the glistening crescent of the
quarter moon. Stones and pebbles crunched underfoot, swept
along by the hem of Amanda's skirt. Slippery, opalescent
light dappled the ground between breaks in the trees and, in
the distance, gleamed wetly on the flooded fields.

Amanda stopped finally under the awning of the huge oak
that stood guarding the front of Rosalie. There was enough
light to see where Verity had been playing earlier in the day.
Hardened mud cakes and moss pies littered the clearing, and

they had to sidestep to avoid stumbling into the pit she had excavated.

"I suppose you are waiting for the explanation I promised," Amanda began quietly.

"I confess, nothing I have seen or heard here today has done anything to alleviate the need for one."

She faced him and her smile was brittle. "Were you expecting to see the family silver and fine china? I'm sorry to disappoint you, but unfortunately, some Yankee captain took a liking to the d'Iberville crest and 'appropriated' it for his dear wife back in Washington. The china was two hundred years old, brought from France by my mother's ancestors. Personally, I would have smashed it before I let some sticky-fingered Yankee take it away, but Mother was more sentimental. She helped him pack it, hoping she could at least protect it from rough handling."

"I didn't mean to imply—"

"I know what you meant to imply," she interrupted flatly. "You were expecting to see evidence of how I spent my ill-gotten gains. Furniture without the stuffing torn out, perhaps, or pictures on the wall instead of faded squares on the paint. Eight matching chairs to put around a dining room table made of something other than two old doors nailed together. Again, I am sorry to disappoint you, but furniture and paintings were not a high priority these past few months. What you saw in the parlor and the dining salon tonight is the sum total of what was left and what we could salvage after your valiant Army took what they wanted."

She waited for him to rise to the bait so she could feel justified in letting go of her temper. But he did nothing. He said nothing. He merely watched her through dark hooded eyes that told her nothing of what he was thinking, too damned civil to be believed.

"I did not say that to brag about who we were or to buy your pity for what we have become. I said it because there have been d'Ibervilles on this land since Natchez was nothing more than a trading post for trappers. Since the post itself was called Fort Rosalie." Her gaze slipped past his shoulder and softened as she looked at the regal, columned splendor of the ghostly shadow that rose up behind them. "This was once a beautiful, gracious home. It was a beautiful, gracious way of life that no one who was not a part of it could ever hope to understand."

"And never will if we are continually blockaded at every turn."

Disdain rippled through her like a wave of ice water. "You do not want to understand. You want to conquer and dictate. You want to make slaves out of the masters and teach us the error of our ways, and the irony of it is—you don't even see the irony. Winning the war wasn't enough for you. You brought in your military rule to degrade and humiliate us, to steal everything we own, to beat us onto our knees. You claim freedom to be the right of every man and slavery to be an offense against God, yet you see nothing wrong with putting those same free men to work on the same land for harder and longer hours in exchange for the 'privilege' of renting ten square feet and calling it sharecropping.

"Then there are those who think freedom means never having to work again. They suddenly discover their benevolent new Yankee masters are not prepared to feed, clothe, and house them for nothing, so they live in shantytowns and murder each other for a scrap of bread. Meanwhile, honest white folk—women and children for the most part, and men who would not have dreamed of treating their slaves as badly as you liberators treat the free-issue darkies now—are thrown out on the streets and are forced to beg for their next meal. Tell me, sir, what have you accomplished in your victory? How have you improved the plight of humanity? And how can you, in any honesty at all, expect anything but blockades at every turn?"

"I guess I shouldn't," he agreed in a bemused murmur. "At the same time, I wasn't exactly expecting a diatribe on politics and social oppression."

Amanda suppressed a childish urge to stamp her foot in exasperation. He had the unnerving ability to touch off her temper then stand back and spread his hands innocently, as if the explosion had been solely of her own making.

"Why, *exactly,* did you buy Briar Glen?" she asked hotly. "Knowing how the people hereabout feel toward Yankees and carpetbaggers and the whole damned Federal Government in general—why would you willingly stick your hand into a nest of angry hornets?"

"Maybe I like living dangerously. Maybe I like the challenge and maybe"—he paused and his gaze fell to the luscious pout of her mouth—"when I see something I like, I don't mind taking a few stings to get it. But I didn't think we came out here to talk about my motives. I thought we were going to talk about yours . . . or, more specifically, what sent you prowling out in the night as Montana Rose."

"*I* thought the reason was obvious. We needed the money. I did what I had to do to get it."

"*Had* to? Someone held a gun to your head and forced you into a gambling salon dressed like a two-bit whore and dealing off the bottom of the deck?"

"I told you, you wouldn't understand," she declared, and started to push past him, intending to return to the house.

"And I told you to try me," he said with a snarl, his hand grabbing her arm without any pretense at civility. His face was a pale blur for the most part, with only the dark slash of his eyebrows and mustache to lend his features any substance. It was his voice and the pressure of his grip that left no room to doubt she had touched a raw nerve somewhere.

But she too felt raw. Raw and very close to tears.

"Maybe I just like living dangerously," she spat, her eyes sparkling as she flung his own words at him. "Maybe I like challenges and maybe"—her breath caught, for his fingers had tightened enough to crush her arm to pulp—*"maybe I had no choice!"*

He brought his face close enough to hers that she could feel the heat of his breath gusting against her lips. "You'll have to do better than that, Mrs. Jackson. Everyone has choices, especially between doing something right and doing something wrong."

"What if it is something *necessary?*" she countered with reckless defiance. "Do you stop to *think* if it's right or wrong?"

He stared at her in silence, his eyes hard and glittering, reflecting pinpoints of light from the slivered moon. The urge washed through him, like a shower of cold water, that he wanted very much to kiss her. It was absurd and he knew if he did not back away, she would win her point by the mere act of him not stopping to debate the right or wrong of it, just the need.

"You keep saying you had no choice," he said, relaxing his grip enough to allow the blood to flow back into her arm.

"I didn't think I did," she replied through her teeth.

"Convince me."

"In '56," she said, "a blight went through the county, affecting the cotton crops along both banks of the river for a hundred miles or more."

"What the devil has that got to do with any of this?" he demanded.

"You wanted an explanation," she retorted. "I'm attempting to give you one."

He clamped his jaw shut. "Your point?"

"My *point* . . . is that Rosalie suffered heavy losses that year. Not enough to ruin us, but enough to put a strain on our working capital and leave very little as a cushion against a second year of blight, should it happen."

"Which, I assume, it did?"

"Three years in a row the harvest yielded less than a tenth of what it should have. We were still all right, what with our stables and what Ryan made each year from breeding and selling his Thoroughbreds. But there was all that talk of war. Father was eager for it, as far back as I can remember. There were always men in the library holding meetings, arguing, haggling, planning for the glorious day when Mississippi would secede and the South would become an independent country."

Tarrington released her arm but he did not back away. He watched her face intently, searching for the first sign of a lie.

"When the day finally came and war was declared, he nearly shot the provost marshal for trying to tell him he was too old to join the Army. He and my brothers enlisted right away, and with everyone convinced the fighting would be over in a month or so, no one worried about failed crops or three years' worth of borrowing on credit. And no one worried that the Confederate bonds we were given in exchange for our horses would eventually be worth less than the paper they were printed on.

"I suppose we were luckier than most when the fighting ended. Two of our men came home. Rosalie was still standing, though most of our slaves had run off and the fields were lying fallow. This close to the river, we were frequently pressed to play host to unwanted guests. The armies of the North and South used our home for their headquarters at varying times over the years. They ate our food and commandeered our livestock, but again we were lucky; the Yankees spared the house instead of burning it or blowing it up for sport. As an infant, Verity used to cry when she heard the sound of boots outside the nursery door. After a while, she even grew too frightened to do that and she would just sit there, shaking in terror while the soldiers ripped apart the bedding and floorboards searching for any hidden valuables."

"Why the hell didn't you leave? Or at least get away from the river?"

"We did leave for a while," she said softly. "Alisha and I went to New Orleans. Verity was born there, but . . . we couldn't stay. There wasn't any point; it was the same everywhere, and we were needed here. Father had been sent home by then, and it was too much for Mother to cope with his injury and . . . and everything else."

Amanda paused and looked up into Tarrington's face. "He tries, he honestly does, but he gets confused so easily. He . . . shuts himself away when things get too difficult, and it sometimes takes days for him to come back to us. He never talks about the war, never seems to notice how things have changed around here. He prefers to act as if Stephen,

Evan, and Caleb are just out of sight somewhere . . . and for the sake of his peace of mind, we have learned to live with it.''

It was the first time she had mentioned her husband, and once again Tarrington found himself battling strange urges—to know what the man was like, to know how much she had loved him, how much she grieved for him now. Questions he couldn't ask, of course. ''It must be difficult for the child. Not having a father, I mean.''

''Verity never knew him; Caleb is just a name to her,'' Amanda said quietly, bowing her head.

''And . . . your husband? Did he know . . . ?''

''Caleb died a month after we were married,'' she said without thinking, without emotion. ''So no, he never knew. He never knew what we went through here.''

''She's a beautiful child,'' he said quietly. ''He would have been very proud of her.''

''She's more than just beautiful, Mr. Tarrington. She is the most important thing in my life, and I would do anything . . . *anything* to keep her safe.'' She lifted her chin again. ''Even dress like a two-bit whore and deal off the bottom of the deck.''

''You still haven't told me why you did it,'' he reminded her gently. ''Or where the hell you came up with the idea, let alone the nerve to try something so outrageous. I don't recall any of my sisters saying five-card stud was a required course at the finishing school.''

''I told you why I did it,'' she said, frowning. ''The loans, the debts, the Confederate bonds. Rosalie is bankrupt, Mr. Tarrington.''

''Banks would still seem a tad more reliable than gaming tables, Mrs. Jackson.''

''Not when they've been taken over by government vultures and land speculators who rub their hands with glee every time they catch the scent of a foreclosure. What's more, we did go to the bank first, to the Natchez Mercantile. They loaned us enough money to buy seed to plant the fields this year. And until a few weeks ago, there was a good chance we could have paid some of the debt back and still have had enough left over to see us through next year.''

Tarrington guessed what was coming and glanced instinctively over his shoulder to where the darkness cloaked the acres of flood-ruined fields.

''God and E. Forrest Wainright conspired to make sure it didn't happen.''

''I am passingly familiar with the one entity,'' Tarrington said dryly, ''but who is E. Forrest Wainright?''

My future husband, she thought abruptly, shaking her head slightly at the irony. ''A speculator and a profiteer. He bought the note on Rosalie and demanded his money within thirty days of giving us notice.''

''Were those the original terms of the loan?''

Amanda smiled bitterly at his lack of understanding. ''There were no *terms,* Mr. Tarrington. Not as you know them. Our family had been doing business with the Mercantile since the day it opened its doors. Our word was our bond, our honor our collateral. Had the bank still been in the hands of men who would no more doubt Ryan's promise to honor my father's debts than they would doubt the sun coming up each morning, we could have survived any number of Yankee bureaucrats.''

Tarrington drew a deep breath and refrained from pointing out the obvious flaws in all of this Southern chivalry. He patted his breast pocket in search of a cigar instead. ''How much do you owe this Wainright? And when is the loan due?''

''Fifty thousand dollars,'' she said calmly. ''By the end of next week.''

Tarrington whistled softly and forgot all about the cigar. ''I admire your initiative, madam. You expected to earn it all in a few hands of cards?''

''I was on my way to doing so, if you'll recall.''

Tarrington waved away her sarcasm. ''I am still pressed to ask how you arrived at that particular method to try to earn the money you needed.''

Amanda hesitated, but only briefly. What did it matter now anyway?

"You are no stranger to the riverboats yourself, sir. Have you ever heard the name Billy Fleet?"

"Fleet?" Now where the deuce was she going with this? he wondered. "He worked the river back in the forties, if I remember correctly. Somewhat of a legend in his own time, he was said to have the fastest hands and keenest card sense of any sharp before or since."

"I shall have to tell Father that," she murmured with a crooked smile. "He would be tickled to hear himself called a legend, I'm sure."

"Father? Your *father* is Billy Fleet?"

"Was, Mr. Tarrington. He *was* Billy Fleet. And it was just a game to him, the bored, spoiled son of a wealthy man who found it exciting and stimulating to ride the riverboats and challenge his own destiny. He gave it up when he married Mother and had to assume the responsibility of the running of Rosalie. For the past twenty-seven years, he has been just plain William Courtland, one of Natchez's most upstanding, law-abiding, eminent citizens."

"Well, I'll be damned," Tarrington muttered, genuinely stunned.

"No doubt you will be," she agreed. "And long before you ever intended if so much of a whisper of this goes beyond these shadows. Judge Moore would shoot you himself, without blinking an eye, if he even thought you knew."

"The Judge knows William Courtland is Billy Fleet?"

"Everyone in Adams County knows, Mr. Tarrington, so it would hardly be worth your while to take out an announcement in the *Gazette.*"

"Your high opinion of me is flattering, Mrs. Jackson."

"It would be even higher if I thought you were the kind of man who would destroy the reputation of an old, broken man in a wheelchair."

"You don't seem to be too worried about your own reputation."

"I am doing a fine enough job ruining it myself."

"Not without a little parental guidance," he countered smoothly. "Or are you going to tell me your esteemed father had no hand in teaching you the art of challenging destiny?"

"It started out as simple parlor tricks," she protested. "As an amusing way for the family to pass a rainy afternoon."

"The family? You mean you weren't the only one to benefit from your father's knowledge?"

"I wasn't even the best. My brother Stephen could have played naked and still won every hand with four aces."

"An enviable talent," he said with a sardonic twist of a smile. "And the others?"

"Evan was cautious, but he usually won if he put his mind to it. Alisha is good, but she tends to get greedy and, when she does, she overplays her hand."

"And Ryan?"

"He used to drive poor Father to distraction. He could gentle an unschooled Arabian with a touch of his hand, but put a deck of cards in those same hands and he was all thumbs."

Tarrington nodded consideringly. "Which explains why you were the one seated in the games and he was merely there to guard your back. Is he the only one who knows?"

"Besides you, yes," she said miserably. "And he would have been quite happy removing you from the list if I hadn't talked him out of it."

Tarrington's eyes glittered strangely. "May I ask why you did?"

"I didn't think Alisha would appreciate gunfire at her wedding," she said bluntly.

"Probably not," he agreed, his smile concealed beneath the full mustache. "All the same, the wedding was several days ago and I am still in one piece."

"You're also Dianna's cousin."

"Ahh. Yes, that might tend to take some of the glow out of her eyes. On the other hand, I don't imagine it put any great shine in his each time he watched you pour yourself into that green velvet dress and sashay onto the deck of a riverboat."

Amanda reached up and closed her fingers around the gold locket. Standing there in the darkness, cloaked in shadows and black bombazine, she herself could hardly believe she had done it. The fights with Ryan—and there had been some monumental confrontations—the appalling risks they had taken . . . it had all been for nothing. They were exactly where they had been a month ago, two months ago, six months ago before the notion had ever occurred to her. In the beginning, she had done it just to put food on the table—and an orange in Verity's hand. In the end, she had been caught up by her own pride and greed, and, in truth, probably deserved nothing better than Forrest Wainright.

Amanda was not aware of the softly filtered moonlight that was giving Tarrington a very good view indeed of the uncertainty and vulnerability that came into her face. Her eyes were wide and misty, her chin no longer firm and stubborn but struggling valiantly to keep the tremors confined to the already much abused lower lip. Wisps of fine silvery hair had floated free of the chignon, curling at her temples and trailing along her throat, drawing his eyes and his less censurable thoughts down to where her hand twisted the chain of the gold locket.

"For what it's worth," he murmured, "if I were in your position, I don't know if I would have had the guts to do what you did."

"For how very little it is worth, Mr. Tarrington, I don't want your praise," she said softly. "Or anyone else's, for that matter. I feel cheap and tawdry enough as it is."

"It wasn't intended as praise. It was a stupid, foolish, recklessly insane thing to do, and you were just plain lucky to have had me for a playing partner that night. Anyone else seeing those magic fingers at work would have put a bullet into you first and pondered the merits of your pluckiness later."

"Regardless if he was cheating himself?" she pointed out wryly.

"As I told you on the *Queen,* I was merely protecting my interests."

"And I was protecting mine."

Tarrington wanted to shake her but, instead, became brusque and businesslike. "Very well, Mrs. Jackson, I have heard your explanation, and for whatever insane and reckless reasons of my own, I believe you."

"Thank you very much," she said her voice tight in her throat, "but I do not need to be patronized either."

"I'm not patronizing you. I'm making you an offer."

Her eyes narrowed instantly with suspicion. "An offer?"

"To forget everything I know about the elusive Montana Rose, and to forget this conversation ever took place. Furthermore"—he paused and seemed to have to give *himself* a little shake in order to comprehend what he was about to say —"I will loan you the money you need to pay off the debts on Rosalie—at a fair rate of interest, of course."

Amanda clutched the locket so tightly the chain bit into the flesh at the nape of her neck. "And what would you expect in return for such generosity?"

"First—a promise. A solemn promise, backed by this code of honor you Southerners claim you hold so dear, that your days as a river pirate are over."

"I have already made myself that promise," she declared bitterly.

"Nonetheless, I'll want your word on it. I know how fickle a woman's mind can be when it becomes inconvenient to recall what she has or has not promised. Five sisters, remember? None of whom ever told a man the straight truth whether it was necessary to lie or not."

Amanda let the sarcasm pass without response. "You said *first,* implying there were more terms?"

Tarrington felt his body tense, felt the hot, slow rush of desire flow into his extremities. It was there, on the tip of his tongue, needing only breath to give it substance. His mind and body had already given it enough consideration to have denied him a single moment's peace since he had confronted her on the deck of the *Mississippi Queen,* since he had first envisioned her naked and welcoming him into her arms. Moreover, if the disdainful light in her eyes was anything to judge by, she knew exactly what he wanted. It would come as no surprise that he wanted her.

"It was merely a figure of speech," he said, smiling tightly. "There are no other terms, no other conditions. Well? Do we have an agreement?"

Amanda's frown was as slow to form as her words. "No. No, Mr. Tarrington, we do not. I can't take your money."

"Why not? You were willing to take it a week ago."

"A week ago . . . the circumstances were different."

"Why? Because we were sitting around a table deliberately trying to cheat each other?"

"No," she said softly. "Because a week ago we needed the money. As of yesterday, we don't."

"The loan has been settled?"

"In . . . a manner of speaking, yes."

"What manner?"

Amanda tensed perceptibly. "I fail to see how it could possibly be any of your business, or your concern, to know."

"You haven't followed your sister's example, I hope, and found some rich, addled bastard to marry yourself to."

Laden with sarcasm, or at the very least with the intent to prod her temper into responding, he was taken aback to hear her small gasp and see the long, pale fingers clasp the locket as if to crush it.

And for a man who had spent the long years of the war holding endless night watches, scanning blackened seas and starless nights for any sign of enemy patrols, the broken moonlight that filtered through the branches of the oak might well have been bright sunlight. He could see the blotches of color rouging her cheeks and he could see the movement in her throat as she worked to ease the dryness in her mouth. Prickling his suspicions further, for the first time all night her eyes refused to meet his, even though she knew he was staring at her—an affront she had never failed to rebuke until now.

"What have you done?" he asked quietly. He tucked a finger under her chin, forcing her to look up at him. "You haven't done something *truly* stupid, like try to renegotiate the terms with Wainright?''

She attempted to pull her chin free, but he would not allow it.

"It wasn't stupid," she declared. "It was the only option we had left."

A tense few seconds passed before he found a way to phrase his next question, hissed as it were, in a voice so silky it sent a shiver down her spine. "And what kind of terms is he demanding?"

Amanda shook her head and this time, when she tried to break his hold, he curled an arm around her waist and brought her up hard against his body.

"Maybe I asked the wrong question," he snarled, his eyes unrelenting as they searched her face. "Maybe I should be asking what kind of terms you offered him?"

"Please," she gasped. "Let me go."

"Not until you tell me what I want to know."

"It isn't any of your affair to know," she insisted breathlessly.

"Wrong turn of phrase to use," he said, drawing her so close against his body, she could feel the buttons of his shirt pressing through her basque. Her heart was pounding and her limbs seemed to have lost all respect for the commands she was giving them to push away, to break free of the wall of muscle that was threatening to overwhelm her.

"Mandy—" His mouth was only inches from hers, his eyes so wide and dark they filled her entire field of vision. "What have you done?"

"It isn't your affair, Yankee," she cried fiercely.

He swore softly and shifted his hand from her chin to the nape of her neck. His mouth covered hers without further preamble, his lips and hands holding her with enough force to prevent any possibility of escape. The kiss was nothing like the light feathering he had tried to seduce her with on the *Mississippi Queen*. There was nothing teasing or tentative about it, nothing that suggested he would stop or even let her gasp at a decent breath until he had had his fill. What

small concessions he did allow, he took ruthless advantage
of, thrusting the wet heat of his tongue between her lips,
probing deeply, penetrating her defenses with an intimacy
bolder than any she had known before.

Caleb's kisses had never flooded her limbs with such a
fiery weakness. They had never sent her hands twisting into
his lapels or her body curling forward with disbelief. He had
surely never painted her mouth with such lush, erotic sugges-
tions that she felt corresponding ribbons of motion begin to
slither and slide between her thighs.

He sank his fingers into the knot of her hair and tore away
the pins holding it prisoner. It tumbled loose, spilling over
her shoulders like liquid moonlight, and he used a silky
fistful of it to draw her head back, to expose the slender
white arch of her throat to his roving lips.

"Stop," she gasped. "Stop . . . please."

"Is it my affair yet?" he demanded huskily.

Amanda's lips throbbed and tingled. Her senses were reeling, her thoughts spinning out of control. His tongue was
unleashing rivers of sensation along her neck, and with a
gasp, she realized his hand was doing the same to her breast,
stroking and kneading the flesh through its thin layers of
bombazine and cotton, brazenly tracing the contours with a
skill that shattered what few illusions she had remaining.

He was not a man to be trifled with. Not a man who liked
to play games or a man accustomed to losing them. She had
challenged him, defied him, and rebuked him, and now he
was telling her, in no uncertain terms, he could take what he
wanted, willingly or not.

"Well?" he growled. "Do I get an answer?"

"No," she cried. "No, you can't change anything now.
You mustn't interfere. It's done. I have given my word—"

Tarrington swore again and reclaimed her mouth, smother-
ing her words beneath the bold insistence of yet another kiss
that threatened to reduce her to a shivering, shuddering puddle of raw nerves.

"Tell me," he grated, his mustache chafing the moist and

ravaged pout of her lips. "Tell me what you have promised to Wainright, or by God . . ."

"I—I . . . have promised to marry him," she stammered, the words so ragged and broken, Tarrington could not be certain his ears had heard her correctly.

"What? *What did you say?*"

"I—" She swallowed hard and her voice improved on the whisper, but barely enough to rise above the solid drumming of her heartbeat. "I have agreed to marry him and he . . . in turn . . . has agreed to extend the loan on Rosalie."

He released her like a red-hot rock and gaped down at her in disbelief. His own senses were none too reliable at the moment. His body was strung as tightly as a bow, the heat was ebbing and flowing through his flesh, causing a confused welter of emotions from anger to arousal, from intense desire to damning fury.

A bead of sweat crawled through his hair and slid down his neck. He backed off a pace, then another, then raked a hand through his hair, across his mustache, around the column of his neck, staring at her as if he were still having trouble comprehending what she was telling him.

"I'm offering you the money you need . . . without any terms or conditions or threats of foreclosure. Take it."

"I . . . can't. I have given Wainright my word."

"Break it," he snarled. "The bloody world will not end if you do. Pay the bastard what you owe him in cash, not by . . . by . . ."

"By selling myself to him?" she finished on a choked cry. "Is that so much different from what you would have expected in exchange for your *generosity?*"

"I told you—"

"You told me there would be no conditions, no demands. But there would have been expectations, would there not?"

Tarrington glared at her, at the brittle contempt sparkling in her eyes. The taste of her was still on his lips, the feel of her impressed on his body, and he was shocked to know a simple kiss could have had such a devastating effect on him.

And from one who was rejecting him. Despite the heat and

passion and raw flame he had felt burning inside her, she was sending him away, denying herself, denying him . . . because of a few ill-spent words and her damned rebel pride.

"Since I have already made my attraction to you quite clear, I won't deny the obvious, madam. But the choice of whether or not you reciprocated would have been yours, and at least you would have had one. With someone like Wainright, I would hazard to guess the only choice you'll have is whether you show him your gratitude on your back or on your knees."

Amanda's face drained in a sickening rush. She reacted instinctively, swinging her hand up out of the darkness and slapping his face with all of the strength and outrage she could muster. It was considerable and Michael Tarrington staggered back a step, his cheek stinging as if it had caught the lash of a whip.

He kept his face turned to the side long enough to win the war against his own reflex to strike back. When he did look at her again, his eyes were tense and brilliant, gleaming with enough fury to stop the breath in her throat.

He moved suddenly and was maliciously pleased to see her flinch. But it was only to offer a formal, if not ingratiatingly polite, bow, saying nothing, sparing her neither another word nor a glance as he walked back to the house.

Chapter 12

Amanda was packed and ready. She stood in the shadows beside Verity's bed and looked down at the sleeping child, resisting the urge to wake her and hug her to her bosom for dear life. She had already adjusted the blankets three times and lifted several golden curls off the little moppet face; she was running out of excuses to linger and knew the clock was ticking slowly, inexorably closer to midnight.

She had tucked everything she would need in a woefully small carpetbag. A book of prayers was carefully wrapped in the folds of her best nightdress. She had a change of underthings and the worn pair of satin slippers Caleb had given to her on their wedding night. The daguerreotype of her husband had been a last-minute addition along with Verity's christening bonnet, both sentimental things. Foolish things her new husband would probably scorn, but sadly enough, the only articles of any value she held dear.

Amanda pressed her brow against the bedpost. Why? Why did it have to end this way? The specter of Wainright had loomed in the background all day and evening. She knew she had to go through with it, but it terrified her to think of what life would be like married to a man like E. Forrest Wainright. Her friends would shun and ridicule her for marrying a Yankee, regardless of the circumstances or necessity. Her family —Ryan in particular—would despise her for showing up his own inadequacy. He might not kill her, as he had threatened to do, but he might never speak to her again for as long as she lived.

But what other choice did they have? A picture of Michael Tarrington came unbidden to mind, and she tried to push it away before his voice could echo in her ears for the thousandth time . . . but she was too late.

"I am offering you the money you need. Take it."

"I have given Wainright my word—"

"Break it! The bloody world will not end if you do!"

A dull rumble of thunder drew Amanda's gaze to the window. It was fitting, somehow, that a storm should be brewing outside. Fitting that the trees should be bending and blowing like old women rocking themselves in despair. Fitting that even God seemed to be frowning down on her with displeasure.

Squaring her shoulders, Amanda walked to the door and picked up her bag. Her hand trembled as she propped the note she had written on the washstand. It was addressed to Ryan, telling him not to worry, she would be back in a few days to explain everything. She had not been able to put her intentions into words even though the deed would be a *fait accompli* long before he had a chance to read the note or do anything to stop her. She asked only that he look after Verity until she returned.

Tears stung her eyelids as she cast a final glance back at the bed. Quietly she let herself out into the hallway and stole down the stairs, knowing which planks to avoid and which were solid enough to bear her weight in silence. The cavernous front foyer was steeped in darkness, but she paused again and looked around one last time, her memory serving her better than any fully lit candlebra. The paintings that had decorated the walls for generations were gone, but she imagined she could see them. The prim and austere d'Ibervilles had glowered down at her since she was a child, scowling at her pranks, passing silent judgment on her beaux, witnessing her marriage to Caleb Beauregard Jackson with solemn approval. She was glad they could not see her now, skulking out of the house in the dead of night, intent on a rendezvous with a common, low-bred Yankee they would have been appalled to see set foot in their family home.

Amanda eased open the massive front door and slipped through on legs that felt as shaky as those of a newborn foal. A gust of wind swirled across the porch and she turned her back to it, hastily drawing the hood of her cloak up and over her head. The clouds were boiling angrily across the sky, their underbellies tinted blue-white and flickering with every rumble and roll. The wind smelled metallic with rain, and even as she gathered the wide wings of her cloak around her and ran for the trees, fat wet drops began to fall. They came lightly at first, then in hard, driving sheets that pelted the branches of the trees and tattooed the packed earth of the lane.

By the time she had run all the way down to the end of the avenue, her cloak was soaked and the cheap soles of her shoes were letting more mud and water through than they protected against. She was out of breath and hugging a stitch in her side. The trees had taken on sinister shapes in the sporadic flares of lightning, with shadows sliding back and forth between the trunks and conjuring memories of a very different kind—memories of soldiers creeping up on the house, hoping to catch the residents by surprise.

Amanda spun around in a full circle, the panic mushrooming in her chest. She had reached the end of the drive and there was no carriage in sight. For a moment she thought the road was deserted and she could not be sure if it was fear or joy that brought a sob forth from her lips. But with the next flash of lightning she saw it. A jagged fork revealed where Wainright's carriage was halted by the side of the road, a shiny blot of black against the rim of blowing trees.

The driver was standing patiently at the head of the team, soothing the two skittish horses and acting as if it were perfectly normal to be waiting there by the side of the road in the middle of a storm-tossed night. He said nothing as she approached, but hurried ahead of her to hold the door of the coach open. He wore a greatcoat with wide multicaped shoulders and a low-brimmed hat that sent a small channel of rainwater funneling over the lip as he bowed slightly and held a hand out to assist her up the low step.

"Mrs. Jackson, I presume," he murmured.

"Yes," she whispered. "Thank you."

Was it her imagination or did his gloved hand squeeze hers reassuringly before he let go?

Amanda groped for the edge of the seat and slid into it

with a small jolt as the door shut behind her. The blinds were drawn and the darkness inside the coach was absolute. The sudden lack of wind and rain was disquieting, and she puffed her breath into the sudden stillness, feeling the cold trickles of rainwater run down her cheeks and under the collar of her cloak.

"Mr. Wainright?"

A grunt came out of the darkness opposite her. "You're late."

She heard him knock twice on the roof of the buggy, and almost instantly the horses leaped forward and the wheels turned, skidding in the mud for the first few moments until the steel rims found a grip on the road.

"You are *twenty minutes* late," he said shortly. "I was beginning to think you had reconsidered."

"The storm delayed me. I had to be sure Verity was settled."

He grunted again but offered no further comment, and Amanda spent the next five minutes striving to settle her own nerves and keep her stomach where it belonged. Somewhere in that time it occurred to her that the buggy had been facing north and, as far as she could determine, had not turned around.

"You are not returning to Natchez?"

"No. Not Natchez. I thought Jamestown would be more appropriate for our needs."

"Jamestown?" she repeated softly.

"You have an objection?"

"No. No, I . . ." She frowned and pushed the hood of her cape off her head, crediting the damp wool for distorting the sound of Wainright's voice.

"You were having second thoughts?"

"No. I gave you my word."

He laughed brusquely. "And your word is, of course, paramount to any other considerations?"

Amanda's frown deepened. It wasn't the wool and it wasn't the buffeting winds and slogging hoofbeats. Something was odd about his voice, odd about the way he asked and answered questions, odd about the way her skin was prickling with alarm.

"Can you light the lantern, please?" she asked on a stilted breath. "I seem to have misplaced a glove."

The sound of a match striking on wood and the subsequent bright flare of the sulfur made her flinch and shrink back into the seat. For as long as it took her eyes to adjust to the glare, all she could see was his hand and the long, tapered fingers. As the darkness melted back, she was able to follow the black sleeve to the massive shoulders, from there to the squared jaw and full mustache, up to the calmly expectant steel gray eyes.

Her breath was expelled sharply on a cry. *"You!"*

Michael Tarrington smiled and touched the flame to the wick of the small coach lamp that hung beside the door. The glare became muted at once as he dropped the sides of the horn panes, casting a soft bloom of light over the rich burgundy upholstery of the buggy's interior.

"Good Lord, you look like a kitten someone rescued from drowning," he mused, for her hair clung in straggling yellow ribbons to her cheeks and throat, her skin gleamed like wet, pink marble. Her cloak was sodden, her hem and shoes coated in mud. "But charming, nonetheless."

"Wh-what are you doing here? Where is Mr. Wainright?"

"I can only hazard a guess, you understand, but I should imagine he is somewhere on the road between Natchez and Rosalie nursing a broken axle and an extremely foul temper."

"How . . . ?"

"You can thank Foley—the rather inventive gentleman topside—for arranging it. He seemed to know just which bolts to loosen to delay your fiancé for an hour or so."

"But . . . this is terrible!" she cried. "You had no right!"

"Not the right, perhaps, but certainly the *sense* to prevent you from doing something you would regret for the rest of your life."

"Precisely my point," she retorted, starting to regain

some of her composure. "*My* life. How dare you presume to interfere?"

"Yes, well, after your parting gesture the other evening, you are damned lucky I *did* presume. You were even luckier I didn't exhibit my fine, barbaric manners and upend you on your fanny then and there."

Amanda leaned forward, her hands clutching the edge of the leather seat. "Why? Why are you here?"

"To save your virtue, of course. Is that not what one of your red-blooded Southern gentlemen would have aspired to do?"

"Save my virtue?" She gasped. "You cannot be serious."

"I assure you, I am very serious. You have blighted my character and I am come to redeem myself."

Amanda collapsed back against the seat. "Do you know what you have done?" she asked in a shocked whisper. "Do you have any *idea* of the damage you have done?"

"I have a good idea of the damage I have prevented," he countered smoothly. "Probably better than you had when you agreed to this madness in the first place—or at least, I am hoping you had no inkling as to the kind of man you were preparing to marry."

Amanda offered only a sullen silence by way of a response, but Tarrington would not let it lie.

"Besides his being a Yankee and a scoundrel and about as immoral a bastard as they come, do you know *anything* about E. Forrest Wainright?"

"Would you please instruct your driver to stop the coach this instant and let me out?"

He ignored the request. "Did you know Wainright was incarcerated in a Federal prison when the war broke out?"

Amanda turned her head, refusing to acknowledge the question or dignify it with an answer.

"Aren't you even moderately curious to know what he did?"

When her only reply was a forced sigh, Tarrington leaned back against the seat and folded his arms across his chest. "He was put behind bars for beating his wife to death."

That won a reaction, albeit a small one, but enough to tell him he had her attention. "It seems he caught her with another man. The lover he merely killed—shot him straight through the heart—but his wife . . . They found her bound and gagged, quite helpless, I assure you, and not able to do a thing to protect herself when he took a knife and began to—"

Amanda whirled around to face him. "I don't believe you. You're making all of this up, and I don't care to hear any more of it."

"I'm not making any of this up," he said quietly, "and you had better believe me, since this is your fiancé we're talking about. As for hearing any more, I would think you would want to know what kind of a man you're selling yourself to, because it wasn't the first—or the last—time he has taken his fists to a woman. It seems he has a taste for roughing up his bed partners. There are more than a few ladies of the evening right here in Natchez who don't think too highly of the way your Mr. Wainright expresses his affection."

"How do you know all of this? How do you know it's true?"

"I haven't had time to ride to New York and back to verify all the sordid details, but I did spend a few hours yesterday and today with a friend of mine who happens to have access to some interesting Army files."

"Obviously not interesting enough to warrant putting him back in jail—*if* what you say is true."

"If the war hadn't broken out when it did, they probably would have hanged him. Unfortunately, however, there was a time shortly after the first Bull Run when the Union was shy of volunteers and thought they might be in some serious trouble. The call even went out to the prisons, and men were offered full amnesty if they agreed to put their killer instincts to good use on the battlefield. If they survived, they were free."

"And Wainright survived."

"Not only survived, but prospered. Enough that he can afford to indulge in his little pleasures, paying off the women he abuses or frightening them so badly they're too terrified to come forward."

Amanda fell silent again, her thoughts in such a turmoil she was not aware of how intently the smoldering gray eyes were watching her through the soft bloom of lamplight.

"Why should I believe you? Why should I trust you?"

"I'm not the kind of man who lies to drowned kittens," he said with gentle mockery. "And up until now, I *was* the kind of man most women trusted . . . although I appear to have slipped up somehow where you are concerned."

"You wonder why? You have cheated and humiliated me; you have antagonized my brother by seeming to court the woman he loves; you turn up at my sister's wedding and nearly ruin the day for everyone. And now you have kidnapped me! Who on this sweet green earth would even think of trusting you?"

"Who indeed," he murmured. "But in my own defense, I must say—at the risk of repeating myself—I was not the only one choosing my cards with care that night on the *Mississippi Queen*. And if your brother cannot see that Dianna loves him as much as he loves her, then he deserves to lose her to an opportunistic rascal like myself. As for the last charge"—he reached over and cradled her cold hands in his —"I wouldn't call it kidnapping to elope in the middle of the night. I would call it quite romantic."

"*Elope!*"

"Certainly. You don't actually think I've gone to all this trouble simply to turn you loose to ply your charms on someone else?"

"You don't actually think I would consent to marry you!"

"Why, Mrs. Jackson . . . Mandy . . . I don't see how you can refuse."

Amanda jerked her hands out of his and pressed as far back in the seat as she could go. "By what madness do you arrive at that conclusion?"

"Simple logic. You still owe Wainright fifty thousand dollars. I'll wager he is beyond furious by now, and even if you crawled to him on hands and knees, I doubt if he would take you back—not on your terms, at any rate . . . if, indeed, he ever intended to.''

"What do you mean, *if* he intended to?''

"My lovely innocent: Anyone could hire a man to say he was a justice of the peace for ten minutes. And as far as believing he would tear up the note on Rosalie . . . I would have to say that was just plain wishful thinking. A man like Wainright would not throw away a chance to own such a plum piece of property, not if, as you say, he has been so keen to have it for so long.''

"But if I marry you . . .''

"Yes?''

"Will he not be even more furious?''

"I'm sure he will. But to get to you, he will have to go through me first.''

Another spray of gooseflesh rose on Amanda's arms. She could not help but notice the gleam in his eyes now and a rush of giddiness swept through her, rendering her more confused than ever. Why would a man like Michael Tarrington go to all of this trouble for her? Why on earth would he ask for more?

"Why would you want to marry me?'' she asked, putting her thoughts into words. "Why could you not just loan me the money as you offered to do in the first place?''

"When I first made the offer, I was not aware of the arrangements you had made with Wainright. I've also had two days to think about it in more general terms—I am a businessman, after all—and you were right when you said I was sticking my hand into a hornets' nest when I bought Briar Glen. Marrying into the Courtland family would greatly lessen the sting of having a newcomer move onto such hallowed ground, so to speak.''

"You would marry me for my name? For the influence of a bankrupt Southern family?''

"From what I have heard about your brother, I have no doubt the family finances will be restored in full, once he is on his feet. In that respect, I would consider the fifty thousand to be money well invested.''

"And is that all you would expect from me? My name?"

"Is that all Wainright expected?"

She reddened to the point where she felt dizzy. "No."

"Then why would you expect me to accept anything less?"

Amanda lowered her eyes and kept them lowered through several taut minutes of listening to nothing but the wheels of the coach churning and the beat of the horses' hooves carrying them through the stormy darkness. She was no better off than she was an hour ago. She would still be selling herself for Rosalie, same price, different buyer. A situation like hers would be laughable if it was happening to someone else, but she was, at that moment, a heartbeat away from dissolving into tears. Tarrington had given her some very good reasons why she should not have been so quick to enter into a marriage with Forrest Wainright, but who was there to give her any advice about Michael Tarrington? How did she know he was not fabricating the whole story about Wainright? How did she know *he* was not the kind of man to hire someone to act the part of a justice of the peace for ten minutes?

Tarrington, studying her from across the width of the coach, smiled inwardly.

"We should be approaching Jamestown soon," he said casually. "The Reverend Peter Jeffries has resided there some thirty years, as I understand it. Do you know him?"

Amanda looked up. "Yes. I know him."

"He might be a little vexed at being wakened at such an ungodly hour. We . . . could wait until the morning, if you prefer."

"And if I prefer just to go back home and face the consequences, whatever they might be—what then?"

He allowed the smile to show as a shadowy crease at the corner of his mouth. "Then I suppose I will have to take you back, won't I?"

Amanda was prepared for any answer but that. And she was prepared for any reaction from her own body but the soft, pulsing throb that began to course through her limbs.

"No, Mr. Tarrington. You won't have to take me back.

And we don't have to wait until morning. I accept your offer.''

The ceremony was simple, hasty, and performed with only Foley the coachman and the Reverend Mr. Jeffries's gray-haired wife as witnesses. The reverend was himself a gruff man and more than a little vexed at being roused from his slumber by repeated banging on the rectory door. It was hardly proper, he informed them imperiously, and initially refused to perform the marriage under such inauspicious circumstances. However, when told by the prospective groom that the lady was, er, in a delicate way, he naturally did his duty to save the Courtland family from a mortifying scandal. This did not prevent him from lecturing Amanda sternly and at great length on familial responsibilities, a lecture that left her burning with humiliation and barely able to hear, much less mouth the correct vows and responses when they were required.

The weakness she had felt in the buggy had not abated any. She stood in the reverend's parlor, a tall, arrogant Yankee by her side, a caped and dripping coachman to bear witness alongside a sleepy-eyed dumpling in a frowsy robe and beribboned nightcap. With Alisha's wedding so fresh in her mind—the flowers, the lace and frills, the music, the laughter—she could not help but bow her head and keep it bowed through most of the ceremony. Her mother would have fainted dead away to see her, salts or no salts. The painted eyes on the d'Iberville portraits would have melted shut with shame.

She got through it somehow, but had no recollection of walking back out to the carriage, or even if she would have managed it without the aid of Tarrington's strong grip on her arm. A gust of wind had extinguished the lantern and there was no attempt made to relight it. The only match that was struck and the only time the utter blackness was disturbed was when her new husband lit himself a cigar.

He smoked it in silence as the carriage proceeded at a

smart pace to Tarrington's home at Briar Glen. Amanda
pushed herself as far into the corner as the leather padding
and wood panels would allow, enmeshed in the privacy of
her own thoughts for an hour or more, until the wheels spun
onto the pebbled drive.

It was too dark to see much of the house as they approached, but Amanda was no stranger to Briar Glen, having
attended many balls and parties thrown by the Porterfields
over the years. The Glen was one of the grandest homes in
Adams County, if not the entire state of Mississippi. A
twelve-columned colonial, it boasted a score of formal bedrooms on the upper floor alone, with a high-ceilinged ballroom, a morning room, afternoon and evening parlors, a
library, solarium, and three separate kitchens, each with its
own culinary function. Before the ravages of war had altered
the design of the outbuildings and landscaping, there had
been whitewashed stables ringing a central courtyard, extensive gardens populated by white marble statues imported
from Rome, and a reflecting pool that could have belonged to
an English country manor.

Most of the stables had been destroyed along with the
slave quarters. The pool was cracked and empty, the gracious
statues missing heads and limbs and pockmarked with bul-
letholes. Amanda had no idea how much the house itself had
suffered, although she had heard that a Yankee general had
been billeted there from the outset of the occupation, thus
saving it from the worst of the looters and scavengers.

It was well past two in the morning when the carriage
drew to a halt at the front of the house. The fury of the storm
had been blown into the next county, leaving only sporadic
echoes of thunder and a stiff, damp wind in its wake. Despite
the lateness of the hour, the windows glowed with scattered
pinpricks of light. A rotund and fully dressed housekeeper
was there to open the main doors and welcome them with the
warm glow of a hurricane lamp before Tarrington had finished assisting his wife out of the coach.

"This is Mrs. Reeves," he said by way of an introduction
as they passed through the door. "She hasn't been here very

long herself, but I'm sure she can help you with whatever you need. Flora—will you take Mrs. Tarrington upstairs and make her comfortable? Is the big room ready?''

''Ye told me to make it ready, did ye not?'' The housekeeper scowled, the gravel in her voice betraying the fact that she was less awake than she appeared. It also revealed, rather pointedly, that she was less accustomed to taking orders than giving them, and not at all shy about giving them to Michael Tarrington.

He confirmed this by tossing a scowl back. ''Mrs. Reeves descended upon me two weeks ago, claiming that while Boston might very well survive without her help, she did not think I could manage on my own in what she considered to be a 'foreign' country. She is a spry old dear, however, and I'm quite fond of her. At times.''

''Fond o' me?'' Mrs. Reeves snorted. ''Ye've an odd way of showin' it then, keeping me out o' my bed until all the wee hours o' the morn. It'll sairve ye right if I sleep till noon. God an' all the saints presairve me—'' She held the lamp aloft and seemed to notice Amanda's bedraggled state for the first time. ''Where have ye had this poor wee child? She's half drenched an' blue with cold!''

''Which is precisely why I am entrusting her to your expert care,'' Tarrington said, and turned to Amanda. ''Foley and I have a few matters to discuss; I will join you later.''

Mrs. Reeves was already bustling toward the stairs. She snatched Amanda's carpetbag out of Foley's hand as she passed, eyeing it with the same mix of suspicion, disapproval, and bursting curiosity that marked each glance she sent Amanda's way.

Amanda trailed after her in silence, lifting the sodden folds of her skirts as she climbed slowly up the broad, banistered staircase. The upper corridors were in darkness, the glowing sphere of the lamp barely penetrated the shadows cloaking the twenty-foot-high ceilings. She noted absently that Tarrington—or someone—had had the walls freshly painted and the wood floors waxed and polished. There were no carpets or wall hangings, but the two ceiling-high windows at either end of the long, central corridor were hung with swagged velvet curtains.

Mrs. Reeves led her all the way to the last door in the hall. Amanda's stomach had been in a state of upheaval since early evening; it rolled over completely and slid all the way down to her toes when she crossed the threshold and found herself standing in what had to be the most enormous, most intimidatingly masculine bedroom she had ever seen.

A vast, cavernous chamber, it was paneled in dark wood and furnished with oversized pieces that could have come straight out of a medieval castle. The four-posted bed was easily three times as wide as her own at Rosalie. The marble fireplace that dominated the opposite wall housed a grate able to seat a six-foot log. Persian carpets underfoot were thick as fur, the armoire and night tables were solid oak, the two leather chairs in front of the fire were studded with brass buttons and sat on feet carved into lion's paws.

"The dressin' room's in here, hen," Mrs. Reeves said, going to a connecting door. "He said as how I should keep a bath hot, but since he didna say as to how long I should keep it, the water might need a bit o' topping up. Aye—" She disappeared behind the door for a moment and emerged a few seconds later wiping her hand down the front of her apron. "I'll fetch up a kettle or two. In the meanwhile, strip yoursel' out o' them claythes afore ye catch yer death. Land sakes, I dinna ken what gets into that man sometimes. Rush here, rush there. Stompin' around the house the blessed day long like a billygoat wi' his ballocks caught in a vise. Where's the hurry, I asked him? Must it be tonight? I asked him. In a storm? I asked him." She stopped and furled a brow in Amanda's direction. "Ye dinna talk much, do ye?"

"I'm . . . a little t-tired . . . and . . . a little over-whelmed by everything," Amanda stammered.

"Aye, well, so ye must be. Anxious too, an' me here blatherin' on like a fishwoman. There now, let me gi' the fire a poke or two to wake it up an' then I'll see aboot that hot water."

"Please don't go to any more trouble."

"Hmphf. Trouble comes when 'is Lairdship doesn't get what he wants *exactly* the way he wants it. Spoilt cock o' the roost, ye ask me. Doted on by his mam and pampered by them addled sisters o' his. Faither's just the same: Spoilt. The pair o' them."

Having made this announcement in motion—she hadn't actually stopped moving or talking since entering the room —Mrs. Reeves sailed on out the door without a pause, still muttering to herself as she walked back down the hall. Amanda listened for a moment, then tiptoed to the door and peeked out. But the bloom of the lamplight had already made the turn down the stairs, and there was nothing but shadows and gloom and silence to emphasize the loud pounding of her heart.

She retreated into the bedroom and closed the door. She stood with her back braced against the carved surface and surveyed her surroundings more closely, deciding it was definitely a man's room, solid and imposing. Yet if she had any doubt she had been taken to the wrong chamber by mistake, it was belied by the sight of the delicate, skirted dressing table that sat against the wall between the door and the fireplace. It looked as sadly out of place as she felt, with its collection of little crystal scent bottles and silver-backed brushes.

Tarrington had obviously been sure of himself. Sure he would not be returning to Briar Glen alone.

Amanda was suddenly chilled to the bone, but not from the soaking she had taken in the storm. A hot bath, if she could stay awake long enough to enjoy it, sounded like ten kinds of heaven, and she tiptoed gingerly into the dressing room, pushing the door slowly, wondrously wide as it revealed shelves upon shelves of neatly folded clothing— shirts, jackets, trousers in every stripe and color, *five* woolen greatcoats, and enough pairs of boots to fill a solid row along one wall. She hadn't seen so many crisp, clean garments in more years than she cared to remember, certainly not outside of a store. The closet itself was larger than most stores these days, with chests of drawers and a mirror on one wall that stretched from floor to ceiling.

Occupying one corner was an enameled, tulip-shaped bathtub. Amanda dipped her fingers into the water and found it more than appealingly warm. She let her clothes fall where they would and stepped naked into the thigh-deep water, sighing as she sank down and let the heat engulf her up to her chin.

She held her breath and submerged her head, working her fingers through the tangled mass of her hair, leaning back as she rose up out of the water again so that it fell in a gleaming gold sheet down her back. She found a small bar of soap, pink and smelling of roses, in a pot by the tub. She worked a thick lather over her skin and hair then rinsed and was lathering again when she heard Mrs. Reeves announcing her return with two kettles of steaming hot water.

"I'll build up the fire afore I go," she huffed, tipping the kettles into the tub, her cheeks as pink as the soap. "Would ye like me to unpack the rest o' yer claythes for ye thenight, or can it wait until the morn?"

Amanda reddened sheepishly as she watched Mrs Reeves start to pick up the garments she had so carelessly discarded. She reddened to the point of fire as she had a sudden vision of what the woman would find if she opened her carpetbag— one tattered nightgown, one pair of worn slippers, a tintype of another man, and a child's knitted bonnet.

"No. No, thank you, Mrs. Reeves. You have done more than enough for me already. I can find what I need myself."

A small, keen eye cast her a glance that suggested Mrs. Reeves was well aware of what Amanda was capable of finding for herself. A handsome, rich husband for a start?

"Aye. Well, I'll just take these filthy things along wi' me, then, shall I? Nay sense lettin' them ripen the whole room. I'll say good night now too, if ye think as how ye can find yer own way into a towel. There's a bell pull on the wall if ye lack owt, an' wine on the table if ye need owt."

"Thank you, Mrs. Reeves," Amanda murmured. "Sleep well."

A snort was the only response and then Amanda was alone again, her body chilled despite the fresh heat of the bathwater.

Michael Tarrington had been *very* sure of himself, ordering a bath, a fire . . . a bottle of wine.

Amanda frowned and stretched out a bare, dripping arm to the decanter sitting on the nearby stand. She was more hungry than thirsty, but she poured herself a glass anyway and, after sampling a mouthful of the sweet red wine, downed the rest of it in several greedy swallows.

She helped herself to a refill and leaned back against the tub, savoring the heat inside and out as she studied the extent of her husband's wardrobe. One entire rack held nothing but gloves. An upper shelf held hats, easily a dozen of them in various shapes and styles.

Amanda sipped her wine and sent a small, milky wave lapping over the crowns of her knees.

He had said he would be joining her later. How much later, and would he be expecting her to fulfill her part of the bargain tonight? A glance at a small, glass-domed clock told her it was ten minutes past three. Too late, she thought. Surely too late.

Chapter 13

Water sloshed over the rim as Amanda stepped out of the tub. She used two big towels to dry her body and her hair, leaving one wrapped around herself as she padded barefoot into the bedroom and searched out her nightdress. The worn flannel looked even nattier than she remembered, and it had been the best of the lot. White, high necked, and shapeless, it made her look like a large moth—a large, half-crazed moth what with her hair straggling every which way over her shoulders.

Mrs. Reeves had indeed stoked the fire, adding a huge log to the embers and banking it liberally with extra kindling. The flames were hot and bright, and by the time she had brushed the majority of tangles out of her hair, the ends were sleek, dry, and curling in the heat.

Absolutely *hours* must have passed since he had dismissed her in the lower hall. Well, one anyway. He had said he was a businessman . . . would it not be a prudent and wise decision to wait until they were both rested and in a better frame of mind to fulfill their *business* obligations?

Only half convinced, she carried her wine over to the dressing table and sat on the cushioned chair. She stared at her own pale reflection, knowing there was no one she could even blame for her misfortune. She had brought it about herself. Ryan would explode when he found out. He would hate her and hate himself, and then he would hate Dianna for introducing Michael Tarrington to Natchez. Sarah Courtland would live on smelling salts for the rest of her life, and Mercy would be driven to murder her mistress with a butcher's axe just to get some peace. Alisha would laugh. Oh, how she would laugh and taunt and hold her up to ridicule for doing *precisely* what she, Amanda, had scorned her twin for doing: marrying for money and convenience.

And Verity. What would Verity make of this big, gloomy house full of strange things and strange people? What would she make of Mrs. Reeves? Did Mrs. Reeves even know there was a child coming to live at Briar Glen? For that matter, *had Michael Tarrington taken Verity into consideration when he had made his grandiose plans?*

Bribing a child with a basket of oranges and a doll was one thing. Assuming responsibility for her upbringing was entirely another.

The sound of a heavy footstep in the outer hallway startled every other thought out of Amanda's mind and sent her hand fluttering to her throat. She gaped at the door in horror and when she saw the brass knob begin to turn, she averted her gaze in a rush of even greater shock. She did not look in his direction as Michael Tarrington came into the room and shut the door behind him. The best she could manage was to snatch up the hairbrush and drag it through her hair, over and over again as if her life was dependent upon her removing every last crimp and tangle.

At least she had the answer to one of her questions. He *did* expect her to live up to her part of the agreement tonight. He expected her to share his bed and fulfill her wifely obligations.

The brush moved with deliberate efficiency through her hair. She had pulled it forward over her shoulder to enable her to carry each stroke the full length, and she used it like a shield to hide behind, acting as if she hadn't noticed him entering the room or that she was not aware of him standing there, watching her every move.

Perhaps she should have looked. She would have seen then that he was not just watching her, he was temporarily frozen to the spot and could not have moved if he had wanted to. The golden shield she had thrown up between them rippled like a curtain of fine silk threads, each stroke of the brush sending a shimmering wave from her shoulder to her knee. The firelight was compounding his mobility problems. It was beside her, strong enough and bright enough to render the worn flannel of her nightgown almost transparent and if not for the veil of hair, she would have appeared to be sitting there naked.

With an effort, Tarrington moved away from the door and walked into the dressing room. Amanda released a pent-up breath and lowered the brush to her lap, meeting her own gaze in the mirror as she looked up.

This is ridiculous, she thought. *I* am ridiculous. What is the worst possible thing that could happen? She wasn't a virgin, for heaven's sake. There were no surprises awaiting her in the marriage bed. He was aggressive and overconfident and he was a dangerous man to underestimate, but Michael Tarrington did not strike her as being either brutish or deliberately cruel.

He was still a man, however, and he would still be trying to prove something—how virile he was, how strong and manly and skillful he was when the lights were out and the covers drawn. And he was still a Yankee—an obstacle that might prove to be insurmountable in the long run. But for all that he had saved her family from falling into ruin, saved Rosalie from falling into Wainright's clutches—she stopped and took a long swallow of wine to drain the glass—it was not such a terrible bargain to have struck.

Michael Tarrington was not the ugliest man she had ever seen in her life, nor the least appealing. She would, in fact, be hard-pressed to name a man with a broader chest or a stronger jaw. He certainly knew how to kiss a woman, how to make her feel as if her whole body were involved in that one simple act of touching mouths, and she hadn't *dis*liked the feeling entirely. In truth, if she remembered correctly, she had been furious with herself for enjoying it too much.

She heard a splash of water and stared at the dressing room door. Using her bathwater, even if it was just to wash away the strain of the last few hours, was an intimacy almost too bold to contemplate, and she found she was holding her breath, listening to every slosh and ripple, feeling it on her skin as if she were there in the water with him.

Which was an absurd image to consider, and it set her to brushing feverishly again, filling the silence with the crackling static from her hair until Tarrington was finished in the dressing room; she had some warning of this when she saw the change in the shadows behind her. A moment later the lamp was doused and he came back into the bedroom, barely glancing at her this time as he crossed over to the fire and gave the log a few adjustments with the iron poker. With a full glass of wine cosseted in his hand, he eased himself into one of the leather wing chairs and gave Amanda his full attention.

She noticed all of this without once taking her eyes away from her own reflection. The shock of glimpsing bare feet and bare chest through gaps in his robe was enough to send her hand groping for the brush again and enough to keep her brushing while she tried to regroup her scattered resolves.

When her arm began to ache and her hair was as shiny as she would ever live to see it, she stopped and began to tame the glossy mane into a single thick braid.

"I wish you wouldn't do that," he said quietly. "I have always thought it a waste to keep something so beautiful twisted in knots and imprisoned with pins and nets. In your case, a terrible waste. Please . . . leave it loose."

Amanda's hands faltered and slipped down to rest on her lap. She heard the leather creak softly as he stood, and she saw the shadows disturbed again as he came over to stand behind her.

"Well, Mrs. Tarrington? Your face is nearly raw from scrubbing, your hair"—his long fingers began to toy with a silky curl—"could not possibly want for more attention. I would say the time has come for you to . . . lay your cards on the table, so to speak?"

Amanda tensed herself against the steady rise of panic in her chest. Her pulse was racing and her heart was beating like a wild thing. All of her lofty determination fled as he buried his hand deeper into the blonde cloud and caressed the nape of her neck.

"Please," she whispered. "I . . . need time."

His hand paused, resting against her neck. "And I," he said evenly, "need you. I need you to prove to me that I haven't completely lost my mind. Call it a test of faith, if you like. Or a test of this code of honor you hold so dear. Call it your duty, or your obligation. Call it whatever you damn well please, just . . . don't make the mistake of thinking you can call my bluff. It was your choice, remember, to play the hand or fold.''

His eyes burned into hers, longer than she would have thought humanly possible without setting her aflame. Something odd flickered in the gray depths, a tension she had not seen before, a darkness she did not want to question . . . a warning she knew instinctively not to challenge.

All the same, she still had some vestiges of pride left—pride that made her lift her chin and square her shoulders. It brought her to her feet with the same resolute dignity she displayed as she brushed past him and walked over to the bed.

''In that case, sir, pray tell me where you would like me. On the left or the right?''

A muscle jumped in Tarrington's cheek. ''Wherever you are more comfortable, madam.''

Amanda shrugged and made for the left-hand side of the bed. She sat primly on the edge of the mattress and faced straight ahead, her eyes angled downward and fixed on the framed picture of Caleb where it lay on the open folds of her carpetbag. He seemed to be staring back at her, his face pale and rigid, stoically accepting the sacrifice she was about to make.

He had been so eager on their wedding night—eager and earnest and clumsy, struggling to temper his passion with the need to preserve and protect her modesty. Caleb had never challenged or defied her. He had never stood so boldly before her, his animal vitality throwing off enough heat to affect her breathing. He had never even come to her naked or given her more than a brief glimpse of his pale, wiry body.

Tarrington was all muscle, hard and sculpted. His robe was, she suspected, left purposefully loose and opened over the deep wedge of his chest so that she might have the opportunity to admire the wealth of bronzed skin and coarse dark hair. That he was naked beneath the blue silk robe, she had no doubt. He probably did not even own a nightshirt nor would he see any reason to wear one to preserve anyone's modesty, least of all hers.

He was only a dark blot at the edge of her vision. He still had not moved. He stood with his legs braced apart, his arms crossed over his chest, his imposing silhouette framed by the glare of the firelight behind him.

"So," he mused, "it is to be played out as the necessary evil, then? Something to be endured but—God forbid—never enjoyed."

"Enjoy? What in heaven's name is there to enjoy about two people fumbling around together in the dark?"

"Absolutely nothing, I suppose. If that is all they do."

"What else is there?"

The question appeared to amuse him, and he offered a husky laugh as he moved toward the bed. "Absolutely nothing . . . if you don't want there to be. Or if you have been told there wouldn't be—which should have been up to your first husband to prove or disprove."

She cast him a fulminating glare, one that held up even as he came within arm's reach. "Caleb was kind and sweet and gentle. He had no need to prove anything to me."

Tarrington laughed again. "My lovely innocent . . . who would have guessed?"

"Guessed what?" she demanded. "That I wouldn't crumble to my knees and beg you to be merciful and swift?"

"No," he drawled speculatively. "That the beautiful, icy, sensual queen of the Mississippi riverboats would look and act as frightened as a virgin staring down the throat—or should I say the breeches—of a Hun bent on rape and pillage."

Amanda's jaw clamped firmly around her indignation. "I should have expected you to be nothing less than vile and vulgar, Yankee."

"Whereas I expected you to be . . . shall we say, a tad more at ease with the physical aspects of marriage. You *have* been in a man's bed before, and you have been enthusiastic enough in your endeavors to have produced a child.''

Amanda lowered her eyes. ''One does not necessarily have to be enthusiastic to be successful in such things, only lucky. Or *unlucky*, as the case may be.''

''True enough,'' he agreed. ''But it can be a lot more fun if both parties are relaxed enough to cooperate with each other.''

''I *am* cooperating,'' she said through her teeth. ''What more would you have me do?''

''I might have you stand up, for a start,'' he said quietly. ''To begin on equal ground, so to speak. That way I wouldn't feel quite so much like the lecturing dean.''

Amanda only laced her hands tighter together on her lap. ''I prefer to remain seated, thank you.''

''Do you now? Very well.'' His hands moved to the knot of his belt and he had it unfastened before Amanda could anticipate the action. As determined as she was to keep her eyes averted and as thick as the shadows were, she caught a glimpse of naked thighs and a smooth, washboard-hard belly. She glimpsed something else as well, pale against the dark explosion of hair at the top of his thighs, and the sight sent her shooting to her feet with a small, airless gasp.

''Ahh,'' he murmured. ''The lecture endeth.''

Standing this close, it was difficult to ignore the sheer size of him. His wide shoulders seemed even wider against the backdrop of firelight, his arms filled the sleeves of his robe so that the silk did not simply hang there, it molded to the muscles with pride. It was difficult not to remember how it had felt to be held in those arms or crushed up against that chest. It was difficult, yet she was adamant about doing so, refusing to quail before him, refusing to fuel his humor at the expense of her own pride.

She drew a deep, determined breath. If he wanted the icy, sensual queen of the Mississippi, that was who he would get. It would be easier for her, in fact, to slip into the skin of Montana Rose and pretend this was all happening to someone else. It was how she had survived all those nights on the riverboats. It would be how she could survive this.

The change that came over her face was subtle and fascinating, and Tarrington realized at once what she was doing; it was like watching a chameleon slowly change colors to adapt to its surroundings. She was going to adapt, she was going to give him the performance she assumed he wanted. And so long as it *was* a performance, she would still feel safe and smug behind her righteousness.

He had not expected anger or vindictiveness to govern his actions this night, but both emotions were suddenly very much in play, a response to the cold wall of indifference she was building around herself. If anyone should have been balking against anything, it should have been him, for he had no idea what mad urge had brought him to this point. Married? He'd never even entertained the thought of an engagement before and had avoided all romantic entanglements like the plague. He had actually regarded it as an added bonus, being a detested Yankee in the heart of the South, knowing there would be no fear of ambush from keening mothers sharpening their claws to snare him for their desperate, grasping daughters.

Yet here he was, feeling his own claws starting to extend, married to a woman who was desperate to pretend she was someone else, grasping at any ploy that would enable her to imagine herself anywhere else than here with him.

"Look at me," he commanded softly.

The tawny wings of her lashes lifted slowly, her eyes wide and calm and very, very blue. He raised his hand and saw her brace herself for the contact, and in that moment he knew, with his ingrained aversion to defiance of any kind, that as soon as she thought to outmaneuver him with that I-dare-you-to-make-me-feel-anything look, there could be but one outcome. Up *until* that moment, he'd had every noble intention of letting her retire alone and undisturbed tonight. Until that moment he had been fully prepared to wait until they were both better adjusted to the circumstances.

"What do you suppose," he mused, "your Mr. Wainright would have done right about now?"

Her eyes showed a brief spark of wariness, but her mouth only pressed into a thinner, more mutinous line.

"A kiss, perhaps?"

Amanda felt his hand twine itself into the silky fall of her hair. There was no avoiding the warm, moist heat of his mouth, no ignoring the soft tickle of his mustache as his tongue trawled lazily across her lips, teasing and tasting until it sought an opening and insinuated itself inside.

Amanda stiffened against the slow, calculated plunder of her mouth. He tasted of red wine and tobacco, the same scents that flavored his breath where it blew warm and fragrant over her skin. After the kiss in the garden at Rosalie, Amanda was alarmingly aware of his skill at seducing a response from a mouth that had never experienced such a thorough and stimulating tryst before, but she had come through it once with her senses intact and she could do it again. *Know thine enemy* was a credo that would serve her well.

The kiss was long and leisurely, and Amanda was quite proud of herself when it ended and she was only slightly out of breath. She was still able to meet him eye to eye, still in full control and in full possession of all her wits. She was, in fact, the model of restraint, the queen of the river tolerating the foibles of an underling.

Tarrington's grin widened, and he said very slowly, very softly, "I don't think so, madam."

"You don't think . . . what? . . . Mr. Tarrington."

"I don't think"—he twisted his fingers deeper into her hair and lowered his mouth to within a heartbeat of hers—"you're as good an actress as *you* think you are."

Her eyes, so large and round in the whiteness of her face, looked up at him with the same bold challenge she had seduced him with on the deck of the *Mississippi Queen.* "What makes you so sure I am acting?"

"If I'm wrong, I'll apologize. If I'm right, you can stop me any time you want to concede the bluff."

Her attempt at a shrug was hampered by the presence of his body crowding against her. She raised her arms, just a little, to keep from tumbling over backward, and found the only thing she could grasp with impunity was the folds of brocaded silk that had swung open over his ribs. A very tiny, very insignificant shiver trickled down her spine in response to the sudden stillness in the air between them. It was the same stillness she remembered seeing and feeling in Caleb the few moments preceding the physical act of consummation, and the realization made her restless, in an odd, tight way, to get it over with.

Sliding her hand up the silk front of his robe, she rested it solicitously on his jaw and smiled. "Why don't you put out the lamps . . . while I get into bed."

She started to pull away, but the hand at the nape of her neck forbade it.

"Aren't you forgetting something?"

Her gaze fell briefly to where her fingers still rested against his jaw. She noted absently how warm he felt, how dark and abrasive the underlying stubble of his beard was despite the fact he had obviously taken the care to shave recently. Her hand looked small and delicate against his brooding masculinity, and she suffered through another sliver of sensation as it rolled icily down her back and swirled around the base of her spine.

She lowered her hand so she could think clearly, and frowned. "I can't imagine what."

"You're forgetting . . . I don't like to see beautiful things covered up."

It took a long moment of staring at his mouth, of absorbing the sound of his voice and the motion of his lips beneath the mustache, for her to comprehend his meaning. It took even longer for her eyes to make the near-impossible climb back up to his, and a further small eternity to mount a defense against the instant and violent rush of color that flooded her cheeks.

"Are you suggesting . . . ?"

The question was cut short on a gasp as she felt his hand

shift from her nape to the row of tiny enameled buttons that ran from the collar of her nightdress to the waist. She froze for as long as it took him to unfasten the top three buttons, but when he started impudently on the fourth, her hand flew up to block his way.

"A gentleman would hardly insist . . . or even expect . . ."

"Coward," he interrupted silkily, quietly. "I didn't expect you to fold so easily. As for my being a gentleman, I was not aware I had been elevated from the ranks of the vile and vulgar."

Amanda's breath left her lungs in a gust. If he thought *for one minute* he was going to use her own words to mock her, he truly was a man beyond all recognizable scruples and conscience.

Pride, hot and fierce, made her push his hand away. It made her jerk the rest of the buttons free, one by one, until the flannel gaped open and trembled visibly with the strength of her anger. Without further ado—or a thought to the consequences—she slipped the gown off her shoulders, letting it crumple unhampered into a soft white puddle around her ankles.

It was worth it, briefly, to see the muscle shiver in his cheek and to know she had taken him by surprise. It was not worth it, not by any measure of pride or sanity or logic, to see the sudden tension ripple through his body, rousing flesh that had, until her misguidedly flaunted insolence, been content with subtle stirrings of interest. There was nothing subtle in the swift, hard rise. Nothing comforting or vaguely reminiscent of any past experiences she could draw upon for comparison. She dared not look down to confirm her shock, but she could feel the enormity of his arousal stretching heatedly across the narrow space that separated them, pulsating with the same ferocity as the thick blue veins that swelled and throbbed in his throat.

And there she stood like a sacrifice before a pagan god, all pale flesh and gleaming gold hair. Opulent curves and elusive shadows enticed his gaze downward, and she felt its heat

scalding her everywhere, opening reservoirs of shame and
spilling the effects across her skin, into her limbs. Her flesh
seemed to shrink on the bones, so tight and hot in places she
felt as if she had caught fire. The focus of her attention—and
his—was also the most intemperate. Jutting from her breasts
like accusing, pointing fingers, her nipples blushed as dark as
her cheeks, turning raspberry red and gathering into tautly
crinkled peaks.

A victim of few surprises, Michael Tarrington had considered himself well beyond discovering anything new or exciting about the female form. He had found pleasure in all
shapes and sizes, all the varying shades from darkest ebony
to palest white, and none had been remembered vividly
enough to leave a lasting imprint on his mind. Not until now.
Now he found himself staring like a fledgling voyeur, wondering if he had ever even dreamed of possessing something
so perfect, so lush, so exquisitely beautiful. And it came as
another unpleasant shock to identify the sensations he was
feeling. His blood thundered in his ears and his arms had to
fight against the tremors that would have sent his hands
reaching greedily out toward her. It was lust, in its most pure
and primitive form, and it was to his credit—and his increasing torment—that he refrained from simply pushing her
down on the bed and taking what he wanted without any
further effort or preamble wasted on the finesse of seduction.

What stopped him was the obvious distress on his wife's
face. She was no longer tense and trembling with anger, but
with fear. Her lips were parted over shallow, rapid breaths,
and her eyes swam with emotions that were unnerving in
their intensity. He remembered then the scorn and derision in
her voice when she had challenged him to tell her what was
enjoyable about two people "fumbling around together in the
dark," and he wondered if her first husband had been so
thoughtless, so inept, so *gentlemanly* he had taken this mag-
nificently sensual beauty into his bed and left her wanting for
no better description than "fumbling"?

Some of the savage beating in his blood waned—not all,
but some. The harsh light went out of his eyes and a more

thoughtful look came over his face as he cradled her chin in his hand and tilted her face up to his. Her hair floated around her shoulders, a thick and glossy contrast to the translucent white of her skin. The flush was still high in her cheeks, dusting them pink, drawing his eyes to the full pout of her mouth, even pinker from the lengthy excess of his first kiss.

He brushed the backs of his fingers across her blush and it was warm to the touch. The heat followed his fingertips as they traced a path from her chin to the pulsing vein in the hollow of her throat. Every nerve in her body was stretched and humming; he could feel it and see it in the shivers that grew pronounced enough to make her sway lightly where she stood. His fingers moved again, draining the heat and color out of her throat as it followed his touch downward onto the smooth rise of her breast.

Her lips parted wider and his mouth was there to capture her gasp. He claimed possession again, his tongue dancing with hers long enough to gentle the new suffusion of fears that shivered through her body. His arm curled around her waist, drawing her closer; his hand curved around her breast and he filled his palm with her softness. He abandoned the wet heat of her mouth and began a slow, deliberate assault on the tender underside of her chin, roving all the way to the dainty curl of her ear and back again, recapturing her mouth for a brief prowl around the sleek, slippery surfaces, only to break away and rove elsewhere.

Amanda fought to maintain command of her senses but his mouth was suddenly everywhere, startling in its ability to find a weakness and lavish it with enough attention to destroy any resistance. His kisses were long and deep and breathtaking, and her efforts to try to ignore what he was doing only made her more keenly aware of his every soft, insinuating caress. His hand was still around her breast. It had not moved, but by the very act of quiescence, it made her wary of where his mouth would rove next. With stunning audacity, he confirmed her fears, bowing his head and taking the nipple into his mouth. He rolled it with just the tip of his tongue first, so lightly it was no more than a delicate tease. And then the force was harder, the suction rousing a strange, stormy intoxication in her blood that had nothing to do with the wine she had consumed. She was compelled to offer a sigh of approbation. But also to rake her fingers into the thick waves of chestnut hair to ensure he did not cease what he was doing any too soon.

With his mouth outrageously overfilled with her flesh, his hand moved restlessly downward, exploring, stroking, skimming curves and crevices where there might be some hidden sensation not yet unleashed. She balked at the first feather-like touch he passed over her thighs, but he easily defeated her efforts to bar his way. He lavished her breasts, her mouth, her throat, her temples with more kisses, leaving her half dazed and without the will or wit to deny the long, deftly skilled fingers anything.

He breached the thatch of pale-yellow curls with a single-mindedness that had her turning her head into the arch of his shoulder, shielding her mortification in the bright cloud of her own hair. She could feel an alarming wetness on his fingers as they slid back and forth between the silky folds of flesh, but the discovery only seemed to make him bolder. He slipped a finger deep inside her, and it was his groan this time that challenged the silence between them, his arms that started to tremble with anticipation. She clenched her thighs around his hand and melted under his expert tutelage. She shimmered and glowed and throbbed with a growing urgency that, in less time than her battered modesty could accept, had her clutching at each wickedly deliberate flutter, gasping with each shocking incursion as the pleasure began to peal and peak within her.

He exploited every little shiver and contraction. Her body was set, tense, vibrating with a dark desire that sent her hands clawing around his shoulders and her nails digging into his flesh.

"Stop!" she gasped. "Please . . . stop!"

The muscles in his arms went rigid in response to her plea. His fingers grew still but he kept them buried inside her, feeling the distinct, definitive pulsations that constricted her flesh and made his own rear with impatience.

"Please," she said, her voice a mere thread of a whisper. "I can't breathe. I . . . can't *breathe*!"

Tarrington's frown relaxed and he withdrew his dampened fingers. He let them drift slowly back up and around the curve of her hip, retracing the path he had taken downward until he once again cradled the luxuriant heaviness of her breast. There he dragged his thumb across the pebble-hard nipple and drew a soft moan from her throat, the sound as helplessly disbelieving as the shivers that brought her arms circling even tighter around his neck.

His hands slid down and pushed aside the silk edges of his robe, leaving nothing between their two bodies but the heated promise of flesh against flesh. Her face was still buried against his throat, but she did not try to bar his way this time when he coaxed her thighs apart and eased himself between them.

"Breathing is nice," he murmured. "But I give you my word . . . this is nicer."

Amanda's mouth slackened and her hands balled into fists. He shifted his weight slightly, angling himself up and into the sleek, quivering passage, waiting until he felt the gusting of her breath on his throat before he picked her up in his arms and, in one smooth motion, lowered her onto the bed and sank between her thighs.

Amanda's head arched back into the bedding as she felt herself being filled, impaled, stretched to the very limit of sensibility. Indeed, she was no virgin but this . . . this enormous intrusion of hard flesh was not like anything she had borne before, and it seemed inconceivable to think she could accommodate all of him. In desperation, she dug her heels into hillocks of feather ticking and tried to push herself away, to keep some small part of her from being overwhelmed. Yet he kept pushing forward, kept furrowing into her, swelling and straining against the tight walls of her sheath until the inability to breathe did, indeed, become the least of her concerns.

She had not seen him cast aside the silk robe, but it was gone. His shoulders, his arms, the great slabs of muscle across his back gleamed in the firelight, rippled with the motion of his hands, his hips, his bowed and questing lips. His breath was hot in her ear, inflaming her senses. Words were there too, blurred and distorted, without substance for the most part, intended only to reassure her, to promise her he would wait. Not too long, he rasped shakily, but he could wait.

Wait for what?

The answer came when he raised his hips and rolled them slowly forward again. Warm and thick and smooth, his flesh slid against nerve endings that were already raw and runny with impatience. A low, ragged groan welcomed his heat in the deepest part of her, and she felt the first bright shiver of ecstasy grip her, shock her into clutching at his waist. He drew back and thrust again . . . and again . . . each stroke causing her body to gather tighter around him. A lush, rich torrent of pleasure began to flow from her toes to her fingertips, curling the one and flinging the other down to ride the increasingly forceful rise and fall of his hips.

The soft pelt on his chest teased her breasts, chafing her skin with the same heady friction as the coarser, darker hairs on his thighs. There was not one single part of her body that was not acutely aware of his strength, his power, his presence. He held her tight, and she felt the driving shock of his need. Deeper and still deeper he thrust until the pleasure swelled and burst within her, swelled again and shook her body with such stunning intensity, it shattered every notion of ecstasy she had known before.

It shattered all of Tarrington's noble intentions as well, and he reared above her one last time, his head flung back, his body held in her pulsing, convulsive grip. The pressure flooded out of him in great throbbing waves that sent him half out of his skin, and he was only dimly aware of Amanda's cry as she tensed beneath him again and strained into the throes of another resplendent orgasm.

A final, harsh groan brought Tarrington's heat back into

her arms, his big body quaking and trembling, his lips pressing each labored breath into the damp curve of her shoulder.

Amanda lay beneath him, perfectly still but for the frantic pounding of her heart. She welcomed the heaviness and the solid reality of his body crowding over hers again, for she needed something to keep her from floating away. The incredible pressure inside her was waning, the tension gone, but his flesh was still very real and very much a formidable presence, thudding with slow, measured beats that filled her with yet another new and unsettling sense of awe.

She relaxed the deathlike grip of her hands where they were still molded to his buttocks, and she eased her limbs slowly down from where they had somehow become twined around his waist. She curled her lip between her teeth when she felt him shift his weight and waited for him to lift his dark head from where it rested on her shoulder.

Closing her eyes, she braced herself, for he would surely not pass up such a fine opportunity to laugh at her. She wouldn't be able to blame him, of course. She had taunted and challenged and defied him. She had mocked his suggestion that there could be anything pleasurable between a man and woman in bed, and he had proved her desperately wrong. So wrong, in fact, her body shivered under an icy spray of pleasure when she felt his mustache tickle the lobe of her ear.

"Well," he murmured softly. And then again, just "Well."

It was almost another full minute before he propped himself on his elbows above her, his silvery gray eyes glowing out of the darkness. Amanda's cheeks flushed with the further realization of how truly, shockingly handsome he was, especially with his hair shaggy and disheveled, and the firelight gilding the bulge of muscles on his arms and torso.

He touched a fingertip to her cheek, brushing away a thread of gold hair. He ran the same fingertip thoughtfully across the fullness of her lower lip before kissing the tip of her nose and nuzzling his way back down onto the fragrant pillow of her hair.

"You are trembling, Mrs. Tarrington," he murmured. "Do I still frighten you?"

She was surprised by the tenderness in his voice, startled by the hard curl of pleasure that rippled through her body in response.

"I wasn't frightened. I was merely . . ."

His head came up again, bringing a fine web of clinging gold hairs with him. One dark wing of an eyebrow was crooked upward over a look that was half curious, half bemused, wholly prepared to disprove whatever she was about to say by whatever means were necessary.

". . . terrified," she finished on a breath.

He studied her a moment longer then smiled in a way that made her wonder about the stern and cynical exterior he presented to the world.

"And do I still terrify you?"

"No. Yes. I . . . don't know."

He stared at her intently for as long as it took to send her lashes wilting down over her eyes again.

"An honest answer, anyway," he mused.

"Will you be equally honest with me?" she asked quietly.

"If I can."

"Would you really have turned around and taken me home tonight if I'd asked you to?"

For all of two heartbeats, she thought he wasn't going to answer at all; then, when she looked up at him again and acknowledged the slow thickening she felt inside her, he whispered, "I don't know. I honestly do not know."

Chapter 14

A manda did not know what time it was. And it took a full
minute of concentrated effort to pinpoint what had wakened her. She was lying on her stomach—sprawled, more
like it—one leg covered, one folded over the rumple of
sheets and blankets. Her head was where her feet should
have been and there were pillows everywhere but under her
head.

She pushed back the thick veil of tumbled hair that was
restricting her view and cautiously looked around. She was
alone in the huge bed, alone in the cavernous room. The fire
was a smoldering pile of gray embers nestled around the
charred skeleton of a log. An empty wine bottle was on the
hearth beside two glasses—one of them tipped on its side.
The sight of two more feather pillows lying alongside the
bottle and glasses sent Amanda sinking back into the tangled
crush of her hair, her fingers pressed over her lips, her eyes
tightly shut against the images flooding back into her mind.

It wasn't possible. It wasn't conceivable that she had done
the things she had done last night. On the bed, on the floor in
front of the fire . . . on the chair, for pity's sake . . .

Far from the swift and perfunctory introduction to his bed
that Amanda had anticipated, Michael Tarrington had taken
devious pains to ensure she would not be left with the impression he was either swift or perfunctory. Or in any way
resigned to accepting half measures. He had not been satisfied with anything less than total exhaustion on both their
parts and total collapse on hers.

Amanda felt a smile pulling at her mouth and tried in vain
to smother it. Her lips were still swollen and sensitive, and
she recalled complaining at one point about the roughness of
his mustache. If she didn't like him kissing her on the mouth
anymore, he had declared, he would just have to kiss her

elsewhere. And all of the various elsewheres he had found had proven not to mind the rugged abrasion at all.

She stretched luxuriantly and rolled onto her back, acutely aware of the bevy of pleasant new aches that made their presence known almost everywhere in her body. She felt soft and glowing inside, tingling and sensitive on the outside. The simple act of stirring beneath the covers made her nipples stand erect and the flesh between her thighs sulk with regret that she had wakened alone.

Where was he?

Nothing of Michael Tarrington's behavior thus far suggested he conformed to anyone's idea of what should or should not be expected from him, yet it was, after all, their first morning—afternoon?—together as man and wife, not to mention her first day as mistress in a new house. One would have thought he would have been there to make the transition easier.

Amanda reached out and touched the depression in the feather mattress where his big body should have lain. There wasn't a hint of the immense heat she had grown so familiar with so quickly. There was only the volcanic disarray of bedding and the musky, earthy scent of long, lush hours of lovemaking.

She gathered up the top blanket and started to wrap it toga-style around her nakedness. At some point during the night her nightgown had been added as fuel to the fire—it had been her halfhearted efforts to rescue it that had created the scene in front of the hearth. It left her nothing to wear, however, and she wondered absently what she would do if Mrs. Reeves had felt the same contempt for her dress and petticoats.

Her first attempt to stand brought her heavily down again as the sheets tangled around her legs. That and the fact that her knees felt as wobbly as a marionette left her sitting and frowning at the edge of the bed for several minutes.

It was while she was contemplating the pattern on the rugs and the sorry state of her own moral decline that she again heard the dull thumping that had originally awakened her.

The sound seemed to be coming from outside, and, with renewed determination, she walked to one of the double panels of heavy blue velvet curtains and pushed it aside.

What she saw made her gasp.

The curtains concealed a deep alcove, complete with a small kneehole writing desk and chair, an ornate brass lamp, and a wide window seat padded with fat cushions covered in the same plush velvet as the draperies. The windows stretched from knee to ceiling height, the panes built to fit the octagonal shape of the alcove, and divided into myriad squares of leaded glass that absorbed and refracted the rays of the sun like crystal prisms.

Amanda stepped delightedly into the self-contained well of sunlight and heat, deciding instantly it could become one of her favorite places. The view from the window seat was magnificent. The alcove overlooked acres of rolling green lawns and landscaped beds of roses, shrubs, and hedges of oleander. The courtyard was off to the left, ringed by a half circle of stables and carriage bays that had recently been repaired and whitewashed—so recently there were signs the painting and repairs were still in progress.

According to Ryan, the Glen had been in need of more than just whitewash on the outbuildings. Michael Tarrington must have had a small army working here these past few weeks to have accomplished so much in so little time. And the cost!

A small shiver raced up her spine and she remembered the night on board the *Mississippi Queen*. He had taken hundred-dollar bills out of his wallet and gambled them away without a blink or a qualm. Exactly how wealthy was he? And how had he come by all his riches? Was it family money? Shrewd business dealings? Speculation? *War profiteering?*

Before she could put him in horns and forked tail again, Amanda was distracted by a fresh volley of muted thumping. Off to the right was a formal terrace enclosed by walls of tall shrubbery and a stone balustrade. The latter was also under repair, and, as she watched, a badly broken pillar was being chipped away completely, hammered into small chunks by a man wielding a large iron maul. He was thin and bony in appearance. His sleeves were rolled above the elbows and the sweat poured off his temples, soaking dark patches across his shoulders and down the back of his shirt. His face was not familiar—there was no reason it should be—but Amanda was treated to an unobstructed view of it when he stopped to wipe the greasy strands of hair out of his eyes and looked directly up at the bedroom window.

Narrow and pockmarked, it was an unremarkable face for the most part. His nose had been badly broken some time in the past and listed to one side. The scraggly tufts of brownish hair that grew on his chin were, she suspected, the best he could probably do by way of a beard. His clothes were ill-fitting, the trousers too loose, the shirt too tight, and as he raised his hand to push his hair out of his eyes again, she saw that two fingers were missing and a third was badly mis-shapen. His teeth were all there, however. Short and stubby, but white enough to show in a leering grin.

She stepped quickly back from the padded ledge, but not before she had given the workman a fetching view of bare shoulders and tousled blonde hair. She retreated farther, hastily drawing the curtains closed behind her and cocooning herself in the cool shadows of the main salon again.

Where was Michael Tarrington?

Where were her clothes?

Dragging the sheets behind her like Lady Muck, Amanda went in search of her carpetbag, thinking she could at least don a shred of dignity by way of her underclothing.

Her bag was gone.

A frantic heartbeat almost made her miss the daguerreotype, bonnet, and prayer book that had been carefully placed on the nightstand. But the bag, along with her meager assortment of linens, was nowhere to be seen.

Had Mrs. Reeves paid her a visit while she slept?

"Oh . . . God." Amanda groaned and bowed her head, shaking it in chagrin. If the housekeeper had come into the room, she had no doubt left it again in shock and indignation. And if Amanda needed any proof of what Mrs. Reeves would have seen, the image reflected in the cheval mirror confirmed it. She looked debauched. Thoroughly, sinfully, wildly debauched.

Where was the man who had left her this way?

With the inner glow rapidly fading, Amanda tried the door to the dressing room. It opened easily enough—small relief to find she had not been locked away for the moral safety of the rest of the household. The bathtub was empty. A pitcher on the washstand held water, and there were fresh towels folded over the harp-back. Beside it, hanging where she could not possibly help but see it, was a frock of cornflower blue muslin, and below it, arranged in neatly folded piles, were new underpinnings: chemise, drawers, stockings, petticoats, corset, and corset cover, all made from the softest, richest foulards and silks, edged in the most delicate lace she had seen in years. Even her ruined shoes had magically disappeared and in their place, delicately cross-laced slippers in soft morocco leather.

Amanda bit her lip and glanced back into the bedroom, but there were no answers there. She tested the doorknob at the other end of the dressing room, but it only revealed a second, much smaller bedroom, empty of any furniture save for a small cot and curtains.

She closed the door again and stared at the clothes. Her hand went out of its own accord and touched the silk chemise. Not even Montana Rose had worn such finery. The silk was so slippery and sheer, it made her blush to think of it next to her skin.

Having little choice between the toga and the muslin, she shed the one and, after washing away the last trace of any lingering glow, she stepped shiveringly into the layers of silk and foulard. She paused after each addition to inspect herself in the mirror, wondering again just how experienced a man her husband was to have estimated her sizes so precisely.

Even guessing at the answer, she was hard-pressed to keep at least a partial glow from returning when she twirled, fully clothed, in front of the mirror. The muslin was the exact shade of her eyes, the style coming surely out of the most recent pattern books, with delicate concertina pleats concealing the front closure. The waist was cut trim enough to make her thankful she'd had a sparse diet these past few months. The sleeves were fitted to the elbow then flared into a gracefully soft bell, edged in lace and banded in a froth of thin blue satin ribbons. There were more ribbons tied in clusters on each of the four scalloped tiers of the skirt, and at the center of each cluster, a perfect pink silk rosebud.

Her hair was the last thing she tackled. There were no pins or combs with which to subdue it properly, but, after recalling her husband's opinion of trapped, confined hair, she settled for purloining a bit of ribbon off one of the flounces and tying the yellow mane loosely at the nape of her neck.

Another slow pirouette in front of the mirror and she was satisfied. Even Alisha would have been bottle green with envy.

Amanda stopped twirling and stared at her reflection.

Alisha had made it painfully clear she had married Karl von Helmstaad just so she could have all of these things—the fine clothes, the grand house, the wealth to support her every whim. Amanda had never aspired to anything of the sort for herself. She would have been content with a roof over her head and a taste of real meat once in a while. She certainly never expected to marry a man like Michael Tarrington: a Yankee, a gambler, a handsome rogue she had seen a total of *three* times before they were wed; a man she knew absolutely nothing about, but one who already knew some of her deepest, darkest secrets.

Cool, level-headed, practical Amanda Courtland Jackson, the serene and devoted widow of a Confederate hero—eloped and wed to a Yankee scalawag in less time than it had taken Alisha to choose a trousseau. She did not even want to think of the stories that would fly around Natchez. She wasn't the first to succumb to the lure of Yankee money and protection, for plenty of other families had been driven to make such desperate sacrifices just to keep food on the table.

A noble sacrifice was one thing. Complete loss of credibility was another. It was probably not as complete as if she had married Forrest Wainright, but the repercussions were bound to make her the fodder of Natchez gossips for months to come.

After a last glance around the bedroom, she ventured out into the hallway. It was as quiet and tomblike as she had last seen it, almost as gloomy with the two windows at either end of the hall so far apart that what little sunlight did come through the swagged curtains was diffused long before it met the middle. Once again she was struck by the enormity of what she had done. Briar Glen, with its stately elegance, its rich history, and haunting grace, was now her home. She, not Emma Porterfield, was its mistress. And her name was no longer Mrs. Caleb Jackson; it was Tarrington. Mrs. Michael Tarrington.

"Mrs. Tarrington. There ye are. I was beginnin' to wonder if I should venture up an' check ye fer a heartbeat."

Mrs. Reeves was standing at the bottom of the grand staircase, her eyes twinkling on the strength of her own humor.

"Slept well, did ye? Nay thanks to that man o' yourn, I vow. Made enough clatter this mornin' to roust the deid, he did. Orthers flyin' here an' there—gi' us this, gi' us that; have this ready, have that cooked *in case,* mind, just *in case* a body might have want o' it. Left strict orthers ye were not to be distairbed, he did. It weren't that sop-eared son-in-law o' mines what woke ye, was it? I told him not to go bangin' and thrumpin' outside Mister Michael's windy, but then Ned Sims never takes heed o' a word I say anyroad. Still, I'll skin his scrawny hide an' take a deal o' pleasure doin' it, ye say it were him what woke ye."

"No. Please, Mrs. Reeves," Amanda said quickly, believing the crusty Scotswoman was more than capable of carrying out her threat. "It wasn't anyone's fault. It was high time I was awake anyway."

"Aye, ye'll hear nay argument from me. Ye ken breakfast is long gone. Dinner's about spoilt an' all, with me not knowin' the wherewithals of who's gonny eat what when. He gave me nay real warnin' ye were comin' an' there was no time to fetch everything he orthered—an' that were assumin' ye had a taste fer any o' the things he's left orthers fer me to fix.''

"I . . . didn't expect anyone to go to any trouble—''

"Trouble's done already," Mrs. Reeves announced flatly. "So we'll just have to make the best o' it." She eyed Amanda closely as she descended the last few steps. "Aye, ma Sally did right by ye. Michael said as how ye were about the same size as his sister Meg, then he sent ma daughter Sal out wi' a shopping list the length o' ma airm. Near wore her feet to the bone, she did, goin' from shop to shop. If ye dinna like what she fotched, ye can blame him. He give her all the orthers, right doon to the color o' ribbons on the shimmy.''

Amanda smoothed her hand self-consciously down the pleated bodice. "Everything . . . the dress . . . everything is wonderful, Mrs. Reeves. And I am sorry to be the cause of so much bother. I had no idea . . . I mean, I did not plan on everything happening so quickly or so . . . unexpectedly.''

"Aye, well, that's the kind o' man ye married, hen. Best ye get used to feathers flyin' every which way every time he blows in off the river. Still an' all." She stalled and seemed to lose some of her steam. "He should have told me sooner, is all. Changed his dresses when he was a bairn, I did. Raised him like he were one o' ma own, an' here he didna even let on he were courtin'. No' a breath, no' a whisper. Oh, aye, he took a lot o' trips doon the river, but he never said as how he were come here to see anyone special. Said as how he were come to look fer a hame fer his wee babbies. *Pfaugh!* Next we know, he's up an' bought this great hulkin' thing an' sent hame fer all his trappin's. Says he were surprised to see me step off the boat? Aye, well, I were so surprised to see what like this place was—an' him barely able to keep a sea chest packed proper—ma bowels missed the basin twice in the one day!''

Amanda, struggling valiantly to keep pace with the thick brogue, did not know whether to laugh or cry. "I promise, Mrs. Reeves, there will be no more surprises.''

"Aye, well." The housekeeper glared pointedly at her new mistress's trim waistline and snorted. "I'd be a rare, ripe old cow an' I believed that one, hen. When's the babby comin'?"

"I . . . beg your pardon?"

"The babby. The bairn. When is she comin'? Did he no' tell me ye had a wee daughter? Purrity?"

"Verity," Amanda said on a breath.

"Vurrity?"

"Verity, yes. It's . . . a family name. On my mother's side."

"Aye, well, he thought as how ye might like to put her in the room next to yourn, but ye'll have tae check the list he gave me o' what ye want aside a cot an' a lavvy. Ma Sally's in a fair swoon about a child comin' to live here. Loves them better than she loves life itsel', she does. Miscarried her own, though, an' tore up so bad it disny look like the Laird is gonny gi' her anither chance."

"I'm . . . so sorry."

"Aye, me an' all. But she's a good wee lass wi' bairns. Ye'll now't find anyone better to look after yer Vurrity, black nor white."

It came as a mild surprise to Amanda to realize Mrs. Reeves was every bit as nervous as she was, worried perhaps, her Mister Michael had married a high-nosed Southern belle who might look down with scorn upon a Scottish housekeeper and her barren daughter.

"Mrs. Reeves—" She laid her hand on the elderly woman's arm and found it stronger than she supposed. "My daughter is very shy and she may take awhile to adapt to her new surroundings, but I'm sure she and Sally will get along just fine."

"She's comin' soon, then?"

Being asked by eyes as bright and eager as Mrs. Reeves's, Amanda doubted Sally was the only one excited at the prospect of a child in the house. Relief made her smile openly for the first time in too many days to recall. "As soon as I can fetch her."

"Aye." Mrs. Reeves nodded brusquely, all smiles herself. "Aye, come along then. I'd best be fixin' ye somethin' to tide ye over till Himself comes back, or he'll be thinkin' he's found an excuse to pack me on the fairst ship back to Boston."

Amanda started to follow her down the hall. "You said he left early this morning?"

"Aye. Gone down to the docks to meet his own babbies. Foley said as how he'd go down an' fetch them, but Mister Michael said no. He'd be goin' too."

Amanda stopped abruptly. And stared. "His own . . . babies?"

"Aye. His babbies. Disny trust anyone else to look after them, although Foley's been wi' him . . . ach . . . ten years now, through the war an' all, on the frigates an' the iron monsters both even though he puked his guts o'er the rails every ither day. Nay, Mister Michael tends his babbies himself. Feeds 'em, mucks 'em, even helps wi' the birthin' when it comes time." She bustled into a large airy room off the main foyer and stood aside to wait for Amanda to catch up. "Canny say as I like the wee beasties maself. Never saw the need fer a horse beneath me while I still had the use o' ma own two legs. But he took a likin' to them, oh, ten years gone—bettin' on 'em mostly, o' course. Now he has it in his brain he can bet on his own. That's why he bought this place, so he says. To give 'em enough room to stretch out proper."

"Horses? His . . . babies . . . are horses?"

Mrs. Reeves grimaced. "A whole flock o' them, hen. Big thunderin' things too. They come trompin' past the house 'bout an hour ago an' kicked up enough dust to choke the Laird Himself up in heaven. Now then, Mister Michael has been takin' his meals in here, no' as I can find fault wi' that. The dinin' room proper would fair swally up a man even the size o' him. But I can take ye around fer a look-see yerself, if ye've a mind to change things."

Amanda was still stalled on the fact that she hadn't even known enough about her new husband to realize Michael

Tarrington raised racehorses. It was all Ryan would need to hear to drive the final nail in her coffin.

"Thank you, Mrs. Reeves," she murmured. "This is fine."

"Flora, hen. Just call me Flora." She bustled back out the door, her starched petticoats rustling with efficiency. "Make yerself to hame an' I'll see what I can find in the pantry to tide ye over."

Amanda nodded and sighed when she was finally alone. The "small" dining room was still twice the size of Rosalie's, with wide, tall windows spanning the length of one full wall. The cherrywood table was long and solidly built, gleaming under several layers of beeswax. A fire crackled cheerfully at one end, at the other, an enormous sideboard stood waiting with half a dozen silver chafing dishes and serving spoons, all polished to mirror brightness.

She crossed over to the wall of windows and looked out over a rose garden. She was glad, suddenly, that a Yankee major had taken a fancy to Briar Glen. There was damage, certainly, for she had seen the burned remains of the slave quarters from the bedroom window, and most of the surrounding trees had been summarily chopped down for firewood by the bivouacked soldiers. The gardens had been trampled and were overrun by weeds, the avenue rutted by heavy wagons and cannon undercarriages. The Roman statues were all but destroyed, and someone had decided the reflecting pool made a good repository for garbage and waste, but all things considered, the Glen had fared better than most.

Mrs. Reeves returned a moment later carrying a tray weighed down with enough fresh-baked bread, butter, and cold sliced meat to feed a score of ravenous field hands.

"Just a wee snack," Flora assured her. "To tide ye over. Sal's bringin' the tea, hot an' strong, an' flavored with a wee bit o' chamomile to put some color in yer cheeks."

She set the tray down and stood with her hands on her hips. "Dinna take ma meanin' the wrong way, now. 'Tis is a grand old house, to be sure, but it's no' what I expected

Himself to be wantin' to tie himself down to. Especially wi' all these big, empty rooms. Too temptin, ye ask me. Mark my words, ye'll have each an' every one o' them gagglin' sisters o' his swoopin' down on ye an' fillin' em afore ye know it. N'owt that they're a bad lot, mind. Just too many o' them wi' their own opinions, all o' them different an' none o' them willin' to bend one way or t'other. They'll be fair sweatin' themselves raw wi' curiosity to see the lassie who finally managed to squeeze a wedding vow out o' their brither's mouth. His mam an' da willny be too far behind either—that is, if they can get it past their gullets he's gone an' married against his own kind. His father were a close friend o' Lincoln's, wouldn't ye know, an' dead set against slave owners o' any kind.''

She saw what little color there was drain from Amanda's face and rushed to correct the impression she had given. ''Ach, dinna fret yoursel' too much, hen. They'll come around soon enough. They'll like you too, once we fatten ye up a little an' teach ye to bring up that smile more often. Lovely thing it was. Lights up yer whole face, did ye know? Aye, an' a pretty pink bloom in yer cheeks when ye ken I'm speakin' out o' turn. I'll be doin' that a lot, ye know,'' she warned sternly. ''I'm no one to keep ma thoughts to maself, nor one to soften ma words when I think a harder one is needed.''

Amanda had guessed that much already. ''You've been with the Tarringtons a long time?''

''Weel, now . . . Mister Michael is thirty an' two, an' I were there at his birthin'. That came two years after his mam an' da were wed, an' I were there to watch them vows too. Only peeped from the kitchen, mind, since I started in the household as a skullery maid—turrible job it was too, but the best I could find fresh off the ship from Glasgow. He were a sickly wee thing when he were born, though ye wouldn't guess it now to look at him. Puked all the time. Couldna take his mam's milk, ye see, an' by the time the bluidy doctors figured that out, he was near gone from starvation. I'd just given birth maself—to the fairst o' eight bairns o' ma own—

an' I crept up from the skullery one day on account o' I couldna bear to hear the wee thing cryin' any more. Aye, well, the long an' short o' it was, he took to ma teat like a leech ta raw meat. Sucked me dry, he did, an' kept it all down, every last drop. Crept up to him three days in a row afore his da caught me. Big bluidy bastard he is, too. Dark as the devil an' twice as ornery when he's riled. I tell ye, I nearly fouled ma britches then an' there when I saw him standin' in the shadows. That's all he were doin'—just standin' there, watchin' me feed his son.

"He didna stop me, though, an' when I were finished an' the babe blew wind an' nothin' more, he came up to me an' took ma hands in his—" Flora paused and held out her hands as if the deed was still a momentous event in her mind. "An' stab me in the heart if he wisna weepin'. He couldna talk, he could just weep an' nod his head, an' squeeze ma hands so tight I thought ma toes would lift off the ground.

"I were his nurse from that day on," she finished proudly. "I've thought o' him as ma own flesh an' blood since then too, which is why I'm here, seein' he disny get into more trouble than he's in already."

Flora made it sound as if most of the damage had been done and the culprit was standing there in front of her.

"Ach, there ye go, risin' up all red an' hot again," the housekeeper scolded gently. "Ye're gonny have to learn to take what I say wi' a grain o' salt, lovey, or I'm fair gonny take advantage. I wasn't meanin' to say *ye* were any kind o' trouble at all; just that he manages to find it quicker than any ither man I know. Like as one o' them magnet things. Trouble just comes to him—or he goes to it, I dinna rightly know which. Ach—" She stopped and tilted her head to one side as the sound of knocking echoed down the hall. "Now who could that be poundin' on the door like a banshee? Like as not it's that worthless snot o' a son-in-law o' mines tellin' me he's out o' this or out o' that an' canny work another hour without what he needs. What Ned Sims needs," she grumbled on her way out of the room, "is a braw clout on the head now an' then."

Amanda sank down onto one of the shield-back chairs, not quite sure what to make of Mrs. Flora Reeves. She was exhausting to keep up with mentally, that much was for certain. And she suspected a good deal of the spit and polish Briar Glen had recently acquired could be attributed directly to the feisty housekeeper.

"Beggin' pardon—" Flora was back a few minutes later. "There's a man at the door askin' to see Mr. or Mrs. Tarrington. I've put him in the study."

Amanda blinked stupidly for a moment. Then she realized, of course, that *she* was Mrs. Tarrington and would be expected to respond to such requests.

"The thing o' it is," Flora continued, halting Amanda halfway to her feet. "He wouldna gi' a Christian name an' he disny look the sort to be one o' Mister Michael's close friends." She paused heavily and lowered her voice as if she were speaking to a slow-witted child. "Would there be anyone else knowin' he has himself a new wife this mornin'?"

Amanda couldn't think of a single solitary soul . . . except for the Reverend Jeffries. And why would he have hastened here from Jamestown . . . unless it was to tell them there was something amiss with the marriage ceremony. That they weren't really married. That she had spent the night in a man's bed without the sanction of the law or the church!

"Should I send to the stables for Mister Michael?"

Amanda blinked again. And shook herself for her own foolishness. It was probably nothing more ominous than a peddlar, or a local merchant who had heard of the repairs taking place at Briar Glen and merely assumed the new owner had a wife. No doubt it was as simple as that, and if so, how could she expect to cope with the more weighty matters associated with the running of Briar Glen if she could not even muster the courage to greet a visitor?

"I'll be fine, Mrs. Reeves. Perhaps . . . perhaps you could just send someone to the stables to ask when we might expect Mr. Tarrington's company for dinner."

"Aye. Aye, I'll do that, then."

Flora accompanied her as far as the door to the study, then hurried off down the hall, leaving Amanda alone for a moment to smooth her skirts and tuck a few loose strands of hair behind her ears before she went inside. She was still smiling, still reasonably calm when she opened the wide gumwood door and swept graciously across the threshold. But the smile died and her hand froze on the brass latch when she saw who turned from the window to greet her.

It was E. Forrest Wainright, and no, there was nothing friendly about his appearance at all.

Chapter 15

The Natchez banker was standing in a bank of sunlight. His hair, already a painfully bright shade of red, looked as if it were blazing on fire. The lower half of his face was prickly with copper stubble; his hawkish eyes were bloodshot and the heavy smudges beneath bespoke a long, sleepless night that had not been spent in pleasurable activity. His clothing was rumpled, his cravat askew. The bottoms of his trousers were stained with mud and water, and one of his shoes was missing a heel.

"Well, well, well," he said slowly, his eyes taking their time sweeping down the length of Amanda's body and back up again. "So it's true."

"Mr. Wainright." Amanda's mouth was suddenly as dry as day-old ashes. "How . . . did you know I was here?"

"How indeed," he mused, his eyes glittering and hard. "I might still be waiting by the side of the road, hat in hand, were it not for the rain . . . and this."

He held up a small gray glove—the one she had thought she had dropped on the floor of the coach last night.

"The fresh wheel tracks were distinctive and easy enough to follow. The preacher was somewhat less cooperative, having been wakened for the second time in as many hours, but he eventually told me all I needed to know."

Amanda tried to moisten her lips, but her tongue had been reduced to chalk as well. "Please, you must believe me. It was not planned."

"What part of it?" Wainright asked casually. "Marrying Tarrington or deliberately humiliating me?"

"Neither," she said. "It just . . . it all happened so quickly . . ."

Wainright's gaze took in the almost perfect fit of the blue

muslin gown, the softly brushed fall of her hair. "Yes, I can see it was all spur-of-the-moment."

Amanda twisted a bit of lace on her sleeve and heard it tear. "Mr. Wainright—"

"You came to me, remember. You made certain promises, certain commitments which I, in all sincerity, was prepared to accept in exchange for relieving you and your family of considerable financial burdens. You gave your word, Amanda," he added in an ominously low voice. "Is it of so little value?"

"I did not deliberately set out to break it. I was there last night, on the road, at midnight. Just as we had arranged."

"Yes, but I wasn't, was I?" he hissed. "Your lover made damned sure of that."

"He . . . wasn't my lover," she insisted softly.

"And none of this was planned," Wainright said belligerently. "Not the broken axle, not the ride to Jamestown or the furtive ceremony. Not the fine house or the fine clothes . . . which, by the way, seem to fit remarkably well for all that you claim to have been so surprised. What game were you playing, Amanda? Was it your idea to humiliate me this way, or was it your brother's?"

"Ryan knew nothing about it," she cried. "He *knows* nothing about it. It was all my idea, and—and my fault, I suppose, that it all went so terribly wrong. You can believe me or not, but I had every intention of keeping my word. I did not know Mr. Tarrington had interfered, or that he'd had any designs toward interfering until it was too late. I saw the coach waiting where it was supposed to be waiting—"

"And you just climbed on board, drove to the nearest preacher, and married the fellow without so much as a by your leave? You're absolutely right, Amanda," he sneered. "I don't believe it."

"It wasn't as simple as that," she whispered.

"No, I don't imagine it was. I imagine it was very difficult to choose which one of us—Tarrington or myself—was best suited to your purposes. Tell me . . . did you decide on merit alone? Was it the size of his bank account, or the size of something else that finally decided you?''

Amanda's flush deepened. ''I have apologized. I'm sorry if you find the apology unacceptable.''

''My dear Amanda, you have not begun to apologize to me. And we have not yet settled the matter of your other debts.''

''You will get your money.''

Wainright moved a menacing step closer. ''Money was not the only consideration.''

''You are wrong, sir. Money *was* the only consideration in our bargain.''

''Why, you haughty little bitch,'' he murmured, his eyes narrowing, his mouth compressing into a thin, harsh line. ''Haughty and arrogant. And obviously overdue for a hard lesson in reality. I'm going to enjoy teaching it to you, Amanda dear. I'm going to enjoy seeing you crawl to me on your hands and knees one day, begging me to take you back.''

''You shall have a very long wait ahead of you, sir,'' Amanda said, with more surety than she was feeling. ''And if you do not leave this instant, I will have you removed by force.''

''Bold words, Mrs. Tarrington.'' He gave a nasty laugh. ''But unlike you or your yellow-bellied brother, I am not a man of idle threats. When I say I am going to make you pay for this, you can believe you are going to pay.''

''And when I say you have five seconds to get out of my house,'' said a deep and bone-chilling baritone, ''you had better believe you won't be alive to count the sixth.''

Amanda whirled around. Michael Tarrington was standing in the doorway, his broad shoulders almost filling it. He was dressed informally in tight black breeches and a loose-fitting linen shirt that had been left open to the waist. Not a hair was out of place to indicate he had hurried in any way, yet there was a latent gleam in his eyes, putting to rest any suspicion he had taken a leisurely stroll. Directly behind him, standing two full heads shorter, was a huffing and puffing Flora Reeves.

"You are Wainright, I presume?" Tarrington asked, stepping casually into the room.

Wainright's keen eyes picked up Amanda's reaction—the pale hand that fluttered up to her breast, the unconcealed look of relief that drained some of the tension from her face. He had heard of the rich Yankee naval officer from Boston, but this was their first meeting face to face. His dislike was instant and intense, and his anger rolled sweetly, savagely into cold, calm fury.

"You seem to think you have some business with my wife?" Tarrington asked, crossing over to his desk and helping himself to a cigar from the carved sandalwood humidor.

"You know I do," Wainright replied evenly. "Just as I am sure you know what it is."

Tarrington glanced at Amanda. She was pale and still as death. The way she was watching him reminded him of a small, trapped animal, poised to run for her life if she could just figure out which way to go. She was also beautiful enough to constrict the muscles in his chest, making it difficult to resist the urge to smash his fists into Wainright's face for frightening her so.

He took his time lighting the cigar, then turned to the banker. "Refresh my memory."

"Personal warranties aside," Wainright said slowly, "there is a small matter of some money owing me. Mrs. Jackson had herself negotiated the terms of extending the loan on Rosalie, which I, in good faith, had agreed to accept in lieu of hard cash. Despite her heartfelt pleas and promises, she failed to meet me at the appointed time and place—but then, you already know that."

"I know full well what *Mrs. Tarrington* was doing last night. As for the loan on Rosalie, keeping personal warranties aside, I'm sure I can offer you terms equally acceptable."

"The loan is due at midnight tonight." Wainright hissed.

"Fifty thousand. In cash. Those are the only terms I will entertain."

Michael exhaled a hazy blue cloud of smoke. He glanced once more at his wife then walked around behind his desk and took a ring of keys from the top drawer. From a deeper bottom drawer he withdrew an iron strongbox, very old to judge by its appearance, heavily scrolled and crested with a foreign coat of arms. The key he slotted into the lock was equally ornate and antiquated; both looked—and indeed had been—salvaged off the wreck of an old galleon.

Michael opened the strongbox and began counting out a neat pile of crisp Yankee greenbacks. Wainright's black scowl wavered between impatience and incredulity before settling once again on outrage.

"Fifty thousand," Michael announced, sliding that amount across the desk. He stuck the cheroot back in his mouth, clamped it securely between straight white teeth, and squinted against the smoke. "Was there anything else? Any other . . . *business* . . . you had to discuss with either myself or my wife?"

Wainright flushed and his eyes glittered with a new malevolence. "The money will do for now, but I am far from finished my business . . . with either one of you."

He leaned forward to scoop up the greenbacks, but before he could, a hand closed securely around his wrist, stopping him cold.

"The note?" Tarrington asked.

"I don't carry it around with me," Wainright spat.

"And I am not in the habit of simply handing this much cash over to complete strangers."

"You don't seem to harbor any deep objections to marrying them."

Michael's expression remained civil, but the slow smile that crept across his mouth came nowhere near touching his eyes. "I'll overlook that for now, considering the circumstances, but I will remind you—and warn you—I do not react well to insults. And an insult to my wife is as good, or should I say worse, than an insult to me. I would advise you not to press your luck.''

Wainright bore the quiet warning with the same disdainful indifference as he bore the crushing pressure around his wrist.

"If you will provide me with a pen and paper, I will write a discharge. You can send one of your men into town to collect the original note . . . *if* that is satisfactory.''

Tarrington's smile turned sardonic. "Greed, as they say, will always win out.'' He released the banker's wrist and pushed a ledger across the desk, watching through slitted eyes as the receipt was hastily scratched out and signed with an inky flourish.

Wainright snatched up the money and tucked it into a breast pocket. His eyes swept around the richly paneled walls of the library one last time before locking with Tarrington's again.

"You've done well for yourself, for a newcomer. Still, a man in your position should know better than to make too many enemies too soon.''

"A man in your position,'' Tarrington countered evenly, "should know when to leave while he still has two good legs to walk on.''

Wainright's eyes darkened briefly. He smirked and took several angry strides toward the door before he halted again and glared over at Amanda. "I suppose you think you're quite clever, do you? All you have done, however, is sold yourself to the highest bidder . . . sort of a slave auction in reverse, you might say, but then I guess old habits die hard.''

"Mrs. Reeves,'' Tarrington said silkily. "Will you show this *gentleman* to the door now?''

"Aye.'' Flora nodded, her chest puffed out with indignation. "By the scruff o' his neck if he's not quick on his feet.''

Wainright was unimpressed, his gaze held steadfast on Amanda. "Don't forget what I said, my dear. I *will* have my day.''

The menacing promise in Wainright's voice put a new

chill in Amanda's flesh. Her hands shook. The torn scrap of lace on her sleeve was a mangled knot of frayed threads and her fingers were so icy cold, there were blue crescents beneath the nails. Some of those same nails had gouged little half circles of red in her palms, painful reminders of the truth that had rung clear in Wainright's voice: She *had* merely sold herself to the highest bidder.

Sensing Tarrington's presence beside her, she lifted her chin, lifted her eyes to his, uncertain of what she would see. Amazingly enough, there was only concern . . . and a trace of gentle humor.

"You do know how to pick your enemies, don't you?"

"I . . . tried to warn you."

He tucked a finger beneath her chin, preventing her from retreating again. "And I made you a promise, did I not? That he would have to go through me first?"

Her lips trembled apart. Tears stood in her eyes, burning unbidden and unwanted across her lashes. "You . . . said yourself, he's a dangerous man," she whispered. "A murderer."

His thumb traced the softness of her lower lip, and he was shocked by the strength of his need to protect her. His chameleon was showing him too many subtle changes, from seductive temptress to naive innocent, from defiant rebel to vulnerable, uncertain captive. Montana Rose . . . Amanda Courtland Jackson . . . Who the devil had he married and why was she equally intriguing, equally capable of bringing him to his knees in either guise?

"Do I detect a wifely concern for my safety?" he mused, catching the shiny wetness of a tear on his fingertip.

"For yours, for mine," she admitted. "For Verity's and Ryan's, for my mother and father . . . for Rosalie," she added in a rush. "I believe him when he says he is not finished with us."

"Good. I'm glad to hear it. Then you'll be careful when I'm not around and you won't go welcoming strangers into our parlor with only Mrs. Reeves to watch your back."

The gentle admonition was delivered with a kiss—a kiss

that left her staring up at him, startled for more reasons than one.

His mustache was gone. He had shaven away the thick chestnut handlebar, removing the saturnine, piratical look with it. Without the camouflage of hair concealing it, his mouth was a generous, wide slash, flawed slightly through one upper bow by a faint white scar.

He smiled self-consciously and brushed a long finger across the hairless expanse. "Tell me you've just noticed and you'll have done untold damage to my vanity."

"Why did you do it?"

"You disapprove?"

"I . . . have no opinion either way."

"You did last night. As I recall, you bemoaned the fact that it was like kissing sandpaper—which, I suppose, is better than the hind end of a goat, but distracting nonetheless."

Amanda felt her cheeks grow warm, but any denial she might have been tempted to offer was smothered under another long, slow, leisurely kiss. One that brought her melting into his arms with shockingly little resistance.

"Clarty no-necked slimy red-topped weevil," Mrs. Reeves announced, returning from seeing that the door had slammed with the proper emphasis behind Wainright. "He'd best no' be showin' his arse on ma doorstep again or he'll feel the stub o' ma boot so far up the crack he'll no' be able to piss proper fer a month!"

Tarrington cursed softly against Amanda's lips and reluctantly lifted his mouth away. "Ahh, Flora. We were just talking about distractions. Was I mistaken when I walked past the kitchens, or was that pork pie I smelled?"

"Pies an' tatties," she said, folding her arms imperiously across her ample bosoms. "An' we'll have nay more o' your lusty goin'-ons until ye've let the wee lassie put some food inside her. Look at the poor thing: pale as a ghost and twice as thin."

Amanda was, in fact, blushing as dark as a rose, and Michael's grin did not improve matters in the least.

"I would sooner disobey an order from an admiral as disobey one of yours, Mrs. Reeves. Lead the way."

"I'm really not very hungry," Amanda protested.

"Well, I am," he said, propelling her forward in Mrs. Reeves's wake. "And we will sup together. I breakfasted alone this morning and have no intentions of letting it become a habit. Besides which, Flora's pork pies are famous throughout all of Massachusetts. Turning your pretty nose up at them could incite graver repercussions than the Boston Tea Party."

Amanda let herself be guided back to the small dining salon. Michael held her chair solicitously, taking the opportunity to study every detail of her appearance as if he were seeing her for the first time that day.

"By God, you truly are a lovely woman," he murmured. "No wonder your Mr. Wainright was a tad piqued."

Amanda watched her husband settle into a chair opposite her.

"It doesn't bother you?" she asked. "It doesn't make you angry at all that he is walking away from here with fifty thousand of your dollars in his pocket?"

"It makes me furious," he said with an easy smile. "But it would have made me more furious to think of him—or anyone like him—putting his hands on you."

Amanda met his gaze across the table. The look in his eyes was intense enough to draw the breath out of her lungs and possessive enough to send a flood of heated sensations rippling along her spine.

Mrs. Reeves saved the day again, swinging her way through the servants' doorway carrying a platter of steaming hot dishes.

"Ach," said Tarrington, mimicking a broad Scots accent. " 'Tis starved I am."

"Aye, well, 'tis starved ye'll stay until ye snuff out that turrible black weed ye're puffin' on." She set the platter down and shoved a glass dish under his elbow, glowering over him until the cheroot met its timely death. "Sally!

Come along, lass. I canny dish out ma pies without a fork or a spoon.''

A slender, dark-haired girl came into the room bearing more dishes of vegetables and crisp fried potatoes. She had the same plump, round cheeks as her mother, and shared a similar lack of height, the top of her head possibly reaching five feet if she stood on tiptoes. Her eyes were a shy, liquid brown and, very unlike her mother, flicked away the instant anyone threatened to take notice of her.

"This is ma own daughter Sally," Flora announced proudly. "She lends a hand in the kitchen, mostly, but on a busy day can scrub the whole hoose an' have it shinin' like a mirror afore noon."

Amanda smiled warmly as the girl risked a glance and a nervous curtsy in her direction. "I'm very pleased to meet you, Sally."

The girl bobbed again and whispered, "Thankee, ma'am. I'm . . . ever so happy to meet you too."

"Aye, well, we'll leave ye to ye're meal now," Flora said with a satisfied glance around the table. "Sound the bell if ye be needin' me fer owt else. An' dinna let him keep all the brown bits o' tatty to himself; he's a right wee pig when it comes to that, an' ye'll have to watch him keen."

"Thank you, Mrs. Reeves," Amanda said. "I will."

Flora nodded brusquely and was gone, ushering Sally ahead of her like a mother hen shooing her chick.

"Well," Michael said, reaching for a serving spoon and a plate. "You seem to have passed the first test with ease. Flora has very definite opinions as to who she takes under her wing and who she kicks out of the nest to fly on their own."

"I like her."

"Good. Because we've been together a long time and, as much of a pain in the . . . neck . . . as she is, I would hate to have to send her packing."

Amanda accepted the heavily burdened plate he passed across the table and held it wavering in midair a moment before setting it down. "You would do that? You would send her away?"

"Well." He pursed his lips and frowned. "If it came down to a choice of having Flora in the kitchen . . . or you in the bedroom . . ." He glanced up and waited for the glorious shade of red to reach her hairline. "I would probably bunk down in the stables and let the two of you have the house to yourselves."

He grinned and set about attacking the small mountain of pork pie and potatoes he had served himself, drowning each mouthful in gravy as he went along. "As for the rest of the household matters, I willingly place it all in your more than capable hands. Change the curtains, hire or fire all the servants you need, order new furniture by the wagonloads if you like: I am relieved to have been saved from Flora's tastes in refurbishing the I-don't-know-how-many rooms still wanting for someone's attention. I have already told Flora I thought you might want to put Verity in the room adjoining ours. I will advise the bank tomorrow so you can draw the funds you need to make it a proper little girl's room—pink, do you suppose?"

Amanda stared at him unblinkingly, her own food untouched.

"One of my sisters had a pink room . . . Beth, I think. I wasn't allowed in any of them very often, but I seem to recall a great deal of pink in Beth's room, and out of all of them, she grew up with the best disposition. On the other hand, she made the poorest choice of husbands—Arveld Pinwater, if you can believe it—a corset maker who can talk for hours on the various types of whalebone he uses in his stays. You're not eating your pie."

Amanda looked down.

"Mrs. Reeves will know," he cautioned blithely. "She probably has her eye and ear to the keyhole now."

A muffled curse from the other side of the kitchen door sent Michael's brow arching with an I-told-you-so expression. "It's part of her charm."

Amanda picked up her fork and tried the pork pie. It was delicious. It was more than delicious, and she ate ravenously, barely swallowing one mouthful before reaching for another.

Michael watched in silence, finishing his own meal and leaning back in his chair to enjoy the last half of his relit cigar.

"Speaking of familial duties," he mentioned casually, "when do you propose to carry the happy news to Rosalie?"

Amanda stopped chewing and lowered her fork slowly to the table.

"I can only assume you left a note of some kind," he continued smoothly. "And being as how Wainright arrived here in relatively good health, I shall also assume you neglected to mention any specifics?"

"I only told Ryan I would be gone a few days, and not to worry."

"The knack of understatement," he murmured, "is one of woman's greatest talents. Aren't you worried he will interpret it the wrong way and think, perhaps, that you've caught up with another riverboat?"

Amanda shook her head. "I would never be able to do something like that on my own."

"My dearest little Rebel chamelion . . . it still surprises me that you were able to do it at all."

The velvety husk in his voice sent another wave of sensation down her spine and she swallowed hard. "I suppose I should tell them soon. They will be worried."

"I suppose you should. And yes, they will."

"Today would be best," she said hesitantly.

"Probably."

"Or first thing in the morning."

Tarrington laughed. "Are you asking me to decide for you? Very well, tomorrow morning is soon enough, and yes, I will stand at your side and share the slings and arrows . . . although I should let you sweat it out alone. It would have been interesting to see how you would have handled the situation had you driven up to the door as Mrs. E. Forrest Wainright."

Amanda's lashes lowered quickly. Was he going to continually remind her of that near disaster?

"Yes," he said quietly, guessing the reason for the sudden

tautness in her jaw. "I am. But that should be the least of your complaints. Do you like horses, by the way?"

"Horses?" His rapid changes of topic were catching her off guard.

"Yes. Four legs and a tail. I'm sure you've seen them around."

Her eyes narrowed at the sarcasm. "I don't consider myself an authority on them, no."

"That wasn't my question. I asked if you liked them."

"As friends, not especially."

His stern expression folded into a grin. "You might find some of them have far more merit than their human counterparts."

"You are probably quite right."

"I *know* I'm right. I was hoping you would agree, since I plan to breed and raise the wee beasties, as Flora so fondly calls them."

"I thought your first love was the sea, not the land."

"Because I joined the Navy, not the Army? Or because our own first auspicious meeting was on a riverboat?"

"You come from Boston. Is it not a seaport?"

"It was also a city that went to war over a few pounds of tea, but that doesn't mean I like to drink the stuff. I take it your rather obvious avoidance of my question means you are not the accomplished horsewoman I presumed all Southern belles to be?"

"I have done my fair share of riding," she said testily.

"Sidesaddle, no doubt. Twirling a parasol and flirting with fellow churchgoers."

"For your information, I happen to loathe riding sidesaddle, and while I cannot attest to the habits of your Yankee women, I would sooner be caught with a few freckles on my nose than be seen carrying a parasol on a horse!"

"Excellent. Then I may expect your company on a riding tour of Briar Glen this afternoon?"

Amanda started to protest, then hesitated. How on earth was she going to get around this one? Of all the things he had to be enamored with: horses!

"I have nothing suitable to wear," she said abruptly. "And I have already promised my time to Mrs. Reeves."

"I believe the lady is stalling. I wonder why."

"I am doing nothing of the kind. I just—"

He arched an eyebrow and waited.

"They don't like me," she conceded with a sigh.

"They?"

"Horses," she snapped without thinking. "Four legs and a tail. I'm sure you've seen them around."

The wolfish grin reappeared and she could have died. "Is there any particular reason why they don't like you?"

"Good heavens, how should I know? I don't know the way the creatures think."

"You might have to learn. There are over forty thousand acres surrounding us that do not take well to a buggy."

"And why should that concern me? I have no intentions of tramping over each and every acre."

The smile reappeared and he stroked the tip of his forefinger over the now-naked upper lip. "My, my. Is this the same woman who was willing to make the ultimate sacrifice to protect her family home?"

"That was different."

"How?"

She knew what he wanted her to say. He wanted her to say Briar Glen was her home now, but she could not bring herself to do it. She could not say it, she could barely bring herself to think it.

"Mandy?"

He had called her Mandy during the night, and use of the endearment brought back the warm, slippery, useless feeling that made her stomach rise up and settle back down awry.

With a start she realized he was standing beside her. His strong hands were on her shoulders, and he was drawing her up and into his arms.

"I am not the kind of man who wants a wife for window dressing only," he insisted softly. "Last night should have proved that much to you anyway. I want you to be as much a part of Briar Glen as you were of Rosalie. I want you to feel like you belong here, Mandy. Here, by God. With me.''

He was too close. She could not think straight with the breadth of his chest at her fingertips, the deep vee of sun-bronzed flesh assaulting her senses with the memory of the taste and feel of him. How was she supposed to concentrate on mundane things like horses and pork pies and un-furnished rooms when all she could think of was how it felt to be held in his arms, how it felt to have his flesh quiver at her touch, how it felt to share the throbbing pressure an instant before he spilled himself inside her?

"No," she whispered.

Tarrington misunderstood and swept her up into his arms.

"Yes, by God," he snarled and kicked the chair out of his way. He strode out of the room and down the hall, passing a startled Flora Reeves along the way. Amanda kept her face buried in the curve of his shoulder and kept her eyes tightly shut until they were up the stairs, in the bedroom, and he was booting the door shut behind them.

Someone—Sally or Flora—had made up the bed and tidied the evidence of the previous night's activities. The curtains were drawn back and tied to let the sunlight in, and the hundreds of square panes in the writing alcove split and refracted the rays of the sun, mottling the floor and walls in a rainbow array of starbursts. The brightest, hottest streamers were hazed with floating dust motes that glittered and swirled with the passage of Tarrington's body as he cut through them to get to the bed. The satin cover gleamed like the still surface of a lake, and as he set Amanda's body down upon it, the satin was drawn into silvery ripples, forming a shimmering halo around her.

He knelt on one knee above her, prepared for another verbal battle. Prepared to prove her wrong if she thought she could regain any of the indifference she had come to him with last night. But then he saw her face. And he felt her hands where they were laced around his neck stopping him from lifting himself too far away. His heart did a curious little spin in his chest as he bowed to the shy pressure, and he could not stop himself from sighing as he lowered himself down into her arms.

He pushed his hands into her hair, freeing it from the scrap of ribbon, spreading it beneath them like a golden fan. His tongue filled her mouth, inviting and winning soft shivers and breathy, soundless gasps in response. His hands urged her up and into a gentle roll so that when he lay back, she was above him and the bindings and fastenings of her frock were easy prey to his searching fingers.

His body was far too impatient to wait for his hands to complete their task, and with a husky groan, he swept the abundance of petticoats and muslin up above her waist and searched out the slitted center of her drawers, cursing his own ignorance when he felt how sleek and ready she was.

His trousers were strained almost to the point of bursting, and it was all he could do to loosen the buttons at his waist and spring free of the confining cloth. He grasped Amanda by the hips and brought her heat sliding down over him, arching his hips at the same time, hearing her shattered cry, hearing his own hoarse rattle of pleasure tear up his throat.

Amanda's eyes were startled wide open above him. After his first imperious thrust, she sat perfectly still, absorbing the shock of feeling him so hard and deep and seemingly immovable inside her. Her hands were stretched straight out, braced on his chest, and as his hips settled slowly back onto the bed, her fingers spread wider in the coarse mat of hair and she gasped his name.

"Tarrington is my father's name," he growled. "You'll have to start calling me Michael if you want to get my attention."

She shook her head, sending more loosened curls tumbling around her shoulders. Her lips parted around a series of short, arrested breaths; she stared down at where they were joined, unable to see anything through the profusion of muslin and foulard petticoats, still too frightened to do more than keep her thighs clamped tightly against his.

"I didn't think it was so terrible a name, or so difficult to say." He shifted his hands higher on her waist and started to guide her back and forth over the rocking motion of his hips.

Amanda groaned with disbelief each time his hands pulled her forward, pressed her back. Her hair engulfed them both in a shining waterfall of sun-bright gold, and as he let her move with faster, bolder confidence, the gleaming waves swept back and forth, back and forth, thrashing with the restless rhythm of a body discovering new limits, discovering there were no limits at all.

Except those governed by the iron grip of his hands. He stopped her midstroke and felt the heat and wetness shudder around him, knowing she was so near the brink, the touch of a feather would push her over.

"You're"—she sucked in a breath and had to wait for a shudder to pass before she could exhale again—"impossible."

"I'm Michael. Say my name. Say it, dammit, or—"

"Michael," she whispered through a shiver. "Michael . . . *Michael!*"

He surged up inside her, his flesh impaling her so deeply she had no room left to question the madness, she only let it carry her away.

Moving in a blur, she pushed herself through crest after crest of glorious rapture. She flung her head back and tightened herself around the white-hot throbs of an orgasm that shuddered through the smallest muscle, the smallest hair that stood on end on the smallest part of her body. There was not enough strength in Michael's hands to hold her, not enough power in his body to withstand the scalding demands of her passion, and he arched up, up, up, blinded by the sunlight and the flaring ecstasy.

When some of the shocking heat abated, Amanda collapsed forward, melting in a limp and utterly helpless quiver of raw nerves on his chest. Michael's arms were waiting to gather her close, holding her tight against a body that continued to pulse with fading echoes of pleasure.

"Stubborn," he murmured after a while. "You're very stubborn, you know."

She groaned and buried her head in the crook of his neck. His shirt had been pushed off his shoulder and she found bare, hard-surfaced flesh beneath her lips, warm and lightly dampened from his exertions.

"I'll take that to be a 'yes, Michael,' " he mused.

She sighed again, a sound loud enough and plaintive enough to draw a wry chuckle from his lips.

"It's not a crime, you know, to enjoy what we've just done. Married couples have been known to lock themselves away for hours, days, sometimes weeks in order to fully explore the potential of their newfound freedom."

"Freedom?" she asked, denouncing the word for its obvious contradictions. "In marriage?"

"You aren't a prisoner here, Mandy," he said quietly. "Nor are you bonded or indentured. You aren't even obligated to share my bed if you find the idea absolutely abhorrent to you."

She lifted her head off his shoulder and looked down at him through the disheveled cloud of her hair. "That wasn't the impression you gave me last night."

"Last night . . . was different," he murmured, his own eyes slipping to where her bodice gaped open and her breasts were almost spilling out, round and full and delectably flushed.

"And just now?"

She was waiting for him to deny his own stubbornness, but he didn't. He grinned with the careless aplomb of a pirate and sent his hands pillaging beneath the parted edges of her bodice. His palms cupped her breasts and his thumbs brushed across her nipples, chasing a shower of fiery bright sparks into her belly. She was conscious of his heat stirring inside her and aware of her own body tightening around him, and she sighed again as he coaxed her forward into the suckling warmth of his mouth.

"You are impossible, you know," she protested softly. "And you don't play fair."

"Not when the stakes are this high, no. I don't."

"But . . . it's all happening so fast. As if it's a dream.

As if it really isn't happening . . . or shouldn't be happening. Not to me, anyway.''

"This is not a dream," he assured her. "It's as real as we want it to be, and it will last as long as we want it to last."

"My family, my friends," she whispered. "They won't understand."

"They don't have to understand. You do. Only you."

"I . . . I only want to feel safe again."

His thumb brushed tenderly along her cheek and down the smooth curve of her jaw. "And do you? Do you feel safe?"

"Here? Now? With you?" Her voice was so hushed it was barely a sound at all. "Yes."

"Then that's all that matters," he said, and drew her mouth back down to his.

Chapter 16

A carriage was coming up the approach to Rosalie, the wheels spinning a faint cloud of dust in its wake.

"Doan know whose it is," Mercy declared, standing and shielding her eyes against the sunlight. "But it sho' is some fancy rig, Miz Sarah."

Sarah Courtland walked to the lip of the veranda and reached down instinctively to reassure the small grasping hands that instantly clutched at her leg.

"There, there now, Verity, dear," she said matter-of-factly, "It's far too bright a day for bogeymen to be out and about. And the carriage is indeed too fine for—" She stopped and gasped, recognizing at once the face of the passenger who leaned her head out the side and waved. It was Amanda. Or at least it looked like Amanda, all fancied up in a new traveling suit and bonnet.

"Mercy," she said weakly, "fetch my salts. And while you're inside, find Mr. Courtland . . . and Ryan . . . and tell them . . . we have found Amanda."

The large black mammy disappeared inside the house as the carriage drew to a halt at the foot of the porch steps. Amanda did not wait for Foley's assistance; she was out of the buggy and running up the stairs before the driver had even climbed out of his seat.

"Verity!" she cried, hugging her daughter and sweeping her up into her arms, spinning her round and round so that the child's skirts and pinafore belled out over her ruffled drawers. "How is my sweetest little girl? Have you been good for Grandma?"

"Amanda!" her mother cried. "Where have you been? Your father and brother have been frantic. We have all been frantic with worry."

"Did you not read the letter I left? I told you *not* to worry, that I would explain everything when I came home."

"Letter? You expect me to read a letter?" she quailed. "We had no idea where you had gone! Why . . . it has just been too terrible for words! Ryan has scoured all of Natchez. He has had the authorities searching the river! Alisha has even come from Summitcrest to keep me from falling into distraction."

"I have only been gone two days, Mother."

"And two whole nights! What could you have been thinking! We have all been sick with worry and imagining the most horrible things. Where have you been?" She peered over Amanda's shoulder. "And whose buggy is that?"

Before she could answer, Ryan came running out of the house. "Amanda? Where the bloody hell have you been?"

"I have just been asking her that very thing," Sarah declared in a quavering voice. "But she refused to tell me. She says I must read it in a letter."

"I haven't refused," Amanda protested. "And I haven't had a chance to—"

"What in thunderation is going on out here?" William rolled out onto the porch in his cane-backed wheelchair. "Has everyone gone completely mad? Shouting and carrying on as if the Yankees were in the woods. Amanda—is that you? Where have you been for the last week?"

"Father, Ryan . . . please, if you will just give me a chance—"

Verity had her mouth pressed to Amanda's ear, whispering a mile a minute, trying to retell every detail of every hour that had passed. She was also spitting copious amounts of enthusiasm into her mother's ear and hugging her so tightly, Amanda's bonnet went askew. "Please, baby—"

"Well, if it isn't the prodigal daughter returned to the fold," Alisha said, emerging from the doorway. "So you've come back, have you? All in one piece too."

"Oh, I just know something dreadful has happened," Sarah wailed. "Mercy . . . Mercy, my salts. Quickly!"

"If you plan on fainting," William roared, "plan to do it

elsewhere. I am waiting to hear an explanation from your daughter, and I cannot do it and listen to your caterwauling at the same time. Obviously nothing too dreadful has happened —she looks perfectly fit to me.''

''She looks more than fit,'' Alisha commented dryly, her gaze taking in every detail of the mint-green velvet suit, gloves, hat, even the lace-trimmed reticule that dangled from her twin's wrist. The outfit vastly outshone her own striped damask and roused the level of her jealousy beyond its normal slow burn.

''Amanda . . . ?'' Ryan began.

''The lot of you,'' William barked. ''Shut up!''

When he had his family's attention, he crooked his finger ominously in Amanda's direction. ''Come over here, Daughter. We'll have no more excuses. And you had best not try any of your female tricks on me, I am wise to them all. I want to know where you have been and what you have been doing. Speak up now, and it best be the truth.''

Amanda glanced around the frowning circle. There was not a friendly face among them except for Verity, and for once it was Amanda who wished she could bury her face in her daughter's skirts for protection.

She heard the faint creak of the carriage step behind her and turned, as did everyone else, in time to see Michael Tarrington stand down and remove his wide-brimmed hat.

''Good afternoon to you all,'' he said easily. ''I hope you have not been too worried about Amanda.''

Sarah let out a strangled cry. Her hand flew to her bosom and she gaped at Amanda in horror. ''Oh, my Lord. She has been with a man!''

''Mercy, the salts,'' William declared dryly. ''Daughter, if you have done anything to shame yourself, or to bring shame upon this family''—he ignored the shriek from his wife and wagged his finger again—''I'll not be responsible for my actions.''

Amanda looked her father straight in the eye and said in a loud, clear voice: ''There is no need for any action whatsoever, Father. Michael and I were married on Wednesday.''

Sarah's mouth dropped open. William's eyebrows lifted so high they seemed to touch his hairline. Alisha, whose eyes had not left Michael Tarrington's face since he had stepped down from the carriage, turned her cold, round-eyed stare on Amanda. Even Mercy, standing with the unstoppered bottle of hartshorn spirits, felt like taking a sniff herself to clear her senses.

"A Yankee?" she muttered. "Miss Amanda done up an' married wid a Yankee? Lordy, Lordy, hell done must've froze when none of us was watchin'."

Ryan gripped Amanda tightly around the upper arm and swung her about to face him. "You've done *what?*"

"Married him," she repeated calmly, her arms tightening around Verity. "Wednesday night. In Jamestown. The Reverend Jeffries performed the ceremony."

Sarah looked from her daughter to the tall, handsome Yankee and back to her daughter. "You *eloped!*"

"We thought it would be best that way."

"But . . . it isn't possible. He . . . you . . ." Sarah gaped at Michael. "You were only here to dinner on *Monday.*"

"Mrs. Courtland." Michael took several steps toward the porch. "Perhaps you will allow me—"

"You keep out of this," Ryan snarled, whirling on him. "So help me God, if you take another step, I'll kill you with my bare hands!"

Michael stopped. He acknowledged Ryan's fury with a cool nod and retraced his steps.

"Ryan, please—" Amanda drew her brother's rage back upon herself. "If you'll just let me explain—"

"Please do," Ryan said bluntly. "Explain. Saturday you could hardly bear to be in the same room as the man. Monday you did your damnedest to be rude to him . . . and now you tell us you have married him. It must be one hell of an explanation; I can hardly wait to hear it."

"Indeed," agreed William, rolling his way between Alisha's and Sarah's skirts. "I should think we do need an explanation, Amanda. Your mother was all but convinced there was some form of foul play and here you stand, telling us you have married the man, just like that.''

''It was not *just like that,*'' she insisted, conscious of the black look in Ryan's eyes. ''I mean, yes, I married him . . . but no, it was not as simple as it sounds. I thought about it a great deal—truly I did—and I am sorry if you have all been overly worried.''

''Worried!'' Sarah clasped her hands together over her breast. ''Why, indeed, should we have worried. Our daughter disappears in the middle of the night. We hear no word for two days. And now you tell us you have eloped. Why, it isn't even decent! What will people think? We cannot survive another scandal, we simply cannot!''

''Mother . . . there will be no scandal. People elope all of the time.''

''Not our people! And not after only one dinner together! It . . . it just isn't decent,'' she finished lamely.

''It wasn't just one dinner, Mother. Michael and I . . . we have known each other longer than you think.''

Sarah, who had thrust her nose into the bottle of hartshorn, stopped and stared. ''What do you mean you have known each other longer? How much longer?''

Ryan's look, if anything, became even blacker, causing the words to stumble when they came off Amanda's tongue. ''We . . . met several weeks ago. We . . . have been acquainted . . . for quite some time.''

Now she could feel Michael's gaze on the back of her neck and she could imagine the gleam dancing in the smoky gray eyes.

Sarah turned to the tall Yankee. ''You have?''

''I am afraid so, Mrs. Courtland,'' he said.

''But when? How? *Where* did you meet?''

''In Natchez,'' he said easily enough. ''I have come to town several times on business.''

''The Judge!'' Sarah exclaimed. ''He said nothing about having introduced you before Alisha's wedding.''

''I'm sure it only slipped his mind.''

''Why, aren't you both just the most wicked and devious

souls," Alisha breathed, partly in surprise, partly in grudging admiration. "Sneaking off and meeting one another for secret trysts. I declare I feel almost guilty myself just imagining it."

Sarah clutched Amanda's arm and gasped, "Tell me that *wasn't* what you did, Amanda! Tell me it wasn't like that at all, or I swear I shall die of utter mortification here and now."

"It wasn't *anything* like that, Mother," Amanda assured her. She smiled at Verity and passed her into Mercy's outstretched arms, then faced her mother with a calmness she was far from feeling. "It is true that I met Michael in Natchez, but there were always crowds of people around and I . . . never deliberately set out with the intention of meeting him. It was purely accidental, I swear it."

"Then why didn't you insist he come to the house like any other proper, decent caller?" Alisha inquired archly. "Like Mr. Joshua Brice, for instance. Oh, the poor, poor man. Whatever will he think when he finds out you were just playing him for the fool?"

Amanda's eyes flashed with sparks as she leveled her gaze on her twin. "I'm sure Josh will have figured out by now just who the biggest fool was in all of this."

Sarah missed the fulminating glares that passed between the two sisters. "But an elopement," she wailed, twisting her hands together in distress. "It all seems so . . . furtive."

"I'm sorry, Mother," Amanda snapped. "Truly, I am. But there just wasn't any other way."

"Quite simply, Mrs. Courtland," Michael said, stepping into the breach again with his lazy charm, "Amanda was wanting to spare you the . . . embarrassment, shall we say, of my . . . status as a Northerner."

"A Yankee!" Sarah wailed again. "Oh, my Lord . . ."

"A Bostonian," Michael said easily, "who has put the war behind him and is hoping to make a home for himself in this beautiful state of Mississippi. I consider it an honor and a privilege to have won your daughter's attention, sir," he added, turning to William and offering a formal bow. "And if I might say, the challenge of wooing and winning her under the circumstances has been one of the greatest of my life so far."

William harrumphed. Then chortled unexpectedly. "Now *that*, sir, I can believe without reservations. I will not say I condone her actions wholeheartedly—not at the moment, anyway—but since the deed is done and cannot be *undone* . . . and you *are* related by blood to Arblaster Moore . . . I suppose we shall have to bear up."

Amanda sank down beside her father's chair and threw her arms around him, heedless of her bonnet slewing sideways and eventually slipping down to hang by its ribbons around her neck.

"Ah-hem." Karl von Helmstaad was suddenly in the doorway. "Is this a private family affair, or can anyone join in? Zounds, is it true? Is Miss Amanda home again?"

"Home," Alisha drawled. "And married. And not the least bit guilty over all the fuss she has caused. For that matter, she doesn't look the least bit repentant about anything, considering . . . what was it she said to me before *my* wedding? . . . she has found herself her own rich Yankee to rub in the noses of our less fortunate neighbors."

Amanda had no defense to offer as everyone seemed to focus on the mint-green traveling suit, the soft kid gloves, the ruffled and beribboned bonnet. It was Sarah, fortified—and left somewhat dizzy—by the hartshorn, who was prompted to remember that her new son-in-law had just purchased Briar Glen, making her daughter the mistress of one of the grandest plantations in the state, if not the whole South.

"Why, Lissy," she said with sudden thoughtfulness. "Love is far more important than a few jealous old gossips. And as your father says, what's done is done. We cannot let the family fall apart over a little . . . brash behavior."

It was everyone's turn to stare at Sarah.

"Well," she exclaimed defiantly, "it *is* rather foolish to dwell on something that is plainly out of our hands now.

Amanda has made her choice, we must all accept it and stand together in welcoming Mr. Tarrington to the family.''

Ryan's patience snapped. ''I don't have to accept it,'' he stated flatly. ''And I won't.''

He strode angrily down the steps and started walking away from the porch.

''Ryan!'' Amanda called after him, but he did not stop. She sprang up from her knees and tried to run after him, but Michael reached out a hand to stop her.

''Let him go,'' he murmured. ''He'll cool off faster if you leave him alone.''

''You don't know him,'' she cried. ''I have to go to him and try to explain.''

She shrugged off Michael's hand and ran after her brother. He was at the stables before she managed to catch up to him, preparing to mount a horse that was already saddled and waiting.

''Ryan! Please wait!''

He barely glanced at her as she came breathlessly up behind him. ''If you don't mind,'' he said brusquely, ''I have work to do.''

''Ryan, please don't do this. Don't ride away angry.''

''Am I supposed to ride away in the throes of delight?''

''If you would just let me explain—''

''What is there to explain? You met the Yankee bastard in a poker game and fell madly, passionately in love with him? What else is there to know? Why else would you have *married* him?''

He said the word as if it was laced with poison and he had to spit the taste of it from his mouth.

''Ryan . . .''

''Surely not for his money? You would never marry a man strictly for his money, would you? That would be low and callow . . . and it would make you not much better than Alisha, who, as we all know, never feels the need to explain her motives either.''

''Or like you, stubborn and pig-headed, and too blinded by his own stupid pride and archaic sense of nobility to allow anyone else to do what had to be done in order to save this family.''

"Allow you?" He gripped the leather saddle as if he would crush it. "*Allow* you? Good Christ, Amanda, what haven't I allowed you to do? I've stood by and watched you dress yourself like a whore and gamble your own pride away on the riverboats. I told you it was too dangerous. I told you something—a million somethings—could go wrong, but you begged and pleaded and threatened to do it on your own if I didn't *allow* you to go, so I did. How noble did you think I felt then? How much blinder do you think I should have to be not to be able to see my own flesh and blood being pawed and ogled by river scum night after night?''

"Ryan . . . we've had this argument a thousand times. And won't you please look at me? I can't talk to your back.''

"Why not? You don't seem to mind going behind it.''

She sighed and tugged at the ribbons that were dragging the weight of her bonnet down her back. She untied them and removed the hat, suppressing an urge to throw it on the ground and grind it under her heel.

"If I did go behind your back, it was because I knew we didn't have any time left to argue or debate what had to be done. It just *had to be done*.''

"You didn't have to sell yourself to the bastard," he hissed.

"No. No, I didn't. And he wasn't even my first choice. When I left the house Wednesday night, I left with the intention of meeting Forrest Wainright. I had gone to see him Sunday afternoon, you see, and I had accepted his terms for setting aside the debt on Rosalie.''

Ryan turned around slowly, his face ashen.

"And *that* would have been a sacrifice worthy of all this outrage," she added quietly. "If not for Michael's intervention, I would be Mrs. E. Forrest Wainright right now and you would be having to extend a welcome to him as the newest member of the family.''

"I would have killed him first," Ryan said tonelessly.

"And I may still kill Tarrington, unless you can give me a damn good reason why I shouldn't."

"Because he is my husband," she said simply. "And as you said yourself, I've been a widow long enough."

Ryan stared, the only movement being in a wisp of tawny hair that had fallen over his forehead.

"Wainright came to Briar Glen yesterday," she continued evenly, "angry and full of threats. Michael paid him off. He bought the note on Rosalie, so it's ours again, free and clear."

"You mean it's Tarrington's, don't you?"

"No. It's ours . . . *yours*. There was never any question of that."

He closed his eyes and shook his head. "What did you have to give him in return?"

"I am his wife."

"In name only?" he challenged.

She hesitated and saw his jaw tauten even before she whispered her reply. "No."

Ryan's shoulders slumped noticeably. "Damn," he muttered. "God*damned* Yankee son-of-a-bitch piece of *shit!*"

Her eyebrows arched gently. "He *is* Dianna's cousin; you probably would have become related to him anyway."

Her attempt at humor fell flat as Ryan glared at her. "Yes, he is her cousin, and I asked her about him. Do you want to know what she said? She said he had been thrown out of nearly every school he attended—for gambling and womanizing, no less. She also said he had a reputation for being the black sheep in the family, and that even his father—who I gather did not exactly have a lily-white past himself—had threatened to disown him on an occasion or two. Being as loyal as she is, she didn't want to share any of the details of his less palatable habits, but I guess you and I know most of them already, don't we?"

"As much he knows mine. I would say that makes us about even when it comes to having secrets we'd rather keep to ourselves."

Ryan shoved his fists deep in his pockets. "It doesn't

make him any more of a saint. He's a gambler, a speculator, and a cheat. What makes you think he'll be any kind of a good husband? A few weeks ago, it was Josh Brice with or without a roof over your head. Now you've got Tarrington and Briar Glen—but is that going to be enough to make you happy? And what about Verity? Have you thought about her at all? About what this marriage might do to her?"

"I have been thinking of her safety and protection every minute of every day since we first found out about the loan," she said harshly. "And I believe I've made the best choice for her too. You may not like the man or his politics, but even you should be able to see that Michael Tarrington will be able to provide a more stable life for her than either Wainright or Joshua Brice."

"He relishes the thought of fatherhood, does he?" Ryan asked sardonically. "You can tell that by a basket of oranges and a goddamn doll? You say he knows all your secrets—does that mean you've told him *everything* about Verity?"

"He . . . knows he will have to be very patient if he wants to win her trust."

"That's it? That's all? You're not planning to tell him anything else?"

"There isn't anything else to tell," she said, chilled despite the bright heat of the sun.

"You have more faith in Alisha's ability to keep her mouth shut than I do. And more faith in a husband you don't know either."

As if on cue, they heard the crunch of boots on the pebbled pathway and turned just as Michael Tarrington came walking into view. His easy gait, the cut of the dark-blue broadcloth jacket, the fit of the stylish trousers, the expensive suppleness of the leather boots all grated on Ryan's nerves and shored up his hostilities.

"I hope I am not intruding," Michael said smoothly. "I thought I should come around and make certain you were both in once piece."

"We can settle our own differences," Ryan said tightly.

"So I see." Tarrington stopped beside Amanda and noted

the soft pink flush in her cheeks. "I trust I haven't had too black a picture painted of me."

"My sister seems to think it could have been worse."

"But she hasn't quite managed to convince you?"

"I need a lot of convincing."

"I'm a patient man."

Ryan's sky-blue eyes narrowed. He felt Amanda's gaze imploring him to keep the peace and he did so with a considerable effort. "Congratulations; I understand you now own Rosalie."

"I own the note on Rosalie," he agreed smoothly. "Which I am assured by my wife you will endeavor to repay as soon as possible."

"I don't have that kind of money," Ryan grated.

"I don't need another farm."

Ryan glared at his new brother-in-law, the fury in his eyes as hot and uncompromising as the fury in his voice. "And I don't take charity. I'm sure you can find some other rich Yankee bastard to buy it."

"I'm sure I could," Tarrington said mildly. A lean, tanned hand disappeared to an inside breast pocket and emerged with a folded document. He held it out to Ryan, who did not have to look at it to know it was the original loan agreement William Courtland had signed with the Natchez Mercantile. "But I doubt I could find another rich Yankee bastard who would feel the same way about the land as you do."

Ryan stared at the document, his fists curling and uncurling. His jaw was so rigid, the pale gold hairs of his beard stubble stood out like porcupine quills.

"Take it," Michael said. "No strings attached."

Amanda held her breath. If Ryan refused—and he was stubborn, proud, and pig-headed enough to do just that—then she would have gone through all this for nothing. She would have incarnated Montana Rose for nothing. She would have gone begging to Forrest Wainright for nothing. She would have married Michael Tarrington . . . for nothing.

Ryan's hand moved an inch. Then another. He took the folded paper from Tarrington and stared down at it for sev-

eral more compellingly taut moments before he spoke.
"There should be enough seed salvageable for a good crop
next year, God willing, and if you will take my hand on it, I
can promise you a fair percentage of your money back by
then."

Michael smiled. "I'm in no hurry. Use it for as long as
you need it."

"At a reasonable rate of interest," Ryan insisted, and
extended his hand.

Amanda felt tears stinging behind her eyes. She knew
what it was costing Ryan just to accept the loan in the first
place.

Tarrington reached out and they shook formally, neither
one wavering his eyes a fraction, neither missing the opportunity to take a close measure of the other's grip. They were
very much alike in general height and build; what Ryan
lacked in breadth across the shoulders, he made up in stamina from the long hours he had spent toiling in the fields.
Amanda had the advantage of knowing what lay beneath the
tailored clothing Michael wore; she hoped Ryan would not
make the mistake of assuming he was soft and citified.

"As I told Amanda," Ryan said, breaking off the contact,
"I was on my way out to the fields. You will have to excuse
me."

"Of course. Your mother has graciously invited us to stay
the night so perhaps we'll have a chance to become better
acquainted later on."

Ryan seemed to take the overture of friendliness in stride
. . . at least, Amanda thought he did. His next words sent
her heart sinking into her belly again.

"I have absolutely no desire to become any better acquainted than we already are, Tarrington. In fact, I should
say what I have to say now, so that we have absolutely no
room for misunderstandings between us. I still think you are
a bastard, Tarrington. This"—he held up the loan papers—
"doesn't change that. Nor does the fact that you've married
my sister. Perhaps you're not as blackhearted a bastard as
Wainright, but you're still a bastard nonetheless. And if you

do anything to hurt Amanda—or Verity—or if you dare to mistreat them *in any way,* I swear to God I will personally tear the life out of you with my bare hands. Do I make myself clear?''

''I would say we understand each other.'' Michael nodded.

Ryan cast a final glance at his sister before he swung himself effortlessly into the saddle. She watched him ride away, and when he was out of sight, she let the air escape her lungs on a sigh.

She looked up at Michael's face but lowered her eyes again almost immediately. ''Thank you.''

''For what?''

''For taking his hand on the loan. For a terrible moment, there, I wasn't sure he would do it.''

''Pride is a pretty powerful obstacle to overcome. But on the bright side, at least he didn't shoot me out of hand; I would consider that a major triumph.''

Amanda's frown only deepened. ''He's worried about me —and about Verity.''

''I don't blame him. In his position, I'd be worried too.''

''He's good for the money,'' she said, curling her lip between her teeth. ''If he says he will pay you back, he will.''

''I'm *not* worried about that, although I would have preferred to take repayment in terms of his expertise rather than see him squander another year on cotton.''

''His . . . expertise?''

''The Judge—among others—has told me he bred and trained the finest horseflesh in these Confederate states.''

''Oh,'' she said with some impatience. ''Horses again.''

He smiled crookedly and gave his chin a rueful scratch. ''Said with such charming disdain, my lovely. How is it you could have lived around them all these years without acquiring some small pittance of tolerance or understanding?''

''I told you—''

''They don't like you, yes. Well, be that as it may, we already have several thousands of dollars invested on the hoof at Briar Glen, and it is my fondest wish to see that investment grow over the coming years. To do that will require special management skills and expert knowledge of stock, bloodlines, and breeding, all of which your brother possesses in abundance.''

''You have invested in horses without knowing anything about them?''

''I know enough to get by, but there is a great deal more I would like to learn.''

Her eyes, blue as a stormy sea and infinitely more dangerous, narrowed down to slits. ''You wouldn't, by any chance, have had that in your mind when you first proposed this marriage?''

He gazed off over the field in the direction Ryan had taken. ''You don't think he would consider working for me?''

''I don't know. Do you think your General Grant would consider declaring he made an error at the Appomattox Court House and rescind General Lee's surrender?''

Michael smiled and glanced down. ''As likely as all that?''

''Even less, I would say.''

His eyes crinkled at the corners. ''Then it should prove to be an admirable challenge.''

''The challenge, sir,'' she said testily, ''will simply be to make it through this evening in one piece.''

''Ahh, yes. This evening.'' He patted his pockets for a moment, frowning as if he had forgotten something of extreme importance. ''I meant to give this to you *last* evening, but . . . where the devil did I put it? . . . but we were a little preoccupied, as I recall. Ahh. Here we are.''

Amanda was watching his face, not his hands, so her surprise was genuine and absolute when he emptied the contents of a small satin pouch into his palm and held the object out to her.

It was a ring. The central stone was a sapphire, dark as ink and easily the size of her thumbnail, surrounded by a fiery circle of twelve diamonds.

Amanda stared at the ring, then up at his face.

"You don't like it?"

She looked down again. The ring was beautiful, and valuable. And it made her wonder again at the source and extent of her husband's wealth.

"I can't wear that," she whispered softly.

"Why not? Your sister has things twinkling in her ears and glittering around her throat; I assumed all women endeavored to glitter and twinkle at great expense to their husbands. The greater the better, I thought."

It was the wrong thing to say and the wrong time to say it with her pride still stinging from the sound of Alisha's mocking laughter.

"You thought wrong," she said, and turned on her heel.

He reached out and caught her around the arm, his grip more forceful than he intended, and certainly more peremptory than she expected, as her gasp proclaimed.

"Mandy?"

"Let go of me."

"What the devil is wrong now? It's a ring, for heaven's sake."

"Yes, it's a ring," she agreed coldly. "My mother had one very much like it, but the Yankees took it, along with everything else of any value we owned whether it twinkled, glittered, or just plain caught their fancy. This"—she passed her hand over the rich velvet of her skirt—"is bad enough to rub in their faces, but since you burned or destroyed my other clothing, I had no choice but to wear it or ride naked in the carriage. I won't wear *that*, however. Not now, not ever!"

She turned and started back along the path, her skirts belling out behind her in her haste. Michael was of half a mind to go after her—he actually took an angry step in that direction before he stopped himself and cursed his own foolhardiness. He hadn't done anything fundamentally wrong. He hadn't deliberately been trying to flaunt his wealth or embarrass her or her family. He had simply thought to give his wife a ring. Nor had he duped her into marrying him just so he could gain leverage over the brother. He would have offered Ryan the job anyway.

He looked down and his scowl deepened. Lying at his feet, the ribbons fanned out across the dusty earth, was her bonnet, cast away in a further gesture of contempt. He stooped over and picked it up, intending to take it back to the house with him. But on a second thought, he swung his arm and sent it spinning away into the rosebushes, not even bothering to see where it landed.

Chapter 17

Sarah insisted they remain the night at Rosalie. She would not hear of them returning to Briar Glen any sooner, and, as she protested time and time again throughout the day, she would have preferred a week or even more to adjust to the idea of Amanda's marriage and to become better acquainted with her new son-in-law. It was Michael himself, however, who insisted—gently—that a day was all they could spare at the present time. There was simply too much to be done at Briar Glen. Soon, though, he promised, they would come back for a longer visit and, of course, with the Glen only an hour's ride away, Sarah and William were welcome to visit Amanda and Verity any time.

Hearing the words said aloud, it occurred to Sarah that her granddaughter as well as her daughter would be moving away. It prompted a fresh flood of tears and a violent fit of prolonged sneezing as she inhaled too much hartshorn.

William Courtland's opinion of Michael Tarrington was fortified over the case of aged Kentucky bourbon the latter had brought with him from Briar Glen. William spent an amiable afternoon verifying the quality of the spirits as well as the mettle of both new sons-in-law. Amanda, meanwhile, spent most of her time with Verity, explaining why they would not be remaining at Rosalie, but would be making their new home at Briar Glen.

"You like Michael, don't you?"

The child's huge, solemn eyes looked up at her. She clutched the doll he had given her and seemed to weigh it against the notion of actually living with him in a strange new house.

Amanda talked for a full hour, extolling the virtues of Briar Glen, knowing she sounded desperate, even to her own ears. She promised they would come back to Rosalie so often it would not feel as if they had left at all. She promised (prayed) Ryan would visit the Glen with William and Sarah. She promised Verity her own pretty new room and a big, soft new bed stuffed with so many feathers it would take ten men to carry it up the stairs—a bed big enough to fit a whole family of new dolls.

Verity did not look convinced. The slightest noise sent her diving into her mother's skirts, and when the entire family gathered together for dinner, she would not venture closer than the width of the room to Michael Tarrington, not even when he attempted to lure her out of hiding with magic tricks and sleight of hand.

Sarah declared herself exhausted beyond all endurance shortly after the meal ended and took to her bed early. Amanda was not far behind, settling Verity into bed, where it seemed to take forever before those accusingly big blue eyes finally stayed closed. Amanda, worn to the bone herself, returned to the drawing room with the intentions only of saying good night. The sound of voices and laughter halted her on the threshold. Alisha, Michael, Karl von Helmstaad, and William Courtland were seated at a table beside the hearth. They were playing cards—poker by the look of it. A layer of smoke drifted over their heads from the three strong cigars Michael had passed around. Alisha's hair glinted gold in the blaze of firelight and lamplight, and, as she leaned forward to pick up a card, Amanda experienced the strangely disconcerting sensation of seeing herself as Montana Rose.

"Ahh! Amanda!" William spied her standing in the doorway and tipped his cigar in her direction. "We had almost given you up for lost. We left a chair for you, over here by me. Come join us and help me welcome these upstarts to the family in style."

"I have only come to say good night." She crossed the room and kissed her father's cheek. "I don't want to leave Verity alone too long."

"Bah! You coddle the child too much. Your mother and Mercy are within earshot if she starts wandering about."

"No. I'd better not."

''But we've just started.''

''I wasn't suggesting you end the game. I only said I was tired; Michael can stay as long as he wishes.''

''Or until his cash runs out,'' Alisha murmured, winding a shiny strand of hair around her finger.

Amanda felt suddenly wide awake. ''You're playing for money?''

''I suggested it might add some piquancy to the game,'' Alisha drawled. ''Michael concurred.''

The familiar use of his name sent Amanda's gaze to her husband's face. She wondered, by the shuttered watchfulness in his eyes, if he was experiencing the same sense of *déjà vu* Amanda had felt at the door, for he was studying her sister with an intensity that raised goosebumps up and down her arms.

''Michael?''

He looked up at her as if her voice had been an intrusion. No, he had not failed to make the association. The gray of his eyes was as hard and cold as slate and did not linger on hers too long before flickering back to concentrate on Alisha.

''You look tired,'' he said. ''Don't wait up for me.''

''I won't,'' she said softly. ''Good night.''

''Night, daughter,'' William waved his hand absently.

''Good night, Amanda dearest,'' Alisha murmured, smiling directly into Michael's eyes. ''I shall try not to take too much advantage of your husband's apparent eagerness to make a good impression.''

Amanda retraced her steps to the door and was certain no one followed her departure, certain she was forgotten the instant she left the room. Unfortunately, her memory was not so obliging, and the image of her sister's sly smile and Michael's attentiveness lingered with her long after she had washed and changed into bedclothes. Verity, as she had often done in the past, had crept from her room to Amanda's and was firmly ensconced beneath the blankets. It gave Amanda a small measure of satisfaction to know the bed was only big enough for the two of them and that Michael, if and when he finally came upstairs, would have to take his comfort from the hard floor. Even so, the urge came over her more than once to tiptoe out into the hall and peer over the railing to catch a glimpse or an echo of the activities in the drawing room. More than once she had to scold herself back into bed and pull the covers up to her chin, envying Verity's deep sleep.

An hour passed. Two. Three. Somewhere out on the river a passing boat whistle blew the midnight watch and Amanda slipped out of bed again and paced to the window, to the door, back to the window again. She stared at the glistening half moon, at the stars, at the blackness of the night; and she wondered what Michael was doing, what he was thinking, how he was reacting to what would be, undoubtedly, one of Alisha's finer performances.

He had not been exactly warm to her since their confrontation at the stable. If anything, he had grown proportionately cooler to her as the day wore on while Alisha, her feline senses quick as ever to detect tension of any kind and pounce on it, had been even quicker to retract her claws and coat her every word and gesture with a healthy layer of syrup. Amanda had watched her sister in action before—watched and studied her well enough to carry off an imitation in the guise of Montana Rose. The slanted eyes, the moistened lips, the soft, breathy voice . . . were they not the same tools of seduction that had lured Michael Tarrington out onto the deck of the *Mississippi Queen* with his initial proposition?

As for Alisha, she had never let anything so trivial as politics or loyalty stand in the way of a conquest. She hated Yankees, but it had not stopped her from flirting with every blue-coated officer who had passed through Rosalie when it was occupied by the Federal Army. Nor had Joshua Brice been the first man to have shown an interest in Amanda and ended up being wholly under Alisha's spell. Each and every man, for that matter, who had ever looked at Amanda had done so only after Alisha had discarded him. Caleb Jackson had been the only one to scorn Alisha's attempts to seduce him, and Amanda had begun to wonder if that was why she had married him. Because he professed to love *her* and not just the mirror image of Alisha.

Josh, on the other hand, had been far too handsome and virile for Alisha to let slip through her fingers, Amanda could see that clearly now. And if Josh was too tempting to resist, what would her sister make of Michael Tarrington, quite simply the most dangerously handsome man to have walked into recent memory? He was also rich and powerful, two intoxicants that would whet Alisha's appetites and lure her like a lioness to raw meat.

Would he find it amusing? Or would he begin to regret he had married the wrong sister?

"I thought I told you not to wait up for me?"

Amanda gasped and was nearly startled off her seat on the window ledge. Michael was standing at the bedroom door, his jacket draped over his arm, his collar unfastened, the ends of his cravat hanging loosely around his neck. There was only one small lamp burning near the bed, the wick turned almost too low for the light to penetrate the shadows, and her reaction was as much due to his sudden appearance as it was to the way he looked—definitely as dangerously handsome as she had just been thinking.

"I . . . couldn't seem to fall asleep."

He regarded her intently for a moment, then closed the door behind him and glanced at the bed.

Amanda followed his gaze to where Verity was nestled against the pillows, one hand clutched around the doll, the other fisted against her mouth with the thumb sucked securely inside.

"I didn't want to leave her alone tonight," Amanda said quickly. "I thought . . . with everything happening so fast . . ."

"You don't have to explain. Or apologize," he said, walking over to the side of the bed to peer down at the sleeping child. "I don't think I made a very good impression on her today."

"Perhaps you should have tried bribing her with more oranges. The bourbon seems to have worked with Father."

The slate-gray eyes found her and she felt the effects of a cold, blank stare slither down her spine.

"Then again, I seem to have lost ground all around," he mused.

"I'm sorry, but what did you expect? Did you think everyone would welcome you with open arms?"

"No. But I didn't exactly expect to find myself the main course in a pool of hungry sharks either."

"What do you mean?"

"What do I mean?" He tossed his jacket over the back of a chair and pulled off his cravat. "I mean, my pet, I would have hated to be on the river with Billy Fleet twenty years ago when his hands were steadier and his capacity for alcohol was not eroded. As it was, even chair-bound and half swacked on Kentucky's finest, I had to keep looking down every few minutes to assure myself I was still in firm possession of *some* of the family jewels."

"My father is a tired old man," she said, biting on her lip. "There is not much in life that gives him pleasure anymore."

"Then I'm glad I could please him—which I did, I might add, to the sum of about four hundred dollars. Enough to keep him in cigars and sugared hams for a while."

"You lost to him? Deliberately?"

He turned to face her, his cambric shirt half open, half untucked from the waist of his trousers. "You say that as if you don't think I'm capable of going against my own better judgment."

When she neither denied nor admitted the charge, he scowled and walked toward her. "I may not be able to live up to your ideal image of the endlessly charming Southern gentleman whose behavior, manners, and morals are above reproach, but I do not purposefully set out to embarrass feeble old men, bribe women, or terrify young children. I bought the damned oranges because you told me a gut-wrenching story that made me feel guilty—which was the object of the excercise, was it not? I wanted to give you the ring today because it was beautiful and so were you and I thought the two of you belonged together. And I lost to your father tonight—yes, *deliberately*—because I suspected his pride would be as thick and crusty as your brother's—as *yours,* for that matter—and I didn't think he would just take the money from me, regardless of whether he needed it to put food on the table or not. Now, if I was wrong doing any of that"—he lifted his shoulders in an exaggerated shrug—"*mea culpa,* and God rot all the Philistines."

Amanda leaned back slightly to avoid the wave of vapors that blew off his breath.

"You're drunk," she surmised with a quietly exasperated sigh.

"I have been drinking a great deal," he corrected her. "But as long as I can still walk and piss in an upright position, I am not drunk."

If Amanda was startled by his crudity, it did not show. Not much showed, for all that the meager light from the oil lamp reached was the corner where they were standing. She was a blur of creamy soft longcloth and misty blonde hair. The locket winked around her neck, drawing his gaze down into the seductively dark valley between her breasts, and he mouthed a soundless oath, having spent the better part of the evening avoiding the temptation of falling into another dusky cleavage that had been presented for his admiration time and time again without a trace of shyness or reluctance.

"Forewarned, they say, is forearmed," he murmured. "Parlor games you called it, if I remember correctly. A pleasant way to pass a rainy afternoon? Christ, madam, between watching your father and trying *not* to watch your sister, I can understand why you're as good as you are at the gaming tables. The marks you met on the riverboats must have been child's play after an evening of family cut-throat. And you say your brothers were better?"

Amanda nodded, uncertain of whether she should be flattered or wary. As casually as she could, she turned and looked out the window. "You . . . said you were trying *not* to watch Alisha?"

"She can be very distracting," he admitted. "Not as distracting as you, however. I kept thinking of you all alone up here and I wondered . . ." She could see his reflection in the glass pane as he moved toward her. ". . . if you were still angry with me?"

Verity could not have asked the question in a more penitent manner, and Amanda felt her resolve weakening. "I wasn't angry."

"Yes, you were."

"No. Anxious, perhaps. Confused."

He pushed aside the thick fall of her hair and bent his lips to the softest part of her nape. When there was no resistance, he curled his arm around her waist, drawing her back against his hard body.

"Does this mean I am forgiven?" he murmured.

This was the discovery he made when he cupped his hand around her breast and kneaded it gently through the thin layer of her nightdress. Her nipple was as taut as a bead, straining against the cloth, straining into the seductive warmth of his fingers.

"Please," she said. "Verity . . ."

His tongue traced a slow, wet line from her nape to her shoulder to the tender white lobe of her ear.

"If she is here," he whispered, "there must be an empty room next door."

Her eyes shivered closed and she tried to ignore the sensations pouring down her spine, pooling in her belly. "I . . . don't want to leave Verity alone. She might waken and call out. And if I'm not here . . ."

He groaned and nuzzled the soft crush of her hair. His hand slid down from her breast and curved boldly into the cleft of her thighs. "If I am not *there*, madam, in a minute or two, I will be the one shouting."

Amanda's eyes fluttered closed, but she twisted out of his grasp and managed to gain a step or two of distance before he caught her and brought her back into his arms.

"Please, Michael," she implored, glancing at the bed to see if Verity had moved. "Not tonight. Not here, of all places."

Perhaps it was the way she said it, that touched on a nerve, for his eyes gleamed darkly and his mouth curled up the corner. "Why not? Are you afraid your family might find out you actually *enjoy* fucking a Yankee?"

Amanda pushed out of his arms. She stumbled back until she came up hard against the wall. "You *are* drunk. You're also vulgar and disgusting and—"

"And about at the limit of my patience," he warned softly. "Now, come over here."

"I will not!"

"I said"—his eyes narrowed to slits and his tongue coiled around a velvety command—"come over here."

"Go to hell."

For all of three seconds, there was no reaction. On the fourth, however, he stalked forward and crowded his body against her, trapping her against the wall. His hands raked into her hair and held her secure while his lips came crushing down over hers, kissing her with all the finesse of a barroom brawler. Amanda gagged on the strong taste of whiskey and tobacco, and she struggled in vain to free herself. She pushed against his broad chest with her fists, but it only made him more determined, his kiss more brutal in its intent. His hands ran down her body and came up again, dragging the hem of the nightdress with them. When she tried to bat him away, he caught her wrists and raised them up over her head, holding them there while his mouth and body crushed into hers. The cool air on her limbs made her renew her efforts to break free. She bit down sharply on his tongue and when he jerked back, she took advantage of the opening to push hard against his chest, then made a frantic dash toward the door.

He was a curse behind, and, even as she was reaching for the latch, she felt the tug of his hand closing around the folds of her nightdress, spinning her around, and throwing her off balance so that she caromed into the side of the bed.

The mattress saved her from a fall, but the sudden jolt unsettled Verity and brought her instantly awake. The child sat up and saw her mother sprawled across the foot of the bed. And she saw the tall, shapeless outline of a man with his hand still fisted around Amanda's nightdress, glowering down over the bed, his face an ominous mask of anger.

Her eyes rounded instantly with terror. She launched herself over the covers and flung herself at Amanda, putting herself and her blue-eyed doll between her mother and the looming shadow.

"Don't you hurt my mommy! Don't you hurt her!"

The cry was shrill and thin, not loud enough to carry beyond the bedroom door, but jarring enough to pierce through the anger and alcohol fogging Michael's senses. He was indeed far drunker than he cared to admit. His blood was pounding behind his eyes, his skin was clammy, and the floor felt like shifting mush beneath his feet.

"Mandy?"

He squeezed his eyes shut several times and raised a hand to wipe at the sweat that was suddenly pouring down his face. He saw Amanda cringing on the bed, gaping up at him in disgust. And he saw Verity, her little face crumpled and set as if she were ready to fly up at him and beat him to death with her doll.

"Christ." He raked his hands through his hair and staggered back a step. "What the hell am I doing?"

"You were hurting my mommy," Verity whispered through a quivering pout.

"No, sweetheart," Amanda said quickly. "Michael wasn't hurting me. I . . . I just tripped and he was trying to catch me. We didn't mean to wake you up. We certainly didn't mean to frighten you . . . *did we, Michael?*"

He blinked the sweat out of his eyes again and met the two accusing stares. Verity had curled her arms around her mother's neck and was burrowed against her shoulder, her chin trembling, her eyes silvered with tears and not blinking at all. Amanda just sat there, holding her daughter's head protectively against her breast. Both of them were so beautiful, so vulnerable, so afraid to move, so afraid of *him* he wanted to cut off his hands and offer them by way of atonement.

Did she have to ask? Was she so unsure of him that she had to ask?

"N-no," he insisted hoarsely. "No, of course I didn't mean to frighten you, honey. And I would never hurt your mother. Never. I'm . . . sorry if you thought I would."

Verity turned her face into Amanda's shoulder, shunning his apology.

He looked at Amanda. "I . . . didn't hurt you, did I?"

"No." Her voice was soft and taut. "You didn't hurt me."

Not this time, she might as well have screamed, and his shoulders sagged, his body swayed unsteadily in the weak light.

"You should have taken the money," he muttered.

"What?"

"You should have just taken the damned money when I offered it to you. And me . . ." He paused long enough to focus on the chair where he had thrown his jacket before he snatched it up and lurched toward the door. "I should never have thought I could buy my way into your life."

"Where are you going?"

"Out. For a walk. A long walk, so you needn't bar the door or worry that I'll be coming back. I won't bother you any more tonight—or ever, if that's the way you want it. In fact, I'll be leaving first thing in the morning, and whether you leave with me or not . . . is your decision. Your choice. Good night."

"Michael . . . wait . . ."

But he was already gone. There was nothing but the closed door to hear her plea.

Chapter 18

S he found him two hours later by the river.

Michael Tarrington had probably walked off a mile or two of monumental frustration, circling the ruined gardens, the summerhouse, the makeshift stables. He had called himself every kind of fool he could think of and some that were newly invented, and, after an hour, when the silent, towering silhouette of the house offered neither sympathy nor answers, he followed the rutted track that led down to the bank of the Mississippi River.

He walked, he smoked, he thought. He cleared his head and paced away the effects of the bourbon, but nothing seemed to help him rid his mind of the image of Amanda sprawled across the bed, her face pale, her eyes full of silent condemnation.

And Verity. Christ Jesus, the child had stared at him as if he had turned into her worst nightmare. Amanda had said she had been frightened as a child by by heavy-booted soldiers kicking in her door, searching her room for valuables. The thought that perhaps he *was* her nightmare made him physically ill, and he wanted to cut off more than just his hands.

He had a wife and a child now. They were his responsibility now and would be for the rest of his life. The reality of what that meant obviously hadn't sunk in yet, hadn't progressed past the challenge of winning Amanda Courtland Jackson and wooing her into his bed.

What the hell was it about her that made him go against every rule he had ever made for himself? His whole life, it seemed, had been spent wandering restlessly, guarding his privacy, maintaining his independence with an almost feverish determination. He had always taken his pleasure where he found it, eluding with ease the countless traps and ploys a woman used to snare herself a husband. He had never wanted a woman badly enough to resort to deceit or entrapment himself. Not until he met Amanda Jackson.

The first moment he had laid eyes on Montana Rose, he had known he wanted her. And he would have paid any price to have her; that was what men did with beautiful women they met on riverboats. It was expected and accepted; the only point of contention was how much and for how long. Their meeting had not been as accidental as it had seemed, or as he had told her, for he had been hearing a great deal about the most beautiful and elusive lady gambler on the Mississippi. He had sailed the river a dozen times with the express purpose of seeing her in action, and when he had finally been able to orchestrate their meeting on board the *Queen,* Tarrington had known he would go to any lengths, any extremes, to possess her.

No one had complimented *him* on his own outstanding performance, or commented on *his* vast reserves of self-control when he had first seen Amanda and Alisha Courtland walking down the wedding aisle. Dianna had said they were twins, and so he had expected to see some similarities . . . but not perfect replicas. Not two perfect candidates for queen of the Mississippi riverboats. And when he had finally determined which of the two had been causing him so many sleepless nights, he had been astonished and confounded again to realize he wanted her even more. He wanted Amanda Jackson in a way he had never wanted a woman before, not just for her body or the pleasure he would find there, but for what he saw in her eyes, what he *wanted* to see in her eyes each and every time she looked at him. Not fear, certainly. Not disgust. Not contempt for the blackhearted Yankee profiteer she assumed she had married.

Not a man who set her and her child cringing in fear.

He never should have assumed he could just touch her, kiss her, whisper a few sweet nothings and have her falling into his arms. Some women, maybe. Not this one. She would need to trust the man she fell in love with. Wholly and implicitly. And she would have to know that he trusted her.

Having reached this pinnacle of knowledge and understanding, had he sabotaged his chances with her through his
own arrogance and ignorance?

"Michael?"

He froze in his tracks and listened. It could have been the
dull roll of the river distorting the sounds around him, or it
could have been the breeze rifling through the cypress beards
that caused them to whisper his name. If so, he was afraid to
turn, afraid to look in case . . .

"Michael?"

He turned, slowly, and saw her standing on the crest of the
embankment, her nightdress and robe a shock of ghost-white
linen billowing gently against the night sky, her hair soft and
loose and flowing like liquid silver over her shoulders.

Michael exhaled through the tightness in his chest and
watched her drift down the slope toward him. She passed
through the slivers of moonlight that cut through the
branches, through blackness into moonlight again as she
slowed to a tentative halt before him. The delicately flounced
robe was open and blown back slightly from the haste that
had brought her out into the night. The nightdress underneath clung to the shape of her breasts, molding to them like
cream melting over warm flesh. Her gaze was unwavering
but her hand trembled noticeably as she lifted it and curled
her fingers around her locket.

"I saw you from the window," she whispered, "and I
didn't want you to leave without knowing how I feel."

"And how . . . do you feel?" he asked, the words
straining to get past the lump in his throat.

She moved a step closer. Her lips were parted and moist,
cool against the fever of his emotions as she reached up and
pressed them with a faltering courage over his.

Michael tossed his half-smoked cigar into the river. He
cradled her face between his hands and bent his mouth to
hers, kissing her with all the tenderness, the gentle passion
and longing that had been building inside him but had not
known how to come out. When they broke apart, it was only
to gasp each other's name and come together again, their

mouths open and searching, slanting hungrily over one another.

"Mandy . . . Mandy . . . dear God, I was afraid I'd
lost you. I was afraid you would never come to me again. I'm
sorry. I'm so very sorry. The things I said . . . what I did
. . . it was inexcusable."

"It doesn't matter," she cried, dragging his mouth down
to hers again.

"No," he said, and his muscles quaked with tremors as he
forced himself to hold her at arm's length. "I want to be
honest with you. I want to tell you how *I* feel before this goes
any further."

"Kiss me and I will know," she implored. "Touch me
and I will know."

The blood roared through his veins with the effort it took
to refuse, but he did. "From the moment I saw you, the very
first moment you walked into my life I knew I wasn't going
to have any peace until you were mine, a part of me. I would
have said anything, done anything, gone to any lengths to
have you."

"Michael . . . you don't have to explain."

"Yes. I do. Because I could have just gone to Ryan and
told him what you were planning to do with Wainright and
together we could have stopped you. For that matter, I could
have gone straight to Ryan in the first place and offered him
the money he needed."

"He wouldn't have taken it. You know he wouldn't."

"He would . . . if I had threatened to expose you as
Montana Rose."

He felt her stiffen in his arms, but she did not pull away
and he continued quickly, "Mandy, I won't lie to you. If I
had it to do all over again, I would still meet you on that road
at midnight and I would still buy the oranges—a whole
wagonload if need be—and I would still do my damndest to
convince you I was your only choice. There is something
good between us, you must feel it. I don't want to lose that
feeling and I don't want to lose you."

"You haven't lost me," she promised softly. "And you

won't . . . so long as you hold me . . . and never let me go.''

Michael swept her eagerly into his arms. His lips sought her temples, her cheeks, they traced the supple path he was coming to know so well to the sweetness of her mouth, and once there, his tongue lashed at hers with a fierce possessiveness neither one could have denied. He heard her shivered cry and smoothed his hands down her back, circling her hips and bringing her hard against him. He groaned himself when her thighs parted of their own accord and she did not wait for his invitation, but began to rub herself sinuously over the straining bulge at his groin.

Michael pulled her down onto the cool thickness of the grass. His hands tore feverishly at the bodice of her nightdress, searching for the ribboned closure that was not there, and with a husky curse, he split the fragile cloth down the seam and filled his hands, filled his mouth, with the soft, exposed flesh.

She arched up off the grass, her hair spilling back in a lustrous wave, her fingers clawing at his shoulders, grabbing at fistfuls of his clothing and trying to rid him of these unwanted restraints. He obliged, without lifting his mouth from her flesh, and stripped off his jacket, his shirt, cursing each and every one of the fashionably small buttons on his trousers that refused to give way.

"Let me," she gasped. "Let me . . ."

Michael conceded with a wry, half-disbelieving laugh and rolled onto his back, content to find her breasts swinging an inch above his mouth. His gaze settled on the bright glint of the gold locket . . . on its border of etched roses . . .

His breath caught again, just as the last button gave way and his flesh surged upward into her greedily waiting mouth. His hands flew down to her hips and he clamped her fiercely between them, lifting her, flinging her aside to land in a tumble of torn white linen and thrashing limbs.

"Michael! Wh-what is it? What's wrong?"

His curse echoed on the air like the crack of a whip.

"Nothing's wrong . . . except that you should be doing this with your husband, not me."

"Wh-what? I don't—"

Michael wrapped his fingers around the locket and jerked it to the limit of the chain, angling it up to the moonlight to sear the boldly etched letter *A* with fire.

"I'm sure you know *exactly* what I mean, Mrs. von Helmstaad."

Alisha stared at Michael Tarrington for a long moment, then slumped back onto the grass with a loud, expressive sigh. "And here I thought we were getting along so marvelously together."

Michael shot to his feet and glared down at his almost naked sister-in-law. He did not trust himself to keep his hands off her—to keep from lifting her by the scruff of her neck and smashing her against the nearest tree.

"Just what the bloody hell kind of game did you think you were playing?" he snarled.

"The same one you were, I thought," she purred, "or is that your idea of a Yankee bluff sticking out of your breeches?"

Michael swore again and pulled his trousers together, turning his back on her laughter as he fought with the buttons again.

"No need to be shy about it," she murmured, licking her lips appreciatively. "I haven't tasted anything half so good in months."

"You haven't answered my question. Why did you follow me out here?"

"I wanted to help you," she said amiably.

"*Help* me?"

"Mmmm. As I said, I saw you from my bedroom window. It wasn't difficult to guess, what with the walls being so thin and all, that my dear sister had sent you and your lusty thoughts out here to cool off. I merely wanted to help you relieve some of your tension."

"By pretending to be Amanda?"

She shrugged. "It wouldn't be the first time. And admit it: You didn't know."

Michael clenched his fists by his sides. He hadn't known. He had been so damned happy and relieved to see who he thought was his wife standing on the embankment, it had blinded him to everything else. Moreover, he would never have known, never have guessed Alisha hated her sister so much actually to attempt a stunt like this.

"I would have known eventually," he said with barely suppressed savagery. "And then I would have killed you."

"Oh, I don't think so," she said silkily. "Not when you realized how much more I can do for you than Amanda. How much more I am willing to do."

She rose up onto her knees and let the robe and torn nightdress fall away from her shoulders. Her breasts stood firm and eager and opaline in the filtered moonlight, the nipples raised, hard, and quivering with the same impudence that brought her up on her feet to stand unabashedly nude before him.

"I'm still willing," she murmured.

"I am a married man."

"And you love your wife," she sneered.

"There is a very good chance that I do."

"So much so you almost made love to her sister? Or was it Montana Rose you were so eager to put yourself into?"

Violence throbbed through every pore in his body. His jaw turned to granite and the steel of his eyes glittered dangerously. He should have turned and strode away from the riverbank without a further word, but something about the malicious smile forming on Alisha's lips cautioned him against it.

"Yes, indeed," she mused. "You did make a grave blunder, Michael, didn't you? Amanda won't be happy at all that you've given away her tawdry little secret. Although I daresay there isn't anything little about it all. Imagine . . . the sweet, demure, prim and proper Widow Jackson . . . secretly the darling of the Mississippi riverboats. You know . . . I wondered sometimes, when men on the riverboats smiled and acted as if they knew me. I thought it was just a case of them mistaking me for someone else, but this . . . this is just too wickedly delicious. Mistaken for my own dear sister, the Queen of the Mississippi gambling boats! My, my, my! I declare, I am scandalized. And . . . just a tad chilly.''

Sighing with lustful delight as her fingers raked through the luxuriously thick mat of hair and climbed up to circle the column of his neck she skimmed her hands up the hard swell of muscles on his chest. Her breasts pillowed against his flesh and she levered herself on tiptoes so that her mouth could nibble hungrily at the underside of his chin.

"If you're chilly," he said, pushing her to arm's length, "you should put your clothes back on."

"But we're not finished our . . . discussion."

"I think we are." He bent over to retrieve his shirt and gathered up her robe and nightdress at the same time. "Get dressed."

He used a tone that would have had anyone else scrambling to obey him, but Alisha just laughed.

"She really has you wrapped around her little finger, doesn't she? Caleb was like that too, so honorable and self-righteous, thinking his precious Amanda was the Virgin incarnate. He didn't know her very well. Neither do you."

He shoved his arms into the sleeves of his shirt and glared at Alisha. "I know all I need to know."

"I'm sure you *think* you do. Just as I am sure I could surprise you with a few things your wife might not *want* you to know."

"If there is something she doesn't want me to know . . . she probably has her reasons."

"Oh . . . my dear sister never does anything without a good reason. Marrying you, for instance. *Puh-leeze* don't try to tell me it was because she was passionately, ravenously in love with you."

Michael finished tucking his shirt into his trousers, and, noting that Alisha still had not moved to cover herself, he took the robe out of her hands and draped it around her shoulders, forcibly sliding her arms into the sleeves and tying the belt at her waist.

"You do know she was practically engaged before you came along. Of course, he was penniless and couldn't have helped out with mortgages and the like, but it didn't stop them from becoming . . . very close friends, if you take my meaning."

I would like to take your throat in my hands and squeeze, he thought, refusing to fall for so obvious a gambit.

"You don't have to believe me," she said. "You can ask just about anyone in the county—including Mother and Father—if Amanda wasn't expected to marry Joshua Brice."

"What happened before our marriage does not concern me," he repeated brusquely, impatience and anger colliding in his voice. "What happens now does, so if you'll excuse me—"

He started back up the slope and Alisha whirled around, hardly able to believe a man was actually walking away from her, *rejecting* her in favor of her prim, mealy-mouthed, self-righteous sister. Outrage and indignation, fueled by the irrational jealousy that had brought her out into the night in the first place, flushed into her cheeks and laced her words with acid as she called after him.

"If she didn't tell you about Josh, she probably didn't tell you about Verity either, did she!"

It was more a statement than a question, and despite his resolve, his footsteps slowed. Then stopped.

"I didn't think so," she grated. "I didn't think she'd want to tarnish her virginal image that much, not even for a Yankee."

Michael drew two deep, measured breaths to gain a firm hold on his composure before he turned slowly back to face her. "What about Verity?"

"Oh?" Her voice was smug and singsong. "I thought you weren't concerned about what went on before your marriage."

He retraced his steps, cutting across a swath of moonlight bright enough to show the fury blazing in his eyes. Alisha stood her ground not even flinching when his fingers went around her arm and he jerked her roughly against his chest.

"I would caution . . . no, I would *warn* you strongly not to make me any angrier than I already am," he snarled. "Now, what is it about Verity that you seem so anxious to tell me?"

"Ask your precious wife!" she hissed.

"I'm asking you," he said, squeezing his hand around her arm, tightening his grip until he saw unwitting tears of pain spring into her eyes. "And I'll keep asking until I get an answer."

Alisha cursed. Her free hand grabbed at his shirt, missed, and her nails gouged the side of his neck, leaving thin red runnels of bleeding flesh over his collarbone.

"Let me go, you Yankee son of a bitch!"

"Not until you've spit out your poison. I won't have you holding anything over Amanda's head . . . or mine."

"You want to know so you can protect her?" Alisha spat, writhing with pain and resentment. "Well, then know this . . . Caleb Jackson was not Verity's father!"

"What? *What did you say?*"

"You heard me. Caleb was such a pantywaist, he couldn't have fathered a jackrabbit. Moreover, they were married when he came home on his last furlough—the first time he'd been home in over a year. Verity was born less than seven months later . . . fat, healthy and not a day too early. She was born in New Orleans too, well away from the eyes and ears of any scandal or gossip. I know because I was with her. Two loving sisters sent away together to await the happy event, lingering there until it was respectable to come home."

Michael stared unblinking at Alisha von Helmstaad. Amanda had said she had gone to New Orleans for the birth, but . . . the rest of it was difficult to believe. No . . . it was impossible to believe.

"You are breaking my arm," she rasped through her teeth.

"Be thankful I don't break your neck," he said, relaxing his grip but not releasing her. "Who else knows about this?"

"No one."

"No one?"

Alisha glared up through narrowed, vindictive eyes. "Father was away fighting and Mother has never been one to ask too many questions if she didn't think she wanted to know the answers. Ryan might know, although he has never said anything to me. But he is her champion and always has been. She wouldn't have been able to keep something like this from him."

"And this . . . Joshua Brice? Is he the father?"

"Heavens, no. He was off playing the hero too. They were all off playing heroes while we women were left behind to fend for ourselves, to barter and trade for what we needed just to stay alive. Of course, we didn't have much to barter with. And wouldn't you just know dear Amanda would be the one to offer the ultimate sacrifice."

Michael's hand began to tremble where it was laced around her arm. *"I don't believe you."*

"You don't believe she would do just about anything to save her precious Rosalie?"

His lips curled back over a snarl. "I don't believe she would do *that.*"

"Why? Because she played the grieving widow so well? Or was it the reluctant virgin? She is such a convincing liar, she could probably make you believe it was an immaculate conception. But then you know better, don't you? You surely must have known she was not protecting any maidenhead when you took her to your bed. And if she's been catting around the waterfront as Montana Rose, goodness only knows what other things she hasn't been protecting."

Michael released Alisha von Helmstaad with an abrupt shove and stared out across the wide swath of the Mississippi River. Amanda . . . *Montana* was a damned good actress, but no one could have fooled him so completely or manipulated him so expertly. Their wedding night . . . she had been genuinely reluctant to consummate their union. Repulsed by the act itself—or so it had seemed. So he had been led to believe. Yet that night, and the next, she had come to accept his body and his attentions willingly enough, even eagerly. Too eagerly, perhaps, for someone who was supposedly a pure and chaste widow, venerating the memory of her dead husband?

No. Alisha was lying. She had to be. She was certainly lying about *something*, that much was as obvious as the jealousy she harbored for her twin. Michael had known too many women like her over the years to be fooled for one instant into believing a fraction of what came out of those lips. And yet . . .

He had thought Amanda was different. And maybe she still was, just not in the way he had hoped. If that was the case . . . If that was the case, by Christ, then she truly had made a fool out of him. A magnificent, blundering fool who had been too blinded by his own lust to see the neatly spun web she had woven around him.

Alisha massaged her upper arm and watched the subtle changes come over Michael's face—the thinning of his mouth, the tautening of a jawline that was already square and solid and unyielding. She took advantage of his distraction to sidle closer, and, when he made no attempt to stop her, she ran her hand down the front of his shirt, smoothing her fingertips over the decidedly impressive swell of muscling, molding her palm and fingers around the iron bulk of his breast.

"What a shame," she whispered, "to waste all of this on someone who doesn't appreciate it."

Michael stared at Alisha. His vision blurred for a moment and he saw Amanda; he saw Montana Rose. He felt her seductive warmth against his chest, her fingers tracing tiny whorls over and around the raised disk of his nipple, his belly, the braced tension in his thighs. He heard her soft, breathy moan and realized his body had not remained as indifferent as his mind. Nor had his blood, singing with the effects of too much bourbon and too rich a need for his wife, cooled to the press of warm white flesh and a wet, silky mouth.

Alisha gasped as his fists twined around thick skeins of

her hair. She gasped again as his mouth came down savagely over hers, his tongue thrusting, ravaging, plundering with a violence that flooded her belly with a heat unlike anything she had felt before. She tasted his anger and his loathing, and she felt the outrage in his hands as he flung her harshly aside. Her ankle twisted painfully in the soft earth and she fell onto her knees, but there was no one beside her to hear her curse, no one there to answer to the fury blazing in her eyes, for when she pushed aside the obstructing veil of her hair, Michael was gone.

In disbelief she scanned the embankment both ways, but the movement of the trees distorted any shadows that might have been a man stalking—or running—away.

Alisha sank back onto her heels and tore two fistfuls of grass out by the roots. How was it that Amanda managed to surround herself with all these noble men? Ryan, Caleb, Josh . . . they were always willing to protect her, forgive her her faults.

Now Michael Tarrington.

Alisha's eyes narrowed and she laughed suddenly. Tarrington might have given her the protection of his name, true enough, but would his pride allow him to forgive her so easily?

Chapter 19

Amanda spent an interminably sleepless night pacing, arguing with herself, arguing with Michael *in absentia*, blaming his drunken arrogance and her own pretentious foolishness for prompting a confrontation that should never have progressed as far as it had. But it had, and now he was off on his own somewhere and she was sitting a tearful vigil over her sleeping daughter, playing and replaying every wretched detail of the day and night through her mind, wondering if there had been any single moment when either of them could have just held up their hands and stopped things going from bad to worse to terrible.

The ring had been presented at an inappropriate time, that was all. And he hadn't lied to her about wanting Ryan's help with his bloody horses, he simply hadn't discussed any of his business activities with her at all. Nor was he obliged to. There were no vows in the wedding ceremony that stated "thou must divulge all of thy plans, motives, secrets . . ."

She had secrets too, and each time Amanda looked at Verity, she suffered a fresh, hot blur of tears. Ryan was right. She should have told Michael everything. The whole sordid truth. She would have been able to tell Caleb, and he would have accepted the child as his own. She *probably* would have been able to tell Josh—before she had known about him and Alisha, of course—but that was because she had known him most of her life and he would have understood the importance of keeping a family together, regardless of the cost or the sacrifice.

She simply didn't know Michael Tarrington well enough to trust him with such fragile pieces of her heart. Or to guess what his reaction toward the child might be.

His parting words echoed in her ears like wind chimes. Stay here, go with him. It was her choice. But with dawn an avalanche of pink and purple clouds rolling across the sky, she still hadn't made that choice, and she left her perch by the window and walked downstairs in search of hot water for a bath.

Maybe, if she only had herself to worry about, it would have been an easier decision to make. She could have learned to cope with his moods, deal with his appetites, adapt to his independent ways. But she had Verity to worry about. Verity, the most fragile piece of her heart, who came first in importance and always would.

Her path to the kitchens took her past the parlor. She might not have seen him, might not have stopped had a stab of reflected sunlight not drawn her eye into the room as she passed. Her footsteps slowed, stopped, and kept her poised on the threshold with her heart lodged in her throat and her hands reaching up to hug her upper arms.

Michael was there, asleep on a chair, his long legs spread and bent at ungainly angles, his arms hanging over the sides. Clutched in one hand was a glass that still held a few drops of amber liquid; beside him, a bottle of whiskey—the culprit that had refracted the bright early rays of the sun. It was a finger's width from being as empty as the second bottle that sat on the floor. His shirt was opened to his waist and his head lolled to one side. His eyes were closed, the lids puffed and red. And though she couldn't see clearly through the milky haze of light that was just beginning to bloom through the curtains, it looked as if there were dried water stains on his cheeks.

The sight sent her leaning against the wall for support. Her throat was dry, her senses suddenly so acute, she swore she could hear the room itself breathing.

She had not yet had the opportunity to observe her husband with his defenses down. How different he looked, especially without the maturing slash of mustache to camouflage the youthful shape of his mouth. Gone too were the etched lines of authority that readily pleated his brow, gone the rigid set to his jaw that made him look so formidable, so unapproachable. So uncompromising. The long sweep of his lashes lay on his cheeks like the fallen wings of a sparrow, and his hair, never completely tidy at the best of times, curled over the top of his collar and lay against his cheek in gleaming, thick waves.

His shirt was spread open across the breadth of his chest, and she could recall quite clearly how it felt to run her fingers through the wealth of coarse dark hairs. Her gaze wandered lower and traced the outline of his thighs, following the creases and folds in his trousers, lingering over the bulge that was impressive even in repose. It did not take much effort to remove the barriers in her mind's eye, to see him naked and standing in the sunlit alcove, or naked and kneeling in front of a glowing fire, or naked and lying beneath her, assuring her he would not break and neither would she.

He had frightened her then, but only with his power and vitality. And he had taken such care to remove those fears, to turn them one by one into eagerness and passion . . . she could not bring herself to believe he would ever do anything to deliberately hurt her.

Lust was not a Yankee monopoly. More than a few honorable Southern gentlemen, overcome by drink and desire, would undoubtedly have behaved the same way. Some men —and here it took no strain to imagine Forrest Wainright's greedy, grasping hands—might not have stopped at all, whether Verity was there beside them or not. Michael *had* stopped. He had been as shocked as she and instantly contrite. And had obviously spent the night drowning in guilt.

Amanda drew a deep breath and pushed away from the wall. She walked across the width of the parlor and stopped beside his chair, and tried not to notice how badly her fingers were trembling as she reached down and touched his arm.

Michael's jaw worked up and down and his chin came up off his chest. His foot stirred and his leg straightened. The hand holding the glass lost its grip, sending the heavy crystal to the floor with a dull thud. The noise brought his eyes open, but it took a long moment for him to bring them into focus.

The gray centers were washed pale by lack of sleep, the whites were veined and bloodshot.

He became aware of someone standing between him and the window, and his eyes made a concentrated effort to squint through the glare the reflected sunlight was throwing off Amanda's dressing gown. He followed the blurred flow of white cloth upward and when he found Amanda's face, he held it for two measurable heartbeats before his eyes widened and he launched himself up and out of the chair.

Amanda flinched back and her hand went to her breast. "I'm sorry. I didn't mean to startle you."

Michael gulped at a lungful of air and his gaze flicked down to where her hand was pressed flat against the base of her throat. His eyes blazed for as long as it took him to search along the delicately ruffled edge of her robe and find the face of her locket. When he found it, when he saw the scrolled initial in its bed of etched roses, some of the anger drained from his face. The shock was slower to fade, for neither the room nor his legs applauded his judgment in leaping so suddenly out of the chair, and he pushed unceremoniously past Amanda to get to the window, where he lifted the sash and pulled the fresh, cool air into his lungs.

"I didn't mean to startle you," she said again. "I only thought to waken you before . . ." Her voice trailed away and she bit down gingerly on the pad of her lip.

"Before anyone else saw me?" he grated. "How very *wifely* of you."

Amanda winced at the bitterness in his voice and clasped her hands tightly together in front of her.

"What time is it?" he asked, hanging his head between his shoulders.

"A little before six, I should imagine."

Michael would have asked what day it was too, but it was taking all of his strength to keep his stomach where it belonged. The blood was pounding in his temples and his mouth tasted like rusted iron. The world outside was too goddamned bright and he had to turn his back to it, but that only brought the glowing white specter of Amanda before him and he had to cradle his head in his hands to keep his skull from splitting apart. The collar of his shirt was displaced further, letting the light fall directly on the ridge of his collarbone.

Amanda moved a step closer, a small frown wrinkling her brow.

"Did I do that?" she asked in a whisper, reaching cool fingers toward his neck.

Michael waved away her hand and pressed his own over the area that had drawn her concern. When he found the quartet of lightly scabbed scratchmarks Alisha's nails had left, his stomach rolled over in another sickly somersault.

"I'm sorry," Amanda said, and looked down at her hands. She could not remember scratching him, but she must have. She remembered pushing and she remembered striking out with her fists, and she was appalled to think she could have done that much, let alone lash out with enough vehemence to draw blood.

"I . . . reacted badly," she said softly. "I shouldn't have been so . . . anxious, and I certainly shouldn't have struck you."

Michael had no reply, mainly because there wasn't one. If he told her she hadn't been the one to leave the marks on his neck, he would have to tell her who did, and then he would have to tell her the rest. He watched her struggling with her conscience, and he tried to see the lie, tried to convince himself he would never find it, but he only saw Alisha's taunting grin and heard the echo of her laughter telling him his wife was proficient at cheating at far more than cards.

"You . . . said you wanted to leave early. I can make you breakfast, if—"

"I'm not bothered about breakfast," he interrupted curtly. "I'll be leaving as soon as Foley brings the carriage around."

Amanda moistened her lips, still avoiding his eyes. "Very well. We should only need an hour or so to get ready, or"— she looked up and her eyes were the same unbearably clear blue as the sky outside—"if you don't want to wait, we can have someone drive us home later."

His head was not pounding so much that he missed the word *home*. Nor did the rushing of his blood drown out the word *we*.

"How is Verity?" he asked tautly. "Are you sure she *wants* to come with me? Are you sure *you* want to come with me?"

Amanda saw the coldness in his eyes and heard it in his voice and she was unsettled by how pale he was, as if her nails had cut across the jugular and bled him dry. His expression was even less reassuring. His lips were flattened into a thin, unforgiving line and pride held his chin so high and rigid, she doubted he would lower it if she prostrated herself on the floor in front of him.

"She just needs . . . time," she whispered. "Maybe we all just need time."

"Maybe we do," he agreed, too quickly and too bluntly to keep the flush from rising in her cheeks.

Amanda bowed her head and twisted her hands together. "I'll . . . go and get Verity ready then, shall I?"

A nerve shivered in Michael's cheek and softened the grim line of his mouth for a moment before it was clamped like granite again. "Suit yourself. I told you last night: The choice of whether you stay or leave is yours."

Amanda weighed the amount of frost coating his words against the chill she felt closing around her own heart . . . and she nodded.

"We'll leave with you, then."

And an hour later, they did.

In complete silence.

Part Two

PLAYING OUT THE HAND

Chapter 20

It took Forrest Wainright eight weeks to discover a weakness in the wall of respectability Michael Tarrington was building around himself. Surprisingly, it came from a most unusual and unexpected source, one of Tarrington's own people: Flora Reeves's son-in-law, Ned Sims.

Ned was not a well-liked man. He was lean and hawkish in appearance, lazy as the day was long, with a knack for doing as little as possible for as long as possible without raising too much of a sweat. He had met Sally Reeves after mustering out of the Army and he had been quick enough, wily enough to recognize the preferential treatment reserved for Flora and her daughter in the Tarrington household. He was even quicker to woo and wed the shy, introverted Sally, justifying his cleverness when the family presented them with a gift of one hundred gold double eagles on their wedding day.

Flora loathed him, of course, and he took perverse pleasure in keeping Sal awake and active all night long just to see the look on the old denizen's face when her daughter wobbled into the kitchen in the morning barely able to straighten her legs. Sally wasn't too keen on him either. The only thing passably pretty about her—her smile—had faded away the first time she walked into the stables and found him naked with the laundry maid. Ned had been the one to get angry, accusing her of spying on him, of sneaking around and following him. He had slapped her some, to stop her wailing, and when she had threatened to lock him out of their bedroom, he had punched her solidly in the gut and taught her a lesson in obedience she would not soon forget.

How was he supposed to have known the bitch was breeding?

He had known it soon enough that night when she started bleeding all over the bed. He had known it the next morning too, when Michael Tarrington had blown into the stable like a thundercloud and nearly beat him to a pulp. He would have thrown Ned out onto the streets of Boston then and there if not for Sally. She was simple and naive and believed a woman's place was by her husband's side, regardless of how he treated her. And if Ned had been banished from the household, Sal would have gone too—he would have seen to it—and Flora Reeves would not have been able to bear it.

The beating had only reinforced Ned's opinion of Tarrington. The big, arrogant bastard had everything—money, looks, charm, women eager to ride him all night long for the price of a smile. Ned had two blown-off fingers and a wife who bleated like a stuck pig if he took too long in one hole or the other.

It did not make matters any better when Tarrington announced he was looking for land in the South. At least in Boston, Ned had had his contacts on the waterfront. He'd known where to sell the odd bits of silver he lifted from the house and he'd known where to find the hottest whores and the cheapest whiskey. More often than not those same whores could tell him who their richest customers were and if they happened to be visiting in the country this particular weekend or that. For a share of the profits and a rollicking good tumble afterward, Ned could be persuaded to scale a wall and find an open window. His hoard of greenbacks and double eagles had grown impressively, and it wasn't long before he had earned himself enough to think about making a clean break and heading West.

That was just about the same time Flora had made the decision to follow Michael Tarrington to Natchez, and the same night that Ned, who would have preferred to follow Jonah into the mouth of the whale, had been caught red-handed in the middle of robbing the home of a prominent magistrate. Ned had been interrupted by one of the maids, and while he thought he had left her for dead, he found out later she had lived long enough to give the authorities a fair description, right down to the missing fingers on his left hand. Natchez had suddenly become a good deal more appealing than Boston. He could still bolt at the first smell of trouble, if need be, and if not . . . well, he knew where Tarrington kept his fancy Spanish strongbox and he knew how to pick the antiquated double-key locking mechanism. He just had to pick the right time.

The *perfect* time had come and gone right under his nose. It had happened so fast, it left him cursing himself breathless to think how close he had come to holding fifty thousand dollars cash. He had known there were sometimes thousands of dollars locked away in the heavy iron box, and he should have guessed, with all the activity going on at Briar Glen, that there would be a need for a hefty cash flow. Still, it had caught him off guard—apparently it had caught a lot of people off guard when Michael Tarrington had announced he would be bringing a new wife to home.

He had been working on the terrace the first time he had seen her, and even then he hadn't half believed his eyes. He'd looked up into a flash of sunlight shining off an upper window, and there she was, a golden-haired angel draped in white sheets. He hadn't even blinked, he'd been so stunned. Sal had spent the previous day in town buying up every frill and gewgaw she could lay a hand to, but either he had been too drunk to absorb what she had told him, or he had just expected some bowed-legged, painted-mouthed floozy with teats the size of water jugs—the only kind of woman he would ever consider marrying again, if he had to. He still hadn't fully recovered from his surprise later that morning when he had crept into the bushes below the library window and observed the less than friendly meeting between the newlyweds and Forrest Wainright.

And when he had seen the fifty thousand come out of the strongbox . . . well, he had nearly gone into spasms then and there. He'd checked that damned box only the day before and there had only been a couple of hundred in greenbacks. Ned hadn't known who Forrest Wainright was at the time, but he was damn quick to find out. He also hadn't recognized the name Montana Rose when Tarrington had said it later on, but because he seemed so adamant about assuring the new

Mrs. Tarrington that her secret would remain safe within the walls of Briar Glen, Ned Sims thought it equally necessary to find out just how valuable a secret it might be.

It did not take him long to determine the answer to both questions.

Ned glanced up at the sound of a footstep on the cobblestone path. His eyes, a nondescript blend of blue and green, screwed down to slits as he saw Amanda Tarrington rounding a copse of tall junipers. She was searching out the last of the late-blooming roses and collecting them in a curved straw basket. She hadn't seen him yet so he allowed himself the luxury of a long, slow perusal. His gaze lingered over the porcelain smoothness of her skin, the delicately sculpted cheekbones, the soft and luscious mouth. The day was moderately warm for late November and she wore a lightly woven shawl draped more over her elbows than her shoulders, affording an unrestricted view of her breasts as they mounded impressively over her bodice each time she leaned forward in pursuit of a rose.

She was certainly a prime cut of womanflesh, Ned decided, and Tarrington spared no expense on clothes and fine trimmings for her. The frock she was wearing today, for example, had lit Sal's eyes up just to touch it. Sateen, she had called it. Midnight blue to show off the whiteness of her shoulders and the pale yellow of her hair, and costing enough to keep a grown man in liquor for a year.

And yet, from what Ned could gather from the scullery gossip, something was amiss between the king and queen. They spent most of their waking hours in separate pursuits, him with his racehorses, her with reading and sewing and fussing around the house. He had even heard they kept separate bedrooms. The brat, Sal had said, had been so leery the first few nights, the new Mrs. Tarrington had slept in her room with her. The fact she had never quite made the move back into her husband's bed had been the subject of many a whispered conversation between Sally and her mother that

Ned was probably not supposed to hear. But he had, and it fascinated him to think a swaggering womanizer like Michael Tarrington could not kick his way past a locked door. That would be the day—or night—Ned would allow such a thing.

The remaining two fingers on his left hand scratched thoughtfully at his crotch as he mentally stripped Amanda Tarrington to her bare skin. He grinned slowly, envisioning her legs wrapped around his waist and her breasts bouncing back and forth as he pumped himself into her, and he wondered if she made those funny little choking sounds when she came, or if she let it all out in a scream.

No, he decided with a speculative chuckle, he wouldn't let a door stand between them. He wouldn't let her out of his sight for too damned long either, or go on buying trips upriver that kept him away from Briar Glen for days at a time. Tarrington was gone now, up to Vicksburg, so Sally said, and was not expected to return until the end of the week. Plenty of time for a beautiful woman to get up to some mischief, especially when she was no stranger to the excitement of the riverboats.

He watched Amanda snip a perfect pink rose and hold it to her nose for a moment, savoring the aroma before she continued down the path. When she turned, she saw Ned Sims standing like a stone watching her, and he could see the sudden tension ripple through her body.

"Afternoon, ma'am," he drawled, his grin widening.

"Ned. I didn't see you there."

"No'm, I didn't reckon you did. Didn't mean to startle you, though. Would've coughed or somethin', but I was kinda takin' a rest, you know; enjoyin' the view. Warm day, ain't it, ma'am? I mean for this time of year, an all. Boston'd be under a foot of snow by now, most likely."

"It must be beautiful."

Ned wheezed deeply through his nose and shook his head. "Nah. Just cold and wet. Here——" He stepped forward and reached out a hand toward the handle of the basket. "Let me take that for you, ma'am. Must be gettin' kind of heavy with all them flowers an' all.''

He stood close enough to smell the perfume in her hair and sneak a good close look straight down into the cleft between her breasts.

''Thank you,'' she said, backing a step away and angling the basket out of his reach. ''But I'm fine. Have you seen Sally and Verity? I am expecting a visit from my brother this afternoon, and I'm sure Verity will need tidying up before then.''

''Saw 'em down by our cabin awhile back. Foldin' linens, I think. I'm goin' that way in a minute or two. I can fetch 'em out if you like.''

''I would appreciate it. Thank you.''

''No trouble a'tall, ma'am. Any time you want me for anything . . . anything a'tall, you just give me a holler. Day or night, don't matter.''

Amanda smiled weakly and hurried on down the path as if he had suggested she take a hot coal in her mouth.

Rebel bitch, he thought. Maybe there was something wrong with *her* and it was Tarrington keeping his door locked at night.

Ned hawked and spat a yellowish wad of phlegm on the ground. He wiped the back of his hand across his mouth and turned his back on Amanda High and Mighty Tarrington. She had given him an excuse to get out of the sun, though, and he took his sweet time sauntering out of the garden and following the neatly groomed path to the servants' quarters. He and Sally shared the last one in a long row of cabins. It was small and neat, with two rooms she had painstakingly tried to cheer up with gingham curtains and lace doilies.

The door was partially ajar and he shoved it open with the flat of his hand. Sal was there, the brat too. Both looked up in surprise as the door slammed back against the wall; Verity dove behind Sally's skirts, narrowly missing being beaned by the small cup of water that was startled out of Sally's hands.

''Ned! What are you doing here?''

"Live here, don't I? Cain't a man come into his own house when the urge takes him?"

"Of course he can," Sally demurred quickly. "It's just that . . . you surprised us, is all."

Ned snorted and walked over to the table she was standing beside. They were sorting linens, dampening some and rolling them into tight sausages to wait for the iron.

"Slave work," he snorted again. "I'll bet that Rebel bitch had a dozen slaves did nothin' but wash and iron her fancies all day long. Look at this—" He snatched up a delicate foulard chemise and swung it from the mutilated claw formed by his thumb and forefinger. "Probably cost an honest man a month's wages. More!"

"Ned, give it back," she hissed.

"Why?" he demanded, holding it up out of Sally's reach. "Too fine for the likes of me to touch? Afraid I'll get my sweat all over it? Well here, what do you think she'd make of this!" He balled the chemise and stuffed it down the front of his trousers, making a good show of rubbing it against himself and groaning with feigned pleasure. "Give it to her now," he said, throwing it onto the table, "and see if she can notice the smell of a real man."

Sally blanched and pushed a stray wisp of dull brown hair back behind her ear. She put the chemise into the pile that needed rewashing for one reason or another, keeping a wary eye on her husband as she did so. He headed straight for the shelf that held his whiskey jug and poured himself out a brimming cupful, drinking it without a break for air. He poured another and when he looked across at Sally, she lowered her head quickly and concentrated on the linens.

"What's wrong now?" he asked. "Did I fart?"

"Please don't start with your drinking," she said softly. "You know what it does to you. And if Mr. Michael ever found you—"

"Mr. Michael ain't here, is he?" Ned sneered. "He's off whorin' upriver somewhere, ain't he? And if I want to have me a drink, I'll have me a drink."

Sally became aware of Verity's hands clutching her thigh. "You . . . shouldn't say such things around the child."

"Why not? She must know what a whore does—she's got one for a mama, doesn't she?"

"Ned, please."

"Ned, please," he mimicked in a whining falsetto. He took another long pull of whiskey and tilted his head toward the bedroom. "Get on in there with me, woman, an' I'll please you, all right. I'll please you till you cain't sit proper for a month."

Sally moistened her lips and glanced at the open door. "Mother is waiting for these linens."

Ned narrowed his eyes. "Let her wait. Your man is here and has an appetite."

"I . . . can fetch some biscuits and ham from the kitchen if you're hungry."

He grinned. "It ain't that kind of appetite I'm talkin' about, gal."

Sally stared at him in growing apprehension. It didn't take much to get him going these days, and she had to tread carefully. Her ribs were still bruised and sore from the last time she had tried to refuse him.

"I'll just take these linens back, then, so Mother doesn't send someone looking."

He seemed content to drink his whiskey and watch her collect up the neatly folded bundles, but when she crossed to the door, her arms fully laden, he was there ahead of her, blocking her way.

"I'm hungry now," he said evenly.

"Ned . . . the child."

He glanced down and saw one blue eye peeping around Sally's skirts. She was as pretty and angelic as the mother, and it only pushed his resentment a notch higher. "Get rid of her. Tell her you and I got to have a little play time together too . . . and tell her if she tattles, why, next time"—he leaned over suddenly and wagged his deformed hand in front of Verity's face—"I just might make her dessert."

"Ned, for heaven's sakes—"

He bellowed out a curse and swung his fist up and across her chest, knocking the pile of folded linens out of her arms and scattering them across the floor.

"Why in Christ's name you always gotta argue with me?" he shouted. "I said get rid of her! Get rid of her and get your skinny ass in that bed before I get a notion to take my belt buckle to you again!"

Sally reached quickly for Verity's hand and all but pushed her out the door. "Go, darling. Run on up to the house."

Verity scampered two steps into the sunlight, then turned and looked back at the cabin. Sally let out a small, anguished cry and tried to follow but Ned was too quick and too determined. He grabbed a handful of her hair and spun her around, away from the door, slamming it shut behind him and shoving the bolt home.

"Why?" he snarled. "Why do you always fight me, bitch? I bet all that Tarrington bastard has to do is crook his little finger at you and you go running."

"N-no, Ned!" she gasped. "No! He's never touched me, I swear it."

"And you've never wanted him to, I suppose."

"I have never been unfaithful to you, Ned. You know I haven't!"

"That wasn't what I asked," he spat, grabbing at her arm. "I asked if you ever *wanted* to be."

"No! No, I have never wanted another man!"

"Liar!" He yanked her up against his chest and spat into her face, "You've wanted *any* other man but me, haven't you? *Haven't you, bitch!*"

"No!" Sally screamed. "No, Ned!"

He flung her in the direction of the bedroom, shoving her with such force she bounced off the wall and fell heavily against a shelf laden with dishes and pans. The shelf broke, spilling crockery onto the floor, and Sally went down with it, landing heavily and awkwardly on her outstretched arm.

Ned, panting and enraged, glowered down at her. "Get up! *Get up!*"

When she didn't move, he reached down with both hands

to haul her to her feet. It was like lifting a rag doll. Her head lolled and her limbs flopped limply side to side, and it wasn't until he saw the ugly red rosette of blood on the floor that he stopped shaking her and saw the deep gash in her temple. A hasty glance at the broken shelf identified the cause of the wound; a second, horrified glance down at his wife told him why she wasn't moving.

"Jesus Christ!" he muttered. "Jesus H. Christ!"

He dropped her back onto the broken crockery and looked around in a panic. There were linens scattered everywhere, even twisted around her ankles, and he thought for one wild moment he might be able to make it look like she had tripped and fallen.

But then he remembered the kid. She had seen them fighting. She would tell her mother and her mother would tell Tarrington, and Ned Sims's life would be worth shit.

In a panic, he stepped over Sally's body and ran into the bedroom. He shoved aside the rag rug at the foot of the bed and pried up the loose floorboard beneath it. He retrieved the small tobacco pouch and tucked it into his shirt. The string tying the neck broke and a handful of coins scattered across the floor, but he was in too much of a hurry, suddenly, to worry about hunting them all down. He gathered up what he could and ran back into the main room. He grabbed his hat, his coat, and a battered old squirrel rifle and, after a careful peek through the door, darted outside and started running for the road.

Chapter 21

Amanda turned at the sound of her name being called. Her eyes widened and her face wreathed instantly with a smile as she saw Ryan and Dianna Moore standing at the edge of the garden. Heedless of the roses that tumbled out of her basket, Amanda hurried to meet them, dropping the awkward burden altogether a moment before Ryan caught her up in his arms and spun her around with enough enthusiasm to lift her skirts and petticoats in a graceful bell.

"Now there's a greeting I could happily accept every day," he said, laughing as he set Amanda down and was subjected to a further moment of fierce hugging.

"Ryan! And Dianna!" She released her brother and exchanged an equally fervent hug with Dianna Moore. "I'm so happy you came."

"Happy?" Dianna's face beamed. "I could just die with happiness every time I think of you here at Briar Glen. And just look at what the two of you have accomplished!"

Amanda followed Dianna's rapt glance around the gardens, the terrace and house, the rows of whitewashed stables in the distance, and the acres of rolling fields that stretched on either side. In the eight weeks Amanda had been at the Glen, Michael's army of workers had swarmed the grounds like ants on a sugar pile. He had spared no expense to haul away the ravages of war and restore the plantation to its former elegance and beauty. The old slave quarters had been completely razed to the ground and neat new cottages built for the workers and household staff. Long lines of stables had been constructed, with fenced paddocks and corrals spreading out across the gentle roll of the hills. He had a stable of forty horses, two dozen of them broodmares, all beautiful, sleek, powerful animals, some of mixed bloodlines, some pure Arabian, some of the Thoroughbreds English born and bred and shipped to Natchez at considerable expense and trouble.

He was away on another buying trip now, which was the only reason Ryan Courtland had deigned to come near Briar Glen.

"Amanda?"

Her head snapped around and she saw Dianna's expectant grin. What the devil had they been talking about? Oh, yes, dying of happiness.

Amanda smiled. "As you can see, it is all still a little overwhelming. I confess I have to pinch myself at times to believe I am really here."

"I know exactly how you feel," Dianna said breathlessly. "I have been pinching myself all week."

Her smile, if it was possible, became even brighter; her grip on Amanda's arm would probably leave bruises. Ryan's mocking scowl confirmed his sister's sudden suspicion their visit was not as casual as their note implied.

"All *week?* Has something happened I don't know about?"

"Oh!" Dianna's nails verged on drawing blood and her knees bounced her through several nervous little jitters as she looked to Ryan with huge, imploring eyes. "I know you said I had to wait. I know you said you wanted to pick the right moment to tell, but . . . I can't wait. I simply can't wait!"

"Apparently not," he said dryly. "Go ahead, before you burst something."

Dianna steadied herself and clutched Amanda's hands fervently in her own. "I took your advice. I told him if he didn't ask me now he may as well not ask me ever, because if he didn't think enough of me to have me when he was poor, he certainly wouldn't be worth having when he was rich."

"The logic of which still escapes me, I might add," Ryan interjected.

Amanda and Dianna both ignored him.

"He asked you to marry him." Amanda gasped.

"Yes."

"And you accepted."

"Yes!"

Both women uttered a little screech and flung themselves into each other's arms. Ryan maintained his stern expression until he found himself engulfed in hugs and flounces again.

"High time too, Ryan Courtland," Amanda declared. "When is the wedding?"

"I have always wanted a Christmas wedding." Dianna sighed. "And just imagine . . . Christmas is only a month away."

"Imagine," Ryan murmured wryly. "And I suppose if this were May, you would have always wanted a summer wedding?"

Dianna rose on tiptoes to kiss him. "Always. Amanda and I have been plotting the demise of your bachelorhood for too long to let weather stand in the way. You were just a little more stubborn than we anticipated."

"Obviously not stubborn enough."

Dismissing the comment with a simultaneous twirl of wide, colored skirts, Amanda and Dianna hooked elbows and started walking back toward the house, their heads tilted together to discuss the details of the upcoming nuptials.

Ryan rescued the basket of roses and followed at a more leisurely pace, taking advantage of their preoccupation to cast a critical and grudgingly admiring eye around the work that had been done to Briar Glen since his last visit. Tarrington was pouring a great deal of money into the plantation —a strong sign he was serious about his commitment to establish the Glen as a fine racing stable. Ryan tried not to show much interest, but the Yankee had managed to acquire some pretty damned impressive bloodstock, and a rush of the old excitement throbbed unwittingly through his veins.

Horseracing was once again a premier sport both north and south of the Mason-Dixon line. People were sick of war and eager to recapture the spirit of former good times. There was money to be made, recognition to be won, standards to be established in the breeding and bloodlines of Thoroughbreds, and Ryan was not too proud to admit he craved the adventure, the excitement of watching a powerful animal become more powerful, more efficient under his tutelage. His hands might be into making Rosalie a working cotton plantation once again, but his heart was on the back of a sleek Thoroughbred, racing for the thrill of the finish line.

"Your husband stopped in at Rosalie last week to speak to me—did you know about it?"

Amanda halted and turned to stare at her brother. "No. No, I didn't know. What did he want?"

"He wanted to make me a new offer." Ryan clenched his jaw. "It seems he hasn't been able to find himself a Southern boy willing to manage his four-legged investments. Not one who's willing to work for a Yankee, at any rate." He paused and looked off toward the paddocks. "The bastard had the nerve to offer me a partnership."

"A *partnership*?"

"So I could tell myself I wasn't actually working *for* him, but *with* him. In exchange for being a trainer, manager, breeder, I would earn a split of the profits."

"What did you tell him?" Amanda asked quietly, aware of Dianna's equally anticipatory hush beside her.

"I told the damned Yankee bastard to get the hell off my land—what did you expect me to tell him?"

Amanda's lungs deflated like a bubble of dough. "Oh, Ryan," she whispered. "You didn't."

"Damned right I did."

"What did Michael do?" Dianna asked.

"Considering he was looking down the barrel of my gun," Ryan said, glaring directly into her soft blue-green eyes, "he got the hell off my land."

Dianna's fingers fluttered up to cover her lips. "Your gun? You threatened to shoot him?"

"No. But I should have. And I would have if I thought either of you had put him up to proposing such an unholy alliance."

"We didn't," they declared in unison, and Amanda added, "I didn't even know he had been to Rosalie, or that he had seen you, or that he had even wanted—or needed—a partner. Does he?"

Ryan's glower remained steady for as long as it took him to determine his sister and fiancée were genuinely ignorant of Michael Tarrington's business dealings.

"I wouldn't know if he needs one or not," he replied sullenly, jamming his hands in his pockets. "And frankly, I don't care."

"Oh, yes you do," Amanda said quietly. "You do care, Ryan Courtland, or you wouldn't have even mentioned his offer. And you would leap at the chance to breed your precious horses again—with both feet stuck in tar—if it wasn't for your damned pride standing in the way."

"My pride has nothing to do with it. He's a Yankee, for God's sake. We fought a war to keep them off our land, to keep them from destroying everything we held dear—now you want me to help him?"

"I want you to help yourself and stop living in the past."

"You seem to be doing that well enough for all of us."

"Yes, and as you can see, we have been utterly and completely destroyed in the process. He beats me blue every other day and locks me away in the cold cellar at night. He terrorizes Verity morning, noon, and night, and has her so petrified, she can hardly wait for him to finish his supper in the evenings so she can ride his shoulders up to bed and have him read her stories and show her magic tricks. He starves us and dresses us in rags. And he never, ever sends any extra supplies or bolts of cloth to Mother, and he has never, ever let any of us forget, by word or deed, that he is the almighty conquering hero and we the simple-minded defeated. Ryan . . . I never thought I would hear myself say these words, but . . . the war is over. We can't keep hating everyone forever. There *are* some decent Yankees. My God, there have to be, otherwise we might as well all take out guns and shoot one another. I know what they did to you in the prison camp and I know how much you hate them—and the guards who beat and starved and tortured you deserve your hatred. But Michael wasn't one of them. He's fine and decent, and he isn't here to destroy anything, he's here to rebuild; to make a new start for himself . . . for us.

"His pride is every bit as fierce as yours," she continued, "but it hasn't blinded him to the point where he'd shoot off his own nose to spite his face. Furthermore, if you can't bear the thought of a Yankee scoundrel making bags of money off the expertise of a Confederate ex-cavalryman, why not look at it as a clever Confederate ex-cavalryman making bags of money off an inept Yankee scoundrel?"

She ran out of breath and steam at the same time and stood almost chin to stubborn chin with her brother, daring him to point out the flaw in her argument. He couldn't, although his mouth opened and closed several times with the effort.

"I think you should listen to her," came a voice from behind a wall of shrubs. "It sounds like good advice—except for the inept part, of course."

Amanda whirled around just as Michael Tarrington stepped into view. His smoky gray eyes touched briefly on Dianna and Ryan before settling on hers and remaining there.

"Michael." Amanda expelled his name on a breath. "You're back."

He looked down the length of his body and smiled. "It would seem so. I finished my business early and caught a fast packet out of Vicksburg. But . . . if you would rather I go away again and come back tomorrow . . . ?"

"No! No, I . . . I'm just . . . surprised, is all."

"Forgive me. I did not mean to eavesdrop or to interrupt your conversation. I was on my way to the stables when I overheard voices and . . . to be honest . . . could scarcely believe the source of such an impassioned plea."

He saw her flush slightly at the unexpected warmth in his voice—a flush that darkened as he took his time appreciating the way the combined effects of the sun and the midnight blue of her dress turned her eyes to aqua and her hair to gleaming silver. He was tired and dusty, which made him all the more susceptible to the whiteness of her shoulders and the soft, clean scent of roses that clung to her skin. His smile remained honest in its pleasure as he moved forward and took her hands into his, raising both and pressing them tenderly against his lips.

"You look lovely. I'm glad I came home early."

Amanda's lips parted over a soft rush of breath. It was the first time she had heard any genuine emotion in his voice since the night they had spent at Rosalie. Since that night, the tension between them had been palpable. The ride to Briar Glen had been an agony of silence; her announced intention to sleep in Verity's room for the first few days had met with barely a glance.

The fact that those few days had stretched into a week, then two, then eight, had roused no comment either. Indeed, there were very few comments at all outside of casual conversations about the weather, the work that was going on, the plans he had for spring. Whenever she tried to steer the subject around to more personal matters, he drew back as if she had held out a live flame and expected him to touch it. Those were the nights she could hear him moving around in his bedroom hours after he had declared himself too exhausted to keep her company in the parlor. Those were the nights when she crept into the adjoining dressing room and saw the slash of light at the bottom of his door; the nights when she would lie awake, holding her breath at every creak and whisper of sound, almost willing herself to see his shadow standing at the door.

Those were also the occasions when she would come down to breakfast the next morning to find Mrs. Reeves waiting with a note explaining he was gone away on business again. He rarely said how long he would be absent and the only messages he left were for Verity, with instructions to give her a hug and a kiss and a promise he would return soon.

The way he behaved toward Verity was nothing less than wonderful, however, for as cool and distant as he was to Amanda, he had gone out of his way to win Verity's heart.

In the beginning, the child had not been too keen on her new stepfather. She hugged the walls if he came unexpectedly into a room, or walked wide, circuitous routes if he happened to be in the path of somewhere she wanted to go. Eventually, however, his seemingly limitless patience had won her over, and now, it was more often than not Verity's running footsteps that announced Michael's return from the stables each day.

Amanda wished their own difficulties could have been resolved so easily.

The effect of Michael's compliment was still tingling up her arms when he released her and turned to Dianna. "Cousin . . . you look exceptionally radiant this afternoon. Damned if you don't look like a woman who has recently accepted a proposal of marriage."

Dianna's mouth dropped. "How did you know?"

"Then it's true?"

"*How* did you know? We've only just told Amanda, and she is the first . . . except for Father, of course. But we swore him to secrecy."

Michael laughed. "On a bible? Before witnesses? You underestimate a father's joy. The Honorable Judge Moore practically fell out of the courthouse window as I passed, shouting the news for all of Natchez to hear."

Dianna sighed. "Oh, dear."

Michael laughed again and kissed her cheek, lingering to whisper something against her ear that made her blush to the roots of her hair. When he straightened, it was with a smooth, unhesitating motion that he extended his hand in Ryan's direction.

"Ryan. My sincerest congratulations to you and Dianna."

It was not a gesture or sentiment Ryan could reject without causing undue embarrassment to Dianna, but he still debated it a long moment before accepting the proffered handshake.

Michael's smile broadened. "It's good to see you here at Briar Glen. Actually, I'm damned glad to see you here; I could use your opinion on something."

He turned and glanced over his shoulder just as Brian Foley came into view rounding the side of the house. A wave

of Tarrington's hand had the lanky groomsman veering off
the path that would have taken him in the direction of the
stables and brought him to the verge of the gardens instead.
He was not alone. Walking behind him, bristling like a high-
spirited child rebelling against a handhold, was an enormous
black stallion, each muscle and sinew straining with power,
each hoof planted with an air of regal diffidence. He was a
brute in size, standing over seventeen hands. His haunches
and flanks were great slabs of muscle that rippled with power
barely held in check. His mane and tail were waves of silk
that lashed like ebony flames at each restless movement of
his head and body.

Ryan stared openly at the sleek, taut lines of the stallion,
his jaw slack, his gaze assessing everything from the long,
beautifully formed legs to the velvet sheen of his finely flared
nose. He found no fault, no flaw anywhere.

"My God," he said softly. "He's magnificent."

"His name is Diablo," Michael said, watching Ryan's
face. "And believe me, the name is appropriate. He put two
handlers over the deck of the packet and kicked another one
clear through the walls of two cabins before they managed to
tie him down."

"Diablo?" Ryan tore his eyes away from the stallion long
enough to read the expectant grin on Michael Tarrington's
face. "Not *the* Diablo . . . from the Tyrell stables in Kentucky?"

"Brought over from England last fall." Michael nodded.

"Good Christ, he must have cost you—"

"The earth and the sun," Michael admitted ruefully. "But
here—" He took the reins from Foley and offered them to
his brother-in-law. "Take him for a run and let me know
what you honestly think of him."

Ryan frowned. "If this is your idea of softening me up,
Tarrington—"

"It is. I can't seem to sway you with my money or my
charm . . . I might as well try to bribe you with something
I know will keep you wide awake at night."

Ryan stood firm, staring into equally unwavering gray

eyes. He could see both Amanda and Dianna out of the corner of his eye, standing motionless, breathless, their faces pale and hopeful. And he could see the stallion, his head held high and challenging.

"He's been eager for a good run since we offloaded him," Michael added quietly. "He might be a little hard to handle."

Ryan looked down at the reins. "It won't change my opinion. I still think you're a son of a bitch, Tarrington."

"Good. Then you won't be reluctant to tell me how big a fool I've made of myself if I *have* squandered the earth and the sun."

Ryan took the reins.

"There are saddles in the livery," Michael offered, but Ryan's mouth only turned down in scorn. He slung the reins over Diablo's neck and swung himself up onto the beast's back, wheeling him around and away without a further word or glance in Michael's direction.

The stallion balked at the unexpected weight and danced sideways along the path, kicking up a spray of dust and pebbles as Ryan urged him toward the open stretch of field. In a few moments they were clear of impeding shrubs and cobblestones, and, with hard-packed earth beneath his hooves, Diablo took the bit in his teeth and stretched out into a thundering gallop.

Michael watched horse and rider streak away into the wind and patted his pocket in search of a cigar.

"Was it really a bribe?" Amanda asked.

He studied her over the flare of a match and was not impressed to feel or see the tremor that passed through his hands. "Would you forgive me if it was?"

Amanda looked up into her husband's darkly handsome face. Into eyes that could melt her knees at a glance. At a mouth that had kissed her to the edge of madness and brought her slowly, tenderly back to reality again.

"Yes," she whispered. "I would forgive you."

He stared into her eyes and felt like a drowning man, like

his whole body was suspended in a warm, heavy liquid and he would not have been able to move if he had wanted to.

"Honestly," Dianna sighed. "If the two of you gave yourselves a decent chance, I think you could truly become fond of each other."

Michael's startled gaze went over to his cousin.

"You and Ryan," she added, her head bent over as she brushed at some dust on her skirt, "are so much alike it's almost frightening."

Michael smiled slowly and tipped his cigar in her direction. "Then we'll have to see what we can do about winning him over to our side. Hell, I like the man already. I haven't been called a son of a bitch to my face since . . . well . . . since the last time he called me one."

While the women exchanged a hopeful smile, he turned to Foley. "Speaking of son of a bitches, see if you can find out what rock Sims is hiding under today—God forbid he should ever be doing any work around here to earn his keep. We'll need one of the big stalls cleaned out for Diablo."

"He was here awhile ago," Amanda offered. "I asked him to find Sally so she could get Verity washed up for lunch."

"And that," Michael said with another sigh of honest affection, "is another reason I came home early. My ears haven't been this dry since the summer."

Foley tipped his head and started off in the direction of the servants' quarters. Amanda followed his progress until she was distracted by the presence of Michael's arm curling around her waist.

She tilted her face up to his. He was hatless and the sun was playing havoc with the color of his hair, refusing to let any one shade of auburn, gold, or brown dominate the chestnut. His wide shoulders were encased in burgundy broadcloth, the collar and cuffs of his shirt bore a faint green stripe. He wore riding breeches of soft chamois tucked into tall black leather boots, and a waistcoat of brocaded green silk with a row of tiny enameled buttons that seemed designed to draw attention upward to the ever-formidable chin and soft, smoky eyes.

For a long, breathless moment, she thought he was going to lean closer and kiss her. The look, the warm hunger was certainly there in his eyes, smoldering and speculative, confirmed by the tremor in the arm circling her waist. But it was not, she realized with another small shock, a tremor of eagerness. It was one of fear. Fear of being pushed away, rejected.

"Mr. Tarrington! Sir!"

Michael, Amanda, even Dianna was startled by the sight of Foley returning at a run. The manservant, normally a pillar of dispassion and competence, was as gray as a masonry gargoyle.

"Sir!"

"Yes? What is it?"

Foley drew to a rigid halt and seemed reluctant to speak in front of the women. "If I could have a word in private . . . ?"

"Out with it, man. You look like you've seen one of Flora's Little People."

"It's Sally, sir. There has been . . . an accident."

"An accident!" Amanda gasped. "Is she all right?"

Foley's mouth worked through several answers before one cleared its way through his lips. "She's taken a bad clip on the head, ma'am. Please, sir?"

Foley's obvious distress caused Michael to throw down his cigar in dawning comprehension. "Where is she?"

"In her cabin, sir. She's . . . in a bad way."

"Sims?"

"Gone. And not long, I'd say."

"Michael?" Amanda looked from one to the other.

"Mandy, go up to the house and find Mrs. Reeves. Tell her—"

Amanda clutched Michael's sleeve, cutting him short. "Verity was with her. Verity was with Sally in the cabin. *If something has happened*—"

Michael rounded on Foley. "Did you see the child?"

"N-no, sir. I just saw Sally."

Amanda was already running down the shaded laneway that divided the main house from the servants' quarters. Michael and Foley, with their long, unencumbered strides, passed her easily and were inside the cabin, searching, before she arrived.

"Verity? *Verity?*"

Amanda arrived at the doorway in a flurry of midnight blue sateen and frothing petticoats. She stood frozen on the threshold while her eyes adjusted to the gloomier interior, and the first thing she saw was Sally's body lying on a crush of scattered linen and broken crockery.

No. The first thing she saw was the blood. It was soaked into the linens, bright crimson against the stark white, a wide, growing stain that originated from the deep and ugly gash on Sally's temple.

Amanda covered her mouth with her hands and was almost too terrified to look around the rest of the cabin. There was only one small window to shed light on the simple furnishings—a table and two chairs, a small stove, some shelves and a cupboard. Nothing that could conceal a child, however small she tried to make herself.

"Verity?" The name was just a whisper on her lips, and she looked up with a desperate hopefulness as Michael emerged from the equally sparse, cramped bedroom.

"Michael?"

His face was waxen as he hurried to her side. "He wouldn't have been stupid enough to hurt the child. Maybe she wasn't even here."

"Michael . . . ?" Dianna arrived at the cabin door, saw the blood and the body, and momentarily forgot what she was going to say. She gave herself a small shake, however, and pointed behind her toward the house. "It's Mrs. Reeves—"

Michael and Amanda both stepped outside in time to see Flora running across the last hundred feet of manicured lawns. She moved with remarkable speed and agility for a short, stout woman who still bound herself in a full spring-wired buckram corset. And for a woman who held a small, frightened child in her arms.

Michael intercepted her in a few long strides and there was no hesitation, either on his part or Verity's, as he relieved Flora of her burden.

"Ma' Sally," she gasped. "Where is she?"

"Inside. I haven't had a chance—"

"The wee one came runnin' up to the house all in a dither," Flora explained as she hurried on toward the cabin, "but I couldna' understand what she were tryin' to say in ma' ear. Sally? Sally?"

Flora disappeared inside the cabin. Michael allowed himself the relief of a fierce hug before he passed Verity into Amanda's waiting arms.

"Make sure she isn't harmed in any way," he commanded grimly.

Amanda did not need any urging. She ran her hands anxiously over little arms and legs, and tipped the child's small white face up for a flurry of fevered kisses before she was able to assure herself her daughter had only suffered a bad scare, nothing more.

Dianna stood beside them, her hand clasped over the tight constraints of her bodice.

"My God," she gasped. "How could a man do such a thing to a woman . . . to his *wife?*"

Amanda could not answer. It was just occurring to her that she had been the one to send Ned Sims down to the cabin, and that if she hadn't, Sally might still be going about her chores with her usual shy efficiency.

Shaken by the thought, Amanda gave Verity a last, reassuring kiss on her cheek and turned to Dianna. "Will you take her back up to the house for me, please? I must go and see if I can do anything to help Flora."

"Of course." Dianna took Verity and tilted her head in the direction of the servants and workmen who were beginning to gather in front of the cabin by twos and threes, having plucked the news out of thin air as usual. "Shall I send someone for the doctor as well?"

Amanda nodded. "Please. And have someone prepare one of the bedrooms; I don't want her staying here a moment longer than necessary."

Dianna left and Amanda issued another series of curt orders to some of the men standing nearby before she went back into the cabin. Mrs. Reeves was on her knees beside Sally, pressing a cloth to her head. Michael and Foley had managed to turn the injured girl gently onto her back; Michael was pouring water into a basin, and Foley was propping her head under a wadding of folded linens. There was still a great deal of fresh blood leaking from the wound each time Flora lifted the cloth away, and Sally's arm, Amanda noticed, was twisted at an odd angle away from the elbow.

Michael was suddenly there in front of her, blocking her view with his big body.

"Go back outside," he ordered quietly. "There's nothing you can do here, but if you want to help, you can send for a doctor and—"

"I've already sent for one. How is she?"

"She's taken a nasty blow on the head, but she opened her eyes a minute ago and tried to say a few words to Flora. Her arm is broken and she has a few cuts . . . but I think she'll be all right."

Amanda raised a trembling hand to her own temple. "I've asked two of the men to find a plank to use as a stretcher, and I'm having one of the bedrooms in the house made ready." She had to stop to catch hold of a painful breath, but when she looked up into her husband's eyes, her voice was firm and clear. "I've also sent someone to find Ryan, and I've ordered a dozen horses saddled. Sims can't have gone far on foot."

Michael's mouth flattened into a bloodless line, cursing himself on the one hand for not having thought of these things himself, while praising her level-headedness at the same time. "It looks like he had a stash of money hidden and took the time to retrieve it before he bolted. And no, he couldn't have gone more than a mile or two on foot. We'll find him. When we do—"

"When ye do," Flora declared vehemently, "I'm gonna kill him maself, I swear I am! Ma Sally's a good wee lassie. She didna' deserve this, no sir. So you gi' on out o' here an' find him! Find the bastard an' tie his ballocks to the saddlehorn, then drag him here by the roughest road ye can find. Anything left of him is mines. All mines!"

Sally moaned softly and Flora was instantly attentive. "There now, Lovey, yer mam's here. Dinna try to talk . . . what? The bairn is fine, hen. She come tae fetch me like a wee angel wi' wings, she did. You just rest now. Doctor's on his way."

Amanda's eyes burned as she watched Flora bend over and whisper soothing words into her daughter's ear. She felt a strong hand clasp her elbow, and she let Michael guide her outside and into the heat of the sunlight.

She turned without a care for the eyes that were watching them and pressed her cheek against his chest. Dianna's query rang in her ears, repeated itself in a muffled whisper. "What kind of man does that to a woman? To his wife?"

Michael's response was delayed by the thunderous approach of a horse and rider. It was Ryan, and, from the stricken look on his face, it seemed he had already heard what had happened. Or part of it anyway. He brought Diablo to a skidding halt and dismounted in a swarming boil of dust.

"Where is Verity?" he cried. "What the hell happened?"

"Verity is fine," Michael said. "She wasn't harmed. She's up at the house with Dianna."

"Wasn't harmed? You bastard, she could have been killed! What the hell kind of maniacs do you have working for you?"

"The kind who won't be able to work for anyone again when I'm finished with him this time," Michael promised coldly.

"*This time?* You mean he has done this sort of thing before? He's beaten his wife to a bloody pulp and you've just let him go on with his chores?"

"Ryan, please," Amanda began.

"No. I'm interested in hearing his answer. Awhile ago you

were singing his praises, telling me what a fine and decent fellow you've married. I'm only curious to know, since he is inviting me to work *with* him and not *for* him, if I would be expected to live up to his sterling expectations of *fine* and *decent.*''

A slow, ruddy flush rose beneath Michael's tan. None of the wide-eyed servants had missed the wrathful derision in Ryan's voice, and none of them missed the graphic two-word expletive with which Michael Tarrington effectively terminated both his invitation to work at Briar Glen and his efforts to make peace with his brother-in-law.

Ned Sims, crouching in his hiding place not a hundred paces away, grinned.

He hadn't planned on staying around to watch, but he hadn't covered a hundred yards before he realized there was nothing but open fields between him and the road or the river, no matter which way he tried to run for it. He needed a horse, and the only way he could get one was to wait for dark and try to steal one out of the stable.

For the time being, he was stuck where he was, watching the entertainment. The big boss and his reb brother-in-law were exchanging insults while the wife jerked back and forth like a puppet, not knowing which one to run after as the husband grabbed up the reins of the stallion and headed for the stables, and the brother stormed up the drive to his carriage. Sims would have laughed out loud had Tarrington not passed close enough to his hidey-hole he could have hawked and spat on his polished Hessians.

Meanwhile, he had five hundred dollars, give or take, in his pouch. Not nearly enough to keep the smile on his face very long, but maybe enough to buy himself some protection while he figured the best way to skin out of town with his neck intact. Too bad he hadn't thought to snatch the kid— they would have paid more than a few measly hundred to get her back alive. Maybe there was another way, though. Knowing what he knew about the prim and proper Mrs. Michael Tarrington, coupled with what he knew about the Yankee captain himself . . . he might just be able to find a buyer interested enough to pay for his information in cold hard cash. And before Tarrington and his hounds sniffed him out.

In a way he was glad he'd stuck around, because at least he knew he wasn't going to be hunted down for murder. He wasn't too keen on the idea of letting Tarrington catch up to him either way, but it wasn't a hanging offense for a man to have a fight with his wife. Still and all, he thought sure he'd left her for a corpse, just like the one back in Boston. Next time, he decided, he would make damned sure when he killed someone, they stayed dead.

Chapter 22

Sally was carried gently to a bedroom in the west wing, one that would benefit from the warmth and cheer of the sun for most of the day. Amanda ordered it aired thoroughly and brought several vases full of the roses she had cut that afternoon to brighten the window ledge. When the doctor came, he sewed a row of large, black stitches across Sally's forehead and temple and declared her to be a very lucky woman indeed. An inch lower would have struck the vulnerable indent of the temple, an inch to the left would have put out an eye. It was common to bleed voraciously from a head wound, he assured them, and so long as there were no signs of distress to the bone—nausea, dizziness, befuddlement—he could predict with some confidence a full recovery. Flora was instructed to wake her every twenty minutes or so to test her alertness. If she had any cause for concern, he would come back at once. If not, he would return first thing in the morning.

Verity had had a bad scare, but suffered nothing more than a scraped knee when she had fallen in her run back to the house. She insisted on seeing Sally with as much stubbornness as Sally insisted on seeing Verity, and, with one tiptoeing timidly on second thoughts and the other wearing a thick turban of bandages around her head and another around her broken arm, the two came together, dissolved in a huddle of smiles and whispers, and left Flora and Amanda both trying very hard not to hug each other in shared relief.

Verity settled easily after that, something that could not be said for Dianna Moore, who had chosen not to leave with Ryan, but had stayed to help Amanda. It became obvious in short order that she was the one requiring attention. It was her first real argument with Ryan and the first time she had been exposed to his temper, neither of which sat well with a woman so recently ebullient over her engagement. She remained brave and stoic enough while there was hot water to be fetched and bandages to be torn, and coffee to be served to the departing doctor. But once it was determined that Sally, Verity, and Flora were settled comfortably, she alternately paced out her own anger back and forth in front of the parlor hearth, or broke down and wept in Amanda's arms.

Michael was out searching for Ned Sims. He and Foley led two large posses to scour the fields and farms north along the river, south toward Natchez. The sheriff had arrived with more men and dogs just as dusk was drifting in a heavy mist over the land; their torches and lanterns could be seen dotting the darkness in scattered groups as the hounds tried to isolate a fresh scent.

Amanda watched it all from one of the tall parlor windows. Dianna was sniffling on a settee behind her, having just forsaken (for the third time) all hope of ever reconciling with the one and only man she had ever loved. Amanda followed the moving blots of light and could hear, even through the thick glass panes and the sniffling, the hollow shouts and restless baying of the dogs.

When they moved off and she could not see them any more, she abandoned her seat by the window and coaxed the exhausted and red-nosed Dianna upstairs to bed. A good night's sleep, she promised, would do everyone a world of good.

Taking her own advice, Amanda retired to the room she shared with her daughter. Verity was fast asleep, surrounded by a protective phalanx of dolls. One of the house servants dozed in a chair in the corner, her dark face gleaming like ebony in the lamplight, her head bowed, her chin touching her chest and riding the soft rise and fall of each breath.

Amanda stood in the doorway for a long moment before pulling the door quietly shut again. Standing in the vaulted hallway, cloaked in the darkness and the silence, she let her hand fall away from the brass knob and, without giving it a conscious thought, walked to the end of the corridor and went into Michael's room instead.

It was dark, full of shadows and shapes of heavy furniture. No one had thought to prepare it for use, and the air was chilly—downright cold, in fact. The curtains across the alcove were swagged open and admitted a pale, milky hint of moonlight from outside. She used it to guide her way to the mantel where she found a tin of matches and two candlesticks. She lit one of the candles and left it by the hearth. The other she carried to the desk in the alcove, shielding the flame with a cupped hand, intending to light the oil lamp. Something stopped her. A shivered spray of alarm went up and down her spine and she started with enough of a jump to splash hot wax over her fingers.

Michael was lying on the bed, his arms folded behind his head, his long legs crossed at the ankles. His collar was gone, his shirt was open at the throat, the whiteness of the cambric a stark contrast to the dark pelt of hair on his chest. He had been watching her. His dark eyes caught the reflected sparks of candlelight, and the intensity of his gaze sent another shower of icy sensations coursing through her body.

It was the same undermining sensation that had robbed her of sensibility earlier in the day when he had told her she looked lovely. The same melting weakness she had experienced when she had seen him run to Flora and hug Verity to his breast, the relief flooding his eyes with naked emotion.

They were shining now and they were all she could focus on as he pushed himself upright and swung his legs with slow deliberation over the side of the bed. His gaze dropped briefly to the erratic movement of the flame, and he reached up with a gentle hand and removed the candlestick from her trembling fingers. He set it down on the bedside table and, still without a word, drew her into the vee of his parted thighs.

The candlelight was bathing her face, gilding her skin in gold. Her hair—never a thing to obey the constraints of pins and orderly curls too long—fell loosely over her shoulders and cascaded down her back. Soft, misty wisps surrounded the pure oval of her face, and the breath he had been holding rattled harshly in his throat as he expelled it.

Michael drew her closer. His hands were on her waist, and he took a moment to admire how trim and slender a thing it was before he leaned his head forward and pressed his lips against the blue sateen that covered her breasts, holding them there so long the heat began to scorch through to her skin. Her body was rendered nerveless, her arms barely strong enough to lift her hands and guide them into the long, wavy thickness of his hair. He welcomed them with a small sigh and turned his head so that he could not help but hear and feel the wild beating of her heart.

Amanda stood helpless in his embrace. She wanted, desperately, to say something, anything, but the words and all ability to form them remained trapped somewhere at the back of her throat. It had been so long. So very long. The nights she thought she would go mad with wanting him, the days she nearly wept just to see him striding across a field or listening intently to some whispered calamity Verity presented him with. It had been so long since he had touched her this way, she could feel her heart breaking and falling to dust around her ankles.

Anything, she thought. I will promise him anything, do anything, be anything he wants me to be . . .

. . . if she will just forgive me, he thought. If we can just start over, start fresh. Start again.

His hands moved slowly up her back, spreading flat, feeling the warmth of her flesh through the satiny layers of fabric, the silk of her hair as it brushed his skin. His fingers carried on up to her nape and threaded into the golden mane, and he lifted his head, tilting his face upward so that it took almost no movement at all to find her mouth and cover it, to mold her lips to his and hold them there until a shallow sigh set them free.

It was a brief freedom, for his hands were suddenly fierce in their possessiveness. His tongue thrust between her lips and deepened the kiss, tracing delicate, searching patterns at first, then lashing her with an urgent savagery that almost brought her down onto her knees before him. He prowled and probed. He swirled around the lush, slick lining of her mouth, teasing and cajoling, delving deeper and deeper until her whole body began to quiver and dissolve.

Michael's hands descended with a trembling violence and sought the fashionably complicated fastenings of her bodice. With no patience for hooks, buttons, and laces, he tore the delicate sateen open from breast to waist, groaning when he found yet another layer of silk and ribbons and dainty lace edgings.

He tore his mouth free and trailed a fiery path of kisses down her throat and onto the swell of her breast. He tugged at the silk and ripped at the ribbons, and Amanda gasped as he bared her breasts to his hungry rovings. Deft, suckling strokes of his tongue had her head arching back and her body pressing shamelessly into the wet heat. Quick, careless sweeps of his big hands stripped her arms from her dress and camisole and left her bare above the waist, with the sateen spilling in a blue wave over petticoats and underpinnings that survived only a few feverish moments more before they too were cast aside and forgotten.

She closed her eyes and tried not to see that she was brazenly naked while he was still fully clothed. She tried not to notice how eagerly and willingly her thighs parted at his invitation, or that she had not just imagined herself all soft and runny inside. His fingers slid into her wetness and emerged shiny and sleek. He stroked them back and forth again, then thrust them deep inside the quivering slickness, his other arm having to brace her now as her body writhed and recoiled with the pleasure.

Michael pressed his mouth against her belly, feeling the distinct clutches and contractions that streaked through her body on every purposeful swirl of his long fingers. It was not enough, suddenly, just to feel her pleasure, and with a husky groan, he brought her down on the bed beside him. He dropped himself onto his knees and buried his mouth in the soft, silky thatch of yellow curls, plunging his tongue into the pearly folds and tasting her ecstasy as it flared bright and hot within her.

Amanda's whole body quaked with the shock and splendor. A wild, breathless rush of pleasure sent her hips arching off the bed, and his hands were there to catch her, to steady her, to hold her hostage beneath his mouth until she was all molten heat and flame. His tongue chased each shudder and shiver, searching and exploring the succulent pink folds, heedless of the ragged cries that warned of an impending climax. He managed, somehow, to push his trousers down past his hips, but Amanda neither noticed nor cared that he was still half dressed, or that the buttons on his shirt chafed her belly and breasts as he rose above her. She only felt the hard and unyielding thickness of his flesh stretching hungrily inside her, and she strained upward with a feverish need, flaring herself wide to welcome him.

She sucked in a breath of undiluted delight, holding it and him as long as she could before relinquishing one on a shallow gust and the other on a warm flood of pleasure. Michael bowed his head to her shoulder and tried to steady himself, to keep his wits about him, but he was too damned close and he wanted her too damned badly to control his hunger too much longer. He forced himself to take up a slow, measured pace, tempering some of his own desperation but doing nothing to moderate hers as she gasped and clutched him through a long, hard spasm. When it released her, she continued to shake with the effects, groaning as his thrusts seemed to gather speed and force and momentum.

She peaked again and this time his hands slipped under her hips and lifted her, pulled her into each stroke so that the shivers rippled along the gliding length of him, tightening and quickening around his flesh like hundreds of greedy little fingers. He groaned and shifted his hands again, hooking them under her knees and raising her limbs so that his penetration was full and absolute, and he rolled his hips harder, faster, testing the very limits of his sanity and reason as she melted around him again and again and again. And when he could no longer deny himself a share of the ecstasy flushing through her body, he pulled her hard against his next powerful downstroke and braced her there while his orgasm ripped through him like wildfire, scorching every nerve and muscle, searing away every definition of pleasure, real or imagined, and replacing it with one word: Amanda.

The world and everything in it disappeared briefly behind a wall of sensation too pure, too inviolate, too exquisitely acute to muddy with anything so mundane as time. It could have been seconds or minutes or hours that they clung together, fused by passion, locked in breathless rapture. Amanda thought she died. Gloriously. Beautifully. In a burning incandescence of light and flame and fury, some of which continued to sparkle and trickle through her limbs in bright, shimmering aftershocks long after the main quake passed.

Michael collapsed forward. He was panting like a drowning man, and she peaked again, softly, for no reason other than the fact she was holding him in her arms again, sharing his heat. The knowledge was exhilarating and she wanted to laugh out loud from the sheer joy of it, but she limited her exuberance to an inward smile and contented herself with the lingering sensation of all that expended power and passion pulsing gently inside her.

Amanda did not want to move or spoil the moment in any way. She scarcely dared to breathe as he raised his head slowly out of the crook of her shoulder and looked down at her.

"I was wrong this afternoon," he murmured. "When I said I'd never seen you look lovelier . . . I'd forgotten how you looked beneath me, all flushed and soft and frightened of giving away too much of yourself."

They were the first words spoken between them since she had come into the bedroom.

"I've missed having you in my bed," he said quietly. The words and the admission obviously cost him more than his pride was worth at the moment, for his hand shook at the seemingly innocuous task of brushing aside a damp tendril of hair that stuck to her temple.

"I've missed being here," she whispered.

He drew a swift breath and tried to contain the eagerness

her words brought with them. "It would be . . . an easy enough situation to rectify."

His mouth was poised above her, outlined in every sensuous detail by the flickering candlelight. His eyes were so close they filled her entire field of vision.

"I'm sure Verity wouldn't mind having her room to herself again."

He needed a few seconds to absorb her words and the meaning behind them before he bowed his head and covered her mouth with a tender kiss. His arms began to tighten around her again when a small rending sound made them both aware that he was still partly clothed. He ended the kiss on a soft oath and rolled onto his back, more than half aroused as he started to rid himself of his boots and trousers.

Another oath, louder this time, made him pause and stare hard at the door.

The knock came again, accompanied by an anxious query. "Sir? Are you in there, sir? I'm sorry to disturb you, but I must speak with you. It's urgent."

"Foley," Michael grumbled, tugging his trousers up to his waist again. "It better be urgent or I'll skin him alive. Coming, dammit," he barked at the closed door, then turning to Amanda, he kissed her hard and fast and touched a finger to her lips. "Hold that thought, I'll be right back."

He bolted off the bed and strode to the door, combing his hands through his hair as he went. Amanda listed dreamily onto her side and saw him open the door just enough to slip through and close it behind him. He heard their voices, but nothing of what they were saying, and so she concentrated instead on the wondrous, throbbing fullness that saturated her senses.

He wanted her back in his bed. And she wanted to be here. Right now, with her body dewy and flushed, she could not even pinpoint the exact reason why she had left it in the first place, or why he had made no effort, in all these long weeks, to bring her back. Pride, no doubt. Damnable Yankee, Rebel pride. Well, she was more than willing to put it behind her. When he came back, she would tell him about Verity, tell him everything. She wanted no more lies or half truths between them. No more secrets. He loved her. He had to. Because she loved him, with all her heart, and she knew—she just knew she could offer to share the deepest, darkest part of her soul with him and he would not cast it away.

The door opened, admitting a crack of light from the hallway. Michael's hand was on the knob—it was all she could see for a few moments—and she heard him say "Five minutes" before he came back into the room and leaned against the closed door.

"Have they found Ned Sims?" she asked, pushing herself upright.

"Not yet," he answered from the shadows. "Someone matching his description stole a horse from a nearby farm and rode off in the direction of Natchez. Best guess is he'll board the first packet out and head downriver. If he makes it to New Orleans, he could be in Galveston, Houston, Corpus Christie, even Mexico within a week, and no one would be able to find him."

"Do you think that's what he'll do?"

"According to Flora, he's talked about heading West. And it's what I'd do if I had someone like me on my heels."

Amanda remembered the "five minutes" and shivered slightly as she drew the edges of the coverlet up and around her bare shoulders. "Are you going after him?"

"You don't think I should?"

"On the contrary. I think you should do exactly what Flora suggested."

"Castrate and kill him?" She could sense his wry smile through the darkness. "I wasn't aware you had such a vindictive streak in you, Mrs. Tarrington."

"He hurt his wife and terrified my child. I would wield the knife myself if I had the opportunity."

He came forward from the niche of the doorway, cutting across the light from the candle by the hearth and coming into the pale glow beside the bed. He put a knee to the edge of the mattress and leaned down, cupping her chin in his hand, tipping her face up to his. The kiss was long and wet

and deep enough to make her forget her tentative hold on the
satin coverlet. It slipped down from her shoulders and lay
rippled around her hips, making her look like a sea nymph
rising from a gleaming pool of water. The image drew a
husky groan from Michael's throat as he pressed another kiss
on the naked curve of her shoulder.

"You're not making this any easier on me."

"Can't you just send Foley?" she gasped. "He seems
capable enough."

"A minute ago you were all in favor of me hunting him to
the ends of the earth."

"That was a minute ago," she said softly, her body straining upward into his warmth.

"Mandy—" He forced himself to hold her at arm's
length. "You know what Flora and Sally mean to me. Yes, I
could send Foley—but he's a valet, for Christ's sake. He's
never hunted anything more dangerous than English tea."

"But the sheriff—"

"Will only spend as much time and effort on Sims as he
thinks it warrants, and that isn't much. After all, he didn't
kill Sally, he isn't wanted for murder. They'll ask a few
token questions, maybe find out in a month or so that he *was*
in New Orleans, but that's about all they'll do."

He was right and she knew it. But to go away now . . .
when *they* had only just found each other again . . .

"Mandy—?"

She looked up and saw how intently he was looking at her.
It was the same tautness and the same guarded reserve she
had come to dread seeing over the past weeks.

"When I get back, there are some things we have to talk
about."

"Things?" she asked on a breath.

"Things," he said, seeming to be at a loss to come up
with a better word. "Things we shouldn't be trying to keep
secret from one another. Things that might work against us if
they came out somewhere down the road, which most secrets
—or lies—tend to do."

He knows, Amanda thought with a sudden shock. *He already knows about Verity.*

The revelation, which at the very least should have brought the four horsemen of the apocalypse thundering across her bed and flaying her to a bloody pulp, left nothing but a cold, calm sense of acceptance in its wake. And more than just a little relief, for if he knew her worst secret and had still made love to her with the passion and fury of a man possessed . . . there was nothing more to stand between them. Was there?

"Yes," she agreed. "You're right, of course. We must talk."

He gave her a queer half smile and his gaze dropped to the luscious fullness of her breasts. The taste of her, the feel of her, the scent of her was still too fresh in his mind to let him think clearly, and he did not trust himself to say any more or do anything more other than to lean over and press a kiss to her temple.

"If I'm going to be delayed for any length of time, I'll send word," he promised.

She nodded and bit her lip to keep from saying anything that might sound fearful or desperate. Which was exactly how she was feeling, suddenly, though she could not have said why.

His hand stroked through the tousled silk of her hair one last time before he went to the dressing room and changed into clean, warm riding clothes.

Amanda remained where she was, wrapped once again in the satin covering. When he left for good, she got out of bed and started to pick up the volcanic disarray of her clothing, but an unexpected spate of dizziness sent her back to the bed and crawling under the warmth of the blankets. Eventually she fell asleep, her arms hugging a pillow as a poor substitution for the comfort of Michael's body.

His note, telling her he had boarded a sloop and would be gone a week, perhaps more, came some time after breakfast.

The note from E. Forrest Wainright came less than three hours later.

Chapter 23

Amanda was still in Michael's bedroom when the second note arrived, though she had moved from the bed to the window alcove sometime during the course of the morning. She was seated by the window, waving periodically at Verity below in the gardens as the child sought more roses to cut for Sally's bedside. The curtains were closed between the room and the window to keep in the warmth from the sun, and she was bundled in Michael's oversized robe, the effects of a hot bath still tingling on her skin.

"Miz Tarrington? Are ye in there, hen?"

"Yes, Flora, I'm here." She uncurled her legs and turned a worried face toward the curtain just as Mrs. Reeves poked her head through. "Is it Sally? Is something wrong?"

"Ach, no, hen. Sal's fine. She's a strong wee lass—stronger than what like she looks. She's got a head on her wider than a door this mornin', but the doctor says it's good and hard; she'll be fine in no time. Best thing for her'll be to hear they've caught that slimy-eyed weasel o' a husband o' hers and strung him from the nearest tree."

She set down the tray she was carrying and started arranging the cup and saucer, small plate, knife, spoon.

"Flora . . . you shouldn't be chasing around after me. You should be with Sally."

"Bah. I sat wi' her all night, wakin' her when she didna want to be woke, an' if I sit wi' her all day, we'll start scratchin' on each ither's nerves sure enough. I told her not to marry that bastard. I told her. But did she listen?" She straightened and puffed out her cheeks. "Christ, but it's warm in here. Ye'll fry yer brain out wi' all this stuffy heat, ye will. Won't do, ye know," she warned, pushing back the heavy panels of curtain. "Ye blister up like a lobster and swoon wi' a sick head—won't do a lick o' good for the bairn yer carryin' either.''

Amanda's expression betrayed nothing as Flora bustled around the alcove, but the wily old Scot's eye had her staked out like an offering on an altar.

''Sick again this mornin', were ye?''

Amanda nodded stupidly.

''Aye, well, ye'll have to eat to keep up yer strength, lovey. Best thing fer the morning heaves is to eat a sweetie right after and wash it down wi' a good dose o' rose hip tea. Does Himself know?''

Amanda shook her head, still mute, still unable to grasp that Flora had guessed what she had only begun to suspect herself.

''Mmmm''—she glanced cryptically at the bed—''I thought as how ye might o' told him last night.'' And Amanda went pink to the ears as Flora added matter-of-factly, ''Not that I'm one to pry into anither person's business, mind. Leastwise not unless I'm invited.''

''He . . . had a great deal on his mind. I didn't think the time was right, and besides, I wasn't even sure myself.''

''Bah! I knew it a month ago. Woman gets a glow in her eyes when she's breedin', all soft and shiny like. I knew straight off when ma' Sally were that way. Knew straight off when she'd lost it too. Glow was gone. Everythin' was gone.'' She pursed her lips and scowled at her own thoughts for a minute before glaring down at her mistress again. ''Ye are plannin' on tellin' him soon, are ye not? Ye've the kind o' hips an' bosom that'll start to spread right away, if they haven't already. Ye're no' afraid o' what he'll do, are ye? Aye, maybe a month or two ago, I might have been too, but have ye no seen the way he is wi' wee Vurrity? He practically dotes on the bairn an' she isna even his!''

The pink darkened to a dusky rose and spread downward to make Amanda's toes curl inside her slippers. She had spent most of the morning pondering Michael's feelings toward Verity, and she knew that, given time, he would love her as deeply as he would love one of his own—if he didn't already. The only question was whether or not her parentage would become a problem in the years ahead.

As to who had told him—there could be only one answer. Alisha. Despite her promises, despite the blood oath she had sworn, Alisha had obviously told the whole sordid story to Michael. When, and for what possible reason, Amanda could not even begin to guess. She had not seen or spoken to her sister since the night they had all spent together at Rosalie. The same night, coincidentally, Michael had seemed to throw up an invisible wall between them.

Now, at least, she knew why. She also knew the wall had been breached last night, despite Alisha's best efforts to destroy them.

Flora was watching Amanda's face. "He's a good man, lovey. He'll do right by ye. When ye tell him, he'll be happy as a lark. Mark ma words, he will. An' if ye'd told him last night, like as ye should have, he'd be here now tellin' ye so himself, not runnin' off tendin' to business."

Amanda was mildly surprised by the prickle in Flora's voice, especially since the business he was tending to was Ned Sims. "He didn't seem to think Mr. Foley could handle things on his own."

"Eh? He said that to ye? Hmphf! Mores the like he was worried about defendin' Brian Foley against a charge o' murther."

Amanda's surprise turned into a frown. She barely knew Mr. Foley. He was always in evidence, but never obtrusively so, as Michael's coachman, valet, butler, groom, and, she suspected, friend. If he had said one complete sentence to Amanda in all the time she had been here, she couldn't think what it might have been, and the idea of the polite, reserved manservant calling up sufficient emotion to kill a man in cold blood (for what else would bring down a murder charge?) was a curious one to say the least.

Flora, apparently not satisfied with the speed of Amanda's thought process, sighed. "He loves her, ye ken. Slow as ice meltin' in a blizzard to let on, but he loves her."

"Foley . . . and Sally?"

"Ye canny always chose who ye love, an' ye canny simply shut the love off, even when ye think it's wrong. Foley come back from the war wi' Mister Michael an' ye'd've thought a bolt o' lightning struck him full in the chest when he seen Sal. She were just a wee bit o' a mouse when he'd gone away, more a nuisance than ought else. Five years, but, makes a big change. Near six, if ye count the time he spent lookin' after Himself while he drank an' gambled his way up an' down the river tryin' to get the taste o' gunpowder an' cannon fodder out o' his mouth. Saw his men trapped in a fire, he did. Turrible things, them ironclads. He never talks about it. Never. But Foley whispered a word or two in his mam's ear when she worried he'd lost his mind, and, well, I were just on the ither side o' the door, wasn't I, an' couldna help but overhear. Ach, but we were talkin' about ma Sally, were we no'? Aye, an' by the time Foley come back to Boston, Sims were already in her bed, married proper, spinnin' her head full o' yarns an' promises. She's a good girl, mind, but a wee bit . . . mmmm . . . innocent. She didna think she could do any better than the likes o' Sims." Flora puffed up her bosom again and crossed her arms in umbrage. "Maybe next time she'll listen to her mam."

"I'm sure she will," Amanda allowed softly, her own mind spinning with the new revelations concerning her husband, Foley, Sally . . .

"Ye know what's best, ye'll take ma advice an' all," Flora continued imperiously. "Ye'll take wee Vurrity and go visit yer own mam for a few days, not sit here cooped up wi' yer frets an' worries. I'll no' be any fit company for the child while Sal needs tendin', an' Sal herself is in a rare state worryin' what the bairn thinks every time she sees all them bandages. O' course, ye don't have to take ma advice about *anything*," she said pointedly as she leaned over and nudged the cup of tea and plate of scones closer to Amanda. "But a change o' scenery might do you some good as well."

"But I don't know how long Michael will be gone. If he comes back and we're not here . . . ?"

"Where will he think ye've gone? To China to wade in the

rice paddies? Nay, he'll think ye're a clever wee lass to go an' see yer mam, to share yer happy news wi' her since he were too clarty to stay here an' hear it himself. Besides, he'll be back afore ye know it. Ach, an' where's ma head anyway?'' She patted down the huge pocket in her apron and produced a sealed envelope. ''This come for ye a wee while ago. The lad what delivered it had the cheek to tell me I'd have to hold it to the light an' I wanted to know who it was from.''

She passed an envelope across and stood waiting with her hands folded over her apron.

Amanda's eyebrows arched.

''Paper's too thick. Couldna see through.''

Amanda smiled, thinking it was probably from Michael. If it was, it was likely sent an hour or so after the first and might mean he had changed his mind about trailing Sims downriver and would be home sooner than he had anticipated.

She was still smiling as she read the opening salutation.

Dear Mrs. Tarrington:
A business matter of some importance has arisen pertaining to a mutual acquaintance of ours from *Montana*. I strongly recommend a meeting at your earliest convenience in order to discuss ways of preventing any of these past indiscretions from becoming general knowledge. I shall expect the pleasure of your company *alone* at my State Street residence at 2 P.M. this afternoon.
     Your humble servant,
     E.F. Wainright

Amanda reread the neat script several times before the actual meaning overrode the shock of seeing Wainright's signature.

A mutual friend from Montana? Past indiscretions?

Amanda let the note sink down onto her lap and stared at the signature again, seeing the bold flourish but not believing her eyes.

It seemed so long ago that she had dressed in desperation and went on board the riverboats as Montana Rose. It seemed like another lifetime, another life, another Amanda. How on earth had Wainright uncovered her secret? And what was he threatening to do—expose her?

"It's no' bad news, I hope?" Flora asked.

Bad news?

Amanda passed a cool, trembling hand across her brow. Wainright knew about Montana Rose. Wainright—a man who would probably go to any lengths, with great delight, to see Michael Tarrington's reputation ruined in Natchez. Letting it become general knowledge that she, Amanda Tarrington, had masqueraded as Montana Rose would not only bring scorn and laughter down on Michael's good name, but would likely dredge up the old ghosts as well, the stories about Billy Fleet and his chicanery on those same riverboats almost three decades ago.

The gossips had not yet stopped talking about Amanda Courtland Jackson's elopement with a Yankee speculator. Fueling those stories with more about Montana Rose and Billy Fleet would not only make her a complete laughing-stock, it would send her mother into a decline that could last for years. It could spill over to affect Ryan and Dianna's marriage and, to a lesser degree, Alisha and Karl's.

"What time is it, please?"

Flora consulted the small oval timepiece she wore pinned to her bodice. "Just gone twelve."

Amanda bit her lip. It would take an hour, at least, to drive into Natchez by buggy, and she wasn't even dressed yet.

She reread the note once more and crumpled it into a small ball. "I need to go into town this afternoon. Will you please have a carriage brought around?"

"It's no bad news, is it?" Flora asked again. "I can spare the time to come with ye, if ye need me."

"No," Amanda said quickly. "No, it isn't bad news. It's just . . . a family matter I must tend to. I won't be long, I promise, and Sally needs you here."

"Mmmm." She twisted her mouth stubbornly. "I dinna like it, you rattlin' off in a buggy all on yer own."

"I'll be fine. Please, just send for the carriage."

Flora gave a parting snort of disapproval but did not press her mistress any further. And, an hour later, after she had seen Amanda into a well-cushioned buggy and threatened the driver to within an inch of his life if he drove over a single rut, she returned to the master bedroom and searched until she found the crumpled ball of notepaper.

Amanda had the driver stop the carriage two blocks from Wainright's State Street residence. She had ignored Flora's instructions concerning the scones and tea, and her stomach felt as if it were pressing against her backbone. She wished with all her heart that Michael was beside her. He was afraid of nothing and no one; he would have known how to handle Wainright with ease.

Making her stomach do even more acrobatics was the uncomfortable memory of her last visit to State Street. The idea of having actually agreed to marry the man—of having sought him out deliberately to accept his proposal—brought a hot, sour taste of bile to the back of her throat.

She had worn a traveling suit of nondescript gray wool that was, if anything in her new wardrobe could be deemed plain, ordinary enough to let her pass unremarked through the crowds of pedestrians. Women walked by arm in arm, chattering like magpies. Free blacks were everywhere, careful to step out of the way if a beaver-hatted merchant passed by, equally arrogant in not moving at all if the gentleman or lady was a Southerner.

Amanda hurried past coaches and soldiers. She stepped cautiously around a man selling small pies off a cart and carried the scent of cooked meat with her through the iron gate and up the stairs to Wainright's door.

It opened before she had a chance to reach for the brass knocker.

"Mrs. Tarrington." Wainright was there himself, swinging the door wide with a mocking gallantry. "How good of you to come. And prompt too, I see. Always an excellent sign when one is considering entering into business arrangements."

Because the sight of a well-dressed woman standing on a doorstep had the potential of drawing more attention than she desired, Amanda brushed past him and stood in the shadows of the foyer.

"I cannot imagine what possible manner of business arrangements you could be referring to, Mr. Wainright. As it happens, I was coming into Natchez today anyway and, I must confess, curiosity was the only thing that prompted me to call. Otherwise I would have advised you to address my husband, since he attends to all of our business matters."

Wainright closed the door and smiled at her. "I doubt very much you would want him to handle this particular bit of business. But where are my manners . . . may I offer you a sip of wine, or a cordial perhaps?"

"No, thank you. I am in somewhat of a hurry, so if you will simply say what you have to say—"

"I prefer brandy in the afternoon," he said, strolling past her and walking through the open door into his study. "Especially on these cool, damp days when you can never quite get the chill out of the air."

He was out of sight before the sentence finished, and Amanda had the choice of following or standing in the empty hall like a leftover coat. She followed, not happily so, and stood on the threshold of the doorway, not taking any more steps than were absolutely necessary. Wainright was at the opposite side of the room pouring himself a glass of brandy. His smile was still firmly in place as he glanced expectantly over his shoulder.

"You're sure you won't join me? I have a rather nice, sweet sherry you might find suitable to your . . . improved tastes."

Despite her efforts at modesty, his narrowed eyes had already roved approvingly over the rich banding of velvet that circled her collar, cuffs, and hem. Her bonnet was simple, but elegant, made more so by the abundance of gold curls gathered at the nape. Her shoes were of the softest gray kid leather, as were the gloves and matching reticule.

"Your husband seems to have acquired a passion for more than fine horseflesh," he mused appreciatively. "But then, I always said you would shine in silks and satins."

Amanda coldly returned his stare. "What is it you want, Mr. Wainright? You seem to think we have some business to discuss, but if this is concerning the note on Rosalie, I assure you my husband will not tolerate any more demands."

"Milked him for all you could already, have you?"

She stiffened. "I don't have to listen to this. If you have anything more to say—"

"I'll just say it to *Montana Rose* . . . shall I?"

She missed half a breath before retorting "Who?"

"Montana Rose. I'm sure you've heard the name before. Hell, there was a time, a few months back, when Natchez fairly buzzed with stories about her." He sipped his brandy and closed the gap between them, walking a slow circle around her, not quite touching but coming close enough for her skin to prickle at his proximity. "They were starting to call her the best on the river. Said she had a sixth sense; eyes in the back of her head; lightning-quick hands; a body to make a grown man weep."

"I'm sure this is all very interesting, but—"

"They called her the Ice Queen," he hissed against her ear, moving behind her again, circling, prowling. "Said she never talked, never smiled, never moved except to rake in the chips. They said she could pull an ace out of thin air and make it disappear again without batting an eyelash. All grossly exaggerated talents, I'm sure, but effective nonetheless."

"Am I supposed to know what you are talking about? Or care?"

"You should care. And you should be damned interested to know the name and reputation of Montana Rose has, if anything, grown by leaps and bounds since her . . . ah, mysterious disappearance. Absence, as we are all told, does indeed make the heart grow fonder—or, as in this case, makes the rumors fly faster. Especially when someone as elusive, as enigmatic, as . . . extraordinary as Montana Rose simply vanishes into thin air. Much like Billy Fleet did, some twenty odd years ago.''

"You are beginning to bore me, Mr. Wainright. I don't know anyone named Montana Rose, and I don't know anyone named Billy Fleet.''

"Well . . . perhaps before you bore *both* of us half to death with your grand protestations, I should tell you that I have come by my information from two separate sources. One was dubious to say the least, but the other was absolutely irrefutable. They both identified you as Montana Rose, Queen of the Mississippi riverboats.''

"Maybe they were both wrong.''

"They were both right, *Montana,* or you wouldn't have come here today.''

"I told you—''

"You were curious, yes. So you did. And so you are still, are you not? Curious to know what I might be tempted to do with this intriguing bit of information?''

"If you were planning to use it to blackmail me, I would warn you not to waste your breath, or your venom. My husband already knows.''

"Ahh, yes, a clever move on his part, if I do say so myself.'' Wainright pursed his lips and propped an elbow on a nearby bookshelf. "To have the pleasure of his wife and his nemesis in bed with him every night? Very clever indeed. Marry thine enemy . . . yes. It should be the eleventh commandment.''

"What are you talking about?''

The watery eyes glinted with even more amusement. "He hasn't told you?''

"Told me what?''

His brow cleared and he tilted his head back through a hearty laugh at her expense. "Priceless. Absolutely priceless. Holding back the trump card on the Queen of the River. Not that I can fault him for his caution. After all, you did

marry him for his money, and a man in his position should
indeed go to any lengths to protect his interests. I, on the
other hand, can only wonder at the audacity of the man and
the generosity of the Fates to have put such delicious ironies
at my disposal.''

Amanda shook her head, not comprehending at all where
his ramblings were coming from or leading to. "If you were
hoping to use this information to blackmail Michael, you
will be equally disappointed. We would both, I think, survive
a little gossip about riverboat gambling. A few eyebrows
might twitch and a few Daughters of the Confederacy might
be scandalized into crossing to the other side of the street a
time or two to avoid us, but I daresay we would survive the
snubs and the whispers.''

"I daresay you could, but what about your family? Would
they be so comfortable becoming the subject of barroom
discussions? Would they appreciate the laughter behind their
backs that would come with the knowledge of their daughter's notoriety as the most famous whore along the riverfront? And please—'' He held up his hand "Spare me the
righteous indignation. Whether the illustrious Montana Rose
ever tucked more than aces up her skirts or not, the idea of a
woman gambling and whoring go hand in hand, don't you
think?''

"I think you are grasping at straws, sir," she said calmly.
"And I should think you would have realized by now that we
Courtlands—indeed, we Southerners do not wilt as easily as
all that.''

"My dear lady, I knew you would not," he agreed. "Nor
did I invite you here solely to discuss your role as Montana
Rose, although it may well be in your role as Montana Rose
that we arrive at an amicable arrangement.''

"I have no intentions of arriving at any arrangements
whatsoever with you, amicable or not. As for Montana Rose,
she no longer exists.''

"She has turned respectable, has she? Found herself a rich
husband and decided to become domesticated?'' He sighed

and shook his head. "I'm truly sorry to hear that. Respectability is not an option that appeals to me overmuch."

"It appeals to me," she said evenly.

Wainright took another sip of his brandy and his eyes turned to slits between the coppery red lashes. "I was told you had few equals when it came to running a bluff. I should warn you I am not so easily duped or deterred."

"And I should warn you *again* that the information you have, and what you plan to do with it, is of little consequence to me, so if anyone appears to be running a bluff here today, it would seem to be you."

Wainright set his empty glass on the bookshelf. Without a word, he crossed the room and opened a narrow door built into the paneling that Amanda had not noticed.

Thinking she had prepared herself for almost anything, she was proved wrong when a small gasp left her lips as the person who had been concealed on the other side came sullenly through the doorway.

"Alisha?"

"Amanda." The name was said as if to a stranger, delivered with a derisive toss of blonde curls.

"What are you doing here?"

"Nothing I wouldn't rather be doing elsewhere, I assure you," Alisha answered tartly.

Amanda stared at her twin, the shock of seeing her in Forrest Wainright's study enough to render her temporarily at a loss. Compounding the shock of seeing her there was the secondary reaction to Alisha von Helmstaad's appearance. There was no color in her complexion aside from what had been hastily applied from pots and jars. Her clothes fit awkwardly, as if she had suddenly lost her sense of style. There were dark-blue smudges under her eyes that the thickest layer of powder could not conceal.

"What are you doing here?" Amanda asked again, her voice softened with genuine concern.

Alisha glared at Wainright. "I'm here because this rat found out about something. Something extremely personal that I had been assured was done in the strictest confidence. I had no idea the doctor was a friend of his, or that my medical problems would be spread around like cheap perfume.''

"Medical problems? Were you ill?"

Her sister laughed mirthlessly. "What a fashionably quaint way to put it. Ill. Yes, Amanda dear, I was *ill*. And for a viciously outrageous fee, the illness was cured.''

Amanda's hand went to her throat. "Cured . . . ?''

"I believe the jurisprudent term would be aborted,'' Wainright interjected smoothly, relishing the instant blaze of loathing that flamed in Alisha's eyes.

Amanda turned slowly to face Wainright. The ugliness of what the word implied sent an unhealthy flush into her cheeks and made her drop her hand, unselfconsciously, from her throat to her belly.

Wainright was not particularly affected by the reaction of either woman and proceeded to elaborate as he fetched his glass from the shelf and refilled it. "It seems the baroness found herself, er, in a family way at a most inconvenient time. For a price, the inconvenience was resolved.''

"And now you think you can take advantage of Alisha's position by blackmailing her?'' Amanda asked, some of her composure returning on a surge of anger.

Wainright's smile was undaunted. "A rare opportunity, wouldn't you agree? Something both the Sons and Daughters of the Confederacy could really sink their teeth into for a good chew.''

Amanda's disgust rose higher in her throat. "You would do it too, wouldn't you?''

"With the greatest of pleasure, my dear,'' he assured her evenly.

Amanda looked at Alisha. "What has he asked for? How much does he want for his silence?''

"More than I could hope to get from Karl. The fat pig is a fraud. He can't buy himself a corset without getting approval from the family back home. As it was, I had to sell some of his precious jewelry to look after my . . . problem. I daren't even try to sell any more or he'll puff up like a quail and explode. Besides—'' She cast a long, icy glare of loathing in Wainright's direction. "I already paid him what he wanted from me."

"And with such vulgar enthusiasm too, I might add," Wainright said dryly, his lecherous grin leaving no doubt what manner of currency he had demanded. "It hardly behooves you to waste your talents on a pig like Helmstaad."

Alisha whirled away in disgust and walked to the window, leaving Amanda to bear the brunt of Wainright's sarcasm. "And here I thought I was complimenting her."

"What do you want, Wainright? How much will it cost to keep your filthy mouth shut?"

"Tut, tut. What makes you think I want money?"

Her eyes narrowed and she fought another sickening wave of nausea. "Because you know you would have to kill me before you got anything else."

He took another slow sip of brandy, his eyes holding hers over the rim of the glass. "In that case, another fifty thousand should compensate quite nicely. For the time being, anyway."

"Fifty thousand? That's insane. *You're* insane."

"Nevertheless, that is my price."

"You heard Alisha, she doesn't have that kind of money. Neither do I."

"Neither does your husband, it might interest you to know," he said wryly.

"Excuse me?"

"The money he spends so freely? It comes from heavy mortgaging and very high risk investments," he explained blithely. "The small fortune he has spent on breeding stock, not to mention the grandiose gesture he made in paying off the debts on Rosalie, have pushed him to the very limit of his creditors' patience."

"How do you know all this?" she gasped.

"I make it my business to know everything about a man who dares to run up against me." He paused and arched an eyebrow. "It doesn't happen very often, you see, yet your husband has managed to outmaneuver me twice. The first time was when he bought a plum piece of land I'd had my eye on for several months; the second was on a dark, stormy night in Jamestown. The mortgages and debt load should take care of his stint as landed gentry. Since you had a hand in meting out the second insult, my dear, I think it only appropriate you should contribute your part of the restitution.''

''I don't have fifty thousand dollars. I have no way of getting it.''

''My dear *Montana,* you are not thinking clearly. There is a perfectly viable way for you to earn all the money you need.''

''On the riverboats?'' she gasped. ''Gambling? What kind of a fool are you, Wainright? Why do you think I embarked on such an elaborate ruse in the first place? I did it to try to win the money we owed on Rosalie! I couldn't do it. In six months, I couldn't do it!''

''Perhaps you didn't choose the right games.''

''Right games, wrong games . . . what does it matter? It would still take months to earn the kind of money you want.''

''Or you could do it in one night. In a high-stakes game with free spenders who are all there for one reason and one reason only: to walk away with the pot of gold.'' He walked closer to her, his red hair glinting like fire. ''I happen to know there will be such a game taking place in the next twenty-four hours. It costs ten thousand just to buy a seat at the table.''

''I don't have ten thousand,'' she said hoarsely.

''I do. And I have that much confidence in you that I'm willing to stake you.''

''What makes you think I could even get into such a game? They're usually arranged between players who know each other and have set up these kinds of games before.''

''You underestimate the reputation of Montana Rose. Even if the game was not being played on board one of your favorite haunts—the *Mississippi Queen*—whose captain is, as I understand it, amiable to making any necessary arrangements in exchange for cash, I have no doubt your name alone could win you a seat in any game on any boat on the river.''

"You seem to have this all figured out, don't you?''

Wainright's small teeth appeared in a smile. "I like to be thorough.''

"Thorough enough to know for certain I will win?''

"You'll win. Your family's reputation depends upon it.''

"Ownership of Rosalie depended upon it before, and I couldn't do it.''

"You were working on your own then, with limited resources. I'm prepared to back you fully, including a little extra help in the game itself, if you need it. You have played with one of the gentlemen before—a Mr. Paul Whitney. He would not be adverse to the idea of working as a team.''

Amanda recalled the man clearly. Skeletally thin, pale, with a scar across his forehead and a lethal reaction to insults. It did not come as any great surprise that he and Wainright should know each other. It did bring a further sense of suffocation, however, as if every exit to the room were being blocked one at a time and her chances for escape were growing smaller and smaller.

"Perhaps I should leave the two of you alone for a few minutes . . . to talk this over in private?''

When neither twin offered a comment, he took up his brandy and strolled through to the other room, pointedly drawing the panel closed behind him.

Amanda stared at the door a moment then looked at Alisha, expecting to see at least a measure of concern, since it was her reputation being placed in the greatest jeopardy. But Alisha did not look perturbed at all. She was adjusting the cuff of lace that spilled artfully from the sleeve of her jacket, behaving as if none of this were her fault. As if this meeting were a minor annoyance to be tolerated and then forgotten . . . as quickly as she forgot anything and everyone else she considered to be of little or no use to Alisha Courtland von Helmstaad.

"How could you have done such a thing?" Amanda asked

quietly. "How could you have let a man like Wainright get such a terrible hold on you?"

Alisha glanced up. "I didn't exactly plan any of this, you know. I was assured of the doctor's discretion, as well as his skill in dealing with such matters."

"What would *you* know about discretion? You told Michael about Verity, didn't you?"

The question was unexpected, and Alisha stalled a moment or two before she offered a casual shrug. "I didn't tell him everything. I only told him Caleb wasn't the father—which he wasn't. I suppose I *could* have told him she was the leavings of a Yankee colonel who thought he could commandeer more than just the use of our home for a few weeks . . . but I didn't think he would really want to know that part . . . do you?"

Amanda grew paler, scarcely able to believe what she was hearing. Her head swam with an insistence that made her sink down on the edge of the settee.

"Obviously not," Alisha continued with quiet venom, "since you apparently didn't want him to know who the real mother was either."

Amanda's lips parted slightly. "You may have given birth to Verity, but you were never her mother."

"And never wanted to be," Alisha spat. "Had I known at the time how easy it would have been to get rid of her, I never would have agreed to go to New Orleans, never would have gone through the hell of giving birth, or let you have her so you could pass her off as the daughter your poor dead husband never knew."

"You don't mean that," Amanda said, shaking her head slowly.

"Don't I? Do you have any idea how much I loathe the sight of that child, knowing where she came from, knowing the pain and humiliation she put me through? Can you even imagine how much I loathe seeing the two of you together, the stoic mother and orphaned daughter, happy as two little periwinkles in a patch? You don't think I would have gotten rid of her? Well, I would have. Just like that," she said, snapping her fingers. "I only rue the day I let you and Ryan talk me out of it."

"Thank goodness we weren't around this time. Now you have nothing to rue at all."

Amanda's sarcasm earned her a long, hard stare.

"And how do you know, even if Wainright gets his money, that he won't come back again in three months or five months or a year, demanding another fifty thousand dollars to safeguard your sordid little secret?"

"I will take steps to ensure he doesn't dare."

"When? The next time he crooks his finger and orders you into his bed?"

Alisha clamped her mouth firmly shut and tried unsuccessfully to keep the hot sparkle of tears out of her eyes. They were not, Amanda realized with a sad shock, prompted by either remorse or shame. They were tears of anger, hatred, and bitter jealousy.

"I'm sorry," she said quietly. "But I won't do it. I can't."

Alisha's eyes widened. "What do you mean you can't do it? Of course you can."

Amanda shook her head. "It isn't worth it."

Alisha gasped. "But you heard what he said. You heard what he is threatening to do."

"You should have thought of that before," Amanda said without emotion. "You should have thought about the possible consequences long before you ever went to see the doctor, never mind before you ever came to see Wainright for the first time."

Alisha's face flooded an ugly red. "I'm your sister! You can't let him ruin me!"

"You ruined yourself."

"If I am ruined, *you* will be ruined too."

"I'll take my chances," Amanda said, and stood.

"I'll take Verity back! I'll tell everyone I'm her real mother—what difference will it make then—and I'll take her back!"

Amanda's face turned to stone. "I would kill you before I

would let you touch her. I'll kill you if you even breathe such a threat to me again.''

Alisha recoiled from the chilling promise in her sister's voice and tried desperately to regain control of the situation. ''But . . . you can't do this to me!''

''You've done it to yourself . . . again . . . only this time, I won't bail you out.''

Amanda turned toward the door, but Alisha was far from finished. ''How dare you! How dare you act so noble and righteous and pass judgment on me!''

''I'm not judging you,'' Amanda sighed. ''I'll leave that to your husband. As for your lover—or lovers, whoever they might be—ask them if it was worth it.''

Alisha's reply came out in a hiss of venom. ''Oh, I'll ask, all right. I'll take them aside, one at a time, all of my lovers . . . *beginning with your husband.*''

Amanda's hand froze against the door jamb.

''That's right, Amanda dearest. You heard correctly. Your Yankee husband, the very bold and *very* virile Michael Tarrington. In the end, not so different from Wainright either, except of course, he wasn't satisfied to try just one twin.''

Amanda swayed a little and had to tighten her grip on the jamb. ''I don't believe you,'' she whispered. ''You're lying.''

''Am I? I guess you'll just have to ask *him* then, won't you? *He* would never lie to you, would he? Ask him about the night we all spent together under one roof as one big happy family. Ask him where he spent the night after you sent him away with his tail between his legs. *Ask him what we did under the moonlight for three long glorious hours.* I swear I was so sore the next morning, I could barely walk, let alone wave a sweet good-bye from the veranda.''

''No . . .''

''He was drunk and he was rough,'' Alisha continued. ''But I got a little rough myself—maybe you saw the scratches on his neck? Here—'' she said, stabbing a finger at her own throat and tracing it down to her collarbone. ''I tried to fight him off at first, but he was too strong and too angry

. . . did you really turn him out of your bed? At any rate, he said one twin was as good as the other and he could always claim afterward he didn't know which one was which. By then, of course, he had his clothes off and he was inside me and . . . frankly . . . I might never have said anything at all''—her eyes narrowed vindictively—*"if it wasn't for the child."*

Amanda's heart stumbled to a halt.

"Karl is impotent, you see, so I couldn't very well pass the thing off as his, now could I?"

Amanda's chest felt as if an iron band was tightening around it. She was staring out into the hallway and the oddest thing—a single, bright mote of dust caught her attention and held it through a slow, spiraling descent.

"After all, I was only trying to do *you* a favor," Alisha added mawkishly. "I was only trying to think ahead to the consequences."

Wainright's low chuckle intruded on the taut silence. He had come back into the library unnoticed and unheard, in time to witness the final exchange between the two sisters.

"My, my, such devotion," he murmured. "Your friends and family will be so proud to hear of such a fine example of sisterly love."

Amanda turned and stared helplessly at Alisha, then Wainright.

"The *Queen* docks tonight. The game is scheduled for tomorrow night. Shall I make inquiries on your behalf with Captain Turnbull, or would you prefer to work out the arrangements yourself?"

Tears shimmered along Amanda's lashes and slipped out the corners unchecked.

"I . . . have to go now," she said in a whisper. "I'm . . . not feeling very well."

"By all means, rest up," Wainright said solicitously. "I can't have my own Mississippi Queen at less than peak perfection."

Amanda fled to the sound of his laughter. She stumbled slightly at the gate and caught the edge of her skirt on the iron grating, but she hardly paused long enough to yank it free. She ran all the way to where the carriage was parked, cutting and weaving past the startled pedestrians, seeing them only as a blur through the thick film of tears that blinded her.

The ride back to Briar Glen was no less of a blur and she was glad Michael was away. She was equally glad Mrs. Reeves had been the one to suggest she go home to Rosalie for a few days, for she asked no questions, posed no obstacles when Amanda bundled Verity and a few of their belongings into the carriage and they left as hastily as she had arrived.

Ryan was working out in the fields, which made it easier to deliver Verity into her mother's safekeeping and explain that she preferred the child stay with her grandparents while Michael was away and Sally was recuperating. It was not all lies, she told herself. Mrs. Reeves had enough to do without chasing after an energetic four-year-old. It only remained then to retrieve the small trunk she had left stored in her old bedroom and to order the coachman to take her back to Natchez. She dismissed him in front of Judge Moore's modest town home where, thankfully, neither the Judge nor Dianna was there to witness her arrival or detain her with questions. From there, she was able to hail a hansom cab to take her to the small, nondescript hotel she had frequented as Montana Rose.

The first thing she ordered was a steaming hot bath; the second was a bottle of brandy. She desperately needed the heat, inside and out, for she had never felt so chilled, so empty, so utterly alone before. She had not allowed herself to dwell on Alisha's charges and accusations during the course of the afternoon, but now, in the privacy of a strange room, in a strange tin bath with the smell and decay of the Natchez waterfront permeating the walls, the bedding, the very air she breathed, she could detach herself from what had become real to Amanda Tarrington and remember the way things had been as Amanda Courtland.

Living apart from Alisha, she supposed she had forgotten

her sister's penchant for treachery and deceit. Or at least relegated it to the past, where it belonged.

Yes, Amanda dear, I was ill. And for a viciously outrageous fee, the illness was cured.

Amanda closed her eyes. She sipped on her brandy and pressed her hand flat over her own belly, sensing the new life growing within her, unable to imagine the extent of Alisha's hatred or desperation that she could do something so cold-blooded, so . . . final . . . without showing the slightest qualm of remorse.

Amanda refilled her glass and sank deeper into the bathwater.

When I get back, there are some things we have to talk about.

Things?

Obviously she wasn't the only one with secrets. The least of his was the fact that Briar Glen was heavily mortgaged and he had persistent creditors. The worst was that he had made love to her twin sister and had left her pregnant with his child.

Were those the *things* he wanted to talk about?

Amanda stared into the amber liquid in her glass and rolled the contents from side to side, watching the clear, runny legs form on the glass and slide back down to the bottom. She stared until the bathwater cooled and the skin on her fingers and toes had turned to crepe.

She would go on board the *Mississippi Queen* and she would buy a seat in the game. She would play as if her life depended upon it . . . because it did. Fifty thousand was not impossible with the right players, but she would settle for forty, thirty, twenty . . . even ten would be enough to take her and Verity away from Natchez. Wainright could choke on his greed for all she cared. Alisha could wallow in self-pity. Ryan, Mother, Father . . . they would survive. Rosalie would survive; it had for over a hundred and fifty years.

As for Michael Tarrington?

He would have to pay for his own sins. She had enough of a burden paying for everyone else's.

Chapter 24

Montana Rose paused in her familiar spot under the arched entryway that led into the main salon of the *Mississippi Queen*. The tables were, as usual, crowded to capacity, but she felt no exhilaration, took no pleasure in the sights and sounds of money, power, and rivalry. If anything, she felt tawdry and uncomfortable in the low-cut emerald gown. Months ago she had thought it elegant and rich, the velvet luxuriant, the flounces and tucks an extravagant necessity to win attention. Now she felt like glaring back at anyone who stared too long. The gown was too tight, the bodice pushed her breasts too high, and the velvet, even though it had hung out all night and she had brushed and steamed it through most of the afternoon, was shiny in places where the cheapness of the fabric was beginning to tell.

There was a showboat docked adjacent to the *Queen,* and frequent bursts of applause, music, and singing echoed across the jetty, becoming lost the instant one stepped from the deck into the din of the gambling salon. Where Montana stood, she could still hear both the music and the shouts of the gamblers. It was distracting—almost as distracting as the knowledge that Wainright was on board the showboat, enjoying the one performance even as another was about to begin. He had met her on the dock and handed her a fat sheaf of money—ten thousand in cash—and wished her luck with a flat, oily grin. Montana had been more unnerved by the meeting than she cared to admit, and did not notice Captain Benjamin Turnbull until he was standing beside her.

"Goddamn, girl. Aren't you just the sight for sore eyes," he exclaimed, planting a large, furry kiss on the back of her hand. "I was beginning to believe some of the stories I'd heard. Some said you moved out West to San Francisco.

Some said you'd grown weary of the game and retired. I even heard one story you'd fallen overboard and drowned.''

Montana smiled wanly. "I assure you, I am alive and well. As for retirement, I have been seriously considering it lately, although I'm not so sure San Francisco would be my first choice. I was thinking more of New Orleans or Baton Rouge.''

"New Orleans," he said promptly. "I guarantee you would shine brighter than any star in the sky.''

"Ahh. But what if I didn't want to shine? What if I just wanted to . . . slip out of sight for a while? A long while, with no one any the wiser for it?''

"My dear Montana." He lowered his voice and raised the back of her hand to his mouth again, tickling her with his beard as he murmured, "Should you want to slip away . . . should you want to vanish completely, you can count upon my utmost discretion to make any arrangements you require.''

"There would be two of us. Myself and a child.''

His eyes betrayed the faintest glint of surprise before descending again into the warm, dusky cleft between her breasts. "It could be done.''

"How much would this . . . discretion . . . cost me?''

He smiled and straightened. "I make it a point never to discuss such business matters with so many large ears flapping around. If you are serious, we can discuss this later on tonight after—I presume—you have concluded your own enterprises.''

"I would be pleased to meet with you later, Ben. And you're right. I was hoping for a little excitement in my life tonight. Anything interesting going on?'' she inquired casually, gazing slowly around the main salon.

"The usual," he said with an easy shrug. "Fat, lazy businessmen with nothing better to do with their time. Couple or three might interest you.''

"That's it?''

"That's about it," he agreed.

Montana met his gaze directly. "I heard there was a big game tonight."

"Where the blazes did you hear that?"

"Is there?"

Ben frowned, drawing his bushy black eyebrows into one solid, thick line. "Hell, Montana, it'd cost you the wind and the sea just to walk into the room."

"I came prepared to work toward my retirement," she said, patting the fringed satin reticule that hung from her wrist. "Can you get me in?"

Turnbull scratched fiercely at his chin. "I don't know—"

"For double your usual percentage, of course."

His eyes narrowed. "Set yourself down over there. I'll see what I can do. No promises, now."

"None expected," she agreed, and found a seat at an empty table along the wall. She followed the captain's burly shoulders through the crowd and up the staircase that led to the second-level tier of curtained alcoves. He disappeared into one of the private booths and was gone so long she began to worry she would not be admitted.

Twenty minutes later Captain Turnbull emerged.

"I had to wait for a hand to play out," he explained when he joined her. "A goddamned big one too—twenty-two thousand and change in the pot, by my estimate. You sure you want to swim in them waters with five hungry sharks, all out for blood?"

"Will they take me?"

"Two of 'em knew your name already. Two didn't want any part of fussing with a woman."

"And the fifth?"

"He's got eyes like a dead fish and hands quick enough to draw a gun as soon as an ace. Said as how he didn't care so long as your money was green."

"Paul Whitney," she murmured.

"You know him?"

"We've met."

"Well then . . . at least you'll know what you're up against."

"So I'm in?"

"You're in."

Montana stood and accompanied Ben back across the salon. They climbed the stairs in silence, and at the top, he stopped her again. "I'll check on you as often as I can, but if it gets too hot in there for you—"

She reached up and patted one of the hairy cheeks. "I can take care of myself. But thank you for worrying."

"Yeah, well, ain't a one of them in there angels."

The hissed warning came just as the curtain opened and a hostess hustled through balancing a tray of empty bottles and dirty dishes. She recognized Montana and nodded to the captain as she held the curtain aside for them to enter.

With Ben's caution still tickling the nape of her neck, Montana saw, seated under the glare of the hooded oil lamp, the pale, cadaverous visage of Paul Whitney. He was dressed all in black as he had been at their last meeting, the wide brim of his hat shielding both his eyes and the angry white scar that traced from one temple to the other. He looked up as she entered and their eyes met. He kept staring as she came fully into the private room, his hands working instinctively to stack the enormous pile of chips he had won into neat columns.

"So. We meet again, Miss Rose," he said in a cold, lifeless monotone. "Stakes are a little higher this time and we don't allow credit of any kind. Cash only. Ten grand to buy in and when that runs out . . . so do you." He stacked the last chip and leaned back. "In or out?"

"In," she said, and started to open her reticule, her mind already scanning back over their last encounter. She remembered his ploy of playing hands where he only needed to draw one card. She also remembered the small pearl-handled derringer he had produced in the blink of an eye.

Her gaze scanned the faces of the other men seated around the table and her recollections stopped there . . . crystallized, more to the truth of it, becoming suspended like a pattern of frost on a window pane. The frost, the sparkling pattern seemed to form a glittering halo around the last face she would, in her wildest of dreams or nightmares, have expected to see there.

He had his back to her. Even so, there was no mistaking the broad, powerful shoulders, the thick chestnut waves of his hair, the slim, inordinately long and fragrant cheroot he held balanced in the square-tipped fingers of his left hand.

Michael Tarrington was supposed to be halfway to Louisiana by now hunting Ned Sims. He was not supposed to be in Natchez, playing poker on board the *Mississippi Queen*.

His face, when he turned it slowly toward her, registered a similar shock, liberally laced with fury and disbelief. *She* was supposed to be safely ensconced behind the walls of Briar Glen, tucked into a feather bed reading bedtime stories to a sleepy, tow-headed four-year-old. She was not supposed to be on a gambling boat, flashing a wad of money and a come-hither smile at men who had already undressed and raped her with their eyes.

Michael's eyes were the color of a harsh winter sky, slate gray and threatening a storm of epic proportions. His mouth was a thin slash, so bleak and forbidding it sounded as if he had to squeeze every word forth.

"Montana. This is indeed a surprise. I hadn't heard you were back in business."

She found her voice somewhere and replied, "I hadn't heard you were back in Natchez."

Whitney spread his hands inquiringly. "We here to reminisce about old times . . . or play cards?"

Montana's hand tightened around the wad of money she had partially withdrawn from her reticule. Had Wainright known Michael would be in the game? Was that how he knew Briar Glen was debt-ridden? Because he knew Michael had gambled his way to the brink of ruin?

Her belly started a slow slide down to her knees and she wanted to turn and run. Wainright should have told her. She would have been better prepared if he had told her how truly heavily the odds would be stacked against her.

At least you'll know what you're up against. Ben's words.

The echo of them was still whispering in her ear as she leaned forward and placed the sheaf of money on the table.

She saw Michael's eyes flick down and his mouth, if it was possible to do so, became even thinner, speculating, she supposed, on where she had come by such a large amount of cash.

"Gentlemen," she said evenly. "Let's play cards."

Chapter 25

Montana stood on deck and breathed the luxury of cold crisp night air. She guessed the dawn was not far off; stars were already beginning to fade and melt out of the sky. A thick layer of mist floated across the surface of the water, sending ghostly fingers up the embankment as if in search of some way to escape the river basin. The showboat was dark, quiet, with only dim lamps mounted at the stern and bow to mark its length in the gloom. The crowds on board the *Queen* had thinned but would never completely go away while the boat was moored to the dock. Even when she sailed, the roulette wheels would still be turning, the faro tables would be working, the hostesses would be hauling their trays and selling their smiles to anyone with the coin to pay.

Michael had left an hour ago, without a word or a glance in her direction. He had lost heavily, due in no small part to the vast quantity of whiskey he had consumed. He had played recklessly and made foolish bets on hands that held nothing stronger than a pair. To prove a point, perhaps? To prove it didn't matter? To prove nothing mattered anymore?

Montana turned abruptly from the deck rail and walked to the stern of the ship, past the monstrous, gleaming paddle wheel. She descended by the crew's afterhatchway, feeling her way along the unlit corridor until she came to the captain's quarters. There was no light showing at the bottom of the cabin door, but there had been no mistaking the look in his eye when she had signaled she was almost finished for the night. She had often met him after a game to settle their account; only once had he been late in joining her.

There was no answer to her soft knock and she tried the latch. It moved freely, as did the door on its well-oiled hinges.

"Ben?"

There was no sound other than her own breathing and the slap and wash of water against the outer skin of the hull.

"Ben . . . are you here?"

The rocking motion of the huge ship was more pronounced in the dark. Sounds had echoes but no source or direction. There was a lantern somewhere, hanging from the center of the ceiling if she remembered correctly, creaking lightly in its metal cradle.

Montana waited for her eyes to become accustomed to the darkness before she tried to search for matches. A chair began to take on shape, a desk, a low beam across the ceiling that must have caused the tall captain a curse or two in passing. A weak, gray light sifted through the small porthole, causing pale reflections from the lights on shore, and as her sight improved the light seemed to strengthen and point the way, like a beacon, to a pair of lamps and a jar of matches on a small table.

Halfway to her goal, her foot snagged on something and she stumbled awkwardly to her knees. Her hands, spread out to break the fall, skidded farther in a pool of water and the dark silence was startled by the sound of her ripe curse. Feeling doubly foolish, Montana tugged at her skirts and felt around the area of her feet to locate what had tripped her. She felt a length of rough wool, and something bristly above it . . . something gaping and wet . . . teeth . . .

Montana choked back a scream and scrambled away from the body. Her hair stood on end and her spine arched, her fingers burned where they had brushed over the arm, the shoulder, the full bearded jaw. It was Captain Turnbull and she did not have to see him in any stronger light to know he was dead.

She stumbled to her feet and ran for the door, swinging it open with a crash in her haste to escape. She did not stop to wonder what had happened. She ran along the corridor and up the stairs; she ran full speed along the deck and did not even stop to offer an apology when she rammed headfirst into a man and woman locked in a passionate embrace beside the rail. The man swore and shouted after her, the woman only stared at the blood that had been left in a smear down her skirt and on her outstretched hands.

Montana kept running down the gangway, along the wharf. She was less than a hundred feet from the main thoroughfare when a shadow detached itself from the jumble of dockside crates and stepped directly into her path. She started to veer around him, to push him out of her way, when two strong hands grabbed her and spun her into a heaving, panting halt.

"Amanda? Hold on up there; what's the hurry? Good God, you look as if the devil is on your heels."

Amanda's mouth dropped open. For the second time that night she found herself staring into the last face on earth she expected to see.

"Josh? *Josh?* Is that you?"

"In the flesh. Alisha told me everything. She sent me down here to look out for you, but I'd all but given up."

"Josh," she gasped. "I don't know where you've come from and, frankly, I don't care. Can you help me . . . *please?* Can you take me back to my hotel?"

"I . . . certainly. Certainly, I can. I have a buggy waiting over—" He stared aghast at her hands, seeing the blood for the first time. "Amanda . . . are you hurt?"

"Wh-what?" She looked down and her eyes widened. Her lips trembled apart and her knees weakened, causing her to sag forward into his arms. "Oh . . . God . . ."

"Come," he said brusquely. "Let's get you away from here and then you can tell me what has happened."

He supported her firmly around the waist as he led her to the waiting carriage. She climbed aboard and pressed herself into the darkest corner while Josh threw the hitching stone on board and cast a wary eye back toward the *Queen,* alert for any signs of pursuit. He scrambled into the driver's seat and slashed the reins over the rump of the dozing horse, and in a few moments they were clattering along the thickly misted, sleeping alleyways, putting a safe distance between themselves and the *Mississippi Queen.* Josh spoke only once, to ask the name of her hotel, then slapped the reins liberally until they had drawn up out front.

He draped his long woolen cloak around her shoulders and circled his arm around her waist again.

"Keep your hands tucked underneath and hold it closed over the hem of your skirt."

Amanda did as she was told, hiding the bloodstains.

"Just keep walking through the lobby, don't stop for anything. Have you the key?"

She nodded again and fumbled in her reticule a moment before handing it to him.

"Good girl," he said, and kissed her lightly on the forehead. "Just act as normal as you can; I'm right here beside you."

"Josh . . . thank you."

"Thank me later. For now, just walk."

She was grateful for his support as they entered the dimly lit lobby. It was not an elegant hotel by any stretch of the imagination, but there was a desk clerk in attendance to discourage vagrants of both the two- and four-legged kind. He was sound asleep behind his stall and there were no other guests venturing in or out this time of night.

As soon as they were in her room, Amanda let out a small cry and ran for the pitcher and washbowl in the corner. She flung off the cloak and splashed water over her hands, scrubbing them until her flesh stung. She soaked a cloth and rubbed frantically at the emerald-green velvet, but the stains were too widespread. She gave up on the cloth and stripped feverishly out of the gown instead, tossing it along with two layers of petticoats on the floor.

Left with only her camisole, corset, and a single thickness of petticoat to guard against the chills shivering through her body, she washed her hands again, to the elbows this time, removing every trace of pink she could find before collapsing, weakly, on the side of the bed.

Josh opened the window and emptied the basin of soap-scummed water. Without being asked, he gathered up the discarded dress and underpinnings and deposited them by the door.

"I'll get rid of these properly when I leave. Don't worry, I'll find a nice big fire so that nothing will remain but ashes. Are you feeling a little better now? Can you talk about what happened?"

"It was the captain," she whispered harshly. "Captain Turnbull. He was dead, in his cabin. I found him."

"Dead?"

"Murdered. Someone murdered him. There was blood everywhere and—" She stared up at him, gritting her teeth as another shiver wracked the length of her body.

Josh spied the bottle of brandy on the bedstand and poured some into a glass. "Drink this," he commanded. "All of it."

She swallowed a deep, biting mouthful and felt it drop like a fireball into her stomach. A second mouthful sent another shudder rippling through her body but she felt better for it. The shivering stopped and she thought she might be able to talk without her teeth chattering.

"His neck . . . I think someone must have cut it. There was . . . an awful lot of blood . . . everywhere."

Josh tilted the glass up to her lips again. "Try not to think about the blood. Just start at the beginning and try to remember everything the way it happened. What were you doing in his cabin in the first place?"

"I went to talk to him. I wanted to ask him about booking passage for Verity and me to New Orleans."

"Passage? On a gambling ship?"

Amanda shook her head as she lowered it. "It's a long story. I knew the captain well; he said he could take us there . . . discreetly."

"So you didn't trust Wainright to keep his word?"

Painfully wide blue eyes looked up at him and Josh cursed under his breath. "It's all right. Alisha told me about the game, about Wainright blackmailing you into playing tonight. She didn't say anything about the captain helping you leave Natchez."

"She didn't know. No one was going to know."

"Not even your husband?"

"Least of all my husband," she said tautly, lowering her eyes again.

Josh released a thoughtful breath through pursed lips. "So. You went down to the cabin and found the captain . . . what did you do then?"

"I . . . just ran. I knew he was dead, there was nothing I could do for him . . . so I ran. I didn't think, I just . . . ran."

"When had you last seen him alive?"

"I don't know. Maybe an hour earlier. Maybe less."

"Then whoever killed him," Josh speculated, "was either waiting for him in the cabin, or followed him from the salon. Did you see anyone else coming or going from the cabin?"

She shook her head. "No."

"Did anyone see you?"

"N-no, I don't think so. Wait . . . yes! A man and a woman were standing on deck. I bumped into them when I ran past."

"Did they see your face? Enough to recognize you if they saw you again?"

Amanda frowned. "I don't know. I think they must have; I nearly knocked the woman down."

Josh scratched a hand through his hair, looking grim. "Then one or both of them will be able to identify Montana Rose as the woman who ran from the scene of the crime."

"Scene of the crime? You make it sound as if they'll think I did it."

When he did not immediately dismiss the notion as foolish, she glanced up sharply.

"A woman running in a state of obvious panic," he said gently. "Blood on her hands and clothes. A man dead in his cabin. What would you think?"

"I think . . . I would want to hear her side of the story first before I condemned her to a hangman's noose."

"And just who do you propose should tell her side of the story? Montana Rose . . . or Amanda Tarrington? Either way the odds are not in your favor. Montana would be convicted on her reputation alone, and Amanda . . . well, what proper young Southern belle rigs herself out like a lady of the evening and plays poker until dawn? Take into account a Yankee judge, a Yankee jury?''

He did not have to finish. The picture he painted was quite clear.

She stood and paced to the window, no wiser for the effort. ''I was planning to leave Natchez anyway. I guess this just makes it all the more imperative.''

''Leaving town now would be the very *worst* thing you could do right now.''

Amanda glanced over her shoulder and frowned. ''I don't understand.''

''You're assuming,'' Josh said slowly, ''all hell will descend on the head of Montana Rose and, in turn, spill over onto Amanda Tarrington. You're assuming the good citizens of Natchez will make the connection—which they won't. A riverboat gambler and the wife of a respected plantation owner? My God, no one in their right minds would ever make the association, let alone believe it. There are just too many women living on the waterfront who fit the same description, and that's where the Yankee authorities will concentrate their search.''

''So what are you suggesting I do: Go back home and take up my knitting and sewing and hope someone else who 'fits the description' will be arrested and hanged in my place?''

''I'm not suggesting you do anything you don't want to do. I'm just suggesting you don't do anything in haste. If Amanda Tarrington up and vanishes in the middle of a sensationalized murder investigation, people who might normally not take a second look will sit right up and start putting two and two together. Leave Natchez now, leave your husband and create a scandal and you will have the bloodhounds sniffing after you as sure as the sun rises every morning.''

''I have already left Michael,'' she said quietly. ''I took Verity to Rosalie yesterday.''

''Then . . . you don't think he'll help you?''

"I don't know," she whispered. "I don't seem to know anything anymore."

Josh saw the sparkle of tears gathering along her lashes and he walked over to the window to stand beside her. He tucked his finger under her chin and gently forced her to look up at him. "I want you to know, I have never forgiven myself for that afternoon in the garden. If there is anything I can do to make it up to you, anything at all, you know I'll do it."

She smiled weakly. "You've already helped me more than you should. You certainly don't want to be seen with the infamous Montana Rose."

"I would be proud to walk down the middle of the street with her," he insisted, bowing gallantly. When he straightened, her expression was still so forlorn, he wrapped his arms around her and pressed a kiss into the glossy golden crown of her hair. "We're not all that dissimilar after all, you and I," he mused. "It appears we have both managed to fall in love with the wrong people."

"I didn't want to fall in love with him, Josh. I really didn't."

"I know. Believe me, I know exactly what you mean." His jaw tensed as he thought of Alisha, of the months of agony she had put him through and of the times she'd used him coldly, heartlessly, and no doubt laughed at his weakness all the while. No. It wouldn't do to dwell too long on Alisha's duplicity. Anger would not help Amanda now.

"Dry your eyes," he ordered with stern tenderness. "Blow your nose like a good little sister and . . . for heaven's sake, find some clothes to put on before I forget I'm a gentleman."

Amanda straightened with a childlike sniffle and realized she was, indeed, wearing only the bare necessities. She went to the armoire where she had hung her gray traveling suit and started to dress.

"What should I do, Josh?"

"First, you check out of this hotel. Once you're safely back at Rosalie, you'll be all right."

"What about Wainright? He will still want his pound of

flesh. He said I was to have his money to him by noon tomorrow or else the whole county would know about Alisha's abortion.''

She had her back to him, hurriedly pulling on clothes, and did not see the sudden stillness that settled over Josh's features. She had blurted it out without thinking, without *caring* to think, assuming, since Josh had said Alisha had told him everything, he meant everything.

"Will you take the money to him?" she asked hopefully.

"What?" It required some fierce concentration for Josh to focus on the question. "What did you say?"

"I know it's a terrible imposition, but will you deliver the money to Wainright?"

"You won tonight?"

In lieu of answering, she crossed over to the bundle of stained velvet and linen and rifled through the cast-off petticoats until she found the slitted opening of the pockets sewn into the side seams. She started pulling out money— stacks of it, bundles of it, folded sheafs that she tossed on the bed in an untidy heap. In a final gesture, she opened the drawstring of her reticule and poured out a glittering stream of gold double eagle coins.

"Christ on a cross," Josh muttered. "How much?"

"Seventy-two thousand, thereabouts. Sixty of it is Wainright's. He doesn't deserve it, of course, but I'll be buying the ease of my conscience. I will have done my sordid little part. If he wants more, he will have to get it from Alisha . . . or her husband. Will you do it? Will you take it to him for me?"

"If you're sure you want me to, but—" He stopped and saw the desperate plea in her eyes. "Of course I will. I promised, didn't I?"

"Thank you, Josh. Thank you for being such a good friend . . . to Caleb and to me."

He smiled grimly and was relieved when she turned her attention to the money again, counting out the twelve thousand she would need to make a clean break from Michael Tarrington. When she was fully dressed, cloaked and hooded against any chance recognition, Josh saw Amanda safely into a carriage and hurried back to the hotel room to clean away the last traces of her presence. He tucked the flat packets of money into his pockets, distributing the bundles evenly so there were no telltale bulges. He stuffed the green velvet gown and the petticoats into a pillowslip and descended to the ground floor of the hotel by way of the servants' staircase. He walked the several blocks to his own hotel, a journey that brought him to the door just as the diamondlike jewel of the sun burst over the eastern horizon.

He was sweating profusely as he mounted the wooden steps to his own dingy room. His heart was hammering within his chest, his mouth was dry, his hands would not stop shaking as he slotted the key into the lock.

Once inside, he thrust a finger between his throat and collar to ease the pressure. He stood with his back braced against the door as if he expected to hear a battery of fists on it at any moment.

There was only silence, however. A dark silence filled with the beating of his heart.

"Well?"

Josh jumped and whirled around. Alisha was lying on the bed, her body clad in a slippery red silk robe, her blonde hair spread across the pillows in a yellow pool.

"Well?" she asked again. "Did the little bitch do it?"

Josh forced his heart back down his throat and tore off his cravat. "What the hell are you doing here? How did you get away from Summitcrest?"

She sighed and stretched, letting the robe fall open across her bare legs. "I persuaded Karl to bring me into Natchez yesterday, and by the time I finished shopping, it was too late to make the drive back, so we took rooms at the Emporium."

"Won't he miss you?"

"Not unless he breaks down the lock to my room and finds I'm not there." She purred and stretched again. "And he knows better than to disturb me until after I've had my beauty sleep."

Josh moved away from the door and searched the cabinet for the bottle of whiskey he kept there.

"You don't look very happy to see me." Alisha pouted, curling her legs beneath her as she rose to her knees. The hazy morning light shimmered faintly over the silk-encased curves of her body, outlining the swell of her breasts and the stiffened peaks of her nipples.

Josh stood rooted to the spot, unable to command either his legs or his brain into a response. She smiled her cat's smile and he could swear she was growling as she stepped off the bed and stalked slowly toward him.

"Joshua Brice," she chided softly, her hands smoothing up his chest. "Joshua," she murmured, and her lips sought the underside of his chin. "Josh," she breathed, her arms falling briefly as she shrugged the red silk robe off her shoulders.

He closed his eyes. "Alisha—"

"Hush," she insisted, her hands trailing up his thighs. "You have obviously had a long and arduous evening—my goodness, but we are tense. Perhaps we should take care of this before we go any further."

She dropped down onto her knees and started to unfasten his trousers.

"Alisha . . ." he hissed, "dammit . . ."

"Hush, I said. You're my man, Joshua Brice, my only man, and if I can't show you how much I love you . . . how much I love to love you . . ."

He swore again and looked down but he did not stop her. He was tense but not aroused, and he watched the stretched and moistened suppleness of her lips teasing his flesh, sliding with an economy of effort, a proficiency of skill that should have had him hard within seconds, but instead left him feeling cheap and disgusted.

"God," he whispered. "You'll do anything to get what you want, won't you?"

Alisha pulled back in surprise. "Why, what a perfectly ungrateful thing to say. What on earth is wrong with you tonight?"

"Nothing," he muttered. "Absolutely nothing. Go ahead, carry on with what you were doing. It would be a shame to waste such a wonderful and talented performance."

Alisha's brow darkened and she pushed away. "I am not your whore, Josh Brice. You have no right to speak to me this way."

She stood and walked to where her clothes were draped across the footboard of the bed. She snatched up a petticoat, but turned to face him without making any move to cover her nudity.

"I gather she wasn't successful? I didn't believe for one minute the little bitch could do it. And I certainly didn't believe half the stories I'd heard about the cunning and clever Montana Rose, let alone that she and Amanda were one and the same person."

"Odd, then, that you were so damned convinced of it yesterday."

"Yesterday I was upset. I told you Wainright wanted *me* to play the *Queen,* but I refused."

"You told me a lot of things," he said harshly. "Nothing that came anywhere near the truth, I would wager to guess."

"Joshua!" Alisha dropped the petticoat and approached him again, her hands pressing flat against his chest, her eyes shining behind a silvery veil of tears as they turned beseechingly up to his. "Why are you so angry with me? Why are you being so cruel?"

"You don't know? You have no idea?"

"No. I don't."

He searched her face for all of two seconds before he jerked away and walked to the chifforobe. He pulled his portmanteau down from the upper shelf and stuffed into it the single change of clothes he had hanging on the pegs.

"What are you doing?" she asked in a querulous voice.

"What does it look like I'm doing? I'm leaving."

"Leaving the hotel?"

"The hotel, Natchez, maybe even Mississippi."

"You're leaving *me?*"

He glanced up at her. "You say that as if the thought never

occurred to you. As if you assumed I would stay at your feet like a puppy, happy to lick your toes now and then, happy to be kicked out of the way when it didn't suit you.''

''You're speaking in riddles, Josh,'' she said petulantly. ''And you're frightening me. Why do you want to leave? Are you tired of me? Is that it? Have you found someone else?''

He snapped the clasp on the portmanteau shut and sighed. ''I'm leaving because it's time to leave. Because I'm tired of the *lies*. Tired of losing little bits of myself every time I'm with you and tired of wondering who the hell I see in the mirror every morning.''

Alisha stared at him, her tears spilling artfully down her cheeks in constant, unbroken streams. ''Lies? What lies have I told you? *What lies has Amanda been telling you?* That's it, isn't it! She's been telling you lies and you believe her!''

''Alisha, for God's sake—'' He lifted his case and started for the door but she ran in front of him, blocking his way.

''Oh Josh, please . . . please don't leave me. Not now, not like this. I—'' Her eyes widened. Her hands, grasping at the folds of his jacket, had come into contact with the bundles of money. Her eyes flicked from one pocket to the other, following her hands as they searched and found more bundles, more sheafs of hundred-dollar bills.

She inhaled sharply and raised her eyes to his. ''She won! She won tonight, didn't she!''

''Yes,'' he conceded with a grudging sigh. ''She won.''

''And you weren't going to tell me? You were just going to *leave*''—she gasped and stumbled back a step—''*with her!*''

''Alisha, don't be absurd. If you must know, there was trouble on board the *Queen* tonight and Amanda gave me the money to deliver to Wainright.''

''She *gave* it to you? She just . . . handed it over?''

Josh reacted badly to the sarcasm in Alisha's voice. ''Yes. She gave it to me. I didn't have to follow her. I didn't have to wait until she'd given the money to Wainright to steal it away from him—though God only knows how you ever talked me into attempting such a foolish piece of insanity.''

"But we have the money!" she cried breathlessly, her hands searching greedily for more bundles. She tossed the bills on the bed behind her, scattering them across the mattress like rose petals. She laughed and dug her hands into the crinkly piles and tossed the greenbacks into the air, watching them flutter down over her head. "My God—how much is here? The whole fifty thousand? Josh . . . we're rich! We're rich!"

"The money isn't ours," he said quietly. "I told you, I was taking it to Wainright for Amanda."

"Like hell you are," she declared, the tears gone, the subservience already a memory. "She doesn't need our help to pay off Mr. E. Fucking Wainright; she can just go to her rich husband and get all the money she needs."

"All the money *she* needs? Exactly what is Wainright holding over her head?" he asked quietly.

"I told you it was a private matter. I really don't think Amanda would want her disgrace bandied about by everyone."

Josh moved closer to the bed. She was kneeling on the money, running her hands through the little piles, pouring handfuls of the Yankee greenbacks over her naked breasts, her hips, her thighs.

The jade-green firebrands that were his eyes scanned the curves and planes of Alisha's alabaster-smooth body. The perfect breasts were perfect again, no longer glowing with burgeoning ripeness. The perfect waist was trim, the soft belly now bereft of its faint hint of plumpness.

He reached down and gripped the slender shoulders with enough force to startle a cry of pain from her lips.

"What was Wainright blackmailing her with?"

"He found out she was Montana Rose!" Alisha gasped. "Isn't that enough? Do you have any idea what gossip like that could do to our family?"

"You didn't seem overly concerned when it was *you* sneaking off to go gambling."

"I didn't care because I was doing it for us . . . for you!"

"Yes, and I begged you, pleaded with you to leave Natchez with me—"

"We didn't have any money!" she countered furiously. "How far could we have gone? How could we have survived —you a farmer without a farm, me waddling around with a bastard inside me—" She sucked in her breath and her expression froze for a fleeting second when she saw the fire blaze into his eyes again.

"Yes?" He snarled. "You were saying?"

"I . . . I meant . . . it could have happened," she stammered. "I could have become pregnant. It happens, sometimes, you know when two people—"

"Happens? *Could have happened?*" His fingers gouged so deeply into her shoulders, the pain sent a flush of red into her cheeks. "What the hell have you done?"

"Wh-what do you mean?"

"Alisha . . . I know every curve of your whore's body. I know when it changes. I knew when it *changed.* I was waiting for you to tell me, hoping it would make a difference—"

"You knew?" she whispered.

"I knew," he spat. "And I guessed that was the real reason why you married von Helmstaad: to buy us time . . . *us* . . . you, me, and the child you couldn't bring yourself to tell me was growing inside you. But it isn't growing inside you anymore, is it?" His eyes narrowed to hard, glittering green shards of contempt and he shook her once, with enough violence to make her teeth snap together. "Is it, Alisha?"

She brought her hand up to his cheek, her fingers trembling with entreaty. "We can have more children Josh. Passels of them if you want. I never meant to hurt you or to deceive you. I never meant to hurt our child—I swear I didn't. It . . . it was Karl. *Karl!* He tried to . . . to force himself on me and when I told him I was with child, he . . . he flew into a rage because I wouldn't tell him the name of the father. He . . . tried to kill me. He beat me, and raped me, and . . . and I lost the baby."

Josh stared at her, unmoved.

"Josh—you have to believe me. I swear it is the truth! I was so frightened, I didn't know what to do. I tried to run but I was hurt and . . . and you were out of town. I was alone . . . and he just kept beating me and beating me, trying to get me to tell him whose baby it was."

"He beat you?"

"Yes!"

"Is that why you went to see Wainright?"

She gasped again and he could actually see the lies hastily rearranging themselves behind her eyes. "I couldn't very well go to see any of the doctors who knew me, could I? I could never have borne the shame. And Wainright *was* courting my sister at one time. I thought I could trust him."

"I know Wainright. I know the kinds of services some of his friends provide—some of his doctor friends? I also know enough about Karl von Helmstaad to believe he wouldn't swat a fly if it was chewing a trench in his arm. What I don't know, what I am almost afraid to know, is exactly what lengths you would go to in order to maintain this little arrangement you so cleverly planned, with the baron's home, his wealth, the comforts he could provide on the one hand . . . and the services of a blinded, dimwitted stud on the other."

"No! No, Josh, no. You're wrong!"

"If I'm wrong, why is Wainright blackmailing *Amanda?* Why wasn't he blackmailing you?"

"He . . . he tried . . . but I didn't have any money. I couldn't get any either."

"But you told him Amanda could?"

Her lips parted around a short gust. "I . . . I had no choice. He already knew everything. I was delirious in the doctor's office. He gave me something for the pain and I . . . I didn't know what I was saying."

Josh's hands tightened around her arms again. "Alisha—I'm coming damned close to beating you myself."

"It's the truth!" she cried.

"Not enough of the truth for me to believe you!" he shouted back.

With a sob of anguish she flung her arms around his neck and let the tears flow free again. "All right! All *right!* I'll tell you what you want to know. I'll tell you the absolute truth about what happened, but you mustn't hate me if I do. You mustn't hate me, Josh, swear it!"

"Just . . . tell me . . . the *truth,*" he grated through his teeth.

"It was the Yankee," she whispered against his throat. "It was the Yankee who raped me, not Karl. He lured me into the garden the night they stayed at Rosalie, and he . . . he threatened to kill me if I told anyone. Afterward . . . he was so rough . . . I knew something was terribly wrong, but . . . I couldn't go to Dr. Dorset because he would have known the child wasn't Karl's. I went to a doctor in town, and . . . and lost the baby right there on his table. Wainright found out what happened and sent for Amanda and me, and told us his silence would cost fifty thousand dollars. That's why Amanda did it. It was his crime she was trying to keep quiet—*Tarrington's.* That's why I wanted you to steal the money, why I still want you to steal it! I want that bastard to pay for what he's done. You should want him to pay too; it was your child!"

"And Amanda? You don't care what happens to her if we do?"

"Amanda!" she raged, pushing out of his arms. "I'm pouring my heart out to you and all you can think of is Amanda!"

"I'm thinking she hasn't done anything to deserve any of this," he said intently.

"And I have?"

Alisha saw a subtle change transform the anger in Josh's face to pity. The wild heat of condemnation faded from his eyes and she saw them cloud over with remorse instead.

"Josh, it's all right," she murmured, pressing close again, running her hands up his chest and curling them around his neck. "Everything is going to be all right . . . as long as the two of us are together. You . . . do still love me, don't you?"

Not only her lips, but her breasts, her belly, her thighs sought forgiveness. Her pleas shivered into whispers, then snatches of breath that smothered him, drowned him, swallowed him into a dark well of conflicting emotions. His lips began to respond despite the numbing confusion. His hands too lifted to the soft indent of her waist, and a shudder welcomed the cool determination of her fingers as she tugged at the waist of his breeches again and peeled them down over his hips.

Her own hips were already in motion, bribing him with slow pelvic thrusts. She sank her teeth into the steely muscle of his shoulder and whispered his name over and over, chanted in the same erotic rhythm, the same beating tempo of her hips as she pulled herself up and over the rock-hard spear of his flesh.

The flames blazed to life in his body and trembled through his limbs as he fell with her onto the piles of money she had scattered on the bed. Her legs were already locked around him, pulling him into the deepest, tightest part of her. The first brutal thrust sent her skidding deliciously over the greenbacks, the second had her crying out in triumph.

His hands were on her breasts, then on the arch of her throat. He closed his eyes and slammed his flesh into hers again and again, feeling her body shake beneath him, hearing her gasp out her pleasure, her ecstasy as his rage mounted. He squeezed his hands tighter around her throat and ignored the sudden shock that rippled through her body. He squeezed and squeezed and squeezed, blinded to the pain in his face and neck as her nails began to claw and score bloody ribbons into his flesh. He roared as he spilled himself within her, bluing the air with curses as his hands crushed the tender cartilage in her throat and kept crushing it until the desperate spasms weakened and faded away, until her body grew still and limp beneath him and her eyes stared sightlessly up at the ceiling.

When his fury waned and he could see and breathe again, he dragged himself upright and looked down at the golden body through a film of scalding tears. Tenderly he smoothed the web of yellow hair off her face, and gently he closed the accusing eyes.

"I'm sorry," he whispered. "I'm so sorry, Alisha, but it had to stop somewhere. The lies had to stop . . . the pain had to stop. And this way, at least, we'll be together."

He straightened slowly and took a deep breath to steady himself. He walked over to where he had left the pillowslip by the door and hesitated only a moment before pulling out the bloodstained green velvet gown that would identify Montana Rose. He draped the garments over the foot of the bed and, calmer now, poured himself a brimming tumbler of whiskey.

As he downed it, he stared at his reflection in the mirror. He raked his hand through his hair and touched a few of the gouges on his cheek, smiling grimly at the blood that came away on his fingers.

The heat of the whiskey blurred his vision and he set the empty glass aside. His shaving kit was on the washstand, and it took only a few seconds to reach inside, to find the straight razor, and test its sharpness on the pad of his thumb. Satisfied, he poured himself another whiskey—odd how his hands were not shaking anymore—and went back to the bed. He stretched out alongside Alisha, waited for the second wave of liquor to blot out any lingering sensations, then bared his wrist to the gleaming edge of the blade.

Chapter 26

Amanda Tarrington was safely back at Rosalie when the news of Benjamin Turnbull's murder began to scorch through Natchez like a brushfire. By midday the gory details were on everyone's lips, expanded and sensationalized out of all proportion. The story spread from house to house, on foot, by horseback and buggy, across the fields and down the mighty Mississippi, missing nothing in its path.

When Mercy carried the news into the family on the same tray she served lunch, Amanda promptly collapsed in a faint on the parlor floor. Sarah, imagining all manner of horrible ailments, sent for Dr. Dorset, who not only confirmed her daughter's pregnancy, but gave additional details of the murder and the furor surrounding it. The authorities, he told them, were scouring the less palatable establishments of Natchez, searching for the whereabouts of the lady gambler, Montana Rose. The *Mississippi Queen* had been shut down by the authorities and would remain so until further notice.

Gruesome, he called it. Maniacal. The captain had been a big fellow and the severed jugular had spouted enough blood to fill a bathtub. If the woman they were searching for did it, he confided to William, she must have come away dripping like a ghoul.

Ryan's fury was awesome. He managed to contain it until the doctor departed, but then he locked Amanda in her bedroom and demanded the entire story, threatening his own brand of violence if she dared omit a single detail. He sat glowering and unresponsive throughout most of the recitation. His emotions ran the gamut from disgust and disillusionment to thundrous denouncements, to calm homicidal hatred for E. Forrest Wainright.

Too calm.

Amanda found him in the disused library a short while

after he left her, cleaning and loading a brace of archaic flintlock dueling pistols.

"May I ask what you are doing?"

"What does it look like I'm doing?"

She frowned down at the pistols, trying to remember when she had seen them last. They had belonged to her maternal great-grandfather, who had bought them in London from Henry Hadley, gunmaker to the Duke of Marlborough. They had gold inlaid barrels and intricate foliate work on the stocks; the escutcheon plates were gold as well, chiseled in relief with grotesques and floral scrolls. The pistols, in their carved mahogany case, had been buried in the garden for most of the war, one of the few precious heirlooms that had not found its way into the hands of Yankee looters.

"Ryan, please . . . for my sake, don't do anything foolish."

"It is precisely for your sake I'm going to rid the earth of that snake once and for all. And when I'm finished with Wainright, I intend to call on your husband."

Amanda watched helplessly as he took each elegantly long-barreled weapon from its velvet pocket and set it on the desktop.

"Ryan." She forced a calmness to match his own. "You don't even know if those guns work. They were buried under a carrot patch for five years."

"I have had them cleaned and primed since Wainright reared his ugly head the first time. I couldn't quite bring myself to go through with it then, but now, dammit . . ." He lifted one of the pistols and poured a measured amount of fine black powder down the long snout.

"Now you intend to go after him and do what? Wave an outdated pistol in his face and demand satisfaction?" She stood in front of her brother and placed her hands on his forearms. "What do you expect him to do? Bow graciously and take ten paces before aiming and politely waiting his turn to fire? You'll be lucky if he doesn't simply shoot you point-blank on his doorstep."

"Then he'll be arrested and hanged for murder," Ryan

said, and shook off her hands. When a felt patch was rammed securely against each charge of powder, he selected a lead ball from the pouch of weighted shot, wrapped it in a second small square of treated felt, and wadded it snugly into the barrel.

"Ryan, I won't let you kill yourself."

He set the first gun cautiously back into its velvet bed as he reached for its mate.

Amanda tapped her fingers on the desktop. She slid her hand along the polished surface and waited until Ryan had lifted the second pistol and was squinting along its barrel.

He heard a metallic *snick* and looked up to find himself staring down the nose of the fully cocked snaphaunce.

"And just what do you propose to do with that?" he asked quietly.

"I propose to shoot you here and now if you refuse to listen to reason."

He arched an eyebrow. "To save Wainright the trouble, I presume?"

"I'm not going to kill you. Only wound you so that you put this insanely noble notion out of your mind."

"Wound me," he mused. "In the arm?" he inquired as he extended a long, muscular appendage for her inspection. "Or would you prefer a leg? The leg is the easier target, but it could prove a bit messy if you hit the artery. Judging from the way your hand is shaking, you might not hit the arm at all, but if I promise to hold it steady—"

"I'm not joking," she warned coldly.

"You're not primed either," he said gently, glancing pointedly at the empty firing pan.

Amanda sighed and lowered the gun. Ryan took it carefully out of her hand and uncocked it. "I'm sorry, but you just don't have the makings of a desperado."

"You do, I suppose?"

"Wainright is overdue. So is your husband."

"So is every other Yankee carpetbagger in Mississippi, but you can't go out and challenge every one of them to a duel."

He glared at her and his jaw flexed into a solid ridge. "Do you honestly think Wainright will just fade away and never bother us again? He knows where to find Montana Rose, and once he finishes playing his little cat-and-mouse games, he'll sell the information to the authorities quicker than you can shout foul."

"He can't point a finger at me without implicating himself. If he tries, I'll swear he set me up to do it. In fact, I'll swear it now—I'll confess to the murder and name him as my accomplice."

"What would *that* accomplish?" he asked in exasperation.

"The same thing as you going off half cocked. I may not be able to stop you with a bullet, but so help me, if you take one step in Wainright's direction, I'll drive myself straight to the sheriff's office and confess everything."

"You wouldn't dare."

"Wouldn't I? What would I have to lose? My reputation? My freedom? I've lost both already, so what does it matter?"

"What about Verity, and the new baby? Does your lack of concern for your own future include condemning them to a life of jeering and taunting about their mother the murderess?"

"You're too damn noble to let anything hurt Verity," she retorted. "As for the baby, Michael's name will protect him. If nothing else, he owes me that much."

Ryan stared into the clear blue eyes and saw the anger, the disillusionment, the stubborn determination, and he knew she was not bluffing.

"If you're not going to let me kill your husband," he said sardonically, "will you at least let me beat the living crap out of him?"

Amanda sighed and turned to the window. After a long moment of quiet contemplation, she shook her head slowly and bowed her chin almost to her chest. "I still can't believe he was there last night. I can't believe he lied to me about going after Ned Sims. I can't even understand why he would have felt he *had* to lie to me. And for the life of me, I can't believe he and Alisha . . ." Her voice faltered and died.

Ryan glanced longingly at the guns again, then moved up behind Amanda and wrapped his arms protectively around her. She sighed again and leaned willingly into the comforting support, her eyes glazing over with the bright sting of tears.

"I had the strangest feeling earlier this morning. In spite of everything that has happened, everything that will surely happen over the coming days, I felt as if an enormous, great weight was suddenly lifted off my shoulders. It was so odd. Like walking from a dark room into one full of sunlight. Who knows . . ." She laced her finger's through Ryan's and held him tightly "Maybe Alisha has done me a favor by bringing all of this out into the open."

"Maybe," Ryan murmured. "But why do *I* have the distinct feeling all hell is about to break loose?"

Amanda sat alone in the parlor, huddled before the warmth of the fire, a shawl pulled snugly around her shoulders. She had been staring into the flames for over an hour, but, as exhausted as she was, she could not stop her mind from spinning long enough to sleep.

"He's here."

She jumped slightly at the sound of Ryan's voice as he walked into the room.

"Your husband is here," he repeated grimly. "Mercy has him blockaded at the front door."

Amanda's earlier show of bravado drained away as quickly as the color from her face. "What shall I do?"

"It's your call: See him or send him away."

"I . . . don't think I'm ready to see him just yet. M-maybe tomorrow. Or the day after."

They both heard shouting from out in the hall, Mercy's voice first, trumpeting a threat against the hazard of crossing the imaginary line she had drawn, and Michael's snarling an equally caustic rebuttal. Ryan turned instantly with the intent to join the fray, but Amanda caught his hand in hers and kept him anchored by her side.

Angry bootsteps approached the parlor. A moment later, Michael loomed in the doorway, his broad shoulders all but filling the space, his expression blacker than the wide-brimmed hat that shadowed his eyes. He looked angry, angrier than Amanda had ever seen him, and she sat stiffly forward on the chair, her hand gripping Ryan's so tightly, it burned.

"Hello, Amanda."

"Michael," she whispered.

"My sister isn't feeling very well." Ryan scowled. "She doesn't need you barging in here uninvited, upsetting her any further."

The cold gray eyes moved slowly from Amanda to Ryan. "Upset her? I have an overwhelming desire to do a great deal more than just *upset* her. For the time being, however, I will settle for a few moments of conversation with her . . . *alone* . . . if it's all the same to you."

"I don't think she has anything to say to you, alone or otherwise."

Michael's gaze shifted back. "Is that your choice . . . or his?"

"By Jesus—" Ryan surged forward again, but Amanda stopped him.

"It's all right. I'd as soon get it over with anyway."

Ryan expelled two heavy breaths, then nodded. "I'll be just outside in the hallway if you need me."

He glared at Michael all the way across the room, the threat implied, the promise made. Amanda thought of the dueling pistols loaded and ready in the upstairs library, and she tried to send her brother a reassuring smile as he strode out of the room and pulled the door shut behind him.

For one full, throbbing minute neither Amanda nor Michael moved. They assessed one another across the silence, each noting the signs of strain and sleeplessness on the other's face.

Michael moved first. He walked over to the fireplace and tossed his hat onto a nearby chair.

"I would have been here sooner," he said, cracking the silence as effectively as a gunshot, "if I had not been delayed by a parade of my own uninvited guests—not the least annoying of whom was your overblown, overwrought, and overly pompous brother-in-law."

"Karl? What did he want?"

"He seems to think your sister has run away. He wanted to know if you had seen her or spoken to her recently."

"Run away? Alisha?"

"She didn't answer any of her summonses and wasn't in her room when he finally got around to checking. Hadn't been there all night, from the look of it."

"Why would he think I knew where she went?" Amanda asked bitterly. "Are you certain he wasn't there to ask you?"

He barely acknowledged her sarcasm with a frown before continuing. "At any rate, the baron no sooner rode off when a detachment of militia rode up to the front door."

What little color had flushed her cheeks drained noticeably away.

"Are you not going to ask why?"

"I'm sure you're about to tell me whether I ask or not."

"It seems they were full of questions too. Questions about the mysterious lady gambler who won an astonishing amount of money in a poker game last night and then simply melted into the night, leaving the body of a dead man in her wake. They wanted to know if I'd had any prior meetings with the elusive Montana Rose; if I might know where she could be found."

His scorn was a painful thing to bear, and she dug the points of her fingernails into her palms to keep from screaming. "What did you tell them?"

"The truth, of course. I told them I had had the pleasure of her company once before, several months ago, and that I'd had no idea *then* how to find her. I also confirmed the fact that she had indeed won a considerable amount of money last night—a large percentage of it mine—but I could not, by any stretch of the imagination, imagine her capable of murdering Captain Turnbull. In that respect," he added tersely, "I was giving you the benefit of the doubt, hoping you could enlighten me further."

There was absolutely no trace of warmth in his voice, no glimmer of compassion in his eyes. No indication at all he had come with the intent of listening to her side of the story and offering her his protection.

Michael saw the shine building in her eyes and grimaced. "If you're thinking of fluttering those big blue eyes at me and weeping out a convincingly coy plea of innocence, I should warn you my patience is worn pretty thin. I would just as soon haul you to the county courthouse and let someone else wring the truth out of you."

"You would turn me in?" she gasped.

"I would not only turn you in, madam, I would take a front-row seat at the hanging if I thought you were guilty. Living with a card sharp is one thing, living with a murderess is quite another. *Sit down!*"

Amanda had begun to rise, an indignant protest on her lips. She saw the blackness flash into his eyes again and wisely sank back down onto the settee.

"You aren't going anywhere until I get some answers," he said evenly.

"I might have a few questions of my own," she countered tautly. "I might want to ask what you were doing there last night."

"You might. But I'm not the one who's being accused of coldblooded murder."

"I didn't kill him."

"You were seen running away from his cabin. You had blood on your hands and on your dress."

"I didn't kill him," she repeated raggedly.

"But you were there, in his cabin."

"Yes."

"Why?"

"We had some . . . business . . . to discuss."

"What kind of *business?*"

"*Private* business, and none of yours."

A muscle shivered in his cheek and his expression became even more thunderous.

"We'll put that aside for a minute," he hissed between his teeth. "So you went to his cabin. What happened then?"

"I knocked on the door, but no one answered. I thought he was still topside and I didn't want to be seen lingering in the corridor, so . . . I went inside."

"And?"

"And . . . he was there."

"Dead?"

"If he'd been sitting up chatting with me," she snapped, "I wouldn't be in this predicament, would I?"

The gray eyes flickered ominously and narrowed on hers.

"Well, I'm sick and tired of everyone asking the same question. Of course he was dead. He was on the floor, and . . . and there was all this blood. It was everywhere . . . on the floor, on the walls."

"His throat was slashed, and not very cleanly; either by an amateur who had to try several times for the veins, or by someone who thoroughly enjoys his work." He saw Amanda blanch and his tone softened for the first time. "Go on. What did you do then?"

"I panicked. I ran."

"Straight into the arms of a Mr. Charles Fry and his companion."

"The couple on deck? I don't remember anything about them. Their faces, everything, is a blur."

"Well, they remember you. Right down to the color of the rosettes on your skirt. Where is it, by the way?"

"The dress? Burned . . . I think."

"You *think?* You don't know for sure?"

"I was told it would be burned."

"By who . . . Ryan?"

She moistened her lips. "No. Ryan knew absolutely nothing about it; he wasn't involved at all. In fact, when he found out about it this morning . . . he was almost as angry as you."

"I doubt that very much. But if it wasn't Ryan, who the hell else would you give your clothes to?"

"Someone I trust!" she cried. "Is it so important for you to know who?"

"Everything that happened last night is important . . . *to both of us.* The dress might well be the single most damning piece of evidence against you, and if you don't have it, it would certainly behoove us both to know where the bloody thing is! Now, who was with you last night, and where did you go after you left the *Queen?*"

"I met Joshua Brice on the dock. He took me back to my hotel and promised me he would burn the dress—and I believe him."

"Brice?" The name caused a second shiver of tension to ripple through his body, and put an edge in his voice that could have cut a diamond. "You trust him implicitly, do you?"

"Yes. I do."

He stared at her a moment longer before turning his back. To cover the awful lapse in concentration her mention of the name had caused, he dug in his pocket for a cigar and lit it, drawing the harsh smoke deeply into his lungs and jolting him back to his senses.

"Why," he asked in as calm a voice as he could muster, "were you on board the *Mississippi Queen* in the first place?"

"I was being blackmailed," she said bluntly, hoping she sounded as ruthless and indifferent as he did.

"Blackmailed?" The word had so little effect, it seemed as if he had been waiting for it. By way of confirmation, he reached into his pocket again and produced the note Wainright had sent her at Briar Glen. "I assume that's what this is all about?"

"He found out I was Montana Rose. He threatened to make it public knowledge if I didn't come up with fifty thousand dollars."

"Fifty thousand?" He crushed the note in his long fingers

and threw it angrily into the fire. "And I suppose he told you exactly how you could get it?"

"He knew there was going to be a big game on the *Queen* last night. He . . . also seemed to know it wouldn't do any good going to you for the money, since you didn't have enough to cover the debts on Briar Glen."

"Very knowledgeable, our Mr. Wainright. What else was he holding over you?"

"You don't think a threat against the noble Tarrington name was enough?"

He flung the cigar after the flaming notepaper and rounded on her. "You're nobody's fool, Amanda. Regardless of what our marriage has or hasn't been to this point, you knew I wouldn't crumble at a bit of idle gossip. I never did give a hang about what you did or who found out. My only complaint was that you kept doing it on my ship."

There was a long, breathless pause.

"Your ship?"

"You didn't know? Wainright didn't tell you I owned the *Queen*?"

Amanda swallowed hard. "He . . . said something about a delicious irony, but no. I had no idea. I guess it was another one of those *things* we were going to talk about?"

Another time she might have noticed the faint ruddiness that crept up beneath his tan. Another time she might have cared.

"I suppose I was suffering under the foolish notion it might embarrass you to know I owned her."

"Then our meeting wasn't so accidental after all?" she whispered.

"I'd already made four or five runs into Natchez, waiting for you to make an appearance. I'd been hearing enough about the lovely and talented Montana Rose to know it was only a matter of time before you started to make some major inroads into my profits. I didn't think the regular dealers could handle you, and I was right. I also suspected Ben was quite taken with you . . . and I was right again. The revenues from the *Queen* are rather handsome and provide me with an admirable if somewhat erratic income. Games like the one arranged for last night make up what I need in ready cash. So you see, my love, when you were sent in to fleece all the lambs at the table last night, you were, in essence, sent in to fleece me.'' He paused a moment and studied her reaction. ''Am I also right in assuming there was something else Wainright found out and was holding over you? Something to do with Verity, perhaps?''

Amanda unclasped her hands, then clasped them together again.

''I know Caleb Jackson wasn't the father,'' he said quietly.

''No,'' she whispered. ''He wasn't. The man who fathered Verity was a Yankee colonel who was quartered here for several weeks during the war. At least, I always suspected it was the colonel; I didn't know for sure until Alisha admitted it in Wainright's office. At the time, she claimed she had been raped. Only afterward, when she started to take less and less care of her comings and goings, did it begin to dawn on me that she probably enjoyed, even enticed, the colonel's attention.''

''Wait a minute,'' Michael said slowly. ''Are you telling me—''

''Verity is Alisha's child. Not that Alisha was ever Verity's mother, or ever had any desire to be, but she was the one who got pregnant and the one who gave birth. She was the one who came to me with the 'perfect solution,' as she called it. For the two of us to change places and let everyone think it was me who was pregnant, and me who was going away to New Orleans to await the birth with my loving sister in attendance.''

''No one questioned it? No one suspected the switch?''

''It wasn't as if any kind of social life existed in the latter years of the war. The only houseguests we had were Yankees, the only visitors we had were strangers.''

Michael cast his mind—not as quick or as clear-thinking as it had been a few moments ago—back over the past few months, but there had never been a hint or a breath of a whisper to suggest Amanda was not the child's real mother. Conversely, he could not recall a single incident when Alisha had paid the slightest heed to the child. She had not betrayed by so much as a glance or secret smile that she felt any attachment whatsoever to Verity. And their conversation that night at Rosalie . . . the lie was so convincing, she might have been talking about a complete stranger, not her own flesh and blood.

"Why didn't you tell me?"

"Why didn't *you* tell *me* you'd been trading secrets with Alisha? It was you who told her about Montana Rose, wasn't it?"

"It was an accident. It slipped out. I was in the middle of apologizing—"

"To my sister? Whatever for?"

The gray eyes bored into hers and he saw something that made the hairs rise across the nape of his neck. "What the hell has she told you?"

"Everything. She was in Wainright's office when I went to meet him and she told me . . . everything."

"It's obvious she's told you *something*. Not necessarily the truth, I warrant."

Her chin trembled despite her determined efforts to keep it firm. "She told me the two of you were outside together the night we stayed at Rosalie. She said it was you who told her about me . . . about Montana Rose."

"What else?"

"She said you were drunk and angry because I sent you away."

"I was angry, yes. Furious. At myself for being such a fool. I was walking it off along the river when she came out of nowhere, and I was just so bloody relieved to see who I thought was my wife coming to forgive me—"

"No," she cried, covering her ears as she shook her head. "I don't want to hear any more lies!"

"Then listen to the truth!" he snarled, coming to her side in two long strides. "She has twisted what happened to suit her own purposes. What did she tell you—that we made love that night?''

''Michael, please—''

''Is that what she told you?'' He gripped her wrists and pulled her up onto her feet. ''Well, I won't lie to you: I came damned close to doing it, all right, and I will even go so far as to admit that had it been anyone else, I just might have been able to go through with it. But I didn't! She was stark naked and using every trick in the book to seduce me, but *I couldn't go through with it!''*

Amanda stared up into his face, wanting to believe him, needing to believe him, and yet—

''Jesus God,'' he rasped, seeing the shimmer of tears, reading the pain behind them. ''There's more, isn't there?''

She nodded and the tears jumped over her lashes and streamed down to her chin.

''Tell me.''

''She was pregnant. She said it was yours.''

Michael's hands tightened around her wrists, scarcely able to believe what he was hearing. ''It's not true. Mandy . . . for God's sake, it's not true! I never touched her!''

Amanda's vision faded and she started to sag under a cloud of darkness. Michael was shouting. A sharp, stabbing pain caught her by surprise and she cried out, doubling over into Michael's arms. He caught her and guided her gently back onto the couch just as Ryan burst through the door.

''Amanda? Amanda, what happened?'' His face was pale and rigid as he shoved past Tarrington and dropped to his knee beside her. ''Are you all right? Is it the baby?''

''I'm . . . fine,'' she gasped. ''It wasn't the baby; it was just a stitch in my side.''

''I'll send for the doctor—''

''No! No, just some water, please. A glass of water, and I'll be fine.''

''Christ,'' he muttered. *''Mercy!''* He strode to the door and nearly collided with the portly maid, who was spun around instantly with orders to fetch water and warm blankets. And to send for the doctor.

Michael had not moved from the foot of the couch. He hadn't moved at all. Not a hair, not an eyelash. Only his eyes, after a few moments, broke away from Amanda's to look at where her hands were cradled protectively over her belly.

"A baby?" he whispered.

"The loving husband"—Ryan snorted contemptuously—"had no idea?"

"No," Michael answered quietly. "I had no idea."

"And I don't suppose you know how she got herself in this condition either?" he sneered.

Michael's face turned a dull, angry red. "Your sister seems to have heard some fairly tasteless things about me which she is willing to accept without questioning the source. Perhaps I should claim the same privilege."

Ryan straightened ominously. "Meaning what?"

"Meaning . . . maybe I know *how* she got pregnant, I just don't know by whom."

Another cry escaped Amanda's lips before she could contain it.

Ryan's response was more direct. He swung hard and fast from the waist, his fist a blur of bunched knuckles as it slammed through the air and connected with Michael's jaw. Michael was sufficiently off balance to stumble sideways with the blow, but his reflexes were superb and he came back swinging, smashing a punch into Ryan's belly with enough force to rock him back on his heels.

"Ryan! Michael! Stop it, both of you!"

Michael appeared to hesitate at the sound of her scream, but Ryan channeled all of his strength and pent-up fury into the series of hard, cutting blows delivered in rapid succession to gut, jaw, ribs, and chest. Michael's reactions were instinctive. He blocked, pivoted, swung with a malicious relish that suggested he too had wanted to feel the crush of flesh under his fists for some time. The calm, passive reserve was stripped away, beaten away by an adversary who roared for blood and charged in time and time again to vent some.

Amanda screamed again and was again ignored. The two men crashed together over the back of a divan and for several minutes were lost from sight, with only the dull thud of flesh impacting on flesh and grunted curses to punctuate their scuffle. Ryan rolled into view and sprang onto his feet, his hands formed into claws as he reached down and hauled Michael upright. A vicious left hook sent a fine spray of Michael's blood fanning the air fractions of a second before his own fist brought Ryan's head into hard contact with one of the carved pilasters that decorated the wall. A volley of hard blows followed, taking advantage of Ryan's temporary dazedness to drive him again and again into the same rippled woodwork.

"Michael! No!" Amanda flew across the room and tore frantically at her husband's grip but he was half blinded by sweat and rage. Two, three more sickeningly solid punches slammed into Ryan's cheeks and jaw before his body began to collapse and he sagged into a bloodied heap on the floor.

Amanda fell on her knees beside him, running her hands over his face, his arms, catching him against her breast as he pitched forward with a pain-filled groan.

Michael swayed where he stood, his breath heaving and hot, his fists stinging and his lip split and dripping blood down his shirtfront.

"Mandy—"

She felt his hand on her shoulder and jerked it away. "Don't touch me! Don't you dare touch me!"

Michael swallowed a gulp of air along with a measure of blood and spat both onto the floor. "For what it's worth, your sister was lying. Do you hear me, Mandy? She was lying!"

"I hear you," she said, glaring up over her shoulder. "And yes. She was lying. About a lot of things, it seems."

"Come home with me. We can work all of this out."

Amanda bowed her head and cradled Ryan's limp body closer in her arms. "Go away, Michael. Please . . . just go away."

He wiped at the blood on his chin and glanced at the doorway where Mercy, Sarah, and William Courtland were crowded around the entrance. For once, Sarah remained on her feet, too shocked to spare a thought to fainting. Mercy's eyes were as round as saucers, nearly popping out of her skull. Michael saw nothing to suggest any of them would be receptive to any manner of explanation he might offer. He saw only the indignation of proud people who knew it had just been a matter of time before he showed his true colors.

He retrieved his hat from the crush of debris and walked slowly to the door. Sarah and Mercy hurried past him to help Amanda with Ryan, leaving only William to block the exit with his wheelchair.

Michael met the older man's eyes and was still able to register some small surprise to see how clear, sharp, and penetrating William's stare was. If he needed any further confirmation as to his father-in-law's state of mind, it came with a dry mutter and a sorry shake of William's head.

"I may pretend to be deaf, dumb, and blind at times, because it suits me to be so. But you, son, . . . you're just plain dumb."

Chapter 27

It was just plain stupid, that's what it was. Arguing, fighting, exchanging insults and accusations like a couple of schoolchildren caught hiding toads in the schoolmarm's desk. Not nearly as harmless, though. Not nearly as harmless.

Amanda twisted to find a more comfortable position for her legs and realized she was still in the parlor. The room was pitch black and had been for some time, to judge by the lack of any glow at all from the fireplace. She was dressed in her nightgown and robe, so groggy she couldn't remember when she had gone to her room or how she had gotten there. Ryan had needed her help, but his pain was more physical than mental. Mercy had seen to Sarah and Verity while Obediah had put William to bed and, on one of the few occasions Amanda could recall, had then locked and bolted the doors before muttering his way to his own rooms out back of the kitchen.

Amanda had gone to her room but she hadn't been able to close her eyes, much less sleep. She had paced and replayed the confrontations over and over in her mind, between her and Ryan, Ryan and Michael, Michael and her, Alisha and her. Even Forrest Wainright's ugly face had intruded on her thoughts, laughing at her ignorance over Michael's ownership of the *Mississippi Queen,* laughing at Alisha's predicament, laughing at her own gullibility and her fatal penchant for assuming responsibility for everyone else's mistakes.

Michael denied having been with Alisha, denied the child was his, and, with hindsight's perfect clarity of vision, Amanda knew it was the truth. How she ever could have believed Alisha's lies, she did not know.

At the same time, Michael had obviously believed Alisha's half truths about Verity. She had told him Caleb wasn't the father and he had assumed—what? That Amanda had taken a lover. And that lover, either by inference or outright lie, was Joshua Brice. In hindsight again, it would suit Alisha's twisted mind to impose her own situation over Amanda's, to make the lie more convincing for the sake of it being half true.

Bitter words, cruel accusations. Was there room for forgiveness, or had too much been said to even hope to repair the damage? She had sent him away and he had not balked. He had not come back either, in spite of the many trips she paced to and from the windows willing him to come riding up the drive, hellfire pride and determination to reclaim his wife blazing from his eyes. It was what had brought her back down to the parlor, she recalled now—the imagined sound of hoofbeats on the hard-packed earth. And it had been the disappointment that had left her slumped on the settee, having checked the view from every window, every vantage.

She couldn't blame him if he didn't come back, if he never wanted to see her again, never wanted to try to work things out between them. No doubt he would be only too happy to see the end of her and her entire troublesome family, for he had surely had enough strife from all of them. He had won the raw end of the bargain with their marriage; he would probably run screaming away from any more noble gestures for the remainder of his life.

Amanda uncurled her legs from beneath her and stretched the crick in her neck, feeling worse for having reached the conclusion she had all but thrown away the best thing that had ever happened to her in her life. She loved him, she knew that now. Completely, utterly and absolutely. Come first light, she would go to him—crawl to him, if need be—and try to make him understand. If he left Natchez hating her, she would not be able to bear it. If he left with the image of her prone at his feet, it would at least be pity, not anger he carried with him in his heart.

In the meantime, she needed to get some sleep. Her head was throbbing, her body ached. She drew her wrapper closer around her shoulders and started to rise. A faint disturbance

—a creaking floorboard and a dull rattle from the other side of the parlor door—intruded on her thoughts and she sighed, wondering who else was awake at this ungodly hour. Mercy, probably. Making hot milk for herself . . . unless there was a problem with Verity?

Wider awake and feeling even more guilt for having neglected her daughter for her own troubles, Amanda padded noiselessly across the darkened room and went through the service door to the kitchen. Expecting to see a light and a shining black face bent over the stove, she was stalled temporarily by the impenetrable darkness. The door whined softly as she pushed it wider, but there was no relief to the heavy shadows. The lamp that was normally kept burning by the stove had been extinguished and the kitchen fire long since banked for the night. The sliver of moon that had helped alleviate some of the gloom in the parlor was blocked by the huge magnolia outside the window, and what little light did manage to filter through was barely enough to vary the shades of black outlining the furniture and fittings.

Amanda huffed a small sigh and turned to go. This time it was not so much what she heard or saw that stopped her at the threshold. It was more of a smell. Foreign, filthy, and salty, it assaulted her senses as surely as a blast of cold air, prompting the same results in a flush of gooseflesh that crawled up her arms.

"Mercy? Obediah?" She heard the creak again and saw the back door swing open on its hinges, pushed by a gusting breeze.

"For pity's sake," she muttered, her heart in her throat, her blood pounding in her temples. Just the door. Just the wind.

She was halfway across the kitchen when she remembered that Obediah had bolted all the doors. She was halfway through a startled cry when the shadows beside her shifted and moved and a pair of hands snaked out of the darkness, one clamping over her mouth, the other curling around her waist and dragging her back to make rough contact against the wall.

"Not a sound, lady," a voice hissed in her ear. "Not one flipping sound or so help me"—the intruder wedged his bony body against her and slid the cold press of a knife blade alongside her neck—"it'll be the last one you make. Understand me?"

Amanda nodded as best she could. The fingers that were mashed over her mouth remained sincere in their threat for another few seconds before relenting, bit by bit, and allowing blood to flow into the bruised flesh again.

"Wh-who are you? What do you want?"

"Aww, you forget me already? I'm hurt, Miz Tarrington. Real hurt."

Amanda's gasp and instinctive cry brought Ned Sims's hand crushing back over her mouth again.

"I told you not to do that," he said, snarling. "Not unless you like the taste of steel down the back of your throat."

He nudged the tip of the knife into the underside of her chin for emphasis, and she felt the faint *pop* and the resultant trickle of warm blood shiver down her neck.

"We'll try it again—real slow this time," he said, easing the pressure from his fingers. They moved from her mouth to the nape of her neck, twining around a fistful of her hair.

"What do you want?" she asked again. "What are you doing here?"

"I come to see you, Miz Tarrington. Real obliging of you to save me the grief of having to search every room, though I must admit"—his body sidled closer and his face drew near enough for her to smell the decay of his teeth—"fetching you out of your bed might have been worth the trouble."

"What are you doing here?" she repeated tersely. "You're supposed to be on your way to New Orleans."

"That's what everyone thinks, ain't it? Truth is, I never went farther than the Swamp. And why should I? Alls I did was try to teach the little woman a lesson in obeying her man."

"You almost killed Sally."

"If I'd wanted to kill her, the bitch'd be dead."

Amanda swallowed hard and wondered if anyone had

heard them yet. Mercy and Obediah slept in a room behind the pantry, the width of a wall away.

"You . . . still haven't told me why you're here."

"Someone's waiting outside to see you. Why don't I let him tell you?"

"Someone's outside?" For one brief, irrational moment, Amanda thought it might be Michael. But then she felt the knife against her throat and the oily grip of Sims's hand in her hair and she knew it was anyone *but* Michael.

"Someone who's anxious to know where his money is at."

A small bubble of panic burst in Amanda's throat. "Wainright? He's here?"

"You say that like you never expected he would find you. Lucky for him, though, he sent me after you last night when you come running off that ship all hell bent for leather. Damn near lost you a time or two, I might admit, but I managed to follow you and your lover boy." He grunted and lowered his voice to an intimate drawl. "Your husband know about him? Is that why you and he don't share that big old bed of his . . . cuz you got yourself some Reb meat on the side?"

Amanda angled her face away from the stench of his breath. He only chuckled dryly and leaned closer, dragging his tongue slowly up the curve of her throat, licking the dark stripe of blood as he did so. "Maybe, when your business with Mr. Wainright is settled, you an' me . . . ?"

Amanda wrenched to one side and brought her knee up hard into the juncture of his thighs. He was able to block enough of the blow by sacrificing his grip on the knife, saving all but a harsh grunt's worth of pain. The knife clattered onto the floor and he jerked her back against the wall; he struck out once, twice with the flat of his hand, the slaps catching her fully on the face and snapping her head side to side.

"Yeah," he promised furiously, slapping her again. "You and me, Miz Tarrington. I'll teach you the same lesson Sal learned."

Amanda's cheeks stung from the pain, her scalp felt as if it were being torn away by the brutal grip he held on her hair. He twisted his fist even tighter and hissed a command for her to move toward the door, shoving her with enough force, she stumbled into the side of the broad-topped cast iron stove. Her hands scraped across the still-warm surface as she regained her balance, but with another shove and another snarled curse, she was propelled out the door and into the chill night air.

Sims half dragged her around the side of the house to where the shadows were inkiest beneath the umbrellalike branches of the huge oak. She stumbled again and lost a slipper, but the shock of feeling cold earth and sharp pebbles gouging into the bare sole of her foot was not to be compared with the shock of seeing E. Forrest Wainright emerge into the mottled moonlight.

"Ah. So you found her."

"More like she found me," Ned said, giving her a final shove forward. "Good thing too, since every other goddamn board squeaks and squeals."

"Southern workmanship is as laughable as their fighting skills," Wainright remarked. "Amanda . . . you've been a tricky little minx to keep track of. One would almost think you were deliberately trying to avoid me."

"What do you want? You have your money, *what more do you want?*"

"*You* have my money," he corrected her wanly. "When I have it, I can promise you I won't want anything—for a while, anyway."

Amanda's jaw still burned from the slaps and her head felt as if it needed a good shake to clear it. "What do you mean, I have it? I don't have it."

Wainright's pause was palpable. "The word is all over town that Montana Rose walked away from the *Mississippi Queen* with over seventy thousand dollars in her clutches."

"Yes, and I gave sixty of it to Joshua Brice."

"You gave my money to someone else?"

"I gave it to Josh. He said he would take it to you in the morning."

"Which morning—yesterday, today, tomorrow? And who the devil is Joshua Brice?"

"Probably lover boy," Ned Sims provided helpfully. "The one who was waiting for her on the docks when she come off the boat."

"He isn't my lover," Amanda insisted. "And he wasn't waiting for me, he was—"

She stopped suddenly, the echo of her own words ringing in her hears. Josh *had* been waiting for her. He had said Alisha had sent him to look out for her, but Alisha had never looked out for anyone other than herself her whole life long. And now Alisha was missing. And Josh had failed to deliver the money!

The baron seems to think his wife has run away . . .

The thought screamed through her mind, drawing her to the inevitable conclusion even though she choked back a gasp denying it. It wasn't possible! It just wasn't. Josh had been sincere when he'd promised to help her. He was her friend. He was Caleb's closest friend! Alisha was another matter. She had only married the baron for his money, but by her own admission, the financial rewards had not lived up to her expectations. Sixty thousand dollars was a lot of money. Was it enough for Alisha to convince Josh to take her away from Natchez?

"By your poignant silence," Wainright hissed, "may we assume it is only just occurring to you that you may have been double-crossed?"

"He . . . promised he would bring it to you," she whispered, lacking anything else to say.

"Stupid bitch," Sims snorted contemptuously. "Or else real smart to claim someone else took the money and ran away."

Wainright glared at him then advanced on Amanda. "If I find out this is true—"

"Why would I do such a thing?" she demanded. "I was the one being blackmailed, remember."

"You were the one protecting her husband's reputation. What if you found out it didn't need protecting? What if you found out your sister was lying, that she was already several months' pregnant when she married?"

Amanda closed her eyes, relief and guilt washing through her in alternating waves. "But I'm still here. If Josh and I were trying to swindle you out of the money, wouldn't I be the first one to leave town?"

"Maybe. Maybe not. At any rate, you still owe me sixty thousand dollars."

"I don't have it," she said flatly. "You know I don't."

"No, and yet I take heart in knowing the loss your husband took Saturday night will have set him back considerably. May I presume he told you who owns the *Queen?*"

"He told me."

"Did he also tell you his grand plantation, his horses, his other little extravagances are all dependant upon the profits he reaps from his floating casino? I confess, I was modestly surprised myself when Captain Turnbull told me how much cash spins around with each turn of the paddle wheels."

"You spoke to Captain Turnbull?"

"As I told you—I believe in knowing everything there is to know about one's adversaries. When I saw you putting your heads together, I thought it prudent to know what about. Passage downriver for you and the child, was it not? To be arranged with the captain's discretion and full protection?"

"Ben wouldn't have told you that," she whispered. "Not voluntarily."

"Between Mr. Sims and myself, we managed to persuade him to cooperate."

Amanda stared at Ned Sims and felt the cool wetness of blood on her neck. "You killed him. You killed Captain Turnbull."

Sims shrugged. "He needed at lot of persuading."

Amanda looked at Wainright again. "You won't get away with it."

"Ah, but it seems I already have. It's Montana Rose the authorities are searching for, not me. And whether or not *you* get away with it''—he reached out and plucked a thick, silvery coil of hair off her shoulder, weighing it thoughtfully in his fingers—''will depend entirely on your husband's willingness to cooperate.''

''He won't bow to your threats,'' she said passionately. ''Not now, not ever.''

''He will if he ever wants to see you again. Alive.''

Amanda felt Sims coming up behind her and she tried to run, to dart away before he trapped her. But Sims and Wainright both anticipated the move and blocked her. She opened her mouth to scream, but something solid and metallic slammed across the back of her skull, causing her mind to explode with the pain and her body to slump forward into Wainright's waiting arms.

Through the agony and the final, fading starbursts, she heard a far-off voice commanding Sims to take her to where their horses were tethered.

Then she knew nothing.

Michael Tarrington jerked awake. He was dressed in shirt, breeches, and boots, and was sprawled across the bed. The sharp crack of a gunshot had traveled from the front hall up the stairs, along the corridor, and into his room without having lost a degree of volume or urgency. The pounding he had taken from Ryan's fists started a chorus of drumbeats hammering inside his head; spots danced in front of his eyes, clouding his vision and hampering his movements as he stumbled from the bed to the door.

Brian Foley was coming down the hall at a dead run.

''The bastard is here, sir, bold as brass. Ned Sims. He shot his way into the front hall and he's using Flora as a shield. Says he has a message for you. Said to give you this and you'd understand.''

Michael looked down into a hand trembling with rage and recognized Amanda's gold locket.

''Where is he?'' he demanded, snatching the locket out of Foley's palm.

"Still in the foyer."

"He came alone?"

"As far as I could see, yes sir."

Michael delayed only long enough to fetch his Remington and tuck it into his waistband at the small of his back.

Ned Sims had his back against the wall and an arm around the portly housekeeper supporting her half-conscious body. There was blood at her temple and a pistol was pressed into her ribs. Her face was twisted with the pain, and her eyes rolled as she fought to keep them open and focused.

"Let her go, Sims," Michael commanded. "You have my word no one will touch you."

"No dice, Tarrington. She stays put until our business is done."

Michael held up the locket. "Where did you get this?"

"From the neck of your purdy little Rebel wife, of course. Chain's broke cuz she put up a bit of a fight, but she's real quiet now. Learned her lesson, you might say."

Michael's fingers squeezed around the locket again, his knuckles glowing white. "Where is she?"

"We got her."

"Who is 'we'?"

"Mr. Wainright. And me."

The steely gray eyes turned as cold and cutting as the edge of an executioner's blade. "Where?"

"That's what you're going to have to pay to find out."

"How much?" Michael asked through the solid ridge of his jaw.

"An even hundred thousand."

"He's getting a little greedy, isn't he?" Michael spat. "Wasn't he satisfied with what my wife already paid him?"

"Mr. Wainright said to tell you he'll get a lot more than cash out of your wife if you don't come across. Uh-uh—" This last admonition was directed at Foley, who had begun to creep up on him from the side. Sims thrust the nose of his gun deeper into Flora's ribs, drawing forth a gasp and a groan of pain. "Don't try it or the old witch buys it. And you got till midnight tonight," he said, addressing Michael again. "Come up with the cash or you ain't never going to see your wife again . . . not all in one piece, at any rate."

"I need more time. I can't possibly raise that much cash in one day."

"Midnight, Mr. Highroller. Or you can start buying her back a finger at a time."

He grinned and held up his own mutilated hand, wagging the two intact fingers and the three misshapen stubs. Flora, finding no restraint around her waist, brought her arm up and drove her elbow back with a vicious stab, ramming both the gun and the hand that held it. The pistol exploded between them and Sims jackknifed to one side, the impact of the bullet sending him careening into a tall wooden hat stand.

Michael sprang into motion instantly, pushing Flora out of the way and knocking the smoking gun out of Sims's hand. He drew his Remington and thrust it up under Sims's jaw, ignoring the hiss of agony that bubbled from between the compressed lips as he hauled him upright. Sims's shirt and jacket were soaking rapidly with blood. The strength seemed to be melting out of his legs and his hands, searching for support, clawed around Michael's forearm.

"Bloody bitch . . . look what she's done!"

"If you don't tell me what I want to know, I'll let her finish the job with a carving knife."

Sims shuddered through a wave of pain and swore.

"Where is my wife?"

"Where you'll never find her."

Michael slammed him hard against the wall. "Where am I supposed to meet Wainright?"

"In hell, you bastard." Ned grinned through pink and bloodied teeth. "You can all meet him in hell."

Flora barreled forward with a ripe Scottish oath and shoved her fist into Sims's groin. She clamped her fingers around his crotch and twisted, tightening and twisting more as he jerked up on his tiptoes and started to howl with the pain.

"Tell Mister Michael what he wants to know, ye sod-brained, foul-mouthed piece o' shit, or I'll break off yer pride an' joy an' stuff it down yer scrawny throat backward!''

''The boat. The riverboat! The *Mississippi Queen!* He'll have her there at midnight. *Christ Jesus!*''

Flora gave an extra twist for good measure before she released him. Sims's eyes rolled into the back of his head and he started to slump down onto the floor, blood and air frothing out of the gaping lips. Michael let him go, knowing it was too late to do anything to help him, even if he had been inclined to do so.

It was Foley who bent over the body and straightened a moment later, shaking his head.

''He won't be able to tell us anything more, sir. He's dead.''

''An' good riddance to him as well,'' Flora declared, balling her hands into fists. ''Good thing I done it with ma own hands too. For ma Sally. Ach, but—'' The harsher reality hit her and she stared up at Michael in horror. ''Ye dinna think it'll hurt our wee lamb none, do ye? What will the other bastard do when this one disny come back?''

''My guess is, Wainright isn't expecting him to come back. He must have known something like this would happen if he sent Sims here with the ransom demand. I doubt he wants too many witnesses or too many hands to share in the profits.''

''But the *Queen,* sir. Isn't that rather stupid of him to arrange the meeting there?'' Foley asked.

Michael considered it a moment while he turned Amanda's locket over and over in his hand. ''No. It's actually quite brilliant. Devious, but brilliant. The *Mississippi Queen* is moored by herself at the end of the jetty and she's still closed down. Anyone coming within fifty yards of her will stand out like a beacon. Moreover, it would be the last place I or anyone else would think to look for her.''

The irony did not escape him either, for what better place to end it all than where it began?

''Have Diablo saddled and ready for me in ten minutes,'' he ordered softly.

"What are ye aimin' to do?" Flora asked tremulously.

"I'm aiming to bring my wife back home, Flora. Where she belongs. And by the way"—he glanced down at Sims's slumped body and winced—"remind me never to get on your bad side."

Ryan Courtland could scarcely believe his ears when he was told Michael Tarrington was waiting on the front porch, demanding to see him. He could scarcely believe his eyes either when he slammed through the door and sure enough, the Yankee was standing there, looking as wild as if the wind had blown him all the way from Briar Glen.

"Wainright has Amanda," Michael said without preamble.

"My sister is upstairs sleeping, Tarrington. If this is another one of your tricks . . ."

Michael held out the gold locket.

The men took the stairs two at a time and burst through the door to Amanda's bedroom without bothering to knock. The bed was rumpled but empty.

It took five minutes longer to search the house room by room before they arrived in the kitchen. Mercy and Obediah were there, frowning over their own discoveries—the ivory-handled knife that had been found under the table, the single satin slipper that had been found outside on the pathway.

"He'll kill her," Ryan said, white-lipped. "He won't let her go, no matter how many times over you meet the ransom."

"I know. But he wants his revenge and he'll wait long enough to see me squirm."

"Do you have the cash to pay him?"

"No. But I have the deed to Briar Glen and the papers for the *Mississippi Queen*. It's everything I own, so I think he'll be satisfied."

Ryan took a long, measured breath and nodded. "How many men do you think he'll have with him tonight?"

"No more than two or three. The river rats he usually

employs to do his dirty work couldn't be trusted not to slit his throat and take the money themselves."

"We can have ten times that many on the dock by midnight."

Michael disagreed. "If we show up in strength, all Wainright would have to do is wrap a length of chain around her ankles and slip Mandy into the river and she'd be gone in the current without a trace. Without a body, we'd be hard-pressed to prove anything against him."

"You have a pretty cold-blooded way of putting it, Tarrington."

"Murder is a pretty cold-blooded business."

"Then what do you suggest we do?"

"We let him think I am alone and doing precisely what he wants me to do."

"Sir." Foley ventured to make a suggestion. "This Wainright person does not know me. I could go down to the docks in advance and keep the *Queen* under close watch. We would at least be able to ascertain exactly how many men we were up against and how we might best be able to outmaneuver them."

Michael nodded, but Ryan shook his head.

"What if he just decides to kill you the minute he sees you?"

Michael studied Ryan's face—a face with enough likeness to Amanda's that his heart ached. "I guess it's a chance I'll have to take. I intend to get my wife back," he added quietly. "Foley and I can do it without your help if need be, but I'd like to know you were with me."

Ryan returned the penetrating stare. His jaw was discolored and throbbing, the cut over his eye was an ugly, scabbed lump. His ribs, belly, and arms were black and blue, and his stomach was roiling, rebelling against the pain and the fear for Amanda's safety.

Tarrington was in no better shape.

"Alisha was lying, wasn't she."

"Yes."

"What about Amanda?"

"What about her?"

"You say you want her back, but what if she doesn't want to go back?"

Michael looked down and studied his hands a moment, turning the locket over and over in his fingers. "Then you're going to be seeing a lot of me around here, because I don't intend to give her up without a hell of a fight."

Chapter 28

The slivered moon was too low on the horizon to cast any effect over the waterfront. A million stars up above and a thousand lamplights that burned in the taverns and saloons below set the entire riverfront glittering. The parties on board the showboat had begun to wind down, but since the canny operators had moved the vessel to another dock to avoid the taint of murder and scandal (while taking full advantage of the morbid curiosity at the same time), the *Queen* rocked gently at her mooring, enjoying her solitude.

Sounds of revelry on shore crept through portholes and down the shadowy passageways, seeping into every cabin, every nook and blackened cranny of the huge, deserted paddle wheeler. Her salon doors were locked, her interiors were hushed and darkened with only the odd whisper of a querulous draft to question the sanity of her owner for keeping her shut down. The enormous crystal chandeliers were cold and dark, their prisms tinkling softly with the motion of the hull. The roulette wheels were still. There was no chattering of dice, no ruffling of cards, no spill of brightly colored glass chips. The crew was ashore, praising the owner's show of respect for the dead captain. The two watchmen left on board were slumped in an out-of-the-way corner; one dead, one nearly so.

Forrest Wainright peered through the slats of the shutters that covered the porthole in the captain's cabin. It was twenty minutes before midnight and so far there had been no sign of movement out on the wharf.

The wick on one of the hanging oil lamps was turned as low as it could possibly go without risking extinction. The meager glow it cast barely reached the narrow cot where Amanda Tarrington lay bound hand and foot. A strip of cotton bunting had been wrapped around her mouth and tied

securely enough to cut into the corners. The sticky, burning
sensation on her wrists told her there was not much more
skin remaining between raw flesh and twined jute yet she
continued to stretch and twist and strain the ropes as stealth-
ily as possible, alert for any sudden movement from Wainright.

She recognized the captain's cabin from previous visits
and knew she was on board the *Mississippi Queen.* Her head
throbbed where Ned Sims had struck her, and if there was a
muscle in her body that was not screaming from the pain and
tension, she could not find it. She had drifted in and out of
consciousness all day long. At some point she had overheard
Wainright discussing with Sims where to arrange the meeting with Michael and the *Queen* had met all their requirements—privacy, isolation, and a convenient means of dis-
posing of the bodies.

*Michael. Michael . . . are you out there somewhere? Do
you know it's a trap? Do you know he has no intentions of
letting either one of us walk away from here alive?*

She pulled feverishly on her ropes. Her ankles were tanta-
lizingly loose and while she was not quite certain of the
advantage she would gain, she kept working to increase the
slack. She redoubled her efforts on the cords biting into her
wrists, forcing her mind to block out the pain, forcing herself
to concentrate on Michael's face, on his smile, his
laugh . . .

Wainright grunted and snapped open his pocket watch,
sending Amanda's heart leaping up into her throat.

"It's almost time. Your husband should be making his
appearance any moment now."

He shut the slats and crossed over to the cot. The lamp was
behind him and Amanda could see nothing of his face other
than the oily sheen of his hair and the point of his beard.

He, on the other hand, had the advantage of muted light
reflecting off the soft white linen of her nightdress and wrapper, neither of which were designed for modesty. Rather,
they drew the eye to the shapeliness of her long, coltish legs,
the trimness of her waist, the round, firm half moons of her

breasts. He was turbulently aware of the response he felt in his own body each and every time he looked at her lying there so helpless and vulnerable. He thought fondly of Alisha's voluptuousness and erotic skills, and he smiled, wondering how the two sisters compared. That too would be part of his compensation. Here, on board the *Mississippi Queen,* he would not only possess Montana Rose, Queen of the Mississippi, he would also possess Amanda Tarrington. Right in front of the agonized eyes of her arrogant husband, who would then know how it felt to be humiliated and shamed.

"Only a little while longer, my dear," he murmured, and his fingertip traced a path from her shoulder to her chin. She tried to flinch away but his hand caught her chin and angled it sharply up toward him, holding it with fingers that pinched and dug cruelly into her cheeks.

"Still playing the Southern belle, are we? Well . . . it won't be long now before we see how haughty you look down on your knees in front of me, begging me to spare your husband's life."

Amanda fought the taste of revulsion rising in her throat. He released her chin and thrust her head back down on the pillow and her eyes blazed back at him, so blue with hatred and loathing they glowed.

He only laughed. "I must leave you for a few minutes, but I'll be back. I assure you, I'll be back."

The blood pumped angrily into Amanda's cheeks. As soon as the key turned in the lock behind him, she poured every last bit of her strength into loosening her bonds. Her ankles sprang apart unexpectedly and, with a gasp of triumph, she squirmed and kicked her feet until she was able to maneuver herself to the side of the cot and sit upright.

She needed to get her hands free, and not knowing how much time she had before Wainright returned, she reached desperately for the first weapon at hand.

There was a small glass jar of matches on a shelf beside the cot. By twisting her upper body she was able to grasp hold of the jar and swing it awkwardly against the side of the bed. The glass was thicker than she thought, and apart from scattering the matches all over the floor, she accomplished nothing.

Damn, she thought. Damn . . . damn . . . damn . . .

She smashed the jar again . . . and again, and on the third attempt it broke, driving several sharp shards into the palm of her left hand. She cursed away the pain and groped blindly among the pieces to find the longest, sharpest edge. Bracing herself for more pain, she sawed the glass back and forth through the jute ropes, feeling the movement driving the shards deeper and deeper into her flesh with each stroke. The rope, when it finally parted, was crimson with blood.

Amanda cradled her damaged hand in front of her and pried out as many of the glittering slivers as she could see. A slash across the base of her thumb was especially deep and painful. It bled profusely and rendered the whole hand almost useless.

Clumsily she tore the gag off her mouth and bound it tightly around the wound. She ran to the door, but it was locked. She opened the shutters and was able to open the porthole, but it was too small to squeeze more than her head through.

In a fever of despair, she listened to the lively sounds of the nightlife along the riverfront. It seemed impossible that it should be so bright, so boisterous, so *close* . . . yet of no help to her whatsoever. If she screamed, no one would hear her but Wainright and the three apelike thugs he had brought on board the *Queen* with him.

Michael was out there somewhere, walking into a trap. She had to warn him away. She had to let him know it was a trap. She had to do *something*.

A gust of air from the open window caught the wick of the lamp and extinguished it. Amanda stared at it for a moment, then fell onto her hands and knees, scouring the floor for the spilled matches. The lamp had an ornate brass front that her injured fingers could not manipulate, but she remembered seeing the stub of a candle on the same shelf as the jar of matches, and, with unsteady hands and unsure intentions, she lit the stub and held it up in front of the porthole.

Michael Tarrington strolled toward the entrance of the jetty and paused to light a cheroot. Calm gray eyes searched the shadows, fully aware of the danger lurking somewhere behind the stacks of crates and bales of cotton that comprised some ship's manifest. Of the dozens of vessels anchored in port, the *Mississippi Queen* was the only one in darkness. He had issued the orders himself, knowing how much the crew respected Benjamin Turnbull, how callous it would be to profit from his death.

Another misguidedly noble gesture, he thought grimly, for now his beautiful *Queen* sat there naked and vulnerable, infested by the likes of Wainright and whatever scum he had picked up from the waterfront taverns. They had obviously already disposed of the inadequate watch he had left on board, as well as the pair of men the sheriff had posted at the end of the dock.

Michael's expression grew grimmer as he came closer to the pier. His footsteps echoed on the wooden slats and he realized he was sweating despite the distinct chill of the river air. He tried to keep all thoughts of Amanda out of his mind, but now and then an image took shape before him of a woman floating downriver, her long silvery hair fanned out across the surface of the muddy water.

Michael slowed as he reached the last stack of crated goods that lined the jetty. He heard the rasp of a match and, in the next instant, was blinded by a lantern held up before his eyes. The sudden glare effectively erased his ability to distinguish shapes and movements in the shadows, and although he raised a hand to try to block some of the light, his night vision had already been destroyed.

E. Forrest Wainright suffered from no such handicap. Half of the lantern was hooded by a metal panel that cleverly shielded his face while intensifying the glare in his adversary's eyes.

"If nothing else, you are prompt, Tarrington. And smart too, I trust? You came alone?"

"I'm alone. Where is my wife?"

"Quite safe. Quite secure. And the man who carried my message to you?"

"Quite dead."

Wainright smiled. "Not prematurely, I hope. You have the required sum?"

Michael started to reach into his jacket and froze. Wainright's hand came up out of the shadows, letting the light fall along the barrel of the Colt .45 he pointed at Michael's chest.

"Thumb and forefinger only," he instructed coldly. "And use the left hand, if you don't mind. I've heard rumors about your dexterity in such matters."

Michael complied, withdrawing a plain envelope from his breast pocket.

"It hardly seems fat enough. I hope you were not foolishly expecting me to accept a promissory note."

"It wasn't possible—as you well know—to raise a hundred thousand dollars cash in a single day. There isn't that much cash in all of Natchez."

"Your wife will be crushed."

"I don't think so." He held up the envelope. "I've had my lawyer transfer the title and deed to Briar Glen as well as the ownership of the *Mississippi Queen* into your name. Together they are worth a hell of a lot more than a hundred thousand dollars."

Wainright arched a brow appreciatively. "You do indeed have a flair for the dramatic. I like your style, Tarrington. How unfortunate we could not have worked together."

He extended his hand for the envelope, but Michael shook his head and tucked it back into his pocket. "Not until I see my wife walking safely away from the dock."

"Ahh." Wainright's bony fingers curled in on themselves like the legs on a dead spider. "Of course. A reasonable request, after all. And it will please you to know she is in perfect condition. Untouched. Unsullied, even though, as you can well appreciate, the temptation was ever-present.''

"She had better be untouched, Wainright," Michael said in an ominously silky voice, "or I'll take ten kinds of pleasure in killing you."

"Charming sentiments . . . but wasted."

He snapped his fingers suddenly and two burly figures stepped out of the blackness beside Michael. The cocking of their Winchester rifles sounded like ratchets, sending Michael's hand plunging instinctively for his Remington. The move was deflected by the stock end of one of the rifles; the second thug was behind him in a flash, shoving the snout of the barrel into his spine.

Michael spread his hands slowly by his sides. The Remington was found and removed, as were the twin silver-handled derringers tucked into the tops of his boots.

"I'll just take those papers now," Wainright mused, plucking the envelope from his pocket. He opened it and scanned the contents under the glare of the lantern, then grunted with approval.

"What now?" Michael asked derisively. "A bullet in the back, or a length of chain around the ankles?"

Wainright folded the papers and slid them back into the envelope. "Actually . . . I thought you might like to see your wife one last time. I thought you might like to see her with her legs spread and her body straining to please me, and to know that long after you are gone, she will still be pleasing me."

Michael roared an explosive curse and lunged for Wainright's throat. He managed to claw his hands around the starched broadcloth before a pair of rifle butts hammered him away. Dazed and bleeding, he was pounded into submission, driven to his knees by repeated blows to his ribs, shoulders, and gut.

"Enough," Wainright ordered quietly. "I don't want him dead just yet. Take him on board and put him in the main salon. Tie him to a front-row seat near the stage and keep his eyes open, even if you have to cut off the lids."

"Yes, sir!"

Wainright watched Michael Tarrington being dragged across the gangway and his mouth thinned into a cruel smile of anticipation. He lingered on the wharf a few seconds longer, raising and lowering the lantern as he glanced behind him to the mouth of the pier. He waited until he saw a match flare to life and carve a slow semicircle into the darkness, the signal that Tarrington had indeed come alone.

It wasn't until he turned back to the ship and doused the lantern that he saw the other light. The single, bright flame of a candle being waved in a desperate arc back and forth across the porthole of a cabin in the rear of the paddle wheeler.

Amanda heard no warning footsteps out in the corridor. The first inkling of disaster came with the sound of the key being twisted in the lock. With hot candlewax dripping over her fingers, she whirled around in time to see the door flung open and Wainright stride into the cabin with the flourish of an actor arriving on stage.

"Your husband sends his regards, madam," he announced. "Unfortunately neither he nor anyone else saw your feeble gesture, so if you were hoping for the cavalry to arrive, or the saints to sing out choruses of Hallelujah, you will be sorely disappointed."

"Where is he? Where is Michael?"

"Waiting for us in the salon. I have promised him a performance he can carry with him into eternity."

He started across the room toward her. Amanda stood perfectly still, the silky threads of her hair drifting forward in the breeze from the porthole, the burning candle clutched in her injured hand, dripping a steady *pat pat pat* of wax onto the floor. In her other hand, concealed behind her back, was the razor-sharp wedge of glass she had used to sever through her bonds.

When he was almost in front of her, Amanda threw the candle and brought the wedge of glass slashing up out of the shadows. Wainright reacted to the threat of the flame first, ducking too late to avoid the sting of glass carving into his cheek. Amanda slashed again, cutting nothing more than the fabric of his coatsleeve, but before she could improve her aim, he was swinging up and out with both arms, striking her hard enough to send her sprawling onto the floor. The glass flew out of her hand, lost in the confusion, but she scrambled for the darker outline of the doorway, kicking and screaming as she felt Wainright's hands grasping at fistfuls of her nightgown.

He caught her and dragged her back, lifting her bodily off the floor and throwing her back against the wall. He groped for the door and slammed it shut, then slotted the key into the lock with a savage twist.

The candle, remarkably enough, was still sputtering on the floor and he picked it up, holding it over the hand he brought down from his cheek. It was shiny and wet with blood, with more pouring down his chin and dripping onto the front of his jacket.

"Why, you little bitch," he raged. "You're going to pay for this. You're going to pay dearly for this!"

Amanda ran to the farthest corner of the cabin. There was nothing she could use for a weapon, but she started hurling anything and everything she could lay her hands on—books, ornaments, a cigar box, a paperweight. Most struck harmlessly on the wall and failed to do more than intensify the anger in Wainright's eyes. He had her cornered and he knew it. Her arsenal was small and finite, and she had nowhere to go, no way to escape.

"It's no use, Amanda," he said, setting the candle down on the table. "There's no cavalry. No saints."

She sobbed and cringed back against the wall. The last thing she threw was a large metal canister and as it bounced off Wainright's shoulder, the lid popped off and a full quart of whale oil sprayed his head and shoulders.

He hardly noticed.

He stooped suddenly, without taking his eyes away from Amanda's face, and picked something up off the floor. It was the shard of glass she had used to cut him and as he turned it over in his hand, the bloodied edge glinted red.

"Yes," he whispered huskily. "We can still give your husband quite a show. One that will send him *screaming* into perdition."

Amanda whimpered helplessly and sank to her knees on the floor. Her hands scraped the wooden matchsticks and she closed trembling fingers around one, scratching it frantically on the smooth floorboards.

The wooden stem snapped and she searched for another.

Wainright was less than five feet away, the blood and oil mingling on his face to make him look like the devil himself. He was grunting, stretching out a hand to snatch at the gleaming tangles of her hair.

Amanda screamed as the glass shard came slicing down at her. A thick, shiny skein of hair was severed inches shy of her scalp, and Wainright laughed, holding his golden trophy aloft.

She struck another match and threw it, but the flame died before it had completed its arc. She saw his hand coming toward her again, saw the oil and the blood and the bright spark of light that reflected off the sliver of glass. She shrank back and bowed her head. Her hand struck the last match and as she felt Wainright's fingers close around her shoulder, she thrust the burning match up and out.

Ryan Courtland rose dripping out of the inky blackness of the Mississippi River and climbed hand over hand up the anchor cable of the silent riverboat. He was shivering from the icy temperature of the water. An oilskin pouch was clamped securely between his teeth and when he was over the rail, he darted behind a large storage bin and unwrapped the pair of modified pepperbox pistols Michael had provided. The chambers carried six rounds of lead grapeshot apiece. When fired at close range, it would have the devastating effects of a shotgun blast.

He heard gruff voices and ducked his head below the bin.

A peek was all he needed to see that Michael was being dragged along the deck by two burly men who had obviously not been pleased to discover the padlocks on the main door of the salon.

"There's always a back way," one of them insisted. "One that won't have so thick a lock."

"Yeah, well, I still say we shoulda just shot the danged thing off and the hell with worrying about the noise."

Ryan smiled grimly and surged up from behind the bin, firing both guns simultaneously before the two startled captors could react.

One volcanic round of scattershot found its mark on a shoulder, tearing away flesh, muscle, and bone, and sending its victim spinning backward along the deck. The second volley was aimed wide, and luckily so, for only half of the shot found its mark, peppering the man's face and barely missing Tarrington's head as he lunged out of the way.

Michael somersaulted across the deck and sprang to his feet. One of the thugs was still standing, groping for an ear that wasn't there, and Tarrington ripped the rifle out of his hands, ramming the butt into the bulging paunch and sending him crunching through the rail and over the side of the boat. The man sank like a stone, but Michael could still hear screaming. Ryan heard it too, but it was coming from the stern of the paddle wheeler, echoing with enough fear and horror to make the hairs on his neck stand on end.

"Amanda!"

Michael was already on the run, pounding past the huge, silent wheel and into the blackness of the ship's belly.

Amanda stared at the flaring match in her hand, then at Wainright's face looming above her. She felt rather than saw the soft hiss and *fwoomph* of the oil-soaked cloth exploding into flame.

For a moment there was no reaction from Wainright other than a frown and a sharp curse. He dropped the wedge of broken glass and began dusting at the flames, his hands moving faster and faster as the flames licked up his arm to his shoulder. His curses turned quickly into shouts as the fire searched greedily for more whale oil. Bright yellow and orange fingers of it spilled down his chest, crawled up his neck and into his hair.

Wainright tore at the burning jacket. He ran up against the wall and rolled his body on the panels in an effort to smother the flames, but his whole torso was engulfed. The oil had penetrated through to his shirt and skin. It had splashed on his hair, his eyes, his mouth.

Amanda screamed as bits of flaming oil were sprayed from his flailing arms. She screamed in horror as the skin on his head and hands turned to burning liquid and began to blister. She ran for the door and tugged frantically at the handle, but it was locked and Wainright had pocketed the key. Behind her, she heard the crash of a body hitting the floor. The thing that was Wainright was still screaming, writhing, bleeding narrow rivers of fire into the oil splashed around Amanda's feet. The edge of the puddle rippled and caught. The flames spread out in a blue sheet, and in seconds, the floor was a pool of fire.

Michael took the stairs to the crew's quarters three at a time. The companionway was filled with thick, oily smoke and a stench that flashed him back onto the deck of a flaming ironclad. Twelve of his crew had been trapped by fire and it was a smell one did not soon forget.

"Amanda?"

"Michael!"

There was terror, pure and clear in her voice, and he flung himself against the door, feeling the heat, hearing the flames crackling hungrily on the other side. Ryan came up behind him and they both put their shoulders to the wood but it was no use; the door was teak and the lock solid brass.

"Move out of the way!" Michael shouted, and aimed the rifle at the lock. The bullet blasted into the wood, splintering the teak and weakening it enough for their weight to shatter the seat of the lock.

The inside of the cabin was an inferno. Michael threw his arm up across his eyes and searched desperately for Amanda. She was standing on the cot, pressed as far against the wall as she could go, kicking frantically at the flames that were lapping at the hem of her gown and wrapper.

Michael plunged into the wall of flame. The air was scorching hot, sucking the breath from his lungs faster than he could think to hoard it. He did not think at all as he ran for the cot and swept Amanda into his arms. He turned blindly and followed Ryan's shouts back to the door, his eyes streaming, his senses beginning to spin from the heat and smoke.

Heaving past Ryan, he heard a shouted warning but was not able to register the words through the thunderous panic beating through his body. He vaulted up the stairs and did not think to do more than tighten his grip on his wife's limp body before he crashed through the wooden rail and plummeted into the swirling darkness of the Mississippi River.

Chapter 29

Dr. Dorset was frowning as he emerged from the hotel bedroom and joined the two anxious men in the sitting room. Michael Tarrington's face was streaked with grime and clotted blood. His cheek was bruised and swollen, a cut over his eye had sliced through his eyebrow and, with the latter all but singed away from the heat of the fire, had given his face a new, somewhat slanted character. His hair had suffered similar damage and stood out in spikes above either ear. His hands were badly scorched and the cause of Dr. Dorset's tongue clucking on the roof of his mouth.

"I'll have a look at those hands of yours now, young man," he said with kindly concern.

"Never mind my hands. How is Amanda?"

Dr. Dorset ignored Michael's rude rebuff and opened his bag. "She has come away with a rather nasty cut on her hand, which I have stitched and which will bear watching closely for any signs of infection. Thanks to someone's quick thinking, she is not as badly off as she could have been —the dunking in the water is what saved her, there is no doubt in my mind. The burns to her arms and legs would have been much worse if time had been wasted trying to treat them some other way."

"Then she'll be all right?"

"For the most part, yes, I would say so."

"What do you mean," Michael asked quietly, "for the most part?"

Dr. Dorset pursed his lips. He was a portly man with sparse gray hair and a multilevel presentation of chins that accordioned in varying shades of red as he bowed his head and sought to choose his words carefully. "It is always a horrific thing to see a human being die from fire. It can only be worse when you feel you are to blame."

"Wainright was going to kill her," Ryan protested angrily. "She did what she had to do out of self-defense."

"Yes. Yes, of course you are quite right and you will hear no argument from me—or anyone else, for that matter. All I am saying is that she will require a good deal of support and understanding. This entire incident is bound to play on her mind for some time, and . . . what with everything else that has happened tonight . . ." His voice trailed away and he shook his head at the incomprehensible tragedy of it all.

The bodies of Alisha von Helmstaad and Joshua Brice had been found earlier in the evening. The military official who had responded to Michael's summons regarding Forrest Wainright's demise had recognized the Courtland name and had told him of the grisly discovery made in a cheap hotel room not half a mile away. Had Michael known his sister-in-law was also the legendary Montana Rose? The bloodstained dress, the money, the furtive waterfront hideaway she had shared with her lover for the past several months . . . they were all pieces to a puzzle that, once put together, would undoubtedly rock the old Natchez society to its foundations.

Michael didn't give a damn about Alisha or Josh Brice or the pinch-faced gossips of Natchez. Nor did he want Amanda to hear about any of it just yet either. In a day or two she might be strong enough to absorb the horror, but not tonight.

"May I see her now?" he asked the doctor.

"In a little while. Let Mrs. Dorset finish fussing with her. I've administered a mild dose of laudanum for the pain and, hopefully it will help her sleep. She needs pampering and bedrest. She will be needing all the care and attention we can give her over the next few weeks, especially if she isn't to lose the child."

Michael's eyes flicked up to the doctor's face.

"Quite frankly, son, I don't know. She's young and she's strong . . . but I won't lie to you. Her body has been subjected to several severe shocks and is likely to endure several more in the coming days. Babies can be tenacious little things, however, and ofttimes, if they are loved enough and wanted enough, they can prove to be just as stubborn as grown men and women. And speaking of stubbornness''— he harrumphed and his tone became businesslike—''if you don't let me have a look at those hands of yours, you'll be going directly against my orders not to upset my patient any further.''

Michael hesitated a moment longer, then relented and allowed the doctor to steer him into a nearby chair.

Ryan paced to the window. The hotel had been the closest building to the waterfront and afforded a spectacular view of the flames shooting out of all three decks of the *Mississippi Queen*. Unable to be saved, she had been cut adrift and pushed out into the middle of the river, there to be nudged and prodded by worrisome little rivercraft whose duty it was to keep her a safe distance from the crowded wharf while she burned gloriously into her watery grave.

The river could easily have become the grave for all of them, Ryan reflected grimly. Brian Foley had earned a broken arm and a bullet in the thigh dealing with the watchdogs Wainright had left on the dock. Amanda had been unconscious and half drowned when she was pulled from the water; Tarrington had not fared much better. How he had not collapsed completely was beyond Ryan's comprehension. Sheer Yankee obstinacy had kept him upright long enough to see them into the hotel and to dispatch help for Amanda, Foley, and the *Queen*.

Ryan was mildly scorched himself, mainly from trying to keep the door clear of flame while Tarrington tried to reach Amanda. His throat was raw from the smoke and from screaming at Tarrington to run for the river, that his and Amanda's clothes were on fire. Two days ago, he would gladly have watched the Yankee bastard roast to death right alongside E. Forrest Wainright. Now, having seen the look of absolute desperation on Tarrington's face when he emerged from the river, he was not so sure he shouldn't be the one roasting for his bullheaded blindness.

When Michael's hands were salved and bandaged, he joined Ryan by the window.

"She's almost gone," Ryan said, staring at the burning hull. "It's a pity they couldn't do anything to save her."

"No. In a way, I'm glad they couldn't. I just hope she takes the bad memories with her."

Ryan glanced over at him. "Surely they weren't all bad—the memories, I mean."

Michael arched what was left of an eyebrow. "Most of them were wild, reckless, without any real aim or purpose. I won her in a card game, just after the war. I was a little wild and reckless myself, wondering what the hell we'd fought all those years over, sick of the blood and the death and the killing. The *Queen* was a beauty. Elegant, lush. A man didn't have to think about anything, worry about anything when he was on board. He just had to sit back and drink it all in, all the life, the laughter, the beauty.

"The first time I saw Amanda," he continued softly, "I felt the same way. She damn near took my breath away and I think . . . I *know* I started falling in love with her the instant she walked up to the table and announced she wasn't like anyone's sister, wasn't like anyone's mother, and sure as hell wasn't like anyone's wife. Because she wasn't. She wasn't like anyone I had ever met before."

The admission came out so matter-of-factly that he and Ryan found themselves staring at one another.

"I do love her, you know. I knew it that first night, and I've known it every day and night since."

"Have you told her that?"

Michael offered a self-deprecating smile. "Do you know the feeling you get when you see something so exquisitely perfect, so inexplicably *right* . . . that you know it must be wrong—or at least wrong for you—and because you fight it, you end up making a complete ass of yourself?"

Ryan thought of Dianna and his jaw worked against allowing any acknowledgment beyond "I think so."

"Believe me, I've wanted to tell her. A hundred times. A thousand times. Things . . . just kept getting in the way."

"Things . . . and people?"

Michael's gaze encompassed the grimy blonde hair, the

bruises and swellings and beet-red sheen to Ryan's skin that was not all entirely due to the recent scorching, and his smile was honest, if slow to form. "You didn't make it any easier."

"Well . . ." Ryan glanced at the bedroom door as it opened and Dr. Dorset's wife came bustling through. "There's nothing—and no one—standing in your way now. Why not go in there and make us all feel a little less like asses?"

Michael continued to search the depths of Ryan's eyes for a long moment, then held out a bandaged hand. "Thank you. For everything."

Ryan took his hand willingly enough, but his smile was wry. "Don't thank me yet. Wait a year or two until we see if this partnership business works."

Michael's spirits remained buoyed until he reached the door to the bedroom. At the threshold, however, his mouth turned to dust and his blood started doing curious little spins through his veins, causing a tightness in his chest and a contrasting looseness in his belly.

Ryan made it sound so easy: Just walk inside, go up to the bed, and tell her you love her. Tell her you didn't really believe her sister's lies, even though she knows you did. Tell her you didn't really think she cheated on Caleb Jackson, or that Verity could have been the product of an illicit love affair, even though you were keen enough and cruel enough to believe it when it was your pride and your manhood being contested. Tell her it was all a big misunderstanding and you're smarter now. Tell her she can't possibly still hate you, or mistrust you, or feel repulsed by you now even though you've given her no earthly reason to do anything but.

Easy.

So easy, he was shaking like a leaf.

The room was small and functional. There were faded yellow chintz curtains over the windows, a matching yellow coverlet on the bed, a utilitarian washstand, armoire, and four-poster bed the quality of which benefited greatly from the low-burning wick in the lamp. There was evidence of

Mrs. Dorset's fussings. Amanda's wet and scorched clothing lay in a bundle in the corner along with the small pile of towels that had been used to bathe her face and clean away the mud from the riverbank. Two open tins of ointment and a glass vial of laudanum sat on the nightstand alongside a partially unraveled roll of gauze bandaging.

Michael noticed all of it and none of it. His eyes, from the moment he had entered the room and stepped tentatively to the side of the door to close it, had remained fixed on his wife.

Amanda looked very pale and fragile against the stark white sheets of the bed. Her beautiful hair had been drawn back from her face and tied with a pink ribbon, artfully arranged in an attempt to conceal the raggedly cut handful over her ear. A single linen sheet was covering her, the lower half tented over her legs to keep the cloth from sticking to the heavy layer of ointment coating her skin. Her graceful, porcelain hands and forearms were slathered as well, the pungent ooze spread thickly over skin that was shiny red and blistered in places. One hand was wrapped loosely in bandages with only the tips of her fingers showing. Those same fingers shook slightly and curled against a tremor and, as he watched, afraid to move or make any sound to draw attention to himself, the brilliant blue of her eyes opened and turned slowly, inexorably to the shadows at the foot of the bed.

"Michael? Is that you?"

He moved closer into the light and saw her eyes widen at the sight of his own lobsterlike hue and battered appearance.

"It's me, all right," he said lamely, passing a hand self-consciously over the singed spikes of his hair. "Not exactly the kind of look Beau Brummel might have introduced to society, but I think it could turn a head or two, don't you?"

His miserable attempt at brevity didn't make her laugh, didn't even tickle a smile.

"I think you look wonderful," she said softly. "Alive and wonderful."

Michael moved closer to the bed, braced for almost anything but the sweet, loving desperation he saw welling in her eyes, shimmering in the rusty light. It was gone in the next instant, swept away by the gasp and the choked sob that caught in her throat.

"Mandy? Is something wrong? Is it the pain? Shall I call Dr. Dorset back?"

She moved her hand, groping the air a moment before she felt the reassurance of his grasp gently closing around her. "Michael . . ." She had to pause to moisten her lips. "The baby. Dr. Dorset said everything was all right, but I thought . . . I mean, he might just have told me that to make me feel better."

"He wasn't just saying it," Michael declared fiercely, believing each word as he said it. "He meant it. He told me the baby and you will both be fine."

"But I can't feel anything. I'm all . . . numb . . . inside. And my head . . . feels like it's floating around the ceiling."

He sat on the edge of the bed and, not knowing what he could touch, what he could dare to touch, he kept her hand cradled to his breast like a precious gem. "That only means the medicine he gave you is working. You have to heal and get your strength back, and to do so, you'll need a lot of sleep."

"I'm too cold to sleep," she said miserably. "You would think . . . being burned . . . I should be hot, but I'm not. And I'm not allowed to have any covers over my legs or on my arms. It doesn't matter anyway. I don't want to sleep," she added tearfully. "If I sleep, you'll go away. You won't give me a chance to tell you . . ."

He frowned and leaned closer to catch the last few words that had been muffled under a sob. "Tell me what, Mandy?"

Amanda's breath gusted between her lips and she stared up at him, her expression so somber and solemn, it rivaled Verity's when the child was confronting one of her gravest dilemmas. "How very stubborn, foolish, pig-headed, ungrateful, and stupid I am."

He straightened slowly and gazed down at her in mild

astonishment. "What on earth do you have to feel stupid or ungrateful about?"

"The way I have treated you," she whispered. "The way I was ready to believe Alisha's lies without even giving you the chance to deny them. I believed her when she told me the two of you had been together that night. I believed her . . . maybe not completely . . . but I was *willing* to believe her when she said the baby was yours . . ."

"Mandy . . . it doesn't matter."

"But it does," she insisted fiercely. "It matters a great deal if you are ever going to be able to forgive me."

"Forgive *you?*" He bowed his head over a muttered oath and raised her bandaged hand to his lips, pressing the gentlest of kisses over her fingertips. "Mandy . . . I've been waiting outside that door for the past hour, wondering what in hell I was going to say to you, how in hell I was ever going to convince you to forgive *me.*"

"You haven't done anything that needs forgiving."

"No, nothing at all," he scoffed. "I'm a real saint, all right, pushing you away, holding you at arm's length because I believed your sister's jealous rantings. I wasn't honest with you, with me. I couldn't even be honest about why I married you."

Amanda's lips parted, then came together again in a thin, trembling line. "Why . . . did you?"

The tension he was feeling was betrayed by the clenched sinew that shivered in his jaw, but for once he made no effort to guard against the emotions kindling in his eyes. "I married you because you were the most beautiful woman I had ever set eyes on. I married you because you had strength and courage, because you were willing to risk your name and your reputation and everything you held dear . . . just to buy your daughter an orange. I married you because you weren't afraid to tell me to go to hell, and because you were prepared to go there yourself, with a man like Wainright, in order to protect your family and your home. I married you hoping some day I might see one-tenth, one-hundredth a part of the love I see shining in your eyes each and every time you look at Verity. I married you . . . because I started falling in love with you the moment I saw you on the *Mississippi Queen,* and have been falling deeper in love every day since. And . . . if you don't forgive me, if you don't tell me we at least have a chance to start over again, I . . . don't know what I'll do.''

Amanda stared. It was all she could do in the face of such an overwhelmingly naked confession. Michael loved her. He loved her and despite his usually uncanny ability to read her thoughts before she could speak them, he sat there, like a condemned man awaiting judgment, watching her.

''All these weeks,'' she whispered, lifting her hand and resting it on his cheek, ''I was afraid you didn't want me anymore.''

''Not want you? You are the most important thing in my life, Mandy. You, Verity . . . the baby. Absolutely nothing else matters. Nothing at all. The rest of the world can go hang, for all I care. I just want you.''

Amanda closed her eyes, her lashes glistening with tears. When she opened them again, she could see by the swift, fierce tension that gripped his features that he had regained his ability to see what she was thinking and know what she was wanting. Desperately.

''Mandy . . .'' He leaned closer and his mouth found hers soft and eager. They broke apart and met again, harder this time, the kiss deeper and longer and expressive enough to leave both of them gasping curses at the encumbrances of bandages and burns.

Ignoring both, she raised one arm and curled it around his neck. ''Tell me again.''

''How much I love you?''

She nodded shyly, the smile drifting across her face even as he bent his mouth to hers and breathed the words over and over and over. This time, when he pulled away—no farther than her arm would let him—the look he had craved to see was there, shining so brightly in her eyes he had to close his own a moment to keep them from filling.

In the end, he didn't care about that either.

"Oh, Michael," she sighed. "I wish he hadn't given me any medicine. I wish—"

"I wish you would let it work so I can get you out of here and take you home."

"Will you stay here with me? Will you stay close by?"

Michael slipped an arm carefully beneath her shoulders and she felt the bedding shift as he stretched out alongside her. With infinite tenderness, he gathered her close against the hard curve of his body, his shoulder pillowing her head, his love promising to keep her warmer than all the blankets in Natchez could have done.

"Is this close enough?" he asked.

"No. But I suppose it will have to do for now."

His arms tightened and she snuggled contentedly against him. Her eyelids grew almost too unbearably heavy to keep open and, with another sigh, she let herself slip further into the gently swirling currents of darkness.

Epilogue

"**M**other, he did it again."

Amanda looked up from her knitting and frowned. "Who is he and what did he do?"

The answer to the first question was obvious as Verity hauled her brother Lucas through the door of the parlor using his ear as leverage. Lucas was five, the youngest of her three brothers and the one who seemed the most determined to make her life a trial.

"He was in my room uninvited, trying to hide this"—she held up a small box, the contents of which jostled side to side and croaked audibly—"in my armoire. Last week it was a snake and the week before it was a fat, hairy spider. I told him if I caught him putting any more creatures in my room, I would make him eat them."

"Lucas." Amanda sighed and rubbed an ache in her back. "Why must you torment your sister so?"

"I dunno." He shrugged and screwed his mouth into a contemplative grimace. "Cuz Bits doesn't scream as loud."

Bits—Elizabeth—was a year older than Lucas and not too ladylike yet to box him on the ears if he tried it, which was a more plausible reason. Verity, on the other hand, had just turned a beautiful, regal fifteen and had spent the past summer in Boston being awed by the blue-nosed society her Northern cousins belonged to.

Amanda rubbed harder at the cramp and shifted awkwardly on the chair. The movement started the baby squirming and she laid a hand over her swollen belly, wincing at a particularly energetic tussle. Another boy, she thought ruefully. It had to be. Elizabeth and Justine had been delights to carry, their movements all like the delicate flutter of butterfly wings. They had been soft, dainty creatures who had mewled when they were born and smiled like the little blonde angels they had become. All three boys, conversely, starting with the first, Samuel William Tarrington, had kicked and pummeled their way through each month of the pregnancy and come out squalling like prizefighters. Dark like their father and devilishly handsome, they were a constant source of aggravation for Verity, who had declared in no uncertain terms that if Amanda gave birth to another boy, she would pack her things and move in with her Uncle Ryan and Aunt Dianna. *They* had the good sense to have only daughters.

"Mother—"

"Verity . . ." Amanda's hand had remained on her belly and she held her breath as another telltale flush of tightness rippled through the stretched muscles. "You will have to feed your brother frogs some other time. Will you find your father for me and . . . tell him to send for Dr. Dorset."

Verity relinquished her hold on Lucas's ear and shoved the box into his hands. "Is it the baby?"

"I think so. Oh!" She dropped her knitting and gripped her stomach with both hands. "I know so!"

Verity whirled on her brother. "Run down to the paddocks and fetch Papa quick as you can. Don't stop or dawdle for *anything,* do you hear me, or—"

"Verity! Where's Flora?"

Verity gave her brother a push out the door and hurried over to help Amanda, who was struggling to her feet. "She's gone to town with Sally and Mr. Foley."

"God, yes. I'd forgotten. They were taking Matthew to the store to buy school clothes."

"And Mrs. Reeves went along to make sure they didn't dress her grandson like a 'wee bleetin' billygoat,' " Verity quoted in the accent.

"I guess it's just you and me, then, for the time being."

"Papa's here too. And it's foaling season; he'll know what to do."

"Thank you very much for the comparison," Amanda mused grimly. "Now, if you could help me upstairs to my stall?"

They heard running footsteps on the porch and a bang as

the door swung open. A moment later, Michael was in the parlor, his face flushed with concern. "Lucas found me in the yard. He said his frog made you sick?"

One look at his wife's face and at Verity's arched brow and he knew. "Oh."

"Yes," Amanda said tightly. "Oh."

"Has someone sent for the doctor?"

"I . . . don't think there's time."

Michael blew out a sharp breath and scooped her up in his arms, shouting orders over his shoulder as he carried her up the stairs. "We'll need hot water. Plenty of it. And towels."

"Hay and oats too," Amanda murmured against his throat.

"What?"

"Nothing," she gasped, clutching him fiercely through another contraction.

Michael kicked the door of their bedroom open and set Amanda gently on a chair for as long as it took him to strip off the bedding (at her insistence) and fetch a loose nightgown from the dressing room. Amanda had already worked most of the fastenings on her bodice free, but surrendered the task willingly to Michael as he knelt in front of her.

His eyes were smoke-gray and intent on every twinge of discomfort that flickered across her face.

"You still maintain it's a boy?"

"I *know* it's a boy. Flora does too."

"Flora has been known to be wrong a time or two."

"She's been right with all of ours so far. And she started knitting blue blankets for both of Sally's boys before Mr. Foley even knew he was going to be a father."

"Dianna fooled her."

"Once. Out of three times. The odds are still heavily in her favor."

"This is all your fault, you know," he murmured.

"My fault?"

"Mmmm. Wanting to domesticate me."

"I was thinking it was all your fault," she said crossly. "Sometimes beds *are* just used for sleeping, you know."

"Is that a complaint?"

Her wide blue eyes looked up and met his. After eleven years of marriage and five children, he still had the ability to melt her insides to jelly with a look or a touch. "I suppose . . . if we run out of bedrooms it could be," she said softly.

He shook his head and kissed her. "We'd just have to move to a bigger house."

She started to smile when another spasm gripped her. Her hands looked for something to grasp and Michael was there, not seeming to mind in the least that the hair on his chest was twisted into her fists.

When the contraction released her, he leaned forward and kissed her hard on the mouth. "Do you know how much I love you, Mrs. Tarrington?"

"Enough to say you wouldn't want to be anywhere else but here with me today?" she said with a gasp.

He gave her the rare, ravishing smile he saved only for her and brushed his lips over the dampness on her forehead. "I wouldn't want to be anywhere else today but here with you."

Amanda smiled weakly and allowed him to ease her out of her dress and shimmy. He had been down at the paddocks all morning and smelled horsy. It was a rich, earthy, wonderful smell she had come to love almost as much as the man himself. There were nearly three hundred Thoroughbreds in the stables, many of them bred from Diablo and all of them trained by Amanda's brother Ryan. He was in Kentucky at this very moment with their entrant for the Breeder's Cup, one of the most prestigious races of the season, and one she knew Michael would not otherwise have missed for anything in the world.

"Do you think Black Silence will win?"

"He's broken every record at every track this year. And if I was still a betting man"—he paused and pressed a tender kiss over the bulge of her stomach before he dropped the nightgown into place—"I'd say the Tarringtons' were going to break two records for speed today."